Hill Country Hijinks

by

Amy Craig

The Wild Rose Press, Inc.
PO Box 708
Adams Basin, NY 14410-0708
Visit us at www.thewildrosepress.com

Publishing History
First Edition, 2025
Trade Paperback ISBN 978-1-5092-5997-7
Digital ISBN 978-1-5092-5998-4

Published in the United States of America

Chapter One

Gripping the railing on his ninety-foot sailboat, Ansel channeled relaxation while his public relations team squawked like seagulls. Kicking the chattering professionals off the yacht tempted him, but he needed the impending photo shoot to publicize his restaurant empire. He lifted his face toward the Caribbean sun and hoped the ship's captain kept the vessel away from the coral reefs. Bad press was the last thing he needed. Reporters already thought he was an egotistical tyrant.

They weren't wrong.

He was strung tighter than a corset, and he should have known better than to schedule the photo shoot on the anniversary of his parents' deaths. Exhaling, he searched for his Zen. Cloud-studded skies and swaying palm trees mirrored the breeze, and soft linen fluttered against his toned chest. "Chef groupies" would eat up this shot. If he unloaded on his staff, he wondered what the groupies would think about his cathartic release.

It would go viral.

His fans ate anything he dished out.

The engine sputtered, and the ship lurched.

Tightening his grip on the railing, he spun toward the sound. "What kind of donkey-chomping meat wipe can't…"

The assembly gaped.

He clamped his lips and worked his jaw. Being a

folksy billionaire restaurateur had its downsides. He could be eccentric, but he couldn't be mean.

Considering the uncertain glances passing between the models and managers drinking his champagne, he was too close to the danger zone. Their surreptitious interest made his insecurities hum, but setting them adrift would lead to unwanted gossip. Instead of making accusations, he forced a smile, saluted, and returned to the ship's prow.

The crowd's chatter resumed.

He rubbed the large, white scar on his palm. While winning a televised cooking competition, he seared his hand, and his creative expletives made him a viral sensation. Who knew calling his competition's meal a "bandit-sack rag sandwich" would turn him into a household name?

Fame garnished his cooking ambitions, but he never looked back. The Chow Channel network gave him a regular show, and he used his income and his notoriety to expand his culinary empire. The boat was a nice perk, but he would rather paddle around buck-ass naked than suffer the attentions of giggling models.

Photographers dragged clattering chairs across the teak deck. A heavy thump landed against wooden decking.

Wincing, he held his tongue and prepared to spend the afternoon polishing scuffs. Cannon fire had to be quieter than a photo shoot.

Collins approached. He possessed a commanding presence honed on collegiate football fields. His indeterminate skin color and deep voice contrasted with his unexpected baldness. Beneath the Caribbean sun, his dome glistened and outshone his strong jaw, aquiline nose, full lips, and golden-brown eyes. His expensive cologne smelled like jackfruit, and Ansel might have mocked it, but Collins could beat the shit out of him. The only people fiercer than he was were his beautiful South Korean wife and his precious twin daughters.

So even though Ansel's heart rate was through the roof, and his right-hand man was also his lead photographer, the pro didn't need to see him sweat. He stretched his neck like a warrior going into combat, squared his shoulders, and held out a hand. "Thanks for coming out. I don't trust anyone else with this shoot."

Gripping his hand, Collins grinned. "Because you're a persnickety bastard?"

"No, because your wife helps me improve my South Korean entrées."

Collins laughed and released his hand. "She's thoroughly American, but when you spend enough time in a place, it sinks into your soul. If you're lucky, she'll let you tag along on our next trip to Seoul and take you to her grandmother's house." He raised his camera, aimed the lens toward the sailboat's prow, and pressed a button. "*Halmeoni* will judge your cooking."

He had no doubt. The prospect of tagging along on a Collinses' family trip intrigued him. He enjoyed the country's green, hilly countryside, cherry trees, and centuries-old Buddhist temples, but he stood out in the high-tech capital like a confused Westerner who needed a guidebook.

After retirement, he could picture himself traversing the world, sampling delicacies, and eating for the pleasure of a satisfying meal. Vagabond lifestyles sounded romantic until you realized no one else

3

appreciated your memories.

"Also, *Halmeoni* knows everything. She gave me the seasickness patch behind my ear. It's the size of Texas."

He laughed. "Everything's bigger in Texas."

Collins cleared his throat. "Remind me why we're building a restaurant in the Texas boondocks?"

Working his jaw, Ansel considered how to explain himself. "That restaurant's my last stand. My pinnacle. As soon as I open Cypress Creek, I'm retiring. I've conquered big cities. Venture capitalists want to see scalability before they make an acquisition. I can't micromanage my empire *and* look good doing it when I'm dead."

Collins tugged his earlobe.

He was a lying prick, but he was too proud to admit the truth. The Cypress Creek restaurant wasn't a pinnacle. It was a spite house. He wanted Aubrey Thomas, the woman who spurned him twenty years ago, to see his success in her hometown.

As a recent culinary school graduate, he had poured his foster father's culinary lessons, his Pine Ridge Reservation influences, and his meager savings into a small, Sioux Falls eatery. When the press lost interest in the Lakota-inspired meals, loyal customers kept afloat the restaurant, but Aubrey and a string of negative reviews sank his efforts.

A year behind him in culinary school, she felt like the antidote to his heavy past. She wore her short, light-brown hair in tight curls, and she framed her wide, brown eyes with false lashes. Rubbing lotion into her glowing, brown skin soothed him, and teasing her into confident, easy smiles set him at ease. She encouraged him to pursue a typical, American menu, but he pushed back and thought they had a good relationship. Every night, he sank into bed, wrapped his arms around her, and drifted to sleep, refining his ambitions.

Then, he'd found her in bed with a culinary student who specialized in Steak *Frites*. The classic French dish was delicious and incredibly easy to prepare, but what kind of chef perfected a New York strip steak and hung up his apron?

He should forget her, but she lingered on his socials like a pack's last cigarette. Ignoring the tantalizing scent was an option, but he was a smug, insecure man addicted to success. He couldn't resist the appeal of one-upping her and making sure her regret lasted as long as his wealth.

He also considered christening his yacht the *Steak Frites*, but *Tranquility* kept him centered, and Aubrey's betrayal taught him to choose discerning associates. No matter the size of the storm, he trusted his management team and his culinary abilities to safely carry him through society's culinary whims.

Straightening his linen shirt, he jerked his head toward the milling assembly. "Don't worry about my reasons for Cypress Creek. Take good pictures and help me build out the site."

Collins cleared his throat. "Talk after the shoot?"

Ansel turned. "Talk now."

Shaking his head, Collins looked out to sea. "Today's the anniversary of your parents' deaths."

He considered his response. Complaining about his past felt more petulant than a toddler denied chicken fingers. Collins was correct, but Ansel kept old scars under wraps. He pivoted toward levity. "It was a long time ago. Tell me, are these pictures going to feature my food or my abs?"

Collins laughed and wiped sweat from his bald head. "Both."

"Liar. Everyone's here for the abs."

Collins bumped his shoulder. "You'll rock the shoot. Just play nice with Jocelyn and Elena."

The models' long legs and soft curves tempted his appetite, but the last time he let a woman get close, he found himself dumped like yesterday's bread. "Will they taste my food?"

"Is that a euphemism?"

He laughed.

"No? Then probably not."

Ansel grunted. Soaking up the companionable, salt-tinged silence, he leaned against the railing and savored the ship's clean lines. Designed for entertaining, the vessel boasted luxurious living spaces and extensive communal spaces. His meteoric rise to the top of the American culinary scene gratified him, but the trim sailboat offered release. The captain, Isla, could also drink him under the table.

If he could trust Collins to aide his empire, he could trust him to talk when ready. Instead of grousing about models who looked like they'd forgotten the taste of a perfectly seasoned duck egg, he could also bury memories of his parents, adopt the easy smile that carried him through twenty years of press interviews, and lift his face toward the sun. "Let's go."

Collins raised the camera, took a quick shot, and looped his index finger through the salt-tinged air. "You heard the man. Let's go!"

Photography assistants stepped out of the shadows

and assumed positions with lights and shades. The models sprawling in the forward lounge area wore white, net cover-ups over swimsuits. They perked up and exchanged glances.

Ansel took his place behind a table set with fine china and plated entrées. He patted the bespoke red leather banquette brought onboard for the shoot and beckoned the beautiful women. "Who's hungry?"

Jocelyn, the brunette model, met his gaze, but Elena, the blonde one, tugged Jocelyn's elbow and whispered in her ear.

"Don't be shy, ladies." He chastised himself for sounding like an old man. *Bitches* would have been too much. The pair's modeling contracts probably precluded them from sharing unapproved snapshots, but he could be approachable. His shoulder-length, sun-lightened brown hair gave him a rakish air that photographed well on professional cameras *and* sleek smartphones. Leaning back, he spread wide his arms. "Settle in and we'll take a few quick snaps so you don't have to wait for Collins' proofs."

Jocelyn slipped into the space to his right and angled her legs toward him. "You're, like, famous and approachable. I thought most chefs were assholes."

He winked. "Don't believe what you hear."

She giggled.

He knew how to play this game. Women assured him his wide shoulders, toned arms, and calloused hands offered plenty of distraction from his gruff kitchen demeanor. A billion dollars in his bank account helped, too. In the last five years, not a single date mentioned his average height or his reluctance to talk about his past. Now, Jocelyn thought he was downright approachable. Maybe he didn't want her to get too close. Standing, he stretched his arms over his head. "Come on, Elena!"

Jocelyn jumped up, wrapped an arm around his trim torso, and posed in front of her friend. "First, one for my followers?"

He smiled indulgently.

Elena took the picture and rushed to his other side. "My turn."

What am I, a carnival ride?

Disengaging her arm, Jocelyn trailed her fingers along his back. "I *love* your restaurants."

"Good to know." Anticipating exactly how the shoot might play out, he sat behind the staged table and divided his attention between the pair. For sixty minutes, he mimed serving plates, pouring champagne, and soaking-up laughter and sunshine.

Responding to Collins' request for a smile, he wondered what his top-performing female kitchen leads would think of his buxom company.

Exposed to the sunlight, the decking warmed.

His bare feet ached on the scorching boards, but Collins' rapid adjustments and clicking shutters reminded him to hold his pose.

Jocelyn rubbed her foot along his calf.

He debated tucking his feet under the table or keeping his legs spread like an asshole. Collins *had* told him to wear shoes. He had a valid point, but Ansel owned the boat. Ignoring Jocelyn's possessive hand on his chest, he lifted seafood ravioli to fake-feed her.

She kept her painted mouth closed.

"Right." Standing, he positioned himself in the shade. "It's all an act."

The ocean swelled and rocked the boat.

Elena dropped a fork onto the deck, and it landed tines up.

Momentum carried him forward. Stepping on the dropped silverware hurt less than he anticipated, but he winced and dropped his food-laden fork. "Shit pellets!"

Collins called for a break, and Jocelyn pouted.

Sauce dripped from the ravioli and pooled on the table. He exhaled. So much good food went to waste. They might as well scrap the props and mime the entire encounter. Something akin to laughter bubbled up in his chest, but he swallowed the sound before he ruined the shoot.

An assistant ran to clean up the mess.

Jocelyn leaned across the table toward her blonde counterpart. "Did you drop something?"

Tilting her head, Elena blinked her eyes.

He might enjoy their catfight, but if Jocelyn weren't careful, Collins would kick her off the shoot and give Elena a single billing. Ansel spread his arms wide. "It's all good. We're here to have a good time."

Elena raised her glass.

Struggling to remember her backstory, he lifted the champagne bottle and refilled the glass. "How're you liking your trip?"

She sipped the brut bubbles. Her lipstick remained in place. "Oh, it's amaze. I mean, Jocelyn here has been everywhere with everyone, but this is my first Caribbean outing."

"Don't sell yourself short." Jocelyn flipped her brunette hair over her left shoulder. "You're so talented and beautiful. Collins said you'll go far—"

The assistant backed out of the shot.

Ansel wondered if he had misjudged the two women. Their interest in doing a good job and garnering Collins' attention for portfolio-worthy shots made perfect sense.

Jocelyn smirked. "—on your knees."

Spitting out her champagne, Elena lunged.

Well, if the pair planned on tasting the food, they'd ruined their opportunity. Stepping back, he watched them go after each other and marveled at their ingenuity. Men threw punches. Women—he winced—ouch.

Jocelyn abruptly stood and upended the table.

China crashed to the decking, and the pair of oiled, coiffed models rolled in the remnants of a delicious pairing of seafood ravioli and chive mousse.

"You said I was a survivor!" Jocelyn yanked down the blonde's hair and shoved a handful of cream into her face. "Survive this, Elena, you bitch!"

He scratched the side of his mouth and stood resolute while two women tangled in a tablecloth.

An assistant handed him a glass of champagne.

Collins' camera clicked.

Looking up from the melee, he wondered if Collins had enough even-tempered, luxurious shots to complete the shoot. Given his brilliance, he might use the models' altercation as an avant-garde advertisement. Until the photographer lowered his camera, Ansel would hold his pose.

He tipped back the champagne and filed away this moment. In less than a year, Cypress Creek would open, Aubrey would regret her decisions, and he would tag along on a Collinses' family trip.

Collins released a shrill whistle.

The models, tangled in their messy ambition, froze.

Collins cracked his knuckles like a football coach.

He shrugged. Handing off the champagne, he walked toward his right-hand man and cleared his throat. "Enjoy the show?"

Collins handed over the camera. "Always."

Laughing, he clicked through the images. He envied Collins' height, but he envied his homelife and pragmatic attitude more. Going through the camera's files, he stumbled onto pictures of Collins' daughters with their arms draped over his shoulders.

Memories of his childhood flashed like faded photographs. In another life, he, too, was a happy-go-lucky kid. His eyes welled, and a lump in his throat threatened to choke him. He should have spent the day doing community service.

Collins fathered his girls, and Ansel sent the biggest gifts, but he also kept his distance. Their happiness proved good things happened to good people, but where did that leave him? He wanted to return to the Reservation, sprawl on an old sofa, and hear Chris Eagle Hawk tell him everything would work out, but the old man was gone, too.

As soon as people grew close, they left, and he carried the scars. Knowing he couldn't explain his regrets while he entertained a crowd, he navigated back to the food fight images, handed over the camera, and stared out to sea.

"You okay, man?"

Clearing his throat, he nodded. "Just a bug."

"Right."

Walking away from his longtime friend, he strode toward the prow and reclaimed the position where nobody could see his face. A heap of snot and tears choked his throat, and he let the enormity of his regrets rip through his consciousness. His chest hurt. Hearing footsteps, he coughed and scrubbed his palms beneath his eyes.

Collins approached his side.

Heading off his friend's concern, he searched for the coverage "Dude, that ravioli went to waste."

A bark of laughter ripped from Collins' chest, but he cleared his throat. "Ansel, I didn't want to tell you before the shoot, but I need help."

The hedged admission sobered his emotions quicker than a call from his legal team. "What kind?"

"The San Antonio work crew can't play nice with the Cypress Creek yokels, and we're behind schedule."

Drawing a breath of clear, salty air, he crossed his arms. Collins solved problems for a living; if he needed help, things were bad. "And?"

Collins scratched his chin stubble. "Also, Jia's pregnant again, and the scans don't look good."

Gauging Collins' tight, massive shoulders, he took a risk and wrapped him in a quick hug. "Go home, man."

Collins shuddered. "Thanks."

Releasing his hold, he reorganized his role in the Cypress Creek restaurant. He planned to roll in a few days before the restaurant's grand opening, check the punch list, and release his best crew, but need begat action. He would go to the construction site, finish the build-out, and cap his long, successful career with a money-making machine that would prove he came out on top. What more did he need from life?

Chapter Two

Riley stared at the architectural samples arranged across her glossy work desk. Texas sunlight shone through the tall windows in her office, but the building materials slipped out of focus. Roofing shingles, paint swatches, fabric samples, and gleaming trim selections mattered. She squinted and considered closing the drapes to filter out the bright, May sunlight. *Did the affluent technology board chair want a media room?*

Downing half her iced coffee, she ran a finger along a swatch of organic fabric and envisioned the house she drew. Sage and emerald-green geometrics created movement, and flowing water channeled a retreat. The chair gave her free rein to drain his bank account, but she struggled to finish the Austin Hill Country project.

Lacey, her assistant, walked into the office, toting a tablet in her capable, sun-kissed hands. "What's wrong? Are you stuck?"

Riley looked back at the samples and imagined one of her fathers, Papi, walking through the organic showplace she designed. "What's wrong with gilding and heirloom vases? Sconces. Everything doesn't have to be practical. We could add a dash of vintage flair."

"Vintage just means old." Lacey wrinkled her nose. "And dusty."

Shaking her head, Riley glanced through the

windows at the arid landscape and recalled the antique stores where she whiled away weekends. Rotating through a mental inventory of gilt pieces, she imagined dinner parties and family game nights. She doubted the chair's wife spent her days searching for make-ahead appetizers. The pair expected restrained luxury, not quirky lamps made from the leather cowboy boots at Mimi's Boot Byre.

Riley had a hard time knocking her childish love for rhinestones. Dad began the family's architectural empire. Although she stepped from his shadow and built a boutique firm catering to preservation and enhancement, her firm's whole-house approach also provided everything from full architectural services to construction assistance and furnishing curation. For the right price, she would even stock a client's bar, and her client waiting list grew every quarter.

Nobody knew she felt like a sunbaked lizard stuck in an empty margarita glass. Rolling up the chairman's design plans, she reached for a clip. A sharp pain radiated behind her eyes.

She dropped the plans and pressed her fingers against her temples. The oversized papers unrolled at her feet. Her vision went hazy, and she saw spots. When the office's sleek, modern design blurred out of focus, she braced a hand on her desk and breathed through the pain.

Lacey scooped up the plans and dropped them beside the samples. "Another headache? Sit for goodness sake. You look like death."

Shaking her head, Riley waited for the sharp pain to subside. She rubbed her hands over her face and pushed through the episode. Gold highlights brightened her chestnut hair, and a stack of jeweled bangles decorated her wrists, but wealth provided weak protection against human fragility. She would have to be stronger. "Really, I'm fine. Have we considered terra cotta?"

"Terra cotta?" Lacey tilted her head. "Is that a new coffee shop?"

"It could be." She tested her balance and rearranged the architectural samples. This design lacked something. She traced the subtle, orange highlights balancing the arid setting and keeping the compound from fading into the landscape. "The house needs a pop of color."

"You need a pop of color." Lacey sat on the edge of the large desk. "Maybe you have a brain bleed. Stroke. Tumor." Furrowing her brow to the extent her preventative toxins let her muscles convey emotions, she unlocked her tablet and ticked off possible diagnoses.

Riley tapped her manicured nails on the desk. "How about a water?"

"Cancer's too obvious." Lacey scrolled down the tablet screen. "Acute poisoning?"

She dropped into her white, leather desk chair and stared at her bookcases while she let Lacey ramble off potential diagnoses. Hardback books summarized decades of design mastery and artistic inspiration. She knew the titles by heart, but the glazed urn sitting on the top shelf held her gaze. It held her twin brother's ashes.

Losing Grant brought her life into sharp focus. He was the golden boy, and he would laugh her ass out of the office for whining about the chairman's future project. She rubbed her temples and gathered her thoughts. "Lacey, pull the Saltillo samples from the storeroom."

Lacey stopped scrolling. "All of them?"

Riley blinked, but she slowly nodded.

"Right." Lacey stood and straightened her pencil skirt. A blonde curl slipped over her eye, and she tucked the curl behind her ear. "There must be fifty boxes in the storeroom. Good thing I packed my flats."

"Think of the workout." Riley suppressed a smile. For a woman who wanted a fulltime job, Lacey showed remarkably little interest in the trade. She would make an excellent project manager, but her design ethos stopped at her wardrobe. Sitting forward, Riley rearranged the samples on her desk. "Put the boxes on the drafting table. I can consider the samples in their boxes. No need to unpack all of them."

"Right." Shaking her head, Lacey turned and walked out of the office. "All of them."

"And a water!" Riley raised her voice.

Waving a hand, Lacey trudged toward the break room like a prisoner.

"You can still go to medical school!"

Lacey flipped her the bird.

She felt the ghost of a smile tug at her lips. Lacey might not be helpful, but she kept life entertaining. Standing, she reached for Grant's urn and hefted its weight. "Was I too bitchy?"

She could imagine Grant doubled over in laughter and offering to help Lacey. He was the vivacious twin always out for a good time. In addition to heading the construction arm of Dad's firm, he was also a volunteer first responder and the life of the party. Until he slipped beneath roiling, muddy floodwaters, she believed he was invincible.

North of Cypress Creek, her hometown, a stream split into two tributaries and flanked Cypress Creek's downtown district. When the water rose, it rose fast, but nobody expected the flash flood that claimed Grant's life. While people lost their homes and businesses to the raging onslaught, she took selfies on the beach in Cabo.

No matter how many times she poured out her regret to her therapist, she worried Grant had paid the price for her selfishness. If she were home, she could have stalled his heroic efforts or saved her dedicated, handsome, and brilliant brother.

Her therapist said grief stayed with a person, but pain dulled with time. Judging by the sharp spasms behind her eyes, she needed years of recovery. Work brought her relief, but if her solution had begun to fail her, she wondered how she would ever regain control of her life. She set the urn back in place on the shelf. "I'm sorry, Brother." Facing her desk, she swallowed and pulled herself together.

Her office phone rang.

Seeing her father's name on the screen, she took a deep breath. Dad's success granted her VIP status, but recognition came with a price. People couldn't resist showing her pictures of kitchen remodels or asking her about Grant's passing. She pressed the speakerphone button. "Hey, Dad."

"How's my girl?"

"Killing it." The lie barely registered. Her father made millions from Travis County's fast-growing expansion, but losing Grant also sent him into a downward spiral. She held out hope he recovered, but she doubted his reserves. "What can I do for you?"

"I need you to take over an unruly client."

She held her breath.

"Ansel Percheron." He coughed. "Who knew one man could cause this much trouble?"

Ansel Percheron was one of the nation's most recognizable chefs. At forty years old, he was the chef-proprietor of ten restaurants in San Antonio, New Orleans, Las Vegas, Miami, and San Francisco. He even lent his name to a restaurant aboard Star Cruise Line's Texas Ship. His success afforded him eccentric leeway, but his insistence on using San Antonio professionals created a heap of trouble for his newest restaurant in Cypress Creek. "What's wrong, Dad? You can't keep up?"

He snorted.

Goading her father might inject vitality into his project management skills. He ran a design, build, and construction company with a celebrity clientele. While she tended toward organic, free-flowing designs, he specialized in pizazz. If anyone doubted his reach, they could send a drone over his Cypress Creek ranch. It needed its own zip code. Admittedly, Dad might shoot down the drone.

"Ansel's a megalomaniac," Dad said, "but I like him."

She snorted. For weeks, Dad whined about the project, but the restaurant would bring cachet to their small, Texas town. Too bad the chef's underlings had little confidence in local construction crews.

His out-of-town craftsmen knew the new restaurant needed floor drains and fireproofing, but they had no idea how to manage inspection wait times and anticipate local quirks. If Dad or his client had taken her advice and hired Nathan Thomas as a local contractor, then Nathan could have anticipated half the problems the out-of-town crew encountered.

Recalling wasted work hours sent her heart rate through the roof. She took a calming breath. Toying with the ends of her long, brown locks, she listened to her father's rant and wondered when she could get a haircut. Having two fathers came with twice the number of dad jokes, but she wouldn't have it any other way. *Papi must be tired of listening to Dad's complaints.*

"What do you think?" Dad asked.

She released her hair and yawned. "Tell Percheron our tradesmen know the city laws, rules, and regulations. If anyone can pass inspections, avoid expensive fines, and interpret codes, they can. Same product, better outcomes, and smaller bills."

"I doubt Percheron cares. His henchmen have triggered enough redesign costs to make me blush when I cash his checks."

She wet her lips. "Is Percheron paying the bills?"

"Hell, yes."

"Okay, then." She let out her breath. "What's the problem? You can handle him."

"My hip." Dad moaned. "I'm too old for this drama."

She rubbed her eyebrows and understood the weeks of grousing phone calls she fielded were a lead-up to this call. After Grant's memorial service, she took over Grant's projects at the family firm, and having set the precedent, she had a hard time backing out of the agreement. If Dad asked her to come to Cypress Creek and get the Percheron project on track, then she would do it. The technology chairman would have to wait for Saltillo tiles. "Okay, Dad. I'll be down soon."

"What's wrong with today?" he asked.

"I have clients…" She let the excuse trail off.

"Ansel arrives on-site tomorrow. I need you here to intercept him." Dad cleared his throat. "With this flare-up in my hip, I can't navigate the construction site, and I don't want Papi to fret."

She exhaled and mentally rearranged her schedule. "All right. I'll be there tonight."

"That's my girl," Dad said.

Smiling, she ended the call. In under a week, she could troubleshoot the Percheron build-out, put in face time with her parents, and soothe her worries. The job would be a piece of cake, and Dad's team had done all the research and legwork. Dad would get his feet back under him. She would return to her design practice. She swirled in her chair, caught the edge of her desk, and kicked up her feet. "Lacey?"

"Coming!" Lacey dropped a box of tiles onto the drafting table. The weathered cypress groaned.

Riley dropped her feet back to the carpet. "I'm heading to Cypress Creek for a week."

Lacey looked up.

"Reschedule my appointments and tell the tech chairman I'm sourcing local goods."

Grinning, Lacey pulled out her phone and walked away from the tiles like a woman ready to abandon her workout buddies in favor of a cold cocktail.

If only Riley's life were that easy.

****

Heading southwest from Austin, Riley kept two hands on the steering wheel of her luxury, black SUV.

She passed miles of suburban development while dictating emails and monitoring traffic surges along Interstate 35. The state's ability to build roads and crossovers made Texas road trips a traveler's dream, but she wiped sweat from her palms and flexed her fingers. Returning to Cypress Creek also made her stomach turn. Everyone in town knew what she lost and where she vacationed when the historic flood nearly wiped out the town.

Staying on the freeway as long as she could, she turned off on Ranch Road 12 and the drive that would take her past Canyon Lake. The residential sprawl dissolved into sparser developments and hilltop estates. She could stop at a number of addresses and pay house calls on previous clients, but she kept her white-knuckle hands on the wheel.

She dodged a pothole and overcorrected. The SUV skittered along roadside reflectors marking a fire hydrant. The rhythmic call to action shook her out of her lethargy, and she straightened in the leather driver's seat.

The tire pressure sensor on the dashboard flashed.

She sighed. Kicking up her feet in the office might have been overkill. Life was never *that* easy. She pulled into a nearby service station and navigated toward the air pumps. Putting the SUV in Park, she grabbed her phone, climbed from the driver's seat, and walked toward the rear tire throwing an alarm.

A nail protruded from the sidewall.

"Great." Shading her gaze, she estimated how long the tire would hold. If she could reach her family's ranch, she could call a service company to replace the tire. More immediate attention for the tire meant she would have to camp out until the local tire repair shop could fix the hole or replace the tire. Sweat ran down her neck.

"You need help?" a man asked.

Turning in the baking hot sun, she made eye contact with a handsome stranger putting air in vintage tires. He wore jeans and a form-fitting, white T-shirt. His blue car, a classic, gas-guzzling monster, might be a few decades older than its inspection sticker, but both specimens looked roadworthy. Lucky for the man, she didn't need his help or a ride in his gleaming roadster.

"I would hate for you to ruin your nails." He winked.

She wondered if she needed a new manicure.

"At least let me put air in your tire. It'll get you to a mechanic."

Before she dismissed his offer, she looked closer. His wide shoulders and toned arms suggested he did something manual for a living, but his defined chest muscles looked honed in a gym. She doubted he laid asphalt for a regular paycheck.

A large, white scar marked the hand he used to hold the air hose, and she considered whether the scar restricted his mobility. Opening her mouth to ask, she considered how intrusive the question might be and swallowed the question. Getting involved with a stranger was the last thing on her list. "No, I've got it."

He straightened and dusted off his hands.

Shy of six feet tall, he wore a low-brimmed hat shading his face, but he looked lean enough to spend his days moving his body instead of occupying a desk chair. If he wanted to offer unsolicited advice, then she would consider the advice, but she would keep her phone clutched tightly in her hand. "Thanks for the offer."

"How far do you have to go?" he asked.

"About twenty miles."

"You like to speed?"

She worked her jaw. Growing up in Texas, she had met enough wannabe cowboys and dance hall junkies who expected nothing but pie and penance from the women in their lives. "Define speeding."

He laughed. "All right then. If I were you, I'd probably get the tire fixed or replaced before I drove more than an hour. I passed a repair shop coming in from San Antonio. The place looked like it carried an extensive selection of new and used tires. Judging by the rust on their corrugated roof, they probably charge fair prices"—he cleared his throat—"not that you need the break."

"What does that mean?" She couldn't fault the man for judging her based on her appearance. She'd done the same thing to him, and life had a way of reinforcing perceptions. Dropping a hand from her gaze, she scrolled through local listings for repair shops. Sure enough, a tire shop matching the man's description appeared at the search page's top. "Everyone wants a good deal."

"True." Circling the SUV, he whistled. "In that case, you might as well get both back tires replaced. I'd hate to find you here again next week."

Her enthusiasm for his down-home advice waned. "Do you own said repair shop?"

He laughed and leaned against his blue car. "Not my line of work, but I'll give you something to keep an eye on. If the mechanic's running his mouth or giving you too much attention, he'll probably grind down on the impact gun and ruin your wheel studs. Some guys don't have a clue how to use a torque wrench."

"And you?" She tilted her head, playing into his handsome arrogance. "You know how to use a torque wrench?"

His lazy smile deepened. "Yes, ma'am, I do. A man who helped raise me was a mechanic, and he taught me to take care of cars, cooks, and women."

I bet he did. She wet her bottom lip and looked him over from his leather boots to his low-brimmed hat. On another day, she might have looked twice at his one hundred and twenty-five thousand dollar car and his three-dollar white T-shirt, but she had limited time for baited flirtations and sunbaked philosophies. Dad needed her, and Mother Nature had set the sun to broil. She slipped her phone in her pocket and cleared her throat to break his easy spell. "I think I can make it home."

He tipped his head. "You have someone you can call? Someone who can follow you down these backcountry roads?"

"Sure." In truth, she leaned on herself, her wealth, and her connectivity, but this handsome stranger and his easy ways were novelties her fast-paced lifestyle kept in check. Another day, she might have lingered over his smile and his perfect white teeth, but unless she found a stiff drink, a mist fan, and heavy shade, she would melt into the sizzling asphalt.

He stepped forward and offered a hand. "My name's Paul. I can follow you for twenty miles. Call it a Sunday drive."

She raised her eyebrows. Texas had its charms, but

she'd rather gore herself on a longhorn than tell a stranger where she lived. Anonymity suited her just fine. "It's Friday."

He laughed and tipped his hat.

The sound of his laughter shouldn't make her insides hum, but it did. She took his hand and felt his rough calluses. Unable to resist the texture, she rubbed a thumb along his skin and savored the texture. "You work with your hands."

"What was that?" he asked.

Dropping his hand in an instant, she felt her cheeks warm. "Nothing. Your grip surprised me."

He rubbed together his thumb and fingers. "You surprised me. Maybe I should tone down the scrub soap. Find a pretty woman to take care of me." He winked. "Know anyone?"

His charm was too good to be true. His laugh made her think of long dinners on back porches and shared jokes. Too nice for broodiness and too good-looking for a rough sell, she wondered what to do with him. Lingering in the countryside would be an easy indulgence, but duty called. "No, you're great just the way you are."

Looking away, she considered her next move. He tempted her, but caution warned her to climb back into the SUV and drive away. She was an award-winning architect and preservationist. If she wanted to spend her days peeling off her panties at the drop of a wrench, she could have had a lot more fun in college. Who knew the smells of engine grease and gasoline could knock out her common sense?

"How about this?" he asked. "I give you my number, and if you don't text me you're safe within an hour, then I'll alert the highway patrol."

She chewed her bottom lip. "But then you'll have my number."

He straightened and adjusted his hat. "Yes, ma'am, I will."

Pulling lip balm from her purse, she considered her options. If she stood outside the gas station any longer, she might offer to buy his hat. Her tire could blow out on the highway, but as long as she had cell service, she could call for assistance. Standing by the air pump chatting with a handsome stranger might fulfill some of her college fantasies, but the longer she dawdled, the more air leaked from her SUV's back tire.

"A name would be helpful," he said.

"It's Riley, but I'll pass, and I'll be fine. Don't worry about me."

He tipped his hat. "Your call."

She turned her back, but failure and denial warred for her attention. If she misjudged the trip home, odds were low the tow truck operator would be half as attractive as Paul and his shiny, blue car.

She reached for the driver's side door handle and opened the SUV's door before she thought twice about her decision. Climbing on the running board, she paused and looked over her left shoulder. "Thanks for doing the gentlemanly thing. It's a lost art."

Dropping the air hose, he looked north. "Some things are worth preserving."

She couldn't agree more, but instead of engaging, she retreated into the safety of her SUV and started the engine. Pulling away from the air pumps, she glanced in the rear view mirror and expected to find him watching her depart.

He took a knee and methodically put air in the car's front tire.

Judging by the vehicle's rims, the tire might be as old as the car, but she doubted he would endanger himself or others on the road by driving on worn-out tires. More likely, he was someone who took care of his belongings. Heeding his advice, she clicked through the SUV's entertainment system until she could call her best friend, Aubrey Thomas.

"I'll bring the kids up to Austin next week," Aubrey said by way of greeting.

"I got impatient." Riley adjusted her sunglasses. "I'm coming to you."

A high-pitched squeal served as Aubrey's response.

She laughed. "Honestly, I'm in town to meet with Dad about a work project, but you're icing on the cake. Join me for drinks before I brave the family compound?"

"Let me check with Nathan. I don't think he has anything scheduled this afternoon, but you never know with these construction types."

She waited and monitored the tire's air pressure on the car's control screen. The number dipped, and she pressed the accelerator toward the floor mat.

"Okay, we're good." Aubrey corrected a kid and shuffled glassware. She came back to the call. "Text me when you get into town, and I'll meet you at Kyle's place."

"Sounds good. See you soon!" Ending the call, Riley focused on the drive and the smooth, black asphalt. Heat shimmered above the road's surface, and a red hawk circled overhead. Paul asked if she had someone she could call to follow her down the backcountry roads, but that person died two years ago.

Grant's death brought tears to her eyes in the most unexpected ways, but nothing could bring back his smile. Aubrey, with her erratic stories, rambling family, and indecisive creativity, was the distraction she needed. Exhaling, she tapped the steering wheel and admitted other forms of distraction might be a good call. She could have stayed at the service station to flirt with Paul or admire his easy smile, but she had twenty miles to cover and a lifetime to make up for abandoning her brother.

Chapter Three

Ansel finished putting air in the tire and wondered what possessed him to approach an uptight, well-manicured woman with shadows beneath her eyes. She was the definition of complications, but he gravitated toward the stubborn way she accepted her predicament. Adding air to her tire and staining her fingers with grease might be the last thing she wanted to do, but if it needed doing, she would handle the task.

If he needed doing, he had a roster of publicity-hungry models willing to flatter him over dinner for the chance to snap a photograph or land in his bed. Hell, he could skip the date. The two models who'd rolled around the deck of his sun-drenched yacht both left messages with his publicist, but he would never call them.

The boat and the models stayed in the Caribbean, but he flew stateside to address the restaurant build-out in Cypress Creek. His preferred limousine company would send a driver to service his foolish whims, but he had two good feet, and Cypress Creek defined "walkable." He only planned to stay in town until opening week.

Instead of speeding into the Hill Country town, he had stopped for air and offered to play knight gallant to a pale-skinned woman with a heart-shaped face, a strong jaw, and big gray eyes that weren't quite blue.

When he gave her his middle name, he hoped she would continue to look at him like a dusty stranger and let him do an anonymous good deed. The world could be full of Pauls, but success made Ansel Percheron a household name.

Instead of accepting his help, she dismissed his offer.

Not that he could blame her. She gave off a responsible air, but the dark shadows beneath her eyes defied makeup. Whatever ghost chased her across the central Texas countryside had enough power to haunt her dreams. Some part of him ached to hold her close and promise everything would be fine. Then again, what did he know about makeup, ghosts, and women?

Shaking his head, he climbed behind the roadster's wheel and turned onto the road leading to Cypress Creek. With Collins safely returned to San Antonio, he cleared his schedule to sort out the problems plaguing the Cypress Creek build-out. He needed a feminine distraction like he needed a norovirus outbreak.

Not that he was against women. They were beautiful creatures, but they were also fierce competition. His most profitable venues boasted a female sous-chef or a female chef de cuisine. The dames did more than instruct his staff. They balanced his intensity. If he could run every restaurant himself, his venues would be more profitable, but his net take would diminish. Nobody built an empire for shits and giggles.

His new restaurant, an ode to Texas glitz and glamour, would borrow the town's name and become its hallmark destination. He preferred to source local ingredients, but practicality tempered his ambitions.

Local supply availability and repeat customer demands shaped his vision for the restaurant, but he limited his forays into dishes featuring wheat, dairy, cane sugar, pork, and chicken. Press write-ups touted his gluten-free, dairy-free, cane sugar-free, soy-free, and pork-free offerings, but diversity came naturally. Chefs accustomed to cooking what nature provided were creative, but chefs accustomed to feeding a packed house were practical. The balance came from honesty and transparency.

He knew chefs who claimed to source locally foraged, fished, and farmed ingredients. The jerks lied through their teeth. "Pacific octopus" spawned in the Mediterranean, "wild venison" lived on farms in Idaho, and "roasted poultry" looked suspiciously like big-box organic chickens. If a popular restaurant had a one-acre farm, he guaranteed ten percent of the restaurant's ingredients hailed from the acreage, and the other ninety percent came from high-end suppliers.

Eagle Hawk taught him to respect the land and look for heritage food sources. But without a national, full-scale agricultural revolution, Ansel had to make-do with America's diverse offerings. He could produce locavore, Lakota-grounded dishes at a small venue, but he couldn't keep up the act for an entire season in a city like Chicago. Serving twenty-five different plates, six nights a week, required more than a token farm. It required discipline, practicality, and compromise.

Compromise had almost undone him.

When he found Aubrey in bed with Steak *Frites,* he tossed *his* white apron on the bed and weighed his choices. He skipped the Culinary Institute of America, the go-to incubator for kitchen stars, because he wanted to retain his connections to South Dakota. He could list the reasons he and Aubrey should be together, but her actions overshadowed his emotions, and he was a man who preferred action.

Instead of reiterating his heart's desires for partnership and family, he turned his back on the naked, gasping pair and seared their adultery into his memory. Then, he walked away.

For weeks, her betrayal haunted him, but he refused to give her the last word. He vented to his peers in the restaurant industry, but they sympathetically bought him beers and told him karma would take care of the situation.

Karma must have been on vacation.

Word about his leaked recipes captured the attention of the cooking school dean, and Aubrey found herself expelled before graduation. A week later, she published an exposé titled "False Promises." The piece tore apart the school, his connection to the Pine Ridge Indian Reservation, and his informal association with the Oglala Lakota tribe.

The piece gutted him.

His foster father, Chris Eagle Hawk, and his peers rallied support. Despite their efforts, reviewers claiming to be disillusioned diners trashed Ansel's reputation. In three months, his first restaurant failed.

Steak *Frites*' restaurant suffered the same outcome. Aubrey called Ansel, but he let her calls go to voice mail and buried himself in his next project. With enough market analysis and innovation, he could sauté his way into success.

Each economic decision left him grinding his teeth and reviewing his first missteps. Early in the mornings, with the kitchen closed, he listened to Aubrey's artificially sweet voice mails and let them fuel his fire. Her betrayal left behind a bitter, metallic aftertaste. He told himself the mistakes made him a stronger man, but the disappointment remained. He breathed his heart and soul into that menu, and it hadn't been enough.

Aubrey's critique of his first restaurant stung because it hit too close to home. He wasn't a tribe member. He was a kid who landed on hard times and found refuge in a loving community. Eagle Hawk witnessed the accident that killed Ansel's parents and almost killed him. A generous, but taciturn, man, he fostered Ansel until Ansel reached legal maturity. He became a second father, and Ansel repaid his generosity by cooking simple dishes and doing hard work. Without him, Ansel would have been lost.

Without Aubrey…well, he preferred not to think about Aubrey Thomas' influence. She wanted to be a chef, but her syrupy interior design business looked successful enough. Selling throw pillows paid her bills, but she would spend her days in the shadow of his success.

He slowed to take in the Hill Country scenery. Tourists flocked to the area for rocky vistas, quaint festivals, spring-fed swimming holes, and iconic rivers. He wondered how few considered the reason their playground abounded with water and wildlife. The Hill Country owed its attributes to the Balcones Escarpment. Cutting through Texas' middle from Waco to Del Rio, the scenic nest created an oasis for Spanish missionaries and new age travelers.

The Escarpment also created danger.

Located in "Flash Flood Alley," Cypress Creek and

the surrounding ranchland occupied a notorious, flood-prone region. Limestone hills drew adventurers and suburbanites, but the tourists sped past flash flood warning signs as easily as they sped past speed limit signs. Below their shenanigans, a fault zone ran more or less even with I-35, and given the right incentive, the region's pent-up energy could wash over them in a heartbeat.

As a lanky reservation kid from South Dakota who knew deals could go bad, he read the insurance report on Cypress Creek from cover to cover before he signed on the dotted line. By purchasing a burnt-out hotel in the small Texas town, he took on the building's past, present, and future, but he also insured the hell out of his gamble. As long as the venue marked his accomplishments and Aubrey Thomas' ire, it could burn, flood, or crumble at nature's whim.

He parked outside the building and considered his investment. Creamy, yellow limestone blocks and rough wooden beams kept the building's exterior standing tall, but fire gutted the interior, and strong winds collapsed the weakened roof front. A blue, plastic tarp flapped in the wind.

The limestone shell had potential, but it needed a lot of work. With his name attached to the project, customers would flock to the restaurant, but it might lose money. Grinning, he hardly cared whether it made him another million dollars. The point was to get under Aubrey's skin.

She might have abandoned her culinary ambitions to start an interior design business in her hometown, but she always coveted wealth. While his new restaurant boomed, she would start and end her days knowing what she had missed. He would have the last laugh from his yacht's prow. As raindrops fell, he pulled an umbrella from his car's trunk and leaned into the well to grab the set of keys that would admit him to the restaurant.

"Of all the gin joints," a woman said.

Recognizing Aubrey's voice, he closed his eyes and wished he were better prepared for this meeting. Based on their relationship, she would yell or throw herself at him, and either outlay would be fine. She could sell all the dust-coated tchotchkes in the world, but she couldn't change her character. "You always said gin was too harsh."

"You always muddled my comments."

Exhaling, he straightened and rocked back on his heels. No matter how many times he psyched himself up to tell her to fuck off, he wondered if she saw something in him no one else did. She treated him like a meal ticket, but having discarded her chance, would she realize what she'd lost? Drawing a deep breath, he adopted a smile and faced her.

The woman who stomped on his heart wore a light-green tank top. A beaded necklace hung between her breasts. No longer straightened, her light-brown curls matched her wide eyes, and a small diamond stud pierced her nasal septum.

She once thought the piercing made her look edgy.

He told her it made her look desperate, but his success in the culinary world depended on more than flashy aesthetics. "Slow day at the store?"

"I heard that piece of shit car coming a mile away." She shook her head. "You always had terrible taste in cars and in women."

He tried to laugh, but the sound died in his throat. Tourists darted to their vehicles, but he stood holding an umbrella. He had nowhere else to go. "How's business?"

She leaned on the front porch railing wrapping her storefront. Water bypassed the building's gutters and dripped off the metal roof. It created a shimmering curtain that separated their worlds. "Do you care? You never returned my calls."

"Funny, I don't remember having time to return them." He shrugged and turned his head to look at the limestone building waiting for a new life. "Running a restaurant empire takes work."

She coughed. "So do relationships."

He pivoted and made eye contact. "Don't tell me I found you in bed with that idiot because you were lonely, Aubrey."

"That *idiot* brought me flowers." She crossed her arms. "He made me feel special."

The absurdity of her statement left him at a loss for words. Rainwater pooled around his boots. He considered storming away, but this conversation had simmered for twenty years. The sooner he brought their confrontation to a boil, the sooner he could move on.

"You, on the other hand…"

Rolling into Cypress Creek was supposed to squash his shortcomings, not enumerate them. He held up a hand. "You were in culinary school, and you knew exactly who you dated. Chefs have long hours and unpredictable days off. Holidays and special occasions are a non-starter. You knew it!"

Yawning, she looked past him. "You were obsessed. Some men can balance their priorities."

Turning to follow her gaze, he looked past Gristmill Road where Kyle Road's Pizza Joint and Brewpub sat on a rise above Cypress Creek. A light-strung patio covered an outdoor seating area. He wondered if the restaurateur could recommend supply vendors. "I was driven."

"Everyone has a love language." She picked at her cuticle. "I needed words, and you excelled at being the strong, silent type."

Frowning, he returned to her rain-shielded gaze. People enjoyed his company. He had loyal friends and a show on The Chow Channel. If she cast him as a stoic genius, she ignored his more colorful traits. He wondered if she had ever seen *him*. "I told you I loved you."

A slight laugh slipped past her lips. "Only while we were naked. Fixing leaking pipes and bringing home stale pastries aren't the same things as acknowledging what makes a woman special. Why were you with me? Convenience?"

He weighed his response. She was more than convenient. By pairing interesting ingredients and complex techniques, she stumbled into culinary success, but replication eluded her, and predictability bored her. Apparently, he bored her, too. "It wasn't convenient."

"What was it? A progressive streak? A taste for the exotic?"

Steak *Frites* were about as exotic as his left shoe. The little acts of service she dismissed so casually were the ways he demonstrated his love. Memories of his parents were too painful for inspiration, and Eagle Hawk let him work through his grief in the garage and in the kitchen. Neither venue required poetry or deep conversation. Of course, Ansel would fail the relationship's soul-baring requirements.

If Aubrey wanted poetry, she should have fallen for someone other than a scarred chef. The only art he made came plated and served with a flourish. "I'm sorry I failed you. I tried my best."

"Well, your best wasn't good enough." She wiggled her fingers and beckoned him toward the storefront porch.

Like a child, he climbed the steps and replayed their relationship. He liked to think he would have made time for her, but long hours and unpredictable days off left him exhausted. Maybe he took her for granted.

"You're here for another chance?" Gripping his shirt, she pulled him close. "You never forgot me, did you?"

Closing his eyes, he resisted her smile's pull and the ginger familiarity of her scent. She was a beautiful woman, and twenty years ago, landing her affection fueled his self-worth. Seeing her bestow her affection on another man and give away his recipes confirmed his weaknesses. He was a fool for thinking he could ignore her influence on his life.

If his assets were the only things she wanted, nothing about her had changed, but he had the upper hand. Clearing his throat, he stepped out of her grasp, turned, and jogged down the steps. "I don't think so."

"You did just what I said." She shrugged and waved a hand toward the future restaurant. "Typical American menus made you rich. Good for you."

Her condemnation stung. Modern, fine-dining

tropes were so extreme that disguising them felt futile. He reflected Native American food cultures and used pre-colonization, indigenous ingredients, but this wasn't 1491. He had to be practical. Rain pooled on the sidewalk, and waves of mulch slipped past the garden beds. He looked up and drew a deep breath. "I'm sorry I wasn't enough."

She looked past him toward the old hotel. "You think this new restaurant will bother me? It'll bring me business. It'll revitalize this town. Or it won't." She shrugged and made eye contact. "Either way, we'll have your investment. Win-win."

Age deepened the lines near her eyes and confined her ambitions to a sleepy, Texas resort town. He wanted to comfort the woman he remembered, but she matured into someone duller than an aspiring chef. "Is that all you care about?"

She wiped a thumb across her nose. "Your presence doesn't affect me in the slightest."

"No, I'm sure it doesn't." He rolled his shoulders. "However, I just realized which one of us has a problem. I can build restaurants anywhere in the world and give myself heartburn, but you have no skin in the game. If nothing affects you, how can you love it?"

She raised her chin and made eye contact. "I love my kids."

"And yourself."

Laughing, she dropped a hand and pulled back from the railing. "Who wouldn't love me?"

He could stand on the sidewalk beneath an umbrella and tell her how lonely she sounded, or he could complete the task that brought him to Cypress Creek. After her exposé, she wrote bad reviews of his restaurant, and her friends mimicked her language. He could call out her bullshit or trash her boutique online, but he was determined to rise above her methods.

His restaurant would succeed, and in doing so, it would prove his achievements outweighed his flaws. Aubrey could stew in the eclectic mess she made, and he could pour his profits into a life he enjoyed. Doubt wiggled through his consciousness, but his reputation remained on the line. He shook his head and walked toward the car.

"Ansel…"

Turning, he waited for a hint of self-reflection.

She waved toward the street. "Don't take up all the parking."

Snorting, he buried his friendship aspirations. "Thanks for the tip."

"And don't—"

Closing the umbrella, he climbed into the driver's seat, slammed the door, and gunned the engine. Facing Aubrey had kept him up at night. Having survived the first showdown, he didn't care if everyone in Cypress Creek knew he had a deeper connection with this town than he let on. He peeled out of the parking lot.

Slowing his breathing, he stopped in front of a blue bungalow situated along a side street past the main thoroughfare. Gray limestone formed the building's foundation, prickly pear cactus lined its front walkway, and a short-term rental sign hung in a window. The property sat within walking distance of downtown, offered high-speed Wi-Fi, and boasted an outdoor kitchen. It would do just fine while he made his point.

Parking the roadster in the gravel driveway, he climbed from the car and sauntered to the bungalow's front door, doing his best Western impression. He could be Paul for another few days. Paul was easy, and the fewer expectations people had, the less disappointment they experienced.

He wondered if any nosy residents appreciated his efforts, and he considered hitching up his jeans, but drawing out the impression might lead to comedic mistakes. His teenage years on the reservation healed his heart, but they curtailed his knowledge of TV Westerns. Although San Antonio offered a colorful blend of Mexican and Texan cultures, it did little to improve his John Wayne impression.

On the other hand, his passport housed a colorful blend of stamps and visas. So what if he couldn't swagger like a macho cowboy too quick with a gun? Between his loaded bank account and his yacht, he had learned to live with his shortcomings.

Punching in a code, he entered the bungalow's living room and surveyed flagstone flooring and leather sectionals. Fresh lilies sat in a vase on the dining room table beside a six-pack of beer. He walked toward the local brew and glimpsed pamphlets and a three-ring information binder.

Texas hospitality had its charms, but whoever laid out the spread wanted him to see the information binder. Picking up the beer, he ferried the bottles to the refrigerator and figured he had time before he cared about trash days and cleaning services.

A knock sounded on the front door.

A middle-aged woman with a wide smile and shiny, black hair swept into a bun poked her head into the bungalow. "Mr. Percheron?"

"Here," he said.

She swung wide the door and stepped inside. "I'm so glad you made it." She took off her shoes and gently arranged them facing the front door. Selecting a pair of slippers from a low shelf, she donned them, extended a hand, and waited. "I'm your landlord, Moeko."

Recognizing the name, he strode forward and gripped her hand. His boots left a trail of dust, but he would clean the floors. She had his corporate credit card number and could rectify his shortcomings. "Ansel. Thank you for having me."

"My pleasure."

He released his grip and caught the subtle scent of cardamom. A swipe of white flour marked her navy shirt. Mid-recipe, she might have rubbed her cheek against her shoulder. He wondered if he should apologize for arriving early.

"My mother-in-law went back to Japan for the summer." Moeko tucked an errant wisp of black hair behind her ear. "This is her house, but she's glad you're using it. Houses without occupants fall into disrepair."

"I'm glad she's nostalgic," he said.

Moeko laughed and set a bright-green flier on the table. "More so that she's practical." She cleared her throat. "Cypress Creek is a lovely town, and I'm looking forward to seeing the old hotel's second lease on life. I hear you're opening a restaurant."

He nodded.

"Please let me know if you need anything. My number's in the information folder, or you can walk next door. Any questions?"

He cocked his head. "What were you baking when I pulled up?"

"Brioche squares with nectarine cardamom jam

and cream cheese." She checked her watch. "They'll be out of the oven in fifteen minutes."

"I'll be over in fifteen minutes."

She grinned. "You're welcome to come for a taste test. On Saturday mornings, I sell pastries from my house, and I wanted to check the recipe before the line forms. I hope you don't mind the foot traffic. The queuing customers are very polite and should stay on the sidewalk."

The prickly pears lined the bungalow's walkway, and he expected their spines would keep the most determined pastry enthusiasts from jumping the line. "Thank you for the offer, but I'll get in line with the rest of your fans."

"Ten o'clock. Cash or Mobile Pay," she said. "I'm retro and modern."

He laughed and rubbed the tight skin on his palm. Weather affected the twenty-year-old burn mark, and he could remember the days before a cell phone ruled his life. "Noted. I won't let payment options slow me down."

"Who does?" Turning, she gathered her things and let herself from the bungalow.

The bungalow was too silent. He could hear people chatting on the sidewalk and closing car doors. The small-town vibe might grow on him, but the town felt nothing like reservation life and the peace his second family created.

Thinking about the unexpected events that shaped his past, he rubbed the old scar and considered how far he had come. Grabbing a hot pot on national television had been a mistake, but he was a chef. His hands bore scars.

The initial sear had brought tears to his eyes. As the heat paralyzed his response, he coped with a string of flavor-infused curse words and refused to let one mistake destroy his big break. At worst, healing the wound might take two to three weeks. He curled his fingers around the wound and played on.

After winning the show and playing to the cameras, he retreated to the bathroom and unclasped his fingers. Stiff from holding a protective gesture, his digits barely moved, and the angry, oozing mess they protected needed more than antibiotic cream and a cold compress.

While the producers celebrated the show, he called a car and rode to the local hospital for emergency services. The second-degree burns required immediate attention. Attending doctors excised his damaged skin and referred him for a follow-up skin graft. The mark secured his fame and paved the way for his future, but it had stayed with him.

By ending his career in Cypress Creek, he hoped to prove he had come full circle and could move on from his past. Unfortunately, the work crews and professionals tasked with supporting his endeavors took off the weekend.

Glancing at the green flier Moeko left, he saw an advertisement for an evening concert at the Jacob's Hole Concert Venue. Mikey Roberts, a semi-famous Texas musician, would perform a show at the outdoor park, and tickets cost about as much as a burrito.

With his hat low over his face, he could form opinions about the town without causing a ruckus. He was a bachelor on holiday in Texas Hill Country, and if he wanted to tap his feet to a twangy guitar, nobody should recognize him or fuss about his choices. "I might as well."

His voice ricocheted between flagstone floors and cypress beams. The dust mote sunbeams ignored his echoing declaration.

He shivered, pocketed the flier, and let himself from the bungalow. His suitcases could wait. Aubrey's hardened demeanor and her nonchalant response to the restaurant could wait. If revenge were a dish best tasted cold, then he waited a long time to plate it. In the meantime, he would pass the night with good music and the heart and soul of Cypress Creek.

Chapter Four

Riley met Aubrey on the newly renovated patio adjoining Kyle Road's Pizza Joint and Brewpub. Embracing her with a hug, she pulled back and checked out the metal necklace hanging between Aubrey's breasts and her light-blue wrap dress. Hill Country locals recognized her as an excellent designer and patronized her shop, Aubrey Thomas Interiors and International Style, but she was a one-woman show. "How do you look so cool in this heat?"

"Good hair products." Aubrey flipped her hair over her left shoulder. "And good genes."

"Oh, is that all?" She laughed and savored the joy of reuniting with her friend. Aubrey's short, light-brown curls defied humidity, and her wide, brown eyes took in small details. Her smooth, brown skin and confident, open smiles encouraged customers to linger, but the small diamond stud piercing her nasal septum hinted at an edge.

Aubrey touched up her hair in a mirror she pulled from her purse. "Inside or out?"

Riley scanned the restaurant patio and admired the renovations. The I-beams supporting a shade structure looked freshly welded, but nobody seemed concerned with the rusty, unpainted steel. Locals and tourists scarfed down happy-hour pizzas and chatted animatedly. A guitarist played pop melodies and delivered easy lyrics. "Let's sit outside."

Aubrey turned to the greeter. "How long?"

"An hour." The woman checked her phone and yawned. "Maybe more."

Stifling a laugh, Riley remembered being sixteen years old and the only mid-afternoon customers in the pizza joint. Even then, Kyle shaped dough behind the counter while she and Aubrey sipped sodas and admired his upperclassman charisma.

Aubrey dug in her purse and checked her phone. "We can sit at the bar."

Her suggestion would work, but Riley wanted the privacy of a table. Weekly text strings maintained their friendship, but Aubrey usually had enough gossip and human-interest stories to fill a local news segment. She scanned the tables for an alternative seating arrangement.

Kyle, grown older and more handsome, stood behind the bar, tracing his finger along a bottle label's fine print. He wore his short, frizzy, brown hair slicked back, and concentration wrinkled his honey-skinned forehead. As he read, he moved his lips, and his medium-length goatee followed.

A server approached.

Kyle straightened.

At full height, he commanded the pizza place bearing his name. His loose, black button-up shirt matched his large, black eyes, but piercings and gauges in his ears reflected the brewery knowledge he accumulated at a college brewpub. His appearance might scare off geriatric bus-trippers, but she had known him her entire life. He had double joints, a fondness for rock climbing, and enough custom art in his backyard to fill half the galleries in Cypress Creek.

The server walked off.

Kyle scanned the restaurant.

Aubrey waved, smiled, and pantomimed tapping a watch.

He looked between her and Riley before jerking his head toward a table sporting a *Reserved* sign.

Thank you, Riley mouthed. Small towns radiated friendliness, but Cypress Creek had weathered enough storms to cement the bonds between its citizens. She might have fallen out of favor with the gossiping biddies, but friends like Kyle would always have her back. Grabbing Aubrey's hand, she pulled her friend toward the reserved table and ignored the older locals who whispered behind their hands.

"Brother died," a man said. "Flood."

Two ladies fanned themselves with paper fans. "Tragic."

She raised her chin. If the locals disapproved of her presence, they could speak up or keep their opinions to themselves. The same women whispering behind their fans used to pinch her little girl cheeks and admire her holiday bonnets.

"How long do you want to stay?" Aubrey asked. "Should Nathan feed the kids?"

"Up to you." She pulled out a bistro chair and caught her middle school principal's furtive review.

The administrator shifted her chair and hid behind a large, paper menu.

No wonder Riley usually shied away from town and went straight to her family ranch. If meeting Aubrey for drinks two years after the flood caused such a commotion, she could have stopped by the liquor store for a bottle of wine and made herself at home on Aubrey's back patio. In the meantime, she flagged down a server with purple hair, who then filled their water glasses. "Two glasses of Chablis." The flinty, white wine would cleanse her palate and erase the snarky, judgey busybodies who judged her.

"Good call on the drinks." Aubrey tapped out a text. "Those sweet, little hellions get freezer pizza for dinner. We'll have our wine, and then I'll go home to help put them to bed."

Riley would go home to two snoring fathers, a sprawling house, and empty hallways. She thanked the server delivering their wine, forced a smile, and lifted her menu. "Perfect. Tell me how you've been."

"Good," Aubrey said. "The shop's doing well, and downtown traffic has been brisk. Your dad's renovating the old hotel next door, but he keeps the site clean and makes the contractors park on the back roads."

Riley raised her glass. "The way to a woman's heart."

Aubrey grinned and sipped her drink. Her hair slipped over her forehead, and she brushed it clear.

Seeing the gesture for the thousandth time, Riley savored coming home and wondered what had changed. The town's residents probably still cradled and constricted teenagers with an auntie's fierceness. Tech entrepreneurs, rock stars, and resort vibes glossed-up traditional roles, but they still lived in Texas's Hill Country. She didn't want to kill tonight's vibe by explaining her return to Cypress Creek. If all went well, she and Aubrey could hang, but she refused to impose. "So how's business? Parking's still at a premium?"

Aubrey rolled her eyes. "If Mimi Lewis stopped

her sidewalk sales, we wouldn't have a problem."

Letting the comment stand, Riley grinned. Mimi's Boot Byre had so many vintage boots that Mimi used handwritten catalogs to describe her inventory. She kept the most desirable boots under shade tents on the street. High school students erected the tents every morning and made minimum wage schlepping boots in and out of her storage shed, but they also made most of her sales.

"Last week, she sold a pair of orange ankle boots to a woman from San Francisco. Six hundred dollars, and the boots made the woman look like a circus clown."

"Ridiculous and impractical." Riley laughed. "She'll probably wear them to Burning Man."

Aubrey raised her glass and sipped.

The server with purple hair approached the table and refilled their water glasses. "What can I get y'all to eat? Do you want to hear the specials?"

"More cold, white wine. This fancy shit is fine, but so is the house white." Aubrey set down her menu. "I'm not even hungry."

"Sure." The server entered Aubrey's selection on a mobile ordering device. He turned to Riley and raised a pierced eyebrow. "And you?"

In the city, the servers would grill Aubrey on her varietal preferences, but Cypress Creek retained enough of a country air to let "white wine" encompass any cold, crisp vintage the restaurant offered. Why had she gone off script? Tossing her menu on top of Aubrey's menu, she smiled and sat back in her chair. "I'll have a ranch water."

"Coming right up." The server scooped up the menus and departed the table. "I'll be back in a few minutes with your drinks."

Tipping back her head, Riley let the early summer evening wash over her. Half the restaurant might be gossiping about her reappearance in town, but right now, she had zero cares in the world.

Kyle's place sat on a rise above the Cypress Creek waterway. Below the light-strung patio, a crushed limestone path led toward a viewing platform overlooking the creek. At this time of year, the creek hardly flowed.

As the town boomed, creek-side developers removed natural vegetation from the creek banks to create amenities for cash-wielding customers who liked waterfront cabins and kayak docks. Kyle kept the vegetation intact outside his restaurant. He said the vines discouraged teenagers, but she thought he enjoyed the wildlife. If she squinted through the trees, she could make out lights from Jacob's Hole peeking through the vegetation like early fireflies. The illusion of a carefree night beckoned, but she focused on her friend.

Aubrey smoothed her napkin over her lap, caught someone's gaze, and winked.

Turning, Riley found Kyle chewing his bottom lip like a debate raged below his surface. His willingness to give them a reserved table suddenly had more to do with Aubrey's flirtation and less to do with small-town loyalty. "No." Turning her body, she sighed and made eye contact with Aubrey. Her husband was a good man, and he worked hard for his family. "Tell me you're not doing what I think you're doing."

The server returned and set down the drinks.

"A minor flirtation." Aubrey sipped her house white. "Don't worry."

Riley picked up her ranch water and downed half the glass. Tequila *blanca*, lime juice, and carbonated water went down easy, but if she had known about Aubrey's affair, she might have ordered shots.

"We agreed to keep it brief, but damn, he's good in bed."

Riley choked on her cocktail and slapped her chest. "Nathan…"

"Works long hours"—Aubrey sipped her wine—"and watches too much porn. If he doesn't want to invest in our relationship, why should I have to do all the work? Don't worry. He'll never leave the kids." She exhaled. "He's lucky to have me."

Catching the server's attention, Riley mimed tipping back another drink. Aubrey's infidelity concerned her on so many levels. Nathan was a good guy, but he was an excellent contractor.

With the Percheron project looming, she planned to fire the San Antonio crew and enlist Nathan's services to get the restaurant back on track. If he accepted the job, he would be a lifesaver, but worksite camaraderie would tempt her to mention Aubrey's secret. She was loyal to her friends, but relationships stretched her so thin she feared she would crack.

"Everyone in this town has affairs," Aubrey whispered. Lifting her glass, she tipped back the final drop. "You've been gone too long. Grow up."

"Thirsty?" Riley asked.

Aubrey wiped the back of a hand across her mouth. "I could drink a bottle."

The server set down two drinks. "I'll be right back to take your order."

Aubrey leaned forward. "Let's talk about you. Did

you know Mikey Roberts is playing tonight? I wish you two would get back together. At least, we would see more of you."

Riley hadn't known about the concert, but she had planned to send her ex-boyfriend a congratulatory text on the release of his latest album. If her old flame planned to romance a steel guitar in front of a crowd of locals, Jacob's Hole was the only venue in town big enough to accommodate his fan base and his ego.

"He never got over you," Aubrey said.

She sipped the remains of her ranch water and sucked on an ice cube. The odds of her getting back together with Mikey were as high as the odds of taming a coyote. A smile seemed like the safest response to Aubrey's prompt, but a smile might be too much encouragement. She shrugged and wondered if running the project from Austin would have been the wiser move. "He never got over the idea of me. I grew up. He expected me to flatter him and acquiesce to his schedule like a high school girl."

"He's always loved you." Aubrey leaned back and crossed her arms. "You were so harsh."

Looking at the relationship from a distance, Riley's behaviors might have seemed cold, but being a musician's girlfriend required equal doses of love, flattery, counseling, and wariness. Aubrey bed-hopped until she picked Nathan. Thinking of all the shattered hearts she left in her wake, Riley mimicked her friend's pose. "Harsh?"

Aubrey's right eye twitched. "I mean, not harsh, exactly."

Bats darted through the trees and steered clear of the patio lights.

Riley uncrossed her arms, finished her drink, and replayed her early romance with Mikey. Trailing him around the southeast wasn't her idea of a career. Their fights and their love letters landed in his songs, and she wondered if she was his muse or his ghostwriter. She sighed. " *'I need Riley June to ride me soon'* isn't my idea of an endearment."

"Honey, he was eighteen." Aubrey stared toward the creek. "We all make stupid mistakes when we're young. Give the boy a chance."

"Like you're giving Nathan a chance?"

Aubrey rubbed a hand across her chest. "It's not the same." She cracked a smile and snickered. "How do you commit to one person for *sixty* years?"

"You should be that lucky!" Chucking a balled-up beverage napkin at Aubrey, Riley wondered if her childhood would ever end. She considered moving to Europe, but this rocky, sunbaked town would always be her home. "You need to end the affair."

"No." Aubrey shook her head. "It'll burn out on its own. These things always do."

Sipping her drink, she quelled her sadness. Marriages should be fulfilling partnerships, not mutual conveniences. Aubrey and Kyle were adults, and if they wanted to risk their hearts for quick flings, she would stay out of their business. Her family obligations held less wiggle room. "I'm taking over the hotel renovations for the new restaurant."

Aubrey tilted her head. "Why?"

"Dad's hip keeps him from the construction site."

"But it's not your style. You do modern, preservationist things."

She laughed and set down her drink. "Thanks for

following my career. I thought you'd be happy to have me around for a while."

"I am"—Aubrey exhaled—"but the restaurant going into the space is too big for Cypress Creek. It'll fail, and the owner will never pay off his construction loans."

"You know him?" She tilted her head. "He's based out of San Antonio."

"Doesn't everyone know him?" Aubrey asked. "He's such an egotistical prick. Before he went big time, he was forever pining about the way things should be in his kitchens and on his menus. Some things work because they work. I don't know why he felt like he had to reinvent the whole, damn industry."

"But he did." Riley replayed Aubrey's career and wondered if she and Percheron clashed egos in culinary school. For Aubrey, the stint in North Dakota was a way to appease her mother's college aspirations. For Chef Percheron, the school must have been so much more. She swallowed and decided to tread carefully. "I mean, I get what you're saying."

Aubrey nodded.

Learning Dad took the job, Riley bypassed Ansel's glossy headshots and focused on his accomplishments and the themes connecting his establishments. As a young chef, he practiced his art in fine restaurants in New York, Boston, and Philadelphia. A lucrative job offer lured him to San Antonio where he helmed the kitchen at a legendary restaurant on the River Walk before extending his reach into more cities. She ate at his original restaurant for client dinners, and the food remained excellent.

A few years ago, he had famously burned a hand

on live television, let loose creative swear words, and kept cooking. The Chow Channel's ratings went through the roof, and Ansel Percheron expanded his empire.

He was the chef-proprietor of ten restaurants in San Antonio, New Orleans, Las Vegas, Miami, San Francisco, and aboard Star Cruise Line's Texas Ship. Aubrey might not have fond memories, but he was the nation's most recognizable chef. Faulting his kitchen credentials was like faulting a billionaire's investment strategy.

Aubrey flicked a loitering fly from the table. "Plus, isn't steak passé?"

She laughed. Passé chefs held court at the bar in neighborhood hangouts. As both a celebrity restaurateur and an accomplished chef, Percheron made media appearances, sold signature products, and ran his restaurants from a gleaming office tower. A mismatch between his empire and Cypress Creek's population meant one of two things. Aubrey was right, or Percheron was ahead of a wave of high-net-worth individuals purchasing Hill Country acreage. She would give him the benefit of the doubt. "As far as I know, he's paid his bills."

"Whatever."

"What aren't you telling me?" she asked.

"Well, I mean, I knew him a while ago," Aubrey said. "When I went to cooking school, I met him. We dated. Of all the places in the world, why is he coming here?"

"Cypress Creek is swimming in new money." She wondered if she should screen her firm's clientele through Aubrey's love life. The chairman's wife might not appreciate throw pillows from Aubrey's store. She shrugged. "No matter where people originate, they see Texas as the last great frontier."

Aubrey toyed with her napkin.

"You know I'm right. Austin's newest ranch owners aren't weathered cowboys. I'm working on a tech CEO's house, and he's dropping more cash than an actor with an ego complex. If wealthy newcomers want to buy ranch land for personal playgrounds, they probably want to buy steaks, too."

Aubrey worked her chin.

"You think he's pining for you?" she asked.

"No." Aubrey smoothed out her napkin. "It's just…"

"Maybe you should stop worrying about past flings and start worrying about your marriage." Spitting out the advice felt cathartic, and she considered a final drink. Boy, the busybodies would enjoy seeing her and Aubrey go at it. Too bad, their teenage spats always ended in hugs. This one would be no different. Aubrey spoke her mind, and Riley did, too. No wonder they'd been friends their entire lives.

"Maybe you should go back to Austin." Aubrey narrowed her gaze. "You always said you'd make it big."

"You did, too." Riley gripped her empty glass and rubbed away the condensation. She wondered if their text-based friendship had fallen into disrepair. Missing their old camaraderie and wondering if diverging paths had turned them into frenemies, she picked up her water glass and sipped. "I'm proud of your store. When I hear people are coming to Cypress Creek, I urge them to visit."

"Do you?" Aubrey dropped her shoulders. "Thanks."

Time slowed, and Riley breathed deeply. Aubrey was right about one thing. She built her life in Austin. Returning to Cypress Creek and muddying the waters by judging Aubrey's decisions made her the worst kind of condescending woman. She took a deep breath and dialed back her impulse to parachute into town and fix the world. Dad's project would be enough. "Tell me about the kids. How's school?"

Aubrey's expression softened. "They're good. Straight *A*s."

After placing orders for salads and a shared pizza, she let Aubrey rule the conversation.

Kyle walked up to the table, carrying two glasses of dessert wine. He set them on the table. "It's on the house."

Riley made eye contact and stared long enough to convey her knowledge of the affair.

He swallowed.

"Come on, Riley." Aubrey nudged her leg.

"I'll run to the restroom." Standing, she turned her back on the pair and skirted restaurant tables until she entered a small, artistically decorated washroom with corrugated iron stalls. After washing her hands, she loitered to fix her hair. *Should I call a car?* If she had to deliberate, she had her answer.

She walked from the restroom and saw Kyle sitting in her chair and laughing with Aubrey. Their clandestine relationship would soon be town gossip. Old friends shared jokes, but they rarely tangled their legs under a table. Riley refused to get caught in another wave of scandal. She pivoted from the newly renovated patio and made her way toward the creek. A path led to Jacob's Hole, the town's swimming spot and concert venue, where Mikey's songs filled the night and teased mindless escapism.

Easing past two lovers kissing on a wooden observation platform, she wondered if something in the water attracted people and offered hope. The creek ran between fragrant, cypress overhangs, gray, water-smoothed roots, and tumbled, limestone boulders. It resisted droughts and flowed year-round. Maybe couples thought the creek's resilience would seep into their affections and preserve them, too.

Maybe the creek depended on irrigation runoff.

She fired off a text to let Aubrey know she had bailed. As darkness fell, the shadows along the creek shifted, but the limestone gorge was as familiar as her reflection. Each crevice held memories. She considered lingering on a boulder to replay happier times, but she craved crowded anonymity. Jumping over the fence lining the access road, she made her way toward the lush lawn beside Jacob's Hole.

True to Aubrey's word, Mikey held court on the lawn's stage, couples danced on the grass, and kids chased light-up toys through the bushes. He was a country musician of reasonable success, and he wore his achievements as easily as he wore his Texas-sized belt buckle.

Fans in Cypress Creek had supported him since he began as a solo act in local bars. Country music superstars covered his songs, but his original versions were feel-good classics, and his debut album remained a mainstay on local playlists.

Every time she heard his voice, she remembered

her early twenties and winced. He looked like a star, but he put a lot of effort into his appearance. Stage makeup compensated for pasty skin that never held a tan. He carried a plastic comb in his back pocket and bought gallons of maximum-strength hair products. His signature pompadour and silky voice lent him a dreamy appeal, but the dreams were fantasies.

Still, he made strangers smile. High school girls loved his softly shaped jaw, well-formed nose, and large lips. No offense to the world's brown-eyed population, but his bright-blue eyes sparkled in publicity photos, and he knew it.

Riley tried not to focus on his crossed eyes and receding hairline. Patio lights swung overhead, and children laughed. Choosing a spot along the seating wall marking the field's perimeter, she let his familiar songs wash over her and wondered if staying in Austin was the right choice. Keeping Cypress Creek's citizens in line was someone else's job, but tending loved ones was hers.

A man wearing jeans and a form-fitting, white T-shirt approached and dipped his hat. "So you made it?"

She recognized the man from the service station and pulled back. "Did you follow me?"

Paul laughed.

His hearty amusement and smooth confidence soothed her nerves. "What are the chances?"

"Well, that's what I aim to find out." He offered a hand. "Dance with me?"

To let him down easily, she checked her phone and hoped he imagined a busy schedule. "I'm sorry…" She looked up and found him staring with a wolfish air. The only commitments he honored were the ones he created. She liked his hat, his humor, and his chiseled jaw. She could dance with him without worrying about entanglements, but she felt selfish and shook her head. "I don't think so."

He blinked and dropped his hand. "Well, that's a first."

"Rejection?" she asked.

"Yes."

She suppressed a laugh. He was handsome and confident, but his trendy, leather bracelet made her question his old car. If his muscled mechanic shtick was manufactured lure, she'd take the bait but not the hook. He had probably tried surfing, wakeboarding, and breathing techniques. Pulling up his shirtsleeve, she might find a little, red kabbalah bracelet hiding behind his cuff. A new age cowboy's rugged ethos knew no bounds. She covered an honest yawn. "Maybe another night. How long are you around?"

He pulled off his hat and scratched his scalp. "Hard to say."

Without the covering, his shoulder-length, sun-lightened brown hair swung loose in the night air and the shadows cast by stage lights. Wolfish or not, he was a handsome man and made an impression at the service station, but after her encounter with Aubrey, she wanted breathing room. She looked toward the stage, stretched out her feet, and tried to get comfortable. "No offense, but I'm a terrible dancer. I would probably step on your toes."

He sat close on the limestone wall. "You couldn't offend me if you tried."

She glanced over and smiled.

He rubbed his thumb into his opposite palm.

The action revealed his calloused hands and confirmed her assumptions about his line of work, but the large burn mark on his palm caught her attention. She wondered if he was a welder or dabbled in the mechanics his father taught him.

Either way, she wanted to reach out and trace the mark, but she had zero scars to share or show for her regrets. Instead of making contact, she clasped her hands in her lap and squeezed until her knuckles ached.

"It's my first night in town," he said.

She jerked her chin toward the stage. "Welcome to Cypress Creek."

He grinned. "Tough nut."

He could herd goats for a living, and she would still feel pulled toward him. She snuck a second glance and noticed his T-shirt pulled taut across his abs. Instead of ogling his muscles, she should give him directions to the Chamber of Commerce. "Cypress Creek is booming, but you can probably see that for yourself. Where are you from?"

"South Dakota."

She struggled to come up with a response. She associated the state with Mount Rushmore and the Badlands, but she had little else to add to the conversation. "Long drive?"

"You have no idea," Paul said.

Mikey transitioned to a new song.

The crowd shifted, and couples came and went from the lawn.

Glancing toward Paul, she made eye contact.

He rubbed his lip. "Tell me one thing, and I'll leave."

She nodded.

"Why is the prettiest woman in the crowd sitting by herself?"

She awarded him points for persistence. Given the drama in Cypress Creek, one dance couldn't hurt, but she was in no position to start something with a footloose man from South Dakota. How many people lived in South Dakota, anyway? She tipped her head and compared Paul's profile to the full-face smiles she'd seen on Percheron's website. The grinning, culinary superstar could take pointers from Paul's laid-back vibe. She'd take a mechanic's charm over Mikey's peers any day of the week. What would the locals say if she bedded another superstar?

She laughed. They'd say she chose men by the size of their bank accounts, but they would have plenty of other things to say, too. The town's sympathetic glances and whispered comments about Grant's death stung, but so did life's ability to move on without her. Maybe if she lost her cool in the town square, she could purge her grief, her hang-ups, and her reputation. Instead, she kept her emotions tucked inside her heart and pressed her nose to the grindstone.

"You think I'm funny?"

"Definitely." She smiled and imagined losing herself in Paul's arms. Would Mikey see? Would he care? Did she care if he cared? The speculative ripples widened her smile. "Hard to say why no one asked me to dance. Maybe I smell bad."

He leaned close and inhaled deeply. "You smell just fine. Better than fine."

She worked her jaw. A hot man was clearly coming on to her, and she could imagine losing herself in his arms. But where would the indulgence take her?

Instead of giving into her attraction, she should nudge Aubrey back toward her marriage or present herself at her parents' house. Paul, with his easy grins, was nothing but trouble. His allure spelled trouble, but he tempted her.

So did an escape. Even though she wanted to lean into his warmth, she held herself stiff and weighed her desires against her responsibilities. A disastrous yoga retreat taught her solitude was never the answer, but she wanted to flee from her attraction to Paul. She didn't deserve his attention.

Needing a deep breath, she looked toward the stage where Mikey played. Her therapist told her to learn from her experiences, but Paul and Mikey were so far apart, she needed a conference room to lay out their discrepancies. One man romanced her naïve heart, and one man tempted her toward pleasure, but where did the liaisons leave her?

Standing, she decided to return to the restaurant before she landed herself in trouble. Dropping her head to make herself heard above the music, she rested a hand on Paul's shoulder to steady her balance. Proximity was a terrible mistake. He smelled like sage, sweat, and fresh, crisp aftershave. She imagined rubbing her cheek along his rough chin. If she met him in an Austin bar, she would definitely take him up on the offer. "Maybe another night."

He cocked his head toward the music, but he remained absolutely still.

She had expected him to pull away. Instead, he radiated heat.

"Maybe another woman. I thought you were made of stronger stuff. Are you as indecisive as this music?"

"This music is good." Eyes wide, she pulled back. "Mikey's kind of famous."

"A dead cat could dance to this shit," he said.

She rallied to Mikey's defense, but a particularly corny lyric punctuated her resolve. Paul was right, but the juxtaposition of a stranger swaggering into town and dumping on a local country star made her laugh. Arrogance worked in the city, but not in Cypress Creek. That man on the stage was Mikey, her old flame, and she would be damned if she would let some handsome stranger dump on her town. First, she needed to mount a defense.

"I'll take your silence for agreement." He stood, put his hat on his head, and tugged a hand toward the remaining audience members. "Dance with me. Last chance."

Thanks to the wine, she fell into step and shuffled her counterarguments. "Why are you dancing to music you don't like?"

"I'm dancing with you." He pulled her toward the crowd, but he turned and caught her gaze. "The music's just background noise. I'd dance with you anywhere."

"Would you now?"

He dropped his mouth toward her ear. "I would."

Familiar faces stared and snapped pictures.

"All right, then." If the busybodies wanted to talk about her, then she hoped they got a good shot. Raising her chin, she followed Paul into the crowd. Two-stepping was walking to a beat, and she could humor Paul with a quick dance before her ineptitude proved her point.

He picked a spot, placed his right hand on her shoulder blade, and held out his left arm in an open invitation.

Taking a deep breath, she laid her arm along his supporting arm and gripped his bicep. It was solid, and she relaxed a bit. Instead of bolting, she slipped her right hand into his left hand and waited to see if he could keep time.

He could.

The quick-quick-slow-slow pattern carried away her worries, and for a brief moment, she closed her eyes and trusted the music. Texas was a big state, and she could lose herself in the swirl of patio lights, laughing couples, and familiar music.

"Everyone's staring," he said. "Did you embezzle money from the flower guild?"

She laughed and knew the carefree moment was too good to last. Shaking her head as the song ended, she slipped from his grip. "Worse. I slept with all their husbands."

He widened his eyes, scanned her from head to toe, and stared. Then he let loose a sly grin. "Doubtful."

"Hmf." If Aubrey could have an affair, then she could, too. If gossip traveled, the only people who could suffer from her indulgences were her, her partners at the firm, and her parents in Cypress Creek. As long as she stayed away from politicians, news of her indiscretions would remain in Hays County. She placed a hand on Paul's chest and felt his heartbeat. "You're not from around here. What do you know about me?"

"Plenty." He pulled her into another dance. "I took you for a sweet, country girl, but you're prettier than a javelina wearing lipstick, and you're just as fierce."

She lost the beat and stumbled. Had he compared

her to a medium-sized, pig-like animal? She'd heard of putting lipstick on a pig, but she never imagined being the pig. Blinking off the spell of his cologne, his warmth, and his alluring presence, she widened the space between them. "What in the hell does that mean?"

"Keep dancing, and I'll tell you," he said.

Lightning cracked.

She jerked away her gaze and counted the seconds until the rolling thunder sounded.

"Skittish?" he asked.

She blinked off the weather's ozone spell. "I don't like storms."

"Lightning never strikes twice."

Paul had about three seconds worth of experience in Cypress Creek. The town weathered floods, droughts, and earthquakes. Any local worth their salt paid attention to the weather and watched out for their neighbors. "What's with the colloquialisms? Read too many fortune cookies?"

He adjusted his hat. "I picked up this folksy habit, and it's worked. The man who helped raise me didn't like swear words, and I would do anything to please him and stay out of trouble."

"Well, shit," she said. "That's almost cute."

"Almost?"

She ran a hand over her face and considered bolting like a startled hare, but liquor provided the courage to be more than...a pig? She shook her head and stared at Paul. His good looks and easy vibe should be catnip for an overachieving city girl, but she was also a townie. "I don't go to bed with cute men."

He worked his jaw. "Well, fuck."

She laughed. "Much better."

He brushed stray hair from her right shoulder. "For the record, you're nothing like a javelina."

"Thank you."

Lightning flashed behind a storm cloud.

She watched nature's outburst fade. Her attraction would fade just as quickly, and the sooner she took shelter and returned to her work, the safer she would be. "Thanks for the upgrade, but I should head out. A storm's brewing."

"What?" He stared.

"Cat got your tongue?" she asked.

He rubbed his jaw. "I thought we were done with the animal comparisons."

She wanted to maintain the banter by pointing out his lupine traits, but a fat raindrop landed on her shoulder. "We are."

Saluting him with one finger, she turned and headed for the creek trail. The flirtation had been nice, and he was handsome enough to tempt her, but anonymity gave her too much freedom. Everyone in town would mark her departure. Instead of indulging her whim, she would slip into the tangled brush that kept tourists from the creek, and she would resume her orderly life.

A line of raindrops fell from the sky and dappled the dusty trail. The dark-brown spots made muddy confetti. Before she could enjoy the innocent splatter, a gust of wind shook a dead branch from an oak tree and dropped it to the ground. The reverberations traveled up her legs, and she froze.

Under the right conditions, the creek, now dry and tame, could become a formidable torrent, and thinking of the possibility reminded her of life's brevity. As families scrambled for cover, she did the same, but as she turned from the creek, she slammed into Paul's chest. He knew nothing of her past or her regrets. She gripped a handful of his shirt and admitted her attraction hadn't faded. It had morphed into a desperate desire to test her vitality. "Where are you staying?"

"A short-term rental. Pretty bungalow. You should see it."

"Is that an invitation?" She held her breath.

He scratched the side of his mouth. "If you were waiting for an invitation, then we could have started this party a while ago."

Grabbing a hand, she pulled him toward the park exit. "Noted, but let me text a few people so they don't worry about me. I'm rarely this impulsive."

"You do you." He matched her stride and plopped his hat on her head. "Until it's my turn."

She laughed. The heavy leather hat kept the worst of the rain from her eyes, but her soaked clothing hung on her frame. As old nightmares and pounding raindrops chased her from the park, she risked a glance at her handsome companion. Something about him had gotten past her reserves, and she wanted to know why.

He grinned.

Unable to pin down her attraction, she returned his carefree smile. Spending the night with a handsome stranger would be good for her mind and her libido. Settling into his gait, she relaxed and let anticipation hum in her blood. Returning to Cypress Creek didn't have to be a drama-filled trial. She would text her parents he had decided to stay at Aubrey's house. She would text Aubrey he had gone home. Nobody would worry about her, and she would get her kicks with Paul.

Safe in his tiny bungalow, she would strip off her heavy garments, chase a moment of bliss, and hope the tension between them burned bright enough to eclipse everything she'd lost.

Chapter Five

Punching in the door code, Ansel pulled the soaking wet woman onto the bungalow's flagstone flooring, slammed the door, and pushed her against the rough wooden wall. He wanted her so badly he had been hard since giving her his hat. Now, a single lamp cast the room in shadows, and his control hung on by a thread. "Yes?"

She nodded.

"Will you tell me your last name before I bury my cock in you?" Screaming the correct name seemed like more than a nicety, but if she didn't hurry up, he would call her "Baby" until the sun rose.

"Riley is enough." She gripped the edges of her shirt and pulled the soaked garment over her head. Adding her bra to the pile, she stepped out of her pants until she stood in her lace-edged panties. "Won't that suffice?"

"It will." He admired her curves and inhaled her unique floral scent tinged with the storm's damp appeal. He could throw her over his shoulder and make for the bed, but he had to stay focused on her pleasure. "More than suffice."

Despite being a woman he met at a highway gas station, she looked like someone who kept weekly nail appointments. He didn't want to end up scratched. He did want to chase the shadows from beneath her eyes, follow her racing pulse, and give her a reason to scream his name until sunrise.

"Maybe you need to see my identification?" she asked. "Blood type? Fingerprints?"

Swearing, he hoisted her onto the dining room table and pinned her hips. "Sassy. I want to see you naked."

She grinned. "So do I."

"Fucking coincidence. You're perfect." He stripped off his wet clothes, yanked her to the edge of the table, and pulled her mouth to his. The heat and precision of her response destroyed his reservations. She kissed as if she was desperate for air and only he could provide it. He was more than happy to oblige.

Changing the angle, he threw her right arm across his shoulder and pressed closer to her full breasts. She tightened her legs around his waist. He laid waste to her lips. Only a thin strip of silk kept him from sinking into her depths. His pulse skyrocketed, and his dick strained against the barrier. He took a deep breath and pulled back. "Will you regret this in the morning?"

She released his shoulder and tilted her head. Her chest heaved. "Will you give me a reason to regret it?"

He laughed and hung his head to catch his breath. "No"—he swallowed—"I won't." Raising his head, he grinned and tipped up her chin. "You're prettier than a convenience store cupcake. I'm happy to eat you out."

She laughed so hard she wiped away a tear. "You with the compliments."

If cheap compliments bought him more time with her, he would spend all night complimenting her eyes and work his way south. He'd been too close to blowing his load and forgetting her pleasure. Exhaling, he guided her back to the table. "Tastier than a roadside weed."

Grinning, she arched and exposed her neck. "Such flattery."

He trailed a hand from her neck to the soft skin between her breasts. "I'm speechless."

Grabbing his right hand, she pulled it onto her breast.

He flexed his fingers, abandoned the last of his reserves, and gripped the heady handful. Nestled between her legs, he leaned forward and kissed her lips without pretense. Skin to skin, he felt her heartbeat and the slick sweat replacing a summer rainstorm.

Her moans inflamed his passion, and his pounding heart sent his blood racing straight to his cock. Breathing deeply, he slowed his response, played with the shadows, and memorized her curves. He imagined kissing every inch of her body, and the task settled his system like a steadying hand. He took his time pulling gasps and sighs from her lips. Her hips flexed against him. He raised his head and made eye contact. "Impatient?"

She trained a hand along the thin line of hair leading to his cock and gripped him. "Yes."

He savored her touch, drew a deep breath, and pinned her hands above her head before she got them right back where they started. "Hold on. I have condoms in my overnight bag."

She braced herself on her elbows. "I love a well-prepared traveler."

He laughed, retrieved the condom, and scanned the room. The brown, leather couch, a former non-entity, suddenly looked like a godsend. Sliding the condom into place, he tossed the wrapper to the floor, returned to the table, and scooped his hands under her ass.

Picking her up off the table, he felt her heat tantalizingly close to his dick. He resisted dropping to the flagstones and letting her ride him. At least with the cold, stone floor against his back, he had a chance to savor her. He lowered her to the couch.

She wiggled out of her lace underwear, spread her legs wide, and slipped a finger between her folds. "Will you watch?"

"I could watch you all night." Dropping to his knees, he braced his weight on one hand, lowered his head, and pulled her right nipple into his mouth. Brushing aside her hand, he teased her pleasure until her back arched off the couch.

"Paul."

"Riley." He raised his head and made eye contact. "You're beautiful"—each word cost him a breath— "and tempting, and mine for the night."

"Yes." Her gaze glinted with promise, and she gripped his bicep and pulled him closer. "When I touch you, I can't think of a reason to stop."

"Then stop trying." Her touch felt like a branding iron, and the bungalow's chilled air pushed him toward her heat. He matched her kisses, and the fear of losing his control slipped from his consciousness. Matched to her rhythm, he relished every sigh and eager thrust against his hand.

Raising her ass from the couch, he dropped his head and savored her taste. Her heat and intensity, glimpsed on a hot summer day, stole his focus. Every lick and smooth, liquid sip was more delicious than the last. He could spend all night going down on her.

When his rhythm sent her tumbling over the edge, she cried out.

He pressed his face deeper into her folds and rode the waves as her body went rigid and limp. Raising his head, he grinned.

She reached for him and ran her nail along his clavicle. "Unless you'd like me to return the favor?"

He could take matters into his own hands and blow his load over her chest, but her satisfied gaze stoked his ego and looked delicious enough to savor. He scraped his jaw along her cheek and pressed a kiss to her hair. "In the morning."

"I like morning sex."

Smiling, he switched their positions and turned her until she straddled his legs. Running a hand down her back, he centered her hips, spread her cheeks, and tightened his grip for a moment. "I do, too." He released his hold. "But tonight, you can run the show."

She lowered herself onto his erection, rocked her hips, and leaned forward. Licking her lips, she teased a kiss from him and pulled back. "I can run the show, huh?"

"Be my guest." Words were a luxury. Every ounce of his control went into governing his pleasure. If he fucked every model who got lost in his test kitchens, he might not give a shit about Riley with the almost-blue eyes. Challenging him to make good on his intentions might be her superpower.

She rocked her hips.

"Fucking beautiful women." He grunted and withdrew. Gripping her hips, he slid into her heat, and the movement was as smooth as silk. She gasped and clenched him. He abandoned his promise and thrust into her depths. Her tight grip on his shoulders conveyed her permission, and he unleashed the fury and heat of his desire.

When the pressure built, he rocked a thumb against her clit, changed the angle, and watched her back arch over his arm.

Mouth open and eyes wide, she gasped.

Freed to chase his release, he plunged into her heat and pumped her hips until he lost control, shuddered, and threw his head back against the couch. His release washed over him, and he rode his pleasure until the pulsing echoes subsided.

She collapsed against his chest.

Holding her close, he unclenched his muscles and slowed his heartbeat. "Nice to meet you."

She laughed and climbed off him.

He slipped off the condom, tied it, and tossed it on top of a tourist magazine. Sure Cypress Creek could produce another copy of the magazine. He grabbed Riley's ankle before she could wiggle away and tucked her under his arm.

Sometime during the night, he rose and carried her to the bed. She slept like the dead, and sliding under the sheets at her side, he envied her oblivion. Whatever she did for a job probably ended the moment she left work. He dreamed up new dishes and reviewed profit sheets.

When the sun rose, its summer rays fought an overcast sky.

Riley raised her head from his chest, ran her tongue along her teeth, and made eye contact. "Morning."

He tucked her hair behind her right ear. "Morning."

She scrambled to her knees. "I didn't mean to stay over."

Backlit by the rising sun, she looked like a priceless statue. He itched to tumble her into the sheets and tease out her pleasure, but he wouldn't stop her from bolting. "It's a rental. Stay as long as you like."

"Huh." Covering her breasts, she glanced at the remainder of her exposed skin and dropped her hands. "No wonder you look out of place in this décor. I should go."

He scanned the lush wood and shrugged. His houses tended toward sweeping vistas and vibrant art. The intricate wall prints in the cottage intrigued him, but he would never have picked them. Riley's ability to peg the mismatch made him wonder what she did for a living. "Will you give me your number?"

"Aren't you just passing through?" She turned toward an en suite bathroom. "I don't live in Cypress Creek, either."

He flopped back on the pillow. A woman who whetted his appetites wanted nothing more than a one-night stand. He wanted to explore every inch of her skin. If he hadn't wooed her with asinine jokes and quick banter, he might stack up as more than a fling, but he spent twenty years guarding his heart. Toys were all he had, too. "Convenient."

"Look"—she walked into the bathroom—"let's call this what it is. A hookup."

Lightning cracked.

In the mirror's reflection, he saw her startle. "Not a big fan of rainstorms?"

She met his gaze in the mirror. "My brother died in a flash flood."

So much for keeping things light. He swallowed. "I'm sorry."

Leaning forward, she cupped a mouthful of water to her lips and turned. "Whenever lightning strikes, I'm skittish. He was my twin. His death rocked me and my family, but we're learning to bear the pain." She turned on the shower and reached for a towel. "Sorry if that admission kills the mood. It's not you, you know. It's the weather."

He piled up the pillows behind his back and let her comment stand. Her quivering voice belied her vulnerability, and the pain of her loss reopened his wounds. After the automobile crash that killed his parents, Eagle Hawk took him in, but every car horn and screeching brake made him jump. Learning to fix vehicles and understand their mechanical systems gave him a way to control his fears, but letting the Oglala Lakota community members guide his grief gave him a refuge.

Coming of age in their culture taught him death was part of the experience of living. He gained a father, but he also gained a community. His new cousins were more like brothers and sisters. A network of aunts and uncles functioned as his extended parents, and he spent as much time with the tribe's elders as with the tight-knit community's youngest members.

Losing his biological parents was a tragedy, but nobody stayed immune to loss. Some years, he felt like he constantly attended funerals. Watching the pallbearers carry their burdens, he absorbed the community's spiritual songs and faced death and mortality. The universality offered comfort. After internments, the tribe came together, and little moments of grief, food, and song became chances to reconnect.

As the years passed, he accepted the people he lost

weren't gone. He could still speak to them. Whether they spoke back was another story. He never had much time for the ghost stories, but he appreciated his peers and their sense of magic, their ceremonies, and the way they honored his memories.

Riley stepped out of the shower and headed toward the living room.

He laced his fingers behind his head and leaned against the headboard. "What was your brother's name?"

She stilled. "Why?"

"Names matter. I'm guessing that's why you won't tell me your last name."

"I told you, Riley's good enough."

"Last night, you distracted me with sex." He sighed. "Ballsy."

She blinked. "That offer expired."

Her steady gaze encouraged him. Despite her impending exit, she wore an interested expression that could tip into lust. "Any other offers?"

She laughed. "I really should go. Thanks for"—she let the towel fall from her hair and scanned his torso—"taking me in. I had a good time. You already look too familiar." She chewed her lip and turned toward the bathroom. "I should say good-bye before I get attached."

He had a dozen reasons to pull her back into bed and continue their association. By day, she might be shadows and sophistication, but under the cover of darkness, she shattered in his arms. He could spend the weekend feeding her impulses.

He considered following her into the bathroom, but having the door slammed in his face might wreck his handsome visage. He unlaced his fingers and braced himself on one elbow. "How about a cup of coffee?"

"Is that a code word?"

"It could be!" He reached for his phone. Three messages from Collins and a list of emails reminded him he had a culinary empire to run. "I'm laid back."

She wiped her damp face with a towel. "Last night, I needed someone laid-back. Storms always do me in."

He wiggled his phone. "Want to check the radar? Today could be a washout."

Lowering the towel, she shook her head. "I don't let my phobia control me, but how can you get lost in a moment when you recognize how much you can lose?"

Reality sobered his lust. He respected the rawness of fresh grief. Sharing emotions hardly lessened their impact, but he could still empathize with her pain. "I lost my parents when I was young. It still hurts."

Her lips quivered.

Sitting straight, he braced his weight on his right hand. "It's not a competition. I can imagine how much you miss your brother, but one day, the storms won't bother you this much. Maybe you'll look up at the dark clouds and think of him looking down."

She wiped away a tear.

Feeling like an asshole, he closed his eyes and shook his head. His game needed so much work. She could tell her friends about his lameness and solicit their laughter. He flopped back and draped an arm across his eyes. "Forget I said anything."

"Thanks." She cleared her throat. "I mean it. Safe travels."

Out of options to prologue their rendezvous, he listened to the cabin door slam and doubted he would ever see her again.

Chapter Six

A clear head, a heady night, and restful sleep kept Riley smiling. If Paul lived closer to Austin, then she would invite him to her house for therapeutic purposes *and* general satisfaction. Thank goodness, she hadn't had that final drink.

Tapping the steering wheel in time to her favorite alternative rock album, she drove her black SUV along the state highway toward her parents' house. After the early summer rains, cloudy, gray skies lingered, but her grin persisted.

The road made a sharp bend. A leaning aluminum mailbox and a jumble of limestone rocks marked the entrance to the ranch her parents owned. To an aimless driver, the break in the trees might look like the gateway to a neglected ranch, but Dad was as meticulous about the ranch property as he was with his new builds. She pulled the SUV onto the narrow, paved driveway apron and climbed out. Ignoring a rattlesnake dummy, she walked up to a chained cattle gate and manipulated a padlock.

The oiled lock popped open.

She tossed the lock toward the dummy snake. Metal hit metal with a satisfying *clunk*. Dad, despite his millions, retained his humor. If he let her reshape the Percheron project under Nathan's crew, he would need it.

Driving the SUV past the gate, she returned to the entrance, grabbed the lock from the dry dirt, and secured the gate. She broke a light sweat, but the perspiration hardly mattered. Her homecoming would be brief and effective.

She followed the crushed limestone drive through the roadside shrubs. The elevation dipped. Soon, the shrubs fell away. Bluebonnets, winecups, and pink evening primrose lined the road and soaked up the sunlight. She'd missed most of the spring blooms, but the two-foot-tall Indian blankets and their showy, red blooms deserved a smile. She adjusted an air-conditioning vent and tapped her fingers on the wheel. "Everything will be fine."

Lightning cracked, and an armadillo ambled across the road.

She slammed on the SUV's brakes. "Watch it, buddy!"

The animal glanced toward the SUV and resumed its journey.

Drumming her fingers on her right thigh, she wiped the sweat off her palms. "People pay me good money for my time."

The armadillo continued its leisurely pace.

She considered revving the SUV's engine, but if her foot slipped, she would have to scrape armadillo off the SUV's fender.

The gray clouds leaked, and raindrops peppered the windshield.

Taking deep breaths, she ignored the rainstorm and replayed her night with Paul. The scent of sage, sweat, and fresh, crisp aftershave lingered on her clothes and calmed her. "Everything's fine." With the drive clear, she followed the limestone until one hundred and fifty acres of Hays County hill country unfolded like a rancher's dream. Between dark storm clouds, sun rays peppered the grasslands with yellow-tinged spotlights, and cattle lulled in green meadows.

A steep, bald hill cast a cooling shadow over her parents' two-story home, and deer pecked at the grass near the tree line. Past the house, a spring-fed canyon led to Blanco River access. Elm and cypress trees lined the creek bed, and horse trails meandered through the hills. Seeing the landscape unchanged, she loosened her grip on the steering wheel.

Her phone rang, and she accepted the call without looking at the phone's screen. "I'm almost there."

"Did you lock the gate?" Dad asked. "Last week, some angler from Maine came to the house looking for river access. Stupid GPS maps."

Hearing his voice slowed her heart rate. "Did you call the cops?"

"Hell, no. I made him a drink."

She laughed and slowed the SUV for a white-tailed deer.

Head high, the animal stepped across the road.

Apparently, the local wildlife had forgotten her speed-fueled teenage years. Drumming her fingers on the wheel, she imagined her cantankerous father shooting the breeze with a trespasser from Maine. Maybe old dogs could learn new tricks. She could return without wallowing in grief. "Will you send the guy a holiday card?"

Dad snorted and ended the call.

She waited for the deer and let the landscape sink into her blood. The ranch occupied a prime spot in

Texas Hill Country. Ancient shallow seas left behind stark, beige limestone, but plentiful springs provided grass and forage for grazing Longhorns. As the sun set, the landscape would take on a soft, pink glow.

"Grant loved this place as much as I did." Wiping a tear from the corner of her eye, she tried not to think about losing him, but her tears fell. He was the first person to jump into the lake, scale rocky cliffs, or dig holes wide enough to swallow a car. Broken bones and stitches resulted, but he laughed off his injuries.

Tempering his enthusiasm proved futile, but she learned to judge hazards and her willingness to leap. Their different approaches created a push-and-pull dynamic common to twins. She kept him in check and followed him into adventures. Then, he went too far and paid with his life. She should have been there. The land's bucolic appearance could charm visitors, but it could also be lethal. Without him at her side, she would handle the days as they came.

The deer left the drive.

She hit the gas and hoped no other animals ventured into her path. The two-story, white ranch house dominated her view. Situated on a rise before the bald hill, the home offered floor-to-ceiling windows, large, shaded decks, rocking chairs, and a screened outdoor dining room. Behind the house, a spring-fed pool with an infinity edge sent water toward the barns. If the horses or the Longhorns noticed a whiff of sunscreen in the water, they never complained about the ranch's amenities.

Pressing a button on her phone for the garage door, she guided the SUV into the fourth bay and spied a bicycle in Grant's parking spot. She wondered who was audacious enough to leave a bike in such a loaded spot. If she found out the jackass from Maine had stuck around and claimed the bay, she would haul his ass back to the country road.

The prospect shouldn't bring her so much pleasure. Closing the garage door, she checked her reflection, added lip gloss, and smacked her lips. Papi had taught her well. She climbed from the driver's seat, clutched her purse, and composed her emotions in the garage's air-conditioned hum. Years of professional success straightened her spine. If she could bust balls in the Austin permit office, she could survive a weekend at her family home.

Gripping the cool doorknob to exit the garage and enter the house, she plastered on a smile and stepped into the mudroom leading toward the kitchen. The farm-style baskets and whitewashed wood from her childhood were gone. Hunter-green paint and brass knobs created a green tunnel that reminded her of mesquite trees. She liked the organic feel.

"Papi, I'm home!" Her voice echoed off woodwork and empty cubbies. Upstairs, secondary bedrooms had private baths, walk-in closets, and balconies overlooking Hill Country, but few people ventured up the stairs. No matter which way a guest turned on the ground floor, the house offered stunning, panoramic views. Clearing her throat, she modulated her volume. "Dad? Papi?"

"Finally! What took you so long?" Papi asked from the kitchen.

His exasperated response teased out a smile. Riley stepped into the kitchen with sunny views of the river. "Wouldn't you like to know?"

Papi danced out of the pantry and rounded the expansive marble island. He wore a yellow button-up shirt, and his manicured nails and highlighted, dark-brown hair looked immaculate in the morning light. Gold jewelry announced his status as a former drag star or a pampered lover, but Riley looked past his bling and frowned. Why was he wearing an apron?

The white, cotton utility hung from his neck, as if he had settled into his domestic roles with chic aplomb. She stared at the out-of-place garment, as if he wore a crumpled cocktail napkin on his head. "What is going on?"

Clicking across the wood floors, Papi pressed a kiss to her cheek, gripped her shoulders, and squeezed. "Oh, I'm so glad you're here. Your father's driving me bonkers."

She inhaled his fresh, familiar cologne. Missing her parents was a perfectly normal reaction. Wanting to buy a bottle of Papi's cologne and spray it on her childhood teddy bear would land her in her therapist's office. She cleared her throat. "What else is new?"

"That's my question." He pulled back and wiggled his jet-black eyebrows. "Why didn't you come home last night? Big date? Huh? Huh?"

Ducking out of his embrace, she set her purse on the island and ignored his probing question. Papi had immaculate manners, but he reveled in gossip. Despite her teasing entrance, she refused to provide it. "Dad's a little intense. What else is new?"

Papi laughed off the defense and patted her cheek. "Good point, but we'll revisit your naughty ways."

She flipped her hair over her right shoulder. Stepping into her childhood kitchen should be easy, but

Papi acted as if everything in the family were the same as it had always been. Had he seen the mudroom? Did he know who owned the bike? Couldn't he hold her a little tighter? Since losing Grant, her worldview would never be the same. She needed the comfort of family, but she refused to ask for another cologne-drenched hug.

Waving toward the kitchen, Papi rounded the island. "What can I get you? Coffee? Mimosa?"

"Both." Individual coping skills mattered, but the house's silence became a physical presence. Where was the sound of a cleaner vacuuming a rug or a landscaper trimming the bushes? Where were Jennifer Lopez's Puerto Rican vocals?

She cocked her head and listened for Callie, the housekeeper, and her barking dogs. Callie's room off the kitchen had a climate-controlled, screened-in porch for her pets, but the little stinkers were never this quiet. Something was wrong in the Golding household. "Where's Callie?"

Papi opened the built-in refrigerator and stuck his head in the opening. "She asked for time off. It's just the three of us. Quaint and cozy."

His buttocks stuck out of the appliance like two sassy, ripe cantaloupes. Dad was forever buying him tailored suits, but Miami lingered in his wardrobe. The idea of Papi wearing an apron and taking on household duties should bring a smile to her face, but he didn't do quaint and cozy. He was the life of the party. She imagined Callie swatting him away from the appliance, settled on a bar stool, and tried to enjoy her homecoming. He made excellent mimosas.

Pulling out Cava and orange juice for mimosas,

Papi tapped his chin.

"Are you getting fancy? Peach purée for Bellinis?"

He added raw shrimp, tomatoes, jícama, and avocado to the island.

Jerking away from the island, she revised her forecast. If Papi wanted to cook, then they were all screwed. "When's Callie coming back?"

"Um?" Papi scratched under his jawline. "Soon?"

His cooking skills fizzled out at macaroni and cheese. If Callie understood his intentions, she would come roaring down the drive to protect her knives from his abuse. "Umm…"

Papi made them drinks and fished out a well-oiled cutting board.

"You're really cooking?" she asked.

"It's been so hot outside, but the storm brought in a breeze." He fanned himself and set down a bunch of cilantro and a handful of limes. Gripping the counter's edge, he inventoried the ingredients. His lips moved, but he made no sound.

Perhaps she had been too harsh. Grief made people do crazy things, and if Papi wanted to cook, then she could have at it. "Do you know how to peel and devein shrimp?"

He wiped the back of a hand across his forehead and looked up from his survey. "I watched a steaming show on The Chow Channel. We can turn on the fans by the pool and enjoy alfresco lunches like the old days. Come help me? I want to hear all about life in Austin. It'll be fun!"

She worked her jaw and considered her options. Dad's newest project was having an outsized influence on their family. He worked in an office, but Papi chaired boards, ran up credit card bills, and organized trunk shows at Cypress Creek boutiques. He was a bright, cheerful presence in her life, but if he wanted to play domestic diva, he had other motivations. "Does Dad know you're cooking?"

"Not exactly." Papi glanced over his left shoulder toward the master suite. "I thought it would be a nice surprise."

Riley held up a hand. "Lunch sounds good, but let me check on Dad. The Percheron project isn't going well. I don't want him to pull me away from lunch prep while we're mid-chop."

"I hear you." Papi pulled a red onion from a basket, sniffed it, and offered it. "Does this onion smell ripe?"

She climbed off the barstool and backed away from the kitchen island. They would be lucky to escape food poisoning. "Honestly, I'm not a great cook. Callie never had the patience for my questions."

A fly buzzed near the trash drawer.

Papi frowned at the onion. "Me, neither."

She had a feeling Callie's vacation had started several days ago. "We, uh, can order delivery. Let me just go check in with Dad."

"Nobody delivers out here." Papi sliced into the onion and pricked his palm. "Oww!" He stared at the wound and tilted his head. "That actually, like, hurts."

Shaking her head, she offered him a paper towel. "More than shaving?"

"I had that shit lasered off. Who invented shaving?"

"Honestly."

When pressure stemmed the blood flow, he looked up and ran his tongue over his bright-white teeth.

"Cooking looks so easy on the network shows. I just need more practice."

"We all do." She gave him a side hug. "While I'm in the office, put a bandage on that war wound and stick the shrimp in the fridge. As soon as I'm done with Dad, I'll give you a hand with your project."

Papi checked beneath the paper towel, and his skin blanched. "Maybe cooking was a bad idea. Warrior's medicine keeps him from drinking. I want to be supportive, but it's so hot outside I could use a refresher."

Summer had barely started.

Papi cupped his chin in his hands and leaned his elbows on the island. "We can stay at the house, but I'm going a little crazy without activities. Please, tell me all about Austin. Have you been to any new clubs?"

Hearing the desperation in his voice, Riley wondered if restless energy was an inherited trait. Playing nurse to Warrior Golding offered few rave reviews. Papi had a case of cabin fever. Last week, he called and asked about grandchildren. She'd been speechless, but now, she understood. He needed a diversion from his Hill Country life.

"I tried accompanying your father to the jobsite, but"—Papi shuddered—"the mess. I'm so glad you're back. Did you know Mikey Roberts is in town, too?"

"Fantastic." Riley offered a smile and felt her stance solidify on familiar ground. Without Callie on hand, the chat would meander toward Riley's love life, and she wasn't about to get back in bed with her ex-boyfriend to satisfy Papi's need for diversion or Aubrey's need for drama. She held up a finger. "Hold that thought. I'll be right back."

Papi topped off his mimosa and waved off her promise. "Go ahead. This mess can wait."

Raw shrimp could definitely not wait. She fled the kitchen for the safety of the master bedroom and the adjoining library. Walking through the hallways, she felt the house's silence once again and quickened her step to open the master suite's door.

The quiet, orderly room offered stunning views and a large drafting table. A cream daybed rested below a bank of windows. Yellow pillows and hothouse flowers marked Papi's touch and kept the room fresh. A stone fireplace kept winter chills at bay. Dad held court in a navy-blue armchair. His muscled breadth and strong jaw lent him a formidable presence. She noted his weight loss and stepped into the room. "Hey, Dad."

He looked up from a magazine, set down a pencil, and beckoned her closer.

She sank into her favorite chair. "More crossword puzzles?"

"I hate them." He kicked out his feet. "Who invented these things, anyway?"

She laughed. On rainy days, she and Grant had whiled away hours on the library floor while he sketched designs for multi-million-dollar houses or raged over crosswords. From her vantage point on the floor, the room's navy shelves held books and *objets d'art* representing mysterious, unspoken wonders. The fact Grant's urn occupied a place on his bookshelf hit her square in the chest, and she thought about the matching urn in her office. Who dusted Dad's reminder of the person he and Papi lost?

Losing her twin in the Memorial Day flood hurt, but she should be capable of entering a family room without breaking into tears. Paul, with his generous kisses and sage advice, had left her with more than a happy buzz. Breathing through the pressure compressing her chest, she replayed his observation. One day, the storms wouldn't scare her quite so much, but she struggled to savor the joy filtering through her memories like sunbeams through a dark sky.

Her entire life, Grant's smile mirrored her happiness, and his tears matched her sadness. Family pictures showcased two babies, two grinning toddlers, and two awkward pre-teens. Every milestone from birth to graduation came with twice the excitement and twice the cheer. Without her sibling, the balloons sagged, and the noisemakers sounded shrill. How could everyone else stand being a party of one?

When people asked if she and Grant were identical twins, she bit back her laughter and waited for their common sense to kick in. She could love Grant for his charms and his quirky mannerisms, but they would never be the same person. Life separated and joined them. They resisted the distance and returned to a shared equilibrium.

Then he was gone.

Gripping the chair's armrests, she breathed deeply. "Do you want to keep doing the crossword?"

"I picked it up to pass the time. I thought you would be in last night. Is the road from Austin down to one lane?"

"Hardly." Whatever a person's feelings about Texas politics, the Lone Star State invested heavily in transportation and infrastructure. "I had a few loose ends to tie up at the office, and I arrived later than I expected." She looked away to avoid detailing exactly why she smelled like a stranger's bodywash. When Dad's silence suggested he might not press for details, she glanced over.

He worked his jaw. "I should be in the corporate office."

Preoccupation saved her. She jutted her chin toward his bad side. "Your hip replacement."

His nostrils flared.

Dad's hip problems started young. He had hip dysplasia, a condition where the hip was slightly dislocated. A midcentury pediatrician missed the diagnosis, and the consequences lingered into adulthood.

When Dad's college sprints became weekend warrior marathons, he experienced problems. His fondness for old-school calisthenics, squats, lunges, and box jumps did a number on his joints and tore his hip cartilage. At his age, he needed surgery and physical therapy, but finding himself sidelined from project sites left him grumpier than a gelding with a bur.

Wondering if she had inherited his bad joints, she kicked out her legs and crossed her ankles. "Most of our projects are new-build construction. This renovation presents a lot of challenges. I'm glad you called me."

He grunted.

She could cast blame, or she could push the conversation toward resolution. Before she took ownership, she wanted to understand how her father landed in such a predicament. "Given your specialty, these project delays make sense. What possessed you to take on a restaurant build-out?"

"I'm tired of eating ribs and tacos in Cypress

Creek's wonderful restaurants. Ansel Percheron will bring something new and different to the table." He rested his elbow on his knee and dropped his chin in his hand. "Have you seen his cooking shows? They're amazing. The things that man can do with a knife!"

The shows popped up as thirty-second clips on her mobile news feed, but her phone remained in silent mode. Thank goodness for vibrating alerts and auto captions.

She scratched her cheek and settled into the conversation. If Dad could admit the problems behind this project, he might avoid future mistakes, and she could move on with her firm's specialized designs. "The chef's from San Antonio. His crew's from San Antonio. Given your age and experience, you know you should have hired locals."

Straightening, Dad stood and winced. "If age is a luxury, I'd rather be poor."

By poor, he meant a basic millionaire. He kept a lawyer on retainer and could expedite materials faster than a short-haul trucker could sprint between state lines. His desire for fine dining was a poor justification for taking on the Percheron project.

To broaden her horizons, she picked the University of Colorado Boulder for a degree in Architectural Engineering and claimed a master's degree in Architecture and Structural Engineering from Berkeley. The years she spent away from Texas excited her, but the Lone Star State called her home. Dad taught her everything about running an architectural and design firm, but he was set in his ways. She moved to Austin to make her professional mark. When he picked up the phone, he knew he wasn't getting a clone.

If nostalgia entailed nannying her brilliant, pigheaded father into compliance, she would corral him with a dose of West Coast efficiency. She leaned forward and braced her hands on the desk. "Dad?"

He raised his eyebrows.

"Callie's not here. Papi's trying to make *ceviche*. If you eat it, you'll probably spend the night riding the porcelain pony."

He paled.

"You taught me to make good decisions, but you need to make them, too." She stood and straightened her shoulders. "I'll sort out the Percheron project, but you need to stop barking orders, play nice with the physical therapists, and get back to doing what you do best."

He ran his hands over his face. "Giving orders."

"Designing!" She cleared her throat. "Also, I hired a consultant to audit my firm's carbon emissions. I'm driving down the sum total of my projects' greenhouse gasses, and this project is no different." She smiled and let the implications of her statement sink in. "I'm taking over everything on this project from sourcing to jobsite."

He stared and shook his head. "You've gone mad. Just work with what I left you!"

She ran her tongue over her front teeth. His rush orders would be the first things to go.

"You'll set us back weeks."

"It's my reputation on the line." Flipping her hair over her right shoulder, she walked toward the door, let her heels click on the library's parquet floor, and kept her back to her father to hide her grin. Papi taught her to make a memorable exit.

"Your father can run interference for me! I'll remote in."

She snorted. "I'm taking Papi out to lunch. Before I leave, I'll bring you a peanut butter-and-honey sandwich. You'll have time to finish your crossword and do your stretches."

"Riley June Golding…"

Pausing with a hand on the door's edge, she looked over her left shoulder and made eye contact. "Do your stretches and be nice to the staff, Dad. I know how much you hate street food. The sooner you're back in the office, the sooner you can dictate menus."

"Weeks!" He sputtered.

Setting boundaries let her manage the project, but it also compelled Dad to get in line with his recovery program. Family took care of family. Without the love she'd grown up with, she would have struggled to find herself. Thank the Texas sun, she'd never been in that position. Dad and Papi raised her to be strong and confident. Now, they would reap the benefits of what they had sowed.

Chapter Seven

Ansel Paul Percheron had booted a few women out of his bed, but watching Riley bail with tears in her eyes made him feel like the king of Southwestern pricks. For a moment, when he awoke with her in his arms, he thought of his undefined future and how much he sacrificed to achieve his culinary success. Riley was someone who inspired dreams. If he spent less time honing his empire and posing for magazines, he might have found a partner like her before a gray hair popped up in his beard. Instead, he went and put his foot in his mouth.

He could rationalize her reaction from here to sundown, but the feeling persisted. So did corporate emails, and he couldn't abandon his achievements to satisfy his whims. Swinging his legs over the edge of the bed, he rubbed his hands over his face, shook his hair out of his eyes, and made for the shower. If one night with Riley could rock his plans, he needed to prove his point to Aubrey and get the hell out of Cypress Creek.

Shuffling through the early morning sunbeams, he spied more indoor slippers waiting in a basket by the toilet. Before Moeko's mother-in-law returned from Japan, he would have to up his hygiene game. Alternatively, he could tip Moeko to prepare the bungalow for the older woman's return, but he doubted she wanted to clean up his mess.

Fresh from a scrub down, he slipped on a clean pair of jeans and wandered into the kitchen. A sleek rice cooker sat on the counter. If he had planned better, he could have set the timer at night so he would have freshly steamed rice for a morning meal. He had other things on his mind when he strode through the door to savor Riley's lush smile.

Ignoring the electric grill, water boiler, and crocks of kitchen gadgets imported from a ¥100 store, he faced a modern, American, single-serve coffeemaker and a basket of single-use plastic cups filled with coffee grounds. His at-home machine could make espresso at the push of a button, but he wanted hot, fast satisfaction.

He thought of Riley. Shoving down that memory before it derailed his morning, he rifled through the basket, selected a morning blend, popped it in the coffee machine, and pressed the brew button.

Steam hissed and popped. Coffee dripped into a cup.

Satisfied the machine finished its machinations, he removed the cup and sipped it. Scalding, tasteless, brown water scorched his tongue. Grimacing, he spat the brew into the sink. "God bless America, but this coffee is shit."

He dumped the brew down the kitchen sink, grabbed a shirt and boots, and strode out of the bungalow like a caffeine-starved maniac. Scanning the blocks of houses surrounding the bungalow, he realized parking might be at a premium. Within a few blocks, downtown shops took over the narrow streets, and he made for the corner coffee shop on foot.

The fresh, mist-tinged air cooled his frustration, and he took a moment to savor the morning air before summer's heat warmed the day. Gripping the door to the coffee shop, he pulled.

The door refused to budge.

"What the…" He scowled and scanned a variety of flyers taped to the shop's windows. The damn place didn't open until seven o'clock. By the same hour in San Antonio, half the population had flooded the freeways, and the other half had dribbled coffee into their laps.

A woman inside the coffee shop hurried toward the door, unlocked it, and peeked out. Her girlish braids contrasted with her lined skin. "We're making coffee, but the croissants aren't ready yet. Come back in thirty minutes."

"Right. Thanks." The reality of Cypress Creek left him struggling to put together two words. The cup of coffee he had dumped down the drain grew more appealing. So did returning to San Antonio. He had sunk a cool million into his spite for Aubrey, and he intended to savor the payback on his investment. Suspecting he would do better with the electric water boiler and tea, he shook his head, turned his back on the coffee shop, and made his way back toward the bungalow.

What time would the workers in Cypress Creek report to work at the new restaurant? If he had to revise the restaurant manual for a mid-morning start, the bakers, cleaners, and prep workers would bump heads with the servers reporting for duty.

A trio of college students climbed out of a car and cut him off.

"Sorry, dude," one teenager said.

The kids headed for an alleyway between the burnout hotel that would house his restaurant and a shabby chic business called Mimi's Boot Byre.

Wondering what kind of mischief the kids would find, Ansel made to follow them.

A gray-haired man stepped out of his silver jewelry store, holding a broom and a pair of clipping shears. He whacked off the dead blooms from hanging baskets and swept the dust and the debris into a neat pile. "Ahh, don't worry about those youngsters. They're hauling out merchandise for Mimi. Most of her sales come from the gear she sets out under sidewalk tents."

Ansel pursed his lips and considered his choices. After the coffee shop, the jewelry store rambled into Mimi's Boot Byre, the old hotel, and Aubrey's interior design business.

Given the spurt of activity on his side of the street, he wondered if Aubrey would be outside washing the windows on a Saturday morning. Apparently, the folksy interior designer who had once dreamed of running a kitchen had decided to sleep in.

Most successful chefs lived off cigarettes, caffeine, and sleep deprivation. They honed their knives with religious devotion, but they dulled their palates with cigarettes. Too bad. Nicotine mellowed out stressful environments and ADHD symptoms. He couldn't spell "neurodivergent," but he could balance his line crew's passions and their interpersonal needs. When Aubrey failed to get what she wanted, she threw fits. Did she ever have the drive to make the cut?

"You waiting on coffee?" the man asked.

Ansel inhaled through his nose. "I thought about

tea."

The old-timer snorted. "Tea never got the job done for me." He set aside the broom and brushed his gray beard against the summer-weight, cotton print shirt covering his shoulders. "What brings you to Cypress Creek?"

"I'm opening a restaurant in the old hotel," Ansel said. "The project's behind track."

The man shaded his gaze. "I've heard about you. Big-shot from San Antonio. Bit off more than you can chew, eh?"

He smiled and shook his head. "Not exactly."

"You're looking for help? Dishwashers and the like? Put up a sign."

At this rate, he could go back to the bungalow or linger around the coffee shop and find his breakfast before noon. "I'm not ready to hire staff. The architect and builder aren't on-site enough of the time, so things fell behind schedule. I'm here to fill in the gaps."

"Mighty big gaps," the shopkeeper said.

Ansel focused on the old hotel anchoring the street. Based on news reports he had read, the fire started in the hotel's kitchen around two o'clock in the morning, and it quickly spread. Built in the 1920s by a city corporation hoping to lure "motoring" tourists to Cypress Creek, the hotel had history, but it also had bare wires and outdated appliances. Any combination of those factors could have triggered the early morning blaze.

The renovation crew Collins selected had scraped out the fire debris and produced a beautiful, smoke-tinged shell to house Cypress Creek's newest restaurant. In the rear of the hotel, a few wood-paneled rooms remained, but a new crew would strip them to the studs and build the five-star watering hole he envisioned.

He rubbed together his palms. "We'll bring it back to its glory."

"You know how much that building means to this town?" The shopkeeper gripped the broom in front of him with two hands. "During the floods, it was a major evacuation center and one of the few places in town that still had power. Over the decades, it has served as the town's hub and the place that grounds us when we're trying to get through a loss."

Ansel loosened his shirt collar.

"The firefighters tried to save it, but an explosion pushed them back. Watching it burn"—the man cleared his throat—"was a hard lick. I doubted the town would bounce back, but we're tough."

"All the guests…"

"Fine," the shopkeeper said. "Smoke alarms sounded, and the guests made their way to balconies. Weren't but a few of them. The intense smoke inside the building sent several to the hospital."

"And the owners?" He'd wondered why the hotel had come up for auction, but the brokerage had remained tight-lipped. "They decided not to rebuild?"

"The stress was too much for them." Picking up his broom, the shopkeeper cleared the two wooden steps leading from the sidewalk to the raised, wooden walkway connecting several storefronts. "Any night of the week, they were in the hotel bar holding court. If you knew them, you made yourself at home. If you were visiting, you might sit and make a new friend."

Ansel worked his jaw and imagined the

monumental task of piecing together a community and ash-tinged lives. If the flood spared the hotel, but the fire ravaged it, the owners might have counted their remaining lives and cashed in their chips before a third disaster changed the odds.

"We loved on them, collected donations, and prayed, but the months after the fire were difficult. Every week, the hotel's walls leaned more and more. They took the community donations and moved to a nearby town. Once in a while, I visit their new hotel, but it's not the same."

"No, it wouldn't be the same." Ansel swallowed. The building occupied a meaningful space in the community's memory, and he had to be respectful of its significance. Gutting a Manhattan high-rise required capital, but crafting a welcoming enclave in Cypress Creek would require respect. "It's a beautiful, old building, but you can't rebuild the past."

"So, you're…"

He extended a hand. "Ansel Percheron."

"Rickie Hays."

The shopkeeper gripped his hand, and heavy calluses left an indention on Ansel's skin. "Pleasure to meet you."

"Ansel Percheron!" a woman yelled.

Rickie rubbed his ear. "Christ, woman, I heard him the first time."

Ansel recognized the woman's voice, and a predatory smile warmed his face. Aubrey Thomas might have traveled outside of Texas to pursue open-sky dreams, but she retained her Hill Country twang, and the accent never left. Turning, he shielded Rickie from the coming onslaught and crossed his arms over his chest.

"I heard about the restaurant, and I wondered when you'd show your face downtown." Aubrey stopped a few feet in front of the jewelry store and planted her hands on her hips. "What the hell do you think you're doing in Cypress Creek?"

He rubbed the stubble on his jaw. With all this excitement, he no longer needed a cup of coffee. Life in Cypress Creek could be downright invigorating. Watching Aubrey play out her indignation would do plenty to awaken his senses. If she wanted to pretend this was their first meeting, he would watch her show. Hell, he expected it. "Well, good morning to you, too, Aubrey."

She shook her head. "Don't you *Aubrey* me. Explain yourself."

The clouds parted, and a ray of sunlight caught the jewel in her nasal piercing. "I'm opening a steak house with a typical, American menu. Isn't that what you told me to do?"

Stamping a foot, she glowered. "Not in my town."

He shaded his eyes and scanned the quaint downtown. He wanted to call her bluff and lay bare her bullshit, but he had no idea how close she and Riley might be. Women were weird. They could spend an hour chatting with a stranger or pass their best friend on the street and slap their ass. If he had unintentionally landed in the middle of a girl pack, he needed to backpedal and find his bearings. "This is your town?"

"You damn well know it. Of all the cities in Texas, why Cypress Creek?"

"It's booming." He jerked his head toward Rickie's jewelry store. "I like to support local businesses. Have you visited Mimi's Boot Byre? I hear it's a hoot."

She dropped back her head. "Go back to Sioux Falls!"

Early morning tourists stared, but they walked on.

Ansel swallowed a chuckle, turned to Rickie, and raised his eyebrows. "Sioux Falls is a lovely town. Aside from the beautiful waterfall, the town has outstanding food and some of the best public art in the Midwest. They don't need my talents."

Rickie picked at his teeth. "You two got history?"

"No more than most." Ansel smiled. "Once upon a time, Aubrey wanted to be a chef, but I heard her interior design store has done well. Maybe she wants to get back in the kitchen. She probably makes a mean Steak *Frites*."

Rickie scratched his jaw. "Doubt it."

"Fucking assholes." Aubrey kicked a tall, porch post supporting an overhang. The overhand wobbled, and its shadow on the sunbaked sidewalk shook. "I don't know why I put up with this shit."

Ansel laughed, slipped a hand in his pocket, and turned toward the bungalow to set up his laptop. He was famous in culinary circles, but Cypress Creek was a small town, and its residents kept tourists hours. Local reporters might mark his exchange with Aubrey. He doubted his conversation with his ex-girlfriend would make the front page, but his restaurant would.

After opening night, he would triumphantly leave town, consider the restaurant the world's best rebuttal, and retire to his sailboat to savor his success like a satisfying *digestif*.

For all he cared, Aubrey could offload lampshades to tipsy lunch guests. He refused to give her the last word in Sioux Falls, but claiming the moral high ground in Cypress Creek would be more fun than he anticipated. Imagining their exchanges, he turned, slammed into a warm body, and reached out to steady the bystander's shoulders. "My bad."

A woman gripped his forearms. "Paul."

He released his grip on her shoulders, inhaled deeply, and took in the expensive perfume, supple skin, and gray-blue eyes returning his stare. Gold highlights brightened Riley's chestnut hair, and her open-mouthed expression told him he should start backpedaling before he found himself on his ass between two formidable women. Dropping his hands from her arms, he smiled. "Riley."

"You know this asshat?" Aubrey asked.

Riley looked past him. "I do. How do you know Paul?"

"His name's Ansel Paul Percheron, and he's the idiot rebuilding the old hotel into a ritzy steak house nobody in this town can afford."

Riley opened her mouth and looked back and forth between him and Aubrey. Her oscillating gaze refused to settle, and she rubbed her forehead before leaning against a lamppost and closing her eyes. "For the love of God. Fuck me."

With pleasure. He looked between the two women and refrained from defending his steak house or savoring Riley's presence. Aubrey's assessment of the restaurant wasn't entirely off base, but the locals could treat themselves for special occasions. The day-trippers and newbie landowners making economic waves were his real targets. Right now, he had two women with which to contend, and they both looked unhappy to see him.

Riley folded an arm against her stomach and leaned over. "I think I'm going to be sick."

Aubrey squeezed past him, offered Riley a hair tie, and rubbed her lower back.

Shit, they were friends. In his defense, sleeping with Riley was spectacular. His restaurant should be opportunity number one, but his half-hard cock had other ideas. If she had roots in Cypress Creek, then he might lure her back into his bed. "Look"—he cleared his throat—"we might have started off on the wrong foot."

Riley narrowed her gaze. "Did you double park me? Knock over a flowerpot? Take the last ounce of creamer?" Her voice rose to a near shout before she clamped a hand over her mouth. "You lied about your identity!"

So much for those *other* ideas. Realizing his problems outweighed his opportunities by a long shot, he decided to backpedal and do it fast. "You're right. I'm dumber than a box of pyrite and thicker than a rough-hewn plank. Of course, I should have told you I was a billionaire, celebrity restaurateur." He let sarcasm leach into his tone. "Imagine our authentic connection."

Aubrey snorted. "Billionaire, my ass."

Riley stepped away from the lamppost. "You should leave town and do it fast. As far as my daddies are concerned, we've never met. I have enough dark clouds hanging over my head. I don't need your egotistical shadow and this town's judgment to block out the remaining sunlight."

A gravely man coughed.

Ansel turned, made eye contact, and wondered why

the well-groomed man wearing the yellow shirt looked so familiar. If he were Riley's relative, the similarities might explain his gut recognition, but something else teased his consciousness. He dipped his chin. "Sir."

The man walked forward and wet his lips. "I'm Papi Golding. You met my husband, Warrior Golding, when you built his house. I believe you saw him during the job site walk-through for this restaurant. I find it impossible to believe you didn't notice me, but I was there, too."

Aubrey laughed.

Riley moaned. "I *am* going to be sick."

Realization dawned, and his amusement faded like the early morning mist. Standing on the cracked sidewalk, sweat dripped down his neck, and a trio of people waited for his reaction. He swallowed. "Yes, sir, I remember you now. You had on a brand-new hardhat."

"That's right!" Papi clapped. "I'm unforgettable."

This meeting was excruciating, and he would be happy to forget it. He cleared his throat.

Papi glanced at Riley. "My daughter, Riley Golding, is taking over the restaurant project while Warrior recuperates. She's an award-winning architect, but it sounds like you two are already acquainted." He winked. "Don't worry. Your project is in good hands. She inherited my style."

He would rather have Riley under his hands, but that ship sailed the minute she uncovered his deception. Closing his eyes, he reminded himself why he steered clear of women and complicated relationships. Young or old, the beauty and pleasure of their company were never simple.

Choosing between Papi's curiosity, Aubrey's wrath, and Riley's unknown reaction, he opened his eyes and faced the woman whose reaction mattered the most to him and to his project. "Riley, I'm pleased to see you again."

She wiped a hand over her face and stared.

Papi coughed.

She forced a strained smile, and the expression failed to reach her eyes. "Pleased to see you, too."

The carefree, rain-soaked beauty he held last night transformed into the pretty, uptight woman with shadows beneath her eyes he'd met at the gas station. He'd heard of Riley Golding and the awards she'd won, but her restrained, preservationist style was so opposed to her father's lavish, gilded creations that her shared last name and potential involvement never occurred. He shifted his weight. "How do you feel about steak houses?"

She pursed her lips. "Not my cup of tea."

"And this project?" he asked.

"Is way off track."

Papi hooked Riley's arm and pulled her to the side. Terse whispers ensued.

Rickie swept.

He rocked back on his heels, avoided Aubrey's glare, and wondered if he should have waited outside the coffee shop like an obedient junkie. By now, the croissants were ready, and a day-old newspaper waited to shield his face. Given a warning by *anyone* in town, he could have reconciled the beautiful, confident woman he bedded on impulse was also responsible for his grudging, gilded swan song. Cypress Creek had failed to afford him that courtesy. He no longer felt bad about eighteen-dollar cocktails made with Hill County shrub.

Riley stomped toward him and planted her hands on her hips.

He cleared his throat. "So, about the project?"

She pursed her lips, opened her mouth, and quickly closed it.

A million dollars said she wanted to tell him off.

Working her jaw, she sighed. "I'll meet you at the hotel in an hour."

He raised his eyebrows. "The restaurant?"

Aubrey flicked a piece of dirt from beneath her nail and moved closer to Riley. "It'll always be the hotel. Won't it?"

"No matter what the building holds, we'll make it beautiful again." Riley wrapped an arm around Aubrey's shoulders and jerked her chin toward him. "You okay with this?"

Aubrey nodded. "It's in the past."

Reconciling Aubrey's blasé response with her prior actions required a quantum computer. He worked his jaw and waited.

"You can't gussy up the past"—Rickie crouched and scooped his dust pile and flower clippings into a dustpan—"but you can learn from it."

Taking the man's advice to heart, Ansel considered how he managed his life thus far. Tragedy took his biological parents. Eagle Hawk taught him to respect the past and live in the present, but he spoke little of the future. The old man said life had a way of unfolding without his help, but he never had to run a restaurant empire.

After a night with Riley, Ansel saw a newfound

appeal in forming relationships. Whether he realized the potential of a relationship with Riley remained entirely up to her reciprocal interest. So far, the odds of rekindling her interest fell ten licks short of a stack.

He might have gotten off to a rough start in Cypress Creek. As soon as he sorted out his relationship with Aubrey Collins, Papi Golding, Moeko, and any other members of the town's creative class, he would woo the woman whose gray-blue, stormy eyes reminded him of the golden light following a storm. He made eye contact. "I'll see you in an hour."

Riley narrowed her gaze.

Holding his breath, he waited for her signal.

She rolled her eyes and jerked her chin toward the residential streets.

Her response wasn't a gilded invitation, but given his omission, he would take what he could get from Riley Golding, AIA, ArCH, LEED AP. He had a feeling a smart man would keep his mouth shut about the passion they shared, but Papi probably had a clue. Dipping his head, he turned, smiled at the man, and made his way toward the charming bungalow that would be his home base in Cypress Creek. He had an hour to get himself together before Riley buried him under a mountain of decisions. For a moment, he had worried she would flat-out bury him, but he was alive, and things were looking up.

Chapter Eight

Riley looked back and forth between Aubrey and Papi. She wondered whether lying about her sleeping arrangements would land her in hot water. "I can explain how I met him."

Her best friend and her father raised their eyebrows sky-high.

Pursing her lips, she decided explanations could wait for another day. If either party wanted the details of her romantic life, they could privately ask her about the tryst. She refused to announce her hookups on Gristmill Road. She risked a glance at Mr. Hays and caught his wink. Eyes wide, she looked away and focused on Aubrey and Papi. "Why don't we settle in at the coffee shop and have a nice visit?"

Aubrey snorted. "Stay away from him, Riley. Ansel's ego is bigger than his dick, and that's saying plenty."

Mr. Hays slapped his leg and hooted.

She bit her lip and avoided catching Papi's smirk, but she could only examine the sidewalk cracks for so long. She looked up and made eye contact.

"Honey, are you sure you can handle this job?" Papi asked.

Professional pride and filial instincts raised her shoulders. "Of course, I can handle this job. In my line of work, egotistical millionaires are a dime a dozen. If my customers aren't demanding titans, their spouses and personal assistants are entitled terrorists."

"Don't get me started on terrors." Papi waved off the characterizations.

"I've met a dozen men like Ansel"—the name tasted strange in her mouth—"and one chef from San Antonio shouldn't be a problem. I'm sure he's a grand cook, but it doesn't matter to me whether he's a four-star chef, a three-Michelin-star chef, or a grand restaurateur with a stick up his ass. He's just a person."

"If you say so." Papi peered into the front window of Rickie's Jewelry Shop and fixed his bangs. Silver charms, intricate beadwork, and pewter platters shone under display lights. "Aubrey, do you have new stock in your store, too?"

"Oh, Mr. Golding." Aubrey took his arm. "I have everything. Let's give you the VIP shopping experience."

Papi smiled. "Thank you, sweetie. I knew I could count on you."

Glaring at Riley in a this-isn't-over stare, Aubrey led Papi toward her interior design store. "Wait until you see the precious, yellow…"

Riley watched them go and pulled out her phone. Despite Aubrey's recognition and Papi's introduction, she had to reconcile Ansel Percheron's professional headshot with the man who made love to her. She believed his ignorance of her role in the restaurant build-out, but she questioned hers.

How could a hat and a string of pretty-boy jewelry hide his identity? The man had a national cooking show, for Pete's sake. She saw who she expected to see, but she should have recognized her client! Zooming in on his website photograph, she found bright-white teeth, blond-streaked hair, and handsome cheekbones. A white chef's apron complemented the highlights on his face, and she wondered how much editing went into producing the image.

The man she tumbled with last night had the shadow of a beard along his jaw, lines radiating from his eyes, and dark recesses between his abs. In hindsight, the two facades undoubtedly belonged to the same man, but she tangled her legs with his raw appeal. If she'd met him in chef's whites or across a boardroom table, she would have recognized a publicist's touch and censored her attraction. No such luck.

She looked up at the old hotel. No matter how she spent her prior evening, she would spend her daylight hours with a well-heeled client who expected professionalism and perfection. Cypress Creek's architectural landscape defined it at this moment in time. Revitalizing the old hotel reflected the town's history, its ideology, and its spirit. Form and architecture worked hand in hand, and she understood Cypress Creek's culture. Straightening her shoulders, she vowed to give Ansel Percheron everything he deserved, but she would not give him an inch more.

"Watch out." A college student's preppy bangs obscured his gaze. "This stack is about to tumble."

Stepping onto the decking in front of the jewelry shop, she watched Mimi's college students fill the white tents between the boot store and the hotel with stacks of boxes. Navigating sidewalk cracks and overflowing planters, the students ferried boots to waiting tables, arranged the boots in neat lines, and returned for a second load. The old barn boasted a hayloft and wide double doors, but time sealed the entryway, and a modern glass foyer directed traffic into rows of packed shelves. Riley plotted her next move.

Mimi pulled up in a 1960s boat.

Riley shaded her gaze. When the automotive beast rolled off the line, it was the biggest car money could buy. Chrome and tail fins marked its status as an oilman's car, but Mimi's brash, unmannerly husband passed away in the eighties. Although times changed, Mimi held onto the car and the instant respectability it once afforded. Pickup trucks supplanted land cruisers during the seventies, but Mimi doubled down on blue jeans and leather boots. Her denim wore out, but her boot collection swelled into a commercial enterprise.

Climbing out of the car, Mimi wiped sweat from her forehead. Near seventy years old, she had spreading hips and dyed-blonde hair that disguised her profuse grays. Spreading lipstick and penciled-in eyebrows were harder to combat. "This blasted heat." She patted powder on her cheeks. "What brings you downtown, Riley?"

Lust, rivalry, and filial responsibility seemed like loaded answers. Riley cleared her throat and acknowledged Mimi's gravely question with a wave. "Daddy asked me to take over the hotel renovations while he recovers from hip surgery. I'm meeting the new owner to do a walk-through in an hour."

Mimi lumbered toward the sidewalk. "Good on you." She patted Riley's cheek. "I don't mind a little outside investment in our community. When the restaurant fails, someone will scoop up the renovated property in a sweet deal."

"I hope the new venture doesn't fail," Riley said.

Mimi waved to the college kids and unlocked the front of the Boot Byre. She glanced over her left shoulder. "Why shouldn't it fail? If Kyle's place is good enough for me, then it's good enough for you. We don't need fancy, city life in Cypress Creek."

"Yes, ma'am." Riley eyed the limestone edifice waiting for a new lease on life. No matter what Aubrey or the other citizens of Cypress Creek thought of the venture, she would give her best to the project. When she laid down her head, she would know she had finished a job well done. However, she would not be laying down her head on Ansel's pillow.

"Just see the restaurant leaves a little history intact." Mimi lingered in the Boot Byre's doorway. Her shop cats meowed around her ankles for their breakfast. "That building's been through more than one renovation, and quality lasts."

"Of course," Riley said. "We'll do it proud."

Dad had designed a gilded altar to Texas steak houses and VIP clubs, but he crammed the new kitchen into the building's recesses. If Mimi wanted to reminisce about the past, she could hang out with the walk-in coolers and prep areas slated for the back wall. Restaurant staff on break would probably give her a smoke on the house.

Making her way to the coffee shop, Riley settled at a small table and reviewed the files Dad sent her. His characteristic flair imbued the documents and warmed her heart. If Dad expected her to sign off on the documents, some of the flair would have to go.

She didn't fault Dad for his style, but he grew up in a different era. Louis "Warrior" Golding left Minnesota and came to Texas to thaw out his frozen feet on Texas

A&M University's sunbaked campus. He earned a bachelor's degree in environmental design and a master's degree in architecture before he met Papi in 1979 at a Miami club. Papi returned his affection and convinced him to settle in Papi's hometown, Cypress Creek. Dad built his homebuilding business from scratch and leveraged Papi's family's connections.

Over the years, Dad's staff of architects, landscape architects, interior designers, estimators, and project managers built three hundred custom homes in the Hill Country. Most recently, the staff created a gated community of twenty exclusive homesites in San Antonio near River Highway and Westlake Drive. The company specialized in very high-end markets and built homes for multimillionaires who could afford premium finishes. Presumably, Ansel hired Warrior Golding for a reason.

Making notes, she paged through the design work until she finished her coffee and needed to meet Ansel on-site. Eager to be five minutes early and get the upper hand, she approached the limestone building and found Ansel peering at its façade.

He turned and met her gaze. "What do you think about painting the limestone exterior white?"

She choked back a laugh. "Absolutely not."

"A retro neon sign?" He craned his neck and shaded his eyes. "Maybe we can find old photographs and bring back some 1920s spice. If I knock around the basement, will I find old prohibition jugs?" He dropped his hand. "This town is full of surprises."

She turned her head and made eye contact. "Such as your name?"

"Paul's my middle name. How many Ansels do

you meet?"

"You're the first one."

"It's an iconic name," he said. "Try living up to it."

"I'll let you know when you fall short."

He snorted and scratched the side of his mouth. "Imagine my surprise when the only woman to catch my eye in years happens to be my new architect." He glanced over. "That is, if you're committed to the job."

She tilted her head. "I'm not yours."

"The memories are mine." Grinning, he rocked back on his heels. "It was an unforgettable night."

She cleared her throat. "Try harder."

He laughed. "We can play it that way. You lied, too. I'm guessing you haven't slept with half the town."

"You'll never know." Ignoring the warmth he kindled in her core, she set down her bags and focused on the building. The former hotel had character, but it also had enough damage to warrant demolition. When Ansel purchased the property, he assumed responsibility for the decision, but she would make the place shine.

She turned in a circle and avoided looking at her customer. Having appreciated him naked and seen the car he drove, she would bet money he cherished quality over quantity. She doubted he truly wanted to slap paint on the building and jazz it up with glowing credentials. To rock the project, she would have to understand his goals and the man behind the empire.

Cypress Creek, although it hosted a number of small bed-and-breakfasts, boutique hotels, and charming stores, was very different from San Antonio and his other restaurant locations. She stopped examining the aged limestone and focused on Ansel.

"Why are you here?"

He moved closer. "To accelerate this restaurant's completion."

She wiggled her finger toward him to redirect the conversation. "No, why are you in Cypress Creek?"

He rubbed his chin for a moment but dropped his hand. "Aubrey and I dated, but she tanked my first restaurant. I want her to wake up every morning and see what she gave up. Success has room for more than one American dream, but this restaurant will outshine her petty definition of success."

She blew out her breath. *Petty* didn't begin to cover his grudge, but he had the cash to carry out his spite fantasies. "And her opinion still matters?"

He inhaled deeply, "Who forgets their first love or their first betrayal?"

Had she experienced either grand emotion? Crushes and casual slights littered her memories, but she struggled to equate Ansel's intense reaction to her casual relationships. Mikey was like a stray dog she kept trying to rehome. Grant was blood, and nothing felt better than blood on blood. Making allowances for different lived experiences, she blew out her breath. Aubrey had plenty going on, and Ansel had little bearing on her best friend's life. "Leave Aubrey and her family out of your schemes. Do what you want with this old hotel. I don't care."

"That's not true," he said. "This building is important to Cypress Creek. I've seen your portfolio. You care about your work."

"But do you?" she asked. "Is this restaurant just for spite?"

He rubbed his jaw. "Maybe it started that way, but

the concept grew on me. Anyone with a construction loan can start a restaurant in a metropolitan area. With a decent menu and the right PR team, they might recoup their investments. Most fail. My restaurants thrive, and this building will have my name on it. If you can't endorse spite, consider pride."

She considered a swift kick to his backside, but evicting him from her life seemed as likely as getting a cactus to root in a puddle. She peeled back the layers of his response. His motivations sounded authentic, and she pondered what kind of man carried a grudge for twenty years and let it drive him to succeed. If she doubted his honesty or his integrity, she could turn over the project to another architect at Dad's firm. Instead, she gave Ansel the benefit of the doubt and decided to move forward, but she would remain in control. "Buy a flashy car and leave tread marks outside her house. You're out of your fucking mind."

He laughed and rubbed his eyebrows. "Probably."

Brushing past him, she unlocked the front door and stepped inside the building. Blue plastic kept out the rain, but sawdust piles in the front of the building looked like they might house rat nests and forgotten tools. Smoke scorched the remaining rafters. Walking through the freshly studded rooms, she aligned the mess with the designs Dad shared.

"It's a work in progress," Ansel said.

His voice came from behind, and she recognized his presence. Lost in the building's possibilities, she had momentarily forgotten his company. She turned and leaned against a stud. The wood held. "It's a mess. This is what happens when egotistical owners insist on using their own crews."

"Noted." He kicked a pile of sawdust. A cockroach scurried out of the mess, and he wrinkled his nose. "Collins' reports said everything was going smoothly with the build-out, but he omitted a few details."

"Apparently." The space had potential, but she needed distance from Ansel to think clearly. Breathing deeply, she took a moment to let the space imprint on her senses.

Ansel thwarted her efforts.

Soaked in rain and desire, he smelled like sage, sweat, and fresh, crisp aftershave. She had mischaracterized him. Surrounded by sawdust, something about the moment felt authentic. She filtered out her trite, early response and honed in on a subtler presence. His woodsy smell carried hints of aged wood. She sniffed again and sneezed on the dust. Agarwood.

"Bless you," he said.

"Thank you." She cleared her throat and paced the room's perimeter. Agarwood's fragrant, dark, resinous aroma lingered in her subconscious, and she wondered if Ansel possessed a matching depth.

When mold infected aquilaria trees, the trees produced an aromatic resin, and the resin-embedded heartwood became a favored ingredient for incenses and perfumes. Much like smoke left behind a lingering depth and highlighted surviving structures, agarwood spoke of a tree's perseverance. She needed more than her fair share of the trait.

"I like Warrior's designs," Ansel said, "but I want to move the kitchens toward the front of the house. Let patrons walk into the space and see the artistry in progress and the fresh ingredients going into their meals."

"Will you be behind the counter?" she asked.

"Occasionally. It's my restaurant."

She pulled up the sketch app on her phone and made a show of annotating Dad's designs. "What aren't you telling me about this restaurant? Aubrey said she met you at cooking school, but there's obviously more than history between you two. Of all the places in the world, why did you come to Cypress Creek?"

"Interesting question."

She raised her head. "Will you answer it?"

He ran a hand through his hair. "We dated for a while. She sabotaged my first restaurant, and she left me for some greaseball who knew how to operate a fryer."

His pared-down explanation raised more questions than it answered. Riley plowed through her architecture coursework and kept tabs on Aubrey's culinary career during Sunday night phone calls. Aubrey had never mentioned dating Ansel.

If Aubrey loved him, why hadn't she mentioned him? Leading on a person or sabotaging their life's work suggested a pettiness Riley feared acknowledging, but she had time to reach the root of Aubrey's actions. Ansel, on the other hand, was an unknown quantity. She needed to know with whom she dealt. "So, you're…"

"Rubbing my success in her face?"

His honesty stole her breath, and she choked out a laugh.

He worked his jaw. "Ending my career on a high note?"

Shaking her head, she swiped to the next page of designs. "If this is how you settle scores, you might be out a million dollars and thousands of pounds of steer. Cypress Creek is awash in new money, but the tech cowboys want more than the last great frontier. They want quality and prestige. If you don't give them those attributes, then they'll bail faster than a vulture over fresh kill."

He smoothed a hand over a page. "I'm here, aren't I?"

"For foolish reasons." Slipping her phone back into her pocket, she walked toward the rear of the restaurant. Wood paneling and limestone arches warred for dominance beneath the original roof. She envisioned the arches leading to an old patio overlooking the creek, but the building had never boasted that feature. If she could convince Ansel to move the kitchen to the front of the house, she could give him alfresco dining. The change would cost him and delay the project. She turned to pitch it.

He pulled at a piece of wood paneling. "This has to go."

"Agreed." She made additional notes and snapped pictures. "Have you considered—"

A crack sounded.

She turned and found him holding a broken piece of siding. "What are you doing?"

"Looking at the structure's original walls?" He tossed the siding into a corner and rubbed a hand on his leg. A ragged nail tore his jeans and left a bleeding scratch. His action smeared the blood, but the wound would heal. "Want to help? I can get you gloves."

Rushing to his side, she gripped his arm and remembered the feel of his sweat-slicked skin beneath her hips. She shook off the memory and tossed her hair out of her eyes. "Wait! We need to brace the roof before you remove any supports."

He glanced at her hand, raised his eyebrows, and pulled at another piece of siding. "Aw, come on, Riley. The wood paneling is just veneer."

She dropped a hand and wondered if her presence on the job was also veneer. If he wanted to be in charge, then she would pull the firm's branding and leave him to his own devices. "Look, you hired me to do a job, and I'll do it, but you're not the boss on this construction site. You either let me manage this build-out, or you find another builder to complete the job."

Working his jaw, he adjusted his grip on the piece of veneer, but the wood remained in his hand.

Proximity clouded her thoughts, and she regretted getting so close. Turning away while he weighed her ultimatum, she scanned the restaurant and envisioned a restaurant coming together. With both their skill sets at work, candlelight and wayward glances would linger over rich, velvety wine. Savory smells would emanate from the kitchen, and brass fixtures would gleam. The vision wavered, and she wondered if midnight desires ruined their chance to collaborate.

"Are you always this difficult?" he asked.

"Yes." She kept her back turned. The space had room for microgreens, seared beef, and aged perfection, but she needed time to sketch her vision. She also needed him onboard. Taking a deep breath, she savored Ansel's woodsy presence and heated proximity, but she had to separate business and pleasure. "Do you understand my terms?"

He tossed the siding into the corner with the first piece. "Loud and clear."

She exhaled. "Also, I want to hire Aubrey's husband, Nathan, as the construction contractor. His crews do excellent work, and he knows the county regulatory environment. We'll have fewer delays and quicker progress with him onboard."

"Absolutely not," he said. "I'm not funneling money into Aubrey's checking account."

And we're back to playground rivalries. She turned and made eye contact. "Nathan's construction company has a solid reputation and a robust portfolio. He understands restaurant construction, and his proven experience dots the Hill Country. Don't let pride make all your business decisions."

He held her stare. "Hire one of his competitors."

"Do you hate her that much?" She tilted her head. "How much control does she have?"

He rubbed a hand along the back of his neck. "Hate is a strong word."

"Then hire Nathan." She crossed her arms across her chest. "He's the best choice."

Dropping his hand, he looked toward the street. "Find another crew. The customer's always right. Other options exist."

"Are you always this stubborn?" Grunting, she turned and kicked an old, glass bottle into the corner. If the bottle had the decency to shatter, she would feel a little better, but the thick-lipped vessel clattered along the uneven floorboards and came to rest in the room's corner.

The back door opened, and Mimi flooded the room with bright sunlight. "You two okay? The cats are hiding under the shelves. At this rate, the police will swing by and ask you to keep the peace."

"Hah." Riley brushed her hair out of her eyes. "Mr. Percheron's version of keeping the peace is"—she met his gaze—"complicated."

He tucked a hand into a pocket. "Doesn't have to be."

Riley laughed. "You suggested painting the limestone white and adding a neon sign to the entrance. What's next? Valet?"

He crossed his arms over his chest. "Valet's a given. Gristmill Road has zero parking." Jerking his head toward Mimi, he smiled. "I'd hate to upset the neighbors."

Mimi walked toward the pile of wooden siding and tipped her shiny, leather boot beneath the refuse. "Folks can park wherever they find a spot and walk past the downtown shops on their way to dinner. Red carpets and velvet ropes have never been part of life in Cypress Creek."

Riley wondered when Mimi had last seen either feature. She opened her mouth to smooth over local relations.

"Riley has a good sense about these things," Mimi said. "If you want the job done right, listen to her, hire her crews, and toast her accomplishments on opening night."

"Is that so?" Ansel peered at the ceiling. Smoke damage left carbon-laced swirls on the old plaster, but the damage required structural and cosmetic repair. "Should I write her a blank check? Sponsor drinks at the local fundraiser? Join a church?"

Mimi laughed. "Yes, indeed—"

"No!" Riley rushed between the pair and held up her palms. Understanding Ansel's motivations required a partnership. He might not be like the demanding titans she encountered in Austin, but people like Mimi could be entitled terrors. The two business owners had to coexist in Cypress Creek, and she had to honor her commitment to her father. "We'll work on this project together."

"Hmf." Mimi scanned the room. "And what will you do in this room?"

Riley lowered her hands. "We'll begin the design process in the front of the building. This space might transition to outdoor dining, but I don't want to jump the gun. I imagine Ansel is the only person who can design the kitchen, so we'll start with his ideas. By the time we reach this renovation phase, we'll be a well-oiled machine."

"So, it'll take time?" Mimi asked.

She nodded toward Ansel. "Plenty of time. You can't roll into town and understand Cypress Creek in an evening. You might think you know everything, but you're dead wrong." His cheeks flushed, and she knew her message hit home. "My reputation depends on producing quality."

He rubbed a palm along his throat.

"Good." Mimi wagged a finger. "But not too long."

Ansel rolled his eyes.

Riley stifled a laugh. Turning, she escorted Mimi out the back door. "Why don't you pull your best boots in Ansel's size? I'm sure he needs a new pair, and who doesn't savor the feel of broken-in, vintage leather?"

"Come by later this afternoon." Mimi stepped out of the building and blinked in the sunlight. "We'll see what fits."

"Sounds like a plan," Ansel said.

Shutting the door on Mimi, Riley turned, took Ansel by the elbow, and led him toward the front of the building. She needed time to draw up plans, lunch, and a full-sized SUV to retrieve everything Papi bought on his shopping trip.

Ansel fell into step.

His smooth gait matched hers, and the realization made her drop the hand on his elbow. She needed to form a connection with him, but physical boundaries would serve her just as well. "Don't worry about Mimi. She's still pissed you outbid her at the building auction. She'll come around."

"But will you?" he asked.

"I'm here, aren't I?" She pulled out her phone and snapped pictures of the building's interior. Dad must have all the legal documentation on his computer. A recent survey would provide an in-depth look at the hotel property, but she could skip the plat map. It showed legal property lines belonging to the owner, but her familiarity with Cypress Creek gave her a working knowledge of the neighborhood. She picked up her bags and shook off the shortcut impulse. To be on the safe side, she would review every document. "Is your timeline firm?"

He stepped over the threshold. "In light of recent discoveries, I'm reconsidering it."

She snorted and locked the door with a key.

He held out his hand.

Staring at the key she gripped, she raised her gaze. "I need access."

"I own the building."

"How am I supposed to—"

He wiggled his fingers.

She relinquished the heavy brass and exhaled. "—access the building?"

Pocketing the key, he jerked his head toward the small houses surrounding Gristmill Road. "You know where I live. You have my phone number. I'm happy to meet you anytime, day or night."

Working her jaw, she considered her options. She could enter the burnt-out building from a number of access points, but if he found out, he might accuse her of trespassing. Little did he know how many times she and Grant poked around the town's old buildings while Papi shopped. Cypress Creek was a place that relied on community involvement over monitored cameras and drop-in daycare centers. Half the downtown shop owners probably had keys to the hotel. If she wanted access, she could get it.

Ansel's celebrity presence might change some aspects of town life, but two hundred years of history and tradition would override his idiosyncrasies. She raised her chin. Her newest client had control issues, but she had dealt with quirkier individuals. "It'll be daytime."

He winked. "You sure about that fact?"

She brushed a stray cobweb from her sleeve. He was still obviously flirting, and his advances flattered her ego, but she had a job to accomplish. If he thought humoring her would help him get his way or get into her bed, he had much to learn. Tilting her head, she adopted the smile she reserved for lost tourists. "Absolutely positive."

Chapter Nine

"Well, if we're sticking to daylight hours," Ansel said, "let me take you to lunch."

Riley frowned. "Here? In town?"

He scanned the street. Cars cruised Gristmill Road for a limited number of parking spots. Flycatchers darted in and out of hanging planters, and groups of shoppers peered in windows. One in ten tourists might wander into his new restaurant, but once they enjoyed a meal at his table, they would tell their friends.

"Unnecessary," she said.

Making a stand in Cypress Creek was the only thing necessitating his presence in the town, but the resort town had unexpected charms. He toyed with his phone to hide his grin. "I researched the town's other restaurants, but tasting their food will tell me a lot about my competition. Call our meal market research. You can bill me for your time." He looked up and found her standing in the building's shadow with her back against the limestone.

She dug her sunglasses from her bag. "No."

Her response sounded so absolute, he cringed.

This morning, she disbanded the conversation with Aubrey and Mr. Golding like a champion mediator. If she had a touch of agoraphobia, she hid it, but he preferred the intimacy of the bungalow and the way she came apart in his arms. Remembering the Jacob's Hole

131

performance and where his blatant interest led, he amended his suggestion. "I hate to eat alone. Why don't we try the honky-tonk BBQ?"

"Jed's Pit?"

He shrugged. "I didn't name the place. Hopefully, Jed's food is better than his marketing plan."

She rolled her eyes. "You're co-opting the town's name for your restaurant. Why not name your new restaurant"—she tapped her lips—"Overindulgence at Cypress Creek?"

"Opulence?" If brainstorming restaurant names kept her at his side, he could play this game for hours. "Ornate?"

She leaned forward and narrowed her gaze. "Don't you mean ornery?"

He laughed.

"Will you consider Nathan's crew for the restaurant build-out? They're your best bet to get back on schedule." She slid her sunglasses into place over her eyes. "The decision has nothing to do with Aubrey."

"Will you consider lunch?" he asked.

She took a deep breath and scanned the street. "I've eaten at every restaurant in town."

"I haven't. Show me the best of the best."

She shook her head. "I don't need the public attention dining with you will bring me. You're a"—she narrowed her gaze and worked her jaw—"celebrity."

Distaste dripped from the word, and he dropped his chin to his chest to hide his smile. Name recognition compensated for his rusty flirting skills, but the woman he wanted in his bed had zero interest in his red-carpet status. She was so beautiful she needed more than a pair of sunglasses to evade public attention. In any restaurant setting, her glossy hair and full lips would shine. He imagined sharing in a long, candlelit meal and taking her home to bed. Instead, he raised his head and grinned. "Why is being a celebrity a bad thing?"

"It's too close to infamy. You have a mouth like a sailor."

"Last night, you had zero complaints about my mouth." He savored her pretty blush and steered her toward the alley between the restaurant site and Mimi's boot store.

"Where are we going?" She looked over her right shoulder.

"Give me five minutes." He stopped in the shadows cast by the limestone building and considered how to approach her concerns. Burning a hand on national television cemented his reputation as a colorful character, but his propensity for creative language was hardly shocking or criminal. Hell, in the twenty-four hours he had known Riley, he had barely muttered an expletive.

"Ansel, I said no kisses—"

He held up a hand. "Tell me why you're hiding from your neighbors, Riley. You grew up in this town. Losing your brother shouldn't make you a pariah."

She let her shoulders sag. "Grant and I ran buck wild through this town. We did everything together. He died in a flash flood. Instead of staying by his side, I went on vacation. I failed him."

If she wanted to join her twin in his grave, then he could chain her to his bed and remind her of a life worth living. Erasing her pain was the thing he couldn't do. Meeting the buck-wild version of Riley would have been a hell of an experience, but he liked her as a stubborn, accomplished, impulsive woman. Biting the inside of his cheek, he urged her to continue with a subdued nod.

"Grant signed up to be a volunteer first responder, and I signed up, too." She swallowed and stared toward the shadows along the creek. "We rescued a few kittens and recounted our exploits over cold beers, but we had day jobs."

"You made a difference."

She cleared her throat. "Maybe. Grant shouldn't have been working alone when the flash flood hit. I should have been there, but instead of supporting him, I was in Cancun shotgunning beers and taking shots with a lime."

He would table the image of her in a bikini for another day. He opened his mouth to respond to her guilt. "You didn't know—"

"Everyone in this town knows I have a selfish streak. Call it the result of competing with my twin. I left for Austin to start my firm. Whispers and rumors followed me out of town. They think"—she frowned—"I'm too high-and-mighty for Cypress Creek. Sometimes, I think they're right. Maybe I should have stuck around and embraced the town's flow, but I needed space."

For fuck's sake, what would the townspeople think of his sailboat and scattered mansions? Instead of dismissing her doubts, he loosened his grip on her arm and stroked her smooth skin. "I'm sorry your brother died. I understand why storms make you skittish. Don't let gossips run you out of town. If you love Cypress

Creek, then the town should have your back." He dropped his hand. "End of discussion."

"End of discussion?" She turned and tilted her head. "Life isn't that easy. Do you make a habit of revitalizing small towns? Your staff members might suck up and give your restaurants five-star reviews, but they're blowing smoke up your ass. Live in the real world!"

He shifted his stance and tensed his back muscles. His accomplishments spoke for themselves. Diners came to his restaurants for quality. If atmosphere and panache created buzz in a community, who could fault him for embracing what worked?

Riley raised her eyebrows.

He worked his jaw. Lavishing flattery on big spenders might be over the top, but he learned their names and their preferences. Riley offered few clues. If he mentioned her eyes reminded him of smoke-tinged skies and pearlescent oysters, she might root through a local antique shop or prime the bellows and burn down his playboy reputation. He backed up a step and reconsidered his approach.

This conversation might have nothing to do with food. He was an outsider who had never glimpsed his neighbor's highs and lows. Loving thy neighbor was easy, but restraining thyself from gossip was a Herculean task. She didn't begrudge the biddies their speculation. Instead, she feared she deserved it.

He feared her self-awareness would cripple her. She was so bright and imaginative. Tragedy cast a pall of self-doubt over her self-confidence. If he could burn her doubts to the ground, he would.

"Without me, your steak house"—she waved a

hand over her head—"would be a year late and a million dollars over budget. I'm your key to this small town. Let me do my work."

"Your work?" He rubbed his jaw. "Do you hate this small town?"

Her jaw quivered.

"What about the people who've known you your entire life? The memories on every street corner? When I drive into Cypress Creek, I see tangled lifelines that stretch from the football field to the graveyard. When you return, you can feel the town's pulse. You're a part of it."

She wrapped her arms around her core and shuddered. "I let down Grant!"

He swallowed his rebuttal. His staff looked to him for success, but when he was on-site as head chef, they also expected him to run the kitchen, set the menu, organize staff, liaison with suppliers, and manage the restaurant's budget. They wanted to sear meat and wash dishes in record time, not grapple with commercial decisions. He knew his role and his responsibilities. At-will employment extended both ways, and he slipped on his chef's whites to define himself. She didn't let down Grant. She loved him. Responsibility and love could go hand in hand, but loving a person required little more than acceptance. He stepped forward. "You took a vacation, Riley."

"I was selfish."

If she chewed her bottom lip any harder, then he would offer her a dipping sauce. Instead, he tried a winning smile. "Take another vacation and spend the rest of the weekend with me. We'll come out unscathed. Let me take care of you."

She narrowed her gaze. "I don't need anyone to mind me."

"Honey, we all need minding from time to time." He raised a hand to cup her face. "We're just human."

She eyed him before jabbing a finger into his chest. "Just because you're good in bed, you can't boss me around and drag me into the shadows to say your piece."

If fire cauterized old wounds, her searing indignation would leave fresh, pink scars. He glanced along the brick alley. "Is that so? Seems like we're there."

She widened her gaze, dropped her hand, and stepped back. "Everyone experiences their losses differently. I'm sorry you lost your birth parents, but I'm still grieving Grant. Stick to your job and let me do mine."

Without her breathing down his throat, he felt a cool, light breeze along his skin and wished for her warmth. Her flip-flopping emotions were like contrasting flavors. Each barbed defense complimented her willingness to fight. She would get through her loss and her regrets, but she needed time, and she was right. He had a restaurant to build. He ran a hand through his hair. "Fine, you want to keep things casual? We can be fuck buddies. Call me Paul. I've been called worse."

"What?" She stared.

"That's what you wanted, isn't it? Mindless, anonymous sex?" He thrust his arms to the sides. "I'm all yours."

"I'm not a one-night-stand kind of girl." She kicked a rock down the alley and swore under her breath. "One day in a person's life doesn't define it.

Just because you've seen me naked doesn't mean you know me!"

He raised an eyebrow. Forgetting her taste would be like forgetting his name. Unraveling her complexities could keep him engaged for decades. "I know you."

"You're missing years of life experiences. Those years shaped me." She pushed against his chest. "If you don't like the outcome, shove it! Go back to San Antonio."

Even in a dusty alley, she was downright adorable. Disgruntled restaurant customers flayed his cooking, insulted his heritage, and spat on his feet. Riley Golding wanted to go tit-for-tat in a shadowed alley like school kids working out a disagreement over who would captain the kickball team. She might be a hellcat, but he could handle her misdirected frustration. Beneath her indignation, uneasiness reigned. He could weather her blows. If she wanted to talk through her emotions—naked over a bottle of wine—then he could altruistically participate in her talk therapy. He was just that kind of selfless, generous man. "You're right."

She jabbed his chest a second time. "And another thing…" She tilted her head. "What?"

Cupping her elbows, he pulled her to his body and hoped proximity was the right move. "You're right." He pressed a kiss to her hair. "I don't know you, but I want to."

Looking up, she stared. "You do?"

Her breasts, now pressed against his torso, could occupy him for hours. He considered dropping his head and burying his face in their warmth, but he fought off the impulse, anchored his hands on her hips, and stopped a hair's breadth from her lips. "I do."

She bristled and turned her head. "That's just sex talking."

He ran his cheek along the curve of her jaw. "Riley, I'm sorry for your loss. If Grant was anything like you, he was special. No wonder you miss your brother."

She let her shoulders sag. "Thank you."

He pressed a kiss below her ear and imagined taking her camping and exploring the soft, morning dew. "I'm sorry the town's full of old biddies who gossip without remembering the stupid shit they did when they were young. They don't deserve you. Maybe I don't, either."

She turned her head and made eye contact. "Biddies?"

"Every single annoying, interfering one. Their mutterings don't mean anything. If someone wants to say their piece, they should say it to your face. You can handle it."

"Can you?"

"A kiss is worth a thousand words." He lowered his head until his lips hovered above her lips. "I see someone on edge who's sticking out her neck to support her family. You're loyal and accomplished. Also, you're sexy as hell. Give me one out of three traits, and I'll be satisfied to be your friend or your lover. Your call."

"Accomplished," she said.

He closed his eyes. "For fuck's sake, I meant to say two out of three traits. Give me sexy and accomplished. Sexy and loyal. Just keep being sexy as hell. I'm yours, you horny, opinionated, prickly woman."

She laughed and lifted her chin. "That's a lot of traits."

Claiming a kiss before she changed her mind, he poured his senses into savoring her sweet taste. The experience overwhelmed his senses. Anger and frustration kept her spine as straight as an arrow, but she succumbed to his touch in the shadows. He would leverage his advantages and keep her in his bed as long as she wanted to join him.

As soon as she pulled away, she was apt to quit the restaurant build-out. He would accept her decision, but he wouldn't like it. He doubled down on his efforts and deepened the kiss. Every naughty desire he had last night replayed in his mind's eye. He wanted to turn her and pin her against the wall, but he settled for a searing kiss and hoped it wasn't his last.

She wrapped her arms around his neck and kissed him back.

At any moment, their kiss could render their rendezvous public knowledge. If she could take that chance, then he would savor the opportunity. He changed the angle and left her breathless. Marveling at her impact, he rested his forehead against hers. "Someone might see us and gossip."

She nibbled his lip. "I'll deny it ever happened."

"Good plan." He stroked a thumb along her lower back. Time stood still while he savored the stolen opportunity. He could hold her weight for an eternity.

A truck's backup warning sounded.

She looked toward the street and frowned. "You're right. We should get back to work."

He tightened his hold. "Or go back to my cabin."

She pushed against his chest.

Releasing his hold, he wondered if the next time she saw him, she would slap him or kiss him. He ran a thumb along his swollen bottom lip.

"I told you not to mix business with pleasure." She stepped backward. "We won't do this again."

He itched to stop her, but he stayed his impulse. "Your comment didn't specify kissing. Who says I find it pleasurable?"

Dropping a hand, she cupped him.

His body betrayed his reaction, but he refused to budge from his defense. "Morning wood. It's damn-near chronic. If you'd stuck around longer after our hookup, you'd know what I mean."

She laughed. "Do all celebrities think they can get away with that kind of bullshit?"

He adjusted his jeans. "Probably."

"Entitled assholes." She brushed her hair out of her face. "For clarity's sake, I meant no kissing, no sex, and no side-alley shenanigans. I don't care how handsome and empathetic you are. We can't hook up and work together. To focus on my job, I need a clear head."

He doubted her inability to multitask. He could run a kitchen, sauté greens, and season meat with his eyes closed. Given her accomplishments and her professional skill sets, a few loaded glances and after-hours organisms shouldn't distract her from her job. Handed an ultimatum, he could replace her on the design team, but he couldn't duplicate his attraction. "You're fired."

She laughed and walked toward the sunlit sidewalk. "For cause?"

Rubbing his right shoulder against the old limestone building, he accepted the building's rough abrasion. It might be the only itch he could satisfy today, but he refused to let Riley hide behind grief or excuses. "Your attitude sucks. Let me do my job, and you do yours? Don't give me shit about my celebrity status. Your dad's name is Warrior Golding, for fuck's sake."

"It's a nickname." She cleared her throat. "His real name's Louis. I'm sure he has a lawyer who would be happy to sue you on my behalf for sexual harassment. You're just pissed I'm calling out your hard-line."

"When I was Paul, you were all over me."

"When you were *Paul*, I could file you away as a one-night stand!"

The itch intensified, and he wrapped an arm across his chest to try to reach it. "You won't sue me. Everything we did was consensual, and you don't like gossip."

She pursed her lips. "You don't know me."

Were any women knowable? His presence in town was temporary, but he could string together facts and draw logical conclusions. Her feelings about her brother and the townspeople were nuanced, but she enjoyed his kiss. Working his jaw, he considered his approach.

"I have things to do," she said.

The itch would have to wait. He straightened. "I know a few things."

She raised her chin.

"Your dad manages architects, landscape architects, interior designers, estimators, and project managers. He builds custom homes for multimillionaires who like to gild their bathroom fixtures. I know you apprenticed with him, and your portfolio speaks for itself. You can handle celebrities."

She narrowed her gaze. "Like you and your staff?"

"My staff? I have ten employees and a couple of product lines."

She opened her mouth.

"I also have a few restaurants under my belt, capable restaurant managers, and the good sense to know I can smile pretty for the camera and entice customers to linger over the wine list. Don't tell me you're shy of spending time with me because I court fame."

"People recognize you—"

"Yeah, notoriety fucking sucks." He knocked his heel against the ground and stared at the imprint left in the soft mud. If the town had a long memory, then he would give the gossips fuel. He lifted his chin. "Notoriety's the only thing keeping us apart. When you thought I was a drifter, you were happy enough in my bed."

"I need to do my job!" She threw down her palms. "Can't you respect my boundaries?"

He had a feeling her boundaries were more about keeping up appearances than keeping her safe. "You kissed me back."

"A mistake." She stomped a foot. "We never could have worked together."

"And what exactly is your job, Riley Golding? You're more than daddy's little girl and Cypress Creek's nepo-baby. You broke off from the family firm, started a business, and made it a success. I'm not the only person standing in this alley with a media presence. How many speeches have you given or classes have you taught? How many internship applications do you receive each year?"

Internships were the most flattering and baffling part of her business. Half the students wanted to be her, and the other half wanted to correct her. Collaboration had upsides, but clients demanded results. She let Lacey weed through the internship applications and hoped for the best. So far, Lacey hadn't let her down. She swallowed. "Yeah, people know me."

"You miss your brother. I'll hold you all night long, but I don't want you to hide behind your regrets. How could you anticipate the flash flood hitting Cypress Creek? It was a hundred-year flood! Maybe you should have been a meteorologist instead of an architect."

"You think you know everything?" She turned her back and stormed toward the sidewalk. Kicking a loose rock, she sent it bouncing along a rut.

Five feet of space never felt like such a chasm, but once he started digging a hole, he was all in. "Grant was your brother and your twin, but live your life on your terms. Let's start with lunch. Skipping a turkey melt won't bring him back. If you can't work with me, then I'll accept your resignation. I won't accept excuses."

She turned and glanced over her shoulder.

Her eyes glistened. Feeling like an asshole, he ran his fingers through his hair. If Eagle Hawk had spoken to him this way, Ansel probably would have run away and hitchhiked toward the coast. Instead, Eagle Hawk put him to work and gave him time to grieve.

Instead of goading Riley, he should give her the same latitude to work through her grief, but he doubted he had the luxury of time. He dropped a hand and sighed. "I'm sorry I said that shit about the sandwich.

Grieve in whatever way makes sense, but don't give me excuses. You *can* mix business with pleasure. I'm not your boss. We're peers."

She turned and made eye contact. "The town will talk, and I will either have to live with the gossip or stay out of downtown."

"So, Jed's?" he asked.

"No." She worked her jaw. "Something low-key. You want to talk about the project? Make me lunch. Aren't you an acclaimed chef?"

He'd found himself in a few difficult situations, but he had backed himself into this limestone wall. His grocery order wouldn't arrive until five o'clock, and as far as he knew, the only things in the bungalow cabinets were aged tea, dried rice, and seaweed wraps. He hoped Riley wasn't a fussy eater. Straightening, he interlaced his fingers, stretched out his palms, and accepted her challenge. "I can whip up a few things. Come to the bungalow."

"For food."

He grinned. "Unless you change your mind and want to see me cook naked?"

She headed toward the alley's sunlit opening, but she looked over her right shoulder and smiled. "I'll think about it, but it's probably off the table. After the job's done, we can reconsider."

"Reconsider?" he asked.

She widened her gaze. "The kissing and whatnot!"

"Shh!" He held a finger to his lips. "The town will hear you."

Rolling her eyes, she merged with pedestrian traffic.

He almost laughed, but he restrained himself and

followed. Completing the restaurant never felt so important. Once he launched his opus finale, he could retire and spend his nights in Riley's arms. Aubrey would spit nails. Watching Riley's hips sway, he couldn't care less. His ex-girlfriend undermined him and tanked his first business, but she fell short of castrating him. Her betrayal was like a cattle prod, cruel and unnecessary, but it *had* put his ass in motion. Maybe he should thank her for bringing him to Cypress Creek.

He walked toward his bungalow and spied a line of people idling on the sidewalk. He zeroed in on his rental's front door like a man searching for his last condom, but the milling crowd seemed uninterested in his presence. Was there a bus stop nearby? Walking over the bungalow's threshold, he kicked off his mud-caked boots and headed straight for the kitchen. He hoped he found more than soy sauce, cooking sake, and *nori* sheets in the cupboards.

Flinging open the wooden doors, he scanned classic Japanese condiments and labeled jars holding bonito flakes, *wakame*, *kombu*, and shiitake mushrooms. The seaweed and the mushrooms were a good base. While a soup simmered, he and Riley would have time to chat. Fast Casual might be sweeping the nation, but lingering meals were fine art. He grinned and took down the ingredients.

A knock sounded on the door.

Leaving the cupboard doors open, he padded toward the entrance, opened the door, and found Riley shifting her weight. He leaned against the doorframe. "Fancy seeing you here."

She smiled. "What's for lunch?"

"Soup."

She shrugged and stepped past him. "Okay. Beggars can't be choosers."

"Beggars?" Turning, he considered giving her a crash course in his culinary achievements, but the yeasty, fresh-baked aroma of hot bread sidetracked his arguments. Sniffing, he untangled her sage-tinged sweetness from sourdough's allure. "Riley, did you bring me fresh bread?"

She laughed and laid her bag on the table with the welcome packet. "That's Moeko's pop-up bakery. On Saturdays, she wakes up early to make sweet and savory breads, but letting the dough rise takes time. She doesn't start selling her goods until ten o'clock."

"That line of people want to buy bread?" He scanned the milling crowd and pitied the coffee shop owner's inability to satisfy the town's needs. Unless the bread line prompted the coffee shop to throw in the towel? Shutting the front door, he peered through the bungalow's curtains and counted close to thirty people waiting for Moeko's bread.

"All those people are locals lining up for treats from the Boutique Bungalow Bread Company. Based on social media, today's menu includes croissants, brioche squares with yuzu marmalade, and nectarine-cardamom hand pies."

He eyed the open cupboards and weighed his soup schemes against the allure of homemade bread. Yuzu was a type of East Asian citrus fruit. The Japanese also used yuzu in the bath, but he doubted Riley would join him in the soaker tub. He would have to settle for brioche squares and a Hill Country 5K to burn off his indulgences. Or, he could make soup. It would be excellent soup. He worked his jaw, eyed his boots, and made a decision. "You know, I'm a shit cook."

Riley laughed.

Slipping on his boots, he reached for his hat and then held open the door. "Let's get in line for gluten. If you don't want to stand beside me, I'll pretend I don't know you."

She gathered her things and walked onto the rental's porch. "Is that possible?"

He pulled shut the door and tested the handle. "Depends."

Slipping on her shoes and sliding her purse over her right shoulder, she started down the steps before she paused and turned. "Depends on what?"

He slid a hand into his pocket. "On whether the men in this town mind me staring at your ass. It might be a community asset."

"Ridiculous man." She shook out her hair and waited at the bottom of the steps. "Try to forget you've seen me naked. Ignore the kisses and the"—she dropped her voice—"sex. We're colleagues. If you can behave, we can stand side by side like normal people."

"Normal, huh?"

She wet her lips. "No alleys."

Taking his place beside her, he opened his mouth to offer a more amicable approach toward their partnership, but the warm, buttery smell of fresh croissants and savory fillings stole his focus. When his stomach rumbled, he promptly forgot everything he wanted to say to Riley. Instead of sweet-talking her into a casual conversation, he took a hand and pulled her toward the end of the bread line. Romance had a time and a place, but at this moment, his stomach led.

Chapter Ten

Ansel looked at Moeko's bungalow bakery like a man sizing up his wartime competition. Riley swore his nostrils twitched, but she felt the same way about well-designed buildings. Deciding to keep her ribbing to a minimum, she pulled out her phone and adjusted her stance. She could answer emails while he geeked out on the smell of homemade bread. When his blood sugar stabilized, and he resumed his ability to participate in adult conversation, then she would put away her phone.

Ten minutes later, the line barely advanced.

He turned. "What's taking so long?"

"Agonizing choices." She kept her gaze on the phone screen. Lacey had forwarded a punch list for a nearly completed job. Riley wanted her artisans to exceed her customers' expectations. Amateurs covered up mistakes, but clever designers offered distractions. Riley would troubleshoot the job. To maintain optics, Lacey would flatter the customer and arrange photo shoots. "Life is full of agonizing choices."

"Brioche shouldn't be agonizing," he said. "It's sweet bread."

Frowning, she blinked and looked up from the phone. "Huh?"

"Or hand pies." He rubbed a thumb along his lip. "Croissants. Why the hell isn't this line moving?"

She swore he wiped away drool. Laughing, she

dropped her phone into her bag and scanned the block. A gravel parking pad took up most of the space where Moeko's front lawn should stand. Various potted plants defined the porch edge and trailed over old, brick piers. Near the front door, a twisted oak leaned toward the light and created the perfect spot for a large spider swing and a patch of bare dirt.

Three kids kept busy on the toy while their adult minders waited in line. The kids' laughter and demands for higher pushes could lighten anyone's mood. "Maybe the kids will let you have a turn on the swing."

He glanced at the kids and resumed his laser focus on Moeko's front door. "I doubt it would hold me."

The swing had to be near forty inches in diameter. Its padded steel frame and nylon webbing looked built to last, and she doubted Moeko would mind if Ansel took a ride. If the toy was large enough for multiple children to play together, it could hold one opinionated, San Antonio chef.

She checked the sidewalk and confirmed nobody waited behind them. Leaning close to Ansel, she waited until he registered her proximity and focused. "Come on, I'll push you."

"You'll push me?" he asked.

"What? You don't like to swing?" She shrugged. "Fine by me. Killjoy."

"I am not a killjoy." He followed the swing's progress and moved his eyes like a metronome.

The wrinkles near his eyes deepened, and he fidgeted. She wanted to smooth away his mystification, but he remained so focused on his goals that he refused to enjoy the ride. Still, his happiness wasn't her problem.

Shifting gears, she hoped talk of the restaurant would refocus him. "What about going over my design ideas for the restaurant? I want to open up the back room and give you patio dining, but we need decent ventilation to keep away the bugs."

He frowned and looked away from the swinging kids. "Bugs?"

She grinned. "Welcome to life by a creek. The system might be expensive, but the hotel's limestone arches will camouflage the infrastructure."

A shrill whistle beckoned the kids toward the front of the line.

Abandoning the toy, the kids retreated to their parents' sides. The swing's forlorn black netting swayed beneath the oak tree against a cloudy gray sky.

Ansel frowned but kept his gaze on the bakery's front door. "How much infrastructure?"

"Industrial fans, directional fans, infrared heaters, and evaporative coolers will maintain temperate conditions at all times." She considered pulling out her phone to show him specifications. "Your customers will feel like it's springtime, and they'll laze over their meals like they're visiting the South of France."

"I assume there will be patio lights," he said. "Grape vines. A fountain."

She frowned. His fresh, woodsy smell had hints of aged wood, but lingering storm clouds and fresh green surroundings intensified its depth. Agarwood evoked perseverance, and the limestone building Ansel purchased had persevered.

The pair deserved more than patio lights and trite references to southern France. She envisioned a patio with a focal-point fire feature. Charcoal-black seating situated over poured concrete pavers would create dining islands with the limestone arches, and new cypress trees, perimeter garden beds, and raised planters would perfume the shadows. A wrought-iron fence would define the property and host lighting to showcase Ansel's creations. "Let's skip the fountain."

Turning his head, he cocked it to the side. "Okay, no fountains."

She jerked her chin toward the spider swing. "Take a seat, and I'll tell you all about my ideas."

He rubbed his chin. "You'll push me?"

"I mean, you can try pumping your legs, but they'll probably scrape the ground."

He snorted. Shaking his head, he abandoned the sidewalk, dropped into the nylon netting, and looked toward the overhead canopy.

If he expected the rope to break, the tree branch to crack, or the swing to lay him flat, he was in for a surprise. Cypress Creek learned to be tough, and the hot, Texas sun weeded out the city's weaker tendencies. Overcast clouds might dim the town's allure and diminish retail sales, but she felt confident the tree would endure. She gripped the nearest rope and pulled it. Using her weight, she set Ansel and the swing into motion. "How do you feel about poured concrete tables? Polished, of course."

"Of course." After a few passes over the grass, he relaxed his hold on the mesh, crossed his arms, and maintained eye contact. "How industrial are we talking?"

"I have a finisher who can make the tables look like leathered granite."

"Shouldn't you use limestone?"

She shook her head. "Limestone's too soft."

He raised his eyebrows. "I presume Nathan isn't the concrete finisher."

She considered jerking the rope and sending him spinning. Instead, she adopted a professional smile. "Nathan's crew would take care of the structural improvements. We'll bring in craftsmen for the finishes."

He lowered his shoulders and looked toward the bungalow. "Sounds pricey."

She smiled. "I'm sure you can afford it."

Turning his head, he made eye contact. "But is it worth it?"

She assumed he meant the restaurant, but his reason for coming to Cypress Creek remained at the back of her mind. For hurt to linger for twenty years, he must feel the effects of Aubrey's burn, but she guessed the restaurant build-out had more to do with overcoming his deepest doubts than sticking his success to his ex-girlfriend.

Every time Riley put designs to paper and presented them to a client, she held her breath. When he plated a new dish, he probably did the same thing. By cornering upscale, urban markets, he proved he could put on a show, but celebrity credentials were a dime a dozen.

Repeating his success in Cypress Creek required quality and restaurant patrons willing to feed their near-fanatical devotion. "I'll give you a palate, and provide the food and the restaurant staff. Let your customers tell you if it's worth it."

He worked his jaw. "Oh, they will."

She kept pushing and mentally designed more of

the restaurant.

With each push, his posture relaxed, and their place at the end of the line inched closer to the bungalow door.

The kids emerged from Moeko's with twice-baked almond croissants. As they passed, the sweet scent of almond and powdered sugar drew her focus.

"Getting tired?" Ansel asked. "This is a little embarrassing. I can push you."

She grinned and put her legs into the effort.

He sighed, but a smile ticked up one corner of his mouth.

She wondered if swing therapy might be a new therapy. For all his intensity and his achievements, Ansel had a bit of a stick up his ass. At the gas station, she attributed his demeanor to the hot, Texas sun. Plenty of good ole boys liked to chat and thought they knew best. At Jacob's Hole, he refused to take no for an answer and leave her in peace. Admittedly, she needed a distraction and gladly accompanied him home.

After their sweat-slicked evening, she climbed out of his bed and thought he looked relaxed. Then, she mentioned Grant. He briefly closed his eyes, and she glimpsed his pain. He kept his grief bottled up tight, but he still felt the pain of losing his parents.

He felt deeply, and his emotions lingered. If those attributes made him an excellent chef, then she appreciated his perfection, but she wondered if strain kept him wound tight. Confronted with her minimal acts of resistance, he dragged her into a shadowed alley and kissed her senseless. She doubted he employed the same techniques with his sous chefs. "Are you a terror in the kitchen?"

He shifted his weight, gripped the nylon ropes, and leaned back over the edge of the spider swing. "What do you think?"

She opened her mouth to tease him about his merciless ways, but at the height of the swing's arc, the strap on the tree branch snapped and dropped him to the packed ground above two inches of measly grass.

Ansel slapped a hand over his chest and breathed deeply.

"What the…" Running toward him, she beat the crowd of helpful Texans and curious busybodies who abandoned their places in line to assess his injuries. "Don't move him."

The crowd paused and eased back.

"I'm fine." He pushed up on one arm and planted a palm in the grass. Leaning toward the fallen strap, he inspected the frayed, black nylon and made eye contact. "Please don't tell me Nathan installed this contraption."

She almost laughed, but he fell from the swing's highest arc, and as his body hit hard dirt, she swore she felt the impacting thud. If the swing snapped with one of the kids on it, they might fracture a bone or require concussive care. He was a grown man. Surely, he was made of stronger stuff? She held her breath.

Shifting his weight, he winced.

She dropped to one knee. "How bad is it?"

"My tailbone." Squeezing closed his eyes, he beckoned. "I can't quite see straight."

She leaned close. "Do you need an X-ray?"

"How about a back massage and a sponge bath?" He opened his eyes and winked.

Releasing her breath, she swung a hand toward his chest. He could take his mock injuries and shove them where the sun didn't shine.

He caught her arm and slowed her momentum. "Riley?"

She made eye contact.

Holding up his other hand, he revealed a narrow gash. "A kiss would help me feel better."

An adhesive bandage would work better, but before she looked away from the scrape, she paused to examine the large, white burn on his hand. He famously burned himself on live television, let loose a creative string of swear words, and kept cooking. Long after the show ended, the scar remained. What other pieces of himself had he sacrificed for his success? What pieces remained?

Even as he watched her flee his rental after their hookup, he comforted her about losing Grant. Assurances that life would get better meant little from the people who had never experienced loss, but Ansel knew the pain.

Until her loss, she didn't understand the ways grief shaped a person. Meeting people where they stood, without questioning why and how they grieved, created a safe space for honest emotions. If Ansel could be supportive and loving, he deserved more than her defensive barriers. He deserved her reciprocal empathy. She hoped no one ever shared her experiences, but she could do something to ease his everyday pains. Given enough time, she might ease his heartache. Drawing the hand to her lips, she kissed it and met his gaze. "Does this feel better?"

"Infinitely," he said.

His handsome face softened, and for a moment, the cloudy sky cradled two people sitting on the lawn in a small, Texas town. Closing her eyes, she savored the moment, but professionalism demanded restraint. She took a deep breath, stood, and pulled him to his feet.

He dropped his head and pressed a kiss to her temple. "I promise I won't sue you."

She gasped and pushed him away.

"Mommy, that's the chef from television who says naughty words," a girl said.

"Why's he kissing Ms. Riley?"

"Nobody's kissing anyone!" Riley rubbed her hands over her face. "Mr. Ansel had a boo-boo. I'm sorry he fell."

"Once, I got a boo-boo," the girl said. "It hurt."

The girl's mother patted her back and led her toward a parked car. "Me, too, honey, but Ansel Percheron didn't kiss me to make it better."

A second parent laughed.

Riley watched the group depart and turned to give Ansel a piece of her mind.

"Ansel and Riley…K-I-S-S-I-N-G," two boys chanted. "First comes love, then comes marriage, then comes a baby in a baby carriage." The kids laughed and hid their interest behind the embarrassing song. "That's not all, that's not all…"

Feeling her face redden, she looked toward Ansel to apologize for the accident and minimize the innocent kiss.

He leaned close and dropped his head. "Was that so bad?"

A cool wind picked up. He beat her to the punch, but she refused to let him get under her skin. "The fall?"

He shook his head. "The kiss."

His hair whispered across her face, and she closed her eyes. In another environment, she could play these flirtatious games, but Cypress Creek meant more than a handsome client. She dropped his hand. "It was a comforting impulse. I shouldn't have done it."

"I have a few more body parts that need your comforting impulses." He raised his eyebrows. "One particular ache…only you can ease it."

She rolled her eyes. "Are your days always this exciting?"

He winked. "They are when you're around."

Stomping her foot seemed like an appropriate reaction, but she pursed her lips and held her ground.

"Pity you're not into playing nurse." He wiped his blood on his jeans. "You made yourself loud and clear about our professional relationship, but I appreciate the attention. Every little bit helps my fragile, celebrity ego."

"Your ego's hard as a rock."

He looked up and winked. "It's not the only thing."

She refused to acknowledge his smile or check his pants for a bulge. Turning away before her interest incriminated her, she found the kids involved in a new game.

Their parents lingered out of earshot and snapped pictures of the downed swing.

Ansel might be okay, but Moeko needed a new swing, and she needed distance. "I should probably head home for lunch. I'm here to spend time with my parents, too."

"Scared of my soup?" he asked.

"Hardly." She permitted herself a smile.

Moeko hurried out of the bungalow, carrying a

white paper bag. She offered it to Ansel. "I am so-so-o sorry. Are you okay?"

He held up both palms. "Just a scratch. No big deal."

Moeko thrust the bag into his arms. "Please, would you tell me if you're hurt?"

He opened the bag and withdrew a pastry. "If I'm hurt, do I get more pastries?"

She tilted her head and frowned.

Worrying Moeko's concern would escalate the situation, Riley wrapped an arm around Ansel's waist, peeled him away from greeting, and redirected him toward his rental. "He's fine, and he doesn't need any more pastries." She slapped his bruised ass for good measure. "Men will do anything to satisfy their appetites."

"True," Moeko said.

He added a jump to his step, raised the white bag like a trophy, and strode off. "Talk shop while I eat. Truthfully, Moeko, I'm all good!"

Riley rolled her eyes and considered billing him for the lunch hour. His interest in the backstreet bakery turned their working lunch into a carb-fueled extravagance, and she doubted he would save her a croissant. Instead of chasing him, she turned to Moeko, whom she had known for close to a decade. "The swing's straps must have worn thin. I'm glad your kids weren't playing on it when it broke."

"Oh! That would have been scary. *Ningen banji saiou ga uma*, the results will turn out good." Moeko shaded her gaze and looked up at the tree. "I never thought it would fall, but maybe it's better that it did. We'll get stronger ropes."

Riley shuffled her feet. "So, thanks for the baked goods. Everything smells delicious. I'll send you the money on my phone."

Moeko looked away from the tree. "My pleasure."

Before she walked back to her SUV, she followed Moeko's gaze toward the old oak. "What did you say about the swing?"

"*Saiou ga uma.* It's a Japanese phrase referencing an old story about a son escaping his obligations to the emperor's army. You never know whether events will turn out to be good or bad. Your friend bruised his backside, but his pain might have spared my kids harsher injuries. Psychologists prompt us to reframe our experiences. Viewed from a slightly different angle, an event's meaning can change dramatically."

Riley wondered if Ansel's tailbone would accept Moeko's perspective. Surely, his restaurant was the only thing he wanted reframed. He was the chef-proprietor of ten restaurants, but he waltzed off with a bag of pastries like he won the lottery.

Thunder cracked overhead, and the line of customers queuing for Moeko's baked goods glanced at the sky.

"I'm almost sold out," Moeko said. "Excuse me?"

A heavy raindrop landed on Riley's cheek. "I'll see you later."

The rain intensified as she hurried to the SUV. Drenched, she slid into the driver's seat and turned on the vehicle's heater. Blasting hot air felt ridiculous on an early summer day, but craving heat, she dialed up the seat warmer, too.

She glanced at Ansel's bungalow and knew exactly where to find heat, but she put the vehicle in Drive and peeled out before she made a serious professional mistake. Recording her thoughts for the restaurant design in a voice memo, she drove the black SUV along the state highway passing her parents' house. Rain fell heavy on the windshield, but she navigated the familiar bends and slowed for the strand of native shrubs marking the ranch.

She stopped the SUV in front of the entrance, popped open an umbrella, and manipulated the padlock. As the oiled lock popped open, rain dripped down her neck. Her father, for all his quirks, should consider an automated gate. She dealt with the gate, moved her SUV, and secured the entrance.

Rain pooled in the driveway and slipped down the red, dirt hills toward the waiting creeks. She opened the garage door and slipped into an open bay. Seeing her parents' cars in their spots, she climbed out of the SUV, left her umbrella to dry, and walked into the mudroom. "Papi?"

The ground floor offered stunning, panoramic views of the ranch and the river, but rain clouds narrowed her field of vision to the first ten feet from the glass. Lightning cracked, and wind shook down tree leaves. Clearing her throat, she dropped her bag on the expansive marble island. "Dad?" Her voice wavered.

"Shhh!" Papi walked into the kitchen holding a finger to his lips. "Warrior scared off the rehab nurses. He's hanging out in the library with Mikey Roberts. Do you want them to know you're home?"

With Mikey in the house, six thousand square feet of covered living space felt like a minimum. She sat on a stool and dropped her head on her arms. If she knew he waited at the ranch, she might have bought out

Moeko's baked goods and carb-loaded on her front steps. "Hell, no, I don't want them to know I'm home."

"Riley June Golding, watch your language!" Papi shook his finger. "I left that language in Miami. I swear, your mouth's worse than Grant's ever was."

Her defiance collapsed. She gripped the countertop and longed to hear Grant drop an f-bomb. Ansel said he had a habit of making up creative swear words, but nobody could cuss in a three-piece suit like Grant. She wiped away a tear and wished like were simpler.

Papi laid a hand on her back. "I'm sorry, honey. I shouldn't have mentioned Grant."

She waved off his apology and debated between wallowing or accepting the sting and moving on. Isn't that what Papi and Dad did? Standing, she wrapped Papi in a hug and dropped her head on his comforting right shoulder. "Papi, who do you think taught me all the bad words? I want you to mention Grant. If we stop talking about him, our memories fade. We loved him too much to let that happen."

Sniffling, Papi tightened the hug. "I miss him so much. He could brighten any room."

"Just like you." She pulled back, smiled, and wiped a tear from Papi's face. She and Grant had their strengths, but their fathers lived for both of them. Mikey, despite his waxed appeal, was less like a brother and more like a lingering threat to their tight-knit family. "It's okay if Dad hears me swear, Papi. He fucking misses Grant, too."

Swatting her right arm, Papi wiped away his tears without smearing his makeup. "Don't let your father hear that mouth. You'll never hear the end of it, and neither will I." Shaking his head, he walked into the pantry.

She shrugged, but his reproach lingered. She hated to disappoint Papi. He spoiled her, and Dad challenged her, but their different approaches to life made her a stronger person.

Rolling her head in soothing circles, she considered her approach to the Percheron job. Dad basically owed her. She could spend the rest of her life swearing like a sailor, and he couldn't do a damn thing. A smile tugged free.

Ansel would come up with a better phrase.

Papi set a jar of coconut oil onto the island. "What has you grinning?"

Before she could answer, she heard Mikey's voice from the back of the house. His presence ruined her good mood, and she pushed back from the island. Retreating to her childhood comforts did nothing for her or her ambitions. She could play nice for her fathers' sakes, but nice ended after dessert. "Fuck him."

"Riley June…"

She lifted a hand in acknowledgement and walked toward the wet bar. "Save it, Papi. I'm breaking out the good rum."

"Oh, Lawd," he said.

"Nope, just Mikey." She dumped ice into a tumbler. "But he hardly knows the difference."

Chapter Eleven

Riley ran a hand over the green velvet armchair in the living room. In the Golding household, Michael "Mikey" Roberts was a semi-famous musician, but he also had a favorite armchair. She refused to sit in it.

For nearly a decade, his presence in the household left her starstruck and uncertain. After exploiting his good looks at county fairs, honky-tonks, and church revivals, he returned to Cypress Creek flush with stories and kisses. Sometimes, she welcomed him. More recently, she turned her head.

Few people understood how his dramatic relationship with Riley fueled his song lyrics, but based on the number of times she tried to end the relationship, her parents should have had a clue. Also, they should have burned the armchair.

Instead, Dad and Papi doted on Mikey's preening, good-boy vibes. Riley alternately loved and hated their connection, and she wasted a decade pinning down why he didn't quite make her happy.

With four years separating their ages, she let his life experiences impress her until the day she felt more mature. She told everyone they parted on good terms, but her maturation left room for his persistence.

After every breakup, he lingered at the edge of her life and wooed her parents with his casual charm. Birthdays merited phone calls, holidays brought gifts, and neighborhood gossip stuck with Mikey longer than indelible tattoos.

One could almost believe he still lived in town.

While they dated, Grant played nice for her sake, but he resented the weekends Mikey stayed at the ranch.

Dad encouraged him to take Mikey out in the truck for quality time and ranch chores.

One memorable weekend, Grant had arranged a series of challenges designed to highlight Mikey's ineptitude at country life. He loaded up shotguns, ropes, and basic fire-making equipment and invited Mikey to spend a day tooling around the ranch's outer acreage.

When they returned before nightfall, aluminum cans remained on the fence rails, cattle lingered in the field, and Mikey accumulated so many blisters he threw away his new boots.

"Why do you put up with him?" Grant asked. "You could do so much better."

Closing her college textbook, she looked up at her twin and wondered if their privileged upbringings made their lives too easy. They attended an excellent, private high school halfway between Cypress Creek and Austin. She aced her college calculus and physics coursework, but sophomore year's structural courses would test her.

Mikey barely knew how to use a graphing calculator, but she could teach him. Grant could teach him to shoot. Working hard was a badge of honor, but so was compassion. She tested out her puppy-dog eyes. "Give him a chance."

"I've given him twenty!" Grant threw up his hands. "The man's useless."

"He might say the same thing about you." She planted her hands on her hips and switched tactics. "You can't sing for shit."

He rolled his eyes. "Singing's for sissies."

"Well, unless you want to date him, you shouldn't care," she said.

"I care about you." He gripped her shoulders and held her at arm's length. "We're a team, but I don't want to make small talk with that loser for the next five decades."

"You'll fail as an architect."

Laughing, he chuffed her right shoulder with the restrained affection she expected.

He had dropped his objections to the relationship and played nice.

The next year, Mikey's musical career took off, and his debut album hit the top of the local charts. As she watched his fame soar, their relationship flickered, but she appreciated his talents. The breakups hurt, but when she finally called off the relationship, she felt at peace and ready to sink into her professional life.

Older and wiser, Riley opened the refrigerator door and pulled out a loaf of bread, peanut butter, and jelly. She needed to eat before her past sucker-punched her present.

"What are you doing?" Papi asked.

"Making myself a sandwich." She dropped two pieces of bread on a wooden cutting board and spread a thick layer of nut butter on the first piece of bread. Wiping the knife's edge along the crust, she dipped it in the jelly jar and coated the second piece of bread with strawberry jam. Callie might be adventuring with her dog squad, but Riley had learned to feed herself.

Papi opened the fridge and removed a glass bowl filled with deveined crustaceans. Plastic wrap sealed the top of the bowl, but the ice beneath the shrimp had melted. "What about the shrimp?"

She eyed the offering and weighed it against her sandwich's appeal. Lime juice could work wonders on the raw seafood, but she feared more than indigestion. "I'm almost done with this sandwich."

Papi's face fell.

"Why don't we make fettuccini for dinner? The greens you cut up will make a nice salad. I've always loved your salads." Lifting the sandwich, she took a healthy bite and waited for him to accept the offer.

Papi's smile faltered, and he opened his mouth, but instead of a rebuttal, he sighed and spun the glass bowl on the smooth countertop. It chattered and left rings of condensation in its wake. "Why is cooking such a chore? In my twenties, I lived off street food, and I looked damn good."

She laughed. "You still look good."

A smile warmed his face. "I do."

"You're doing a great job with the cooking and the aging." She stopped chewing to form her words. "I can't wait for the pasta. You know how much Dad indulged in a good cheese sauce."

Papi nodded. "It's his weakness."

"I thought you were his weakness," she said.

Papi looked up and winked. "I am."

In her family's home, she let her smile bloom.

Mikey sauntered into the kitchen and peered into the shrimp bowl. "Dinner?"

Turning, Papi beamed. "Shrimp Alfredo."

He hopped onto a barstool. "I love Alfredo shrimp,

and I make a mean garlic bread."

The sandwich lodged in Riley's throat. Swallowing, she ran her tongue along her teeth. "You're staying for dinner?"

"Just dropped by to chat with your dad about a few real estate prospects." He wiped a peanut butter smear from her plate and popped it into his mouth. "Papi mentioned the guest room's made up."

She edged her plate closer. "It's always made up."

Mikey shrugged. "Lucky me. Did you know I'm working on a new album that goes back to my quintessential sound? I want listeners to consider where I'm going and where I've been. Maybe while I'm here, I could play you a few songs."

"Catchy," Papi said. "I'd love to hear them."

Riley would love to finish her lunch in peace. Mikey's second album lacked the authenticity and fresh lyrics underpinning his debut. In the past decade, country music superstars had covered his early songs, but she preferred his feel-good, classic renditions. Happily, she no longer heard herself in every song. As far as she knew, songwriting credits brought in most of his income, and he carved out a decent life in the Hill Country. She licked clean her finger and looked up.

Mikey met her gaze, blushed, and looked toward Papi. He cleared his throat. "If the album sells as well as it should, I want to buy the 130-acre ranch next door to this one. It has an authentic dance hall that would make a nice rental for Hill Country weddings. Your dad said he would give it a look-see."

She could support his career without having him in spitting distance. With Grant gone, she would inherit the ranch, but she preferred not to inherit a constant reminder of her misspent youth. Blowing out her breath, she stood, rounded the kitchen island, and filled a glass of water. Dad wanted a wedding venue next door like he wanted a tour bus to stop by the river. His encouraging Mikey's interest in the property felt a lot like meddling in her life. Instead of confronting Mikey, she would keep life simple and focus on Dad.

Draining half the water glass, she kept her concerns to herself. Her parents could lavish as much attention on Mikey as they wanted, but she refused to climb back into his bed and fuel his creativity. If push came to shove, she would buy the next-door ranch.

Dad made his way into the kitchen.

His slow, measured steps belied the surgery and physical therapy rehabilitating his hips. She wished he would use a walker, but stubbornness ran in the family. Her indignation faded, and she nudged her plate along the countertop. "Care for a sandwich?"

Dad pulled down a worn baseball cap from a mudroom hook. "Nah, Mikey and I will ride over to see the neighbor's ranch." He set it on his head. "Wouldn't it be nice to have him close?"

Empathy shouldn't derail her life. Walking toward the painted cubbies, she lifted down a pair of worn boots and stood beside Dad without relinquishing the tooled leather. "It's pouring down rain."

"It's clear enough for a drive."

She took a deep breath. "Having Mikey next door is a little too close for comfort. We're over."

He shrugged. "It's his money."

Resting a hand on his arm, she stalled his progress. "First, you hand me the restaurant flip with Percheron, and now, you're kindling Michael's interest in the neighborhood." Dropping her voice, she leaned close. "I would expect these ploys from Papi, but you should know better. Stop meddling. I don't need you to line up suitors like a meddling matchmaker."

He winced.

She offered the boots. "Are we clear?"

Clearing his throat, he accepted the boots and slipped his foot inside the first boot shank. "I built Ansel's house in San Antonio, and I've always liked the man. Are you two getting along?"

As clear as mud. Planting her hands on her hips, she exhaled. "I get along with all my customers."

"Then what's the problem?" Dad asked.

She struggled to reframe her situation in a way that didn't reveal she had shacked up with her customer before meeting him on the job site. "He's too full of himself."

Dad laughed and slipped on the second boot. "Welcome to Texas."

Mikey tucked in barstools, and the legs clattered on the kitchen floor.

Riley winced.

"Honey, don't stay out too long," Papi said. "We're having shrimp Alfredo for dinner, and Mikey's joining us."

Dad planted a kiss on his cheek. "I love shrimp. Mikey, you're a lucky man."

"Really? I find them bland," Riley said.

Three men stared.

Each man was successful in his way, and he deployed charisma to advance his brand, but the trio couldn't be more different. One more meal with Mikey meant little in the grand scheme of things, but pleasing her fathers meant the world. She cleared her throat. "Except when Papi makes them."

Papi's smile beamed.

Returning his affection with a wink, she turned toward the main house and walked out of the kitchen. Out of sight of her fathers and her ex-boyfriend, she abandoned her façade, kicked the newel post, crossed her arms over the elegant stairway marker, and dropped her head. The pain in her foot anchored her to the present, but her past loomed. Mikey belonged firmly in her past. "Actually, I do hate shrimp. Without the right seasoning, they're just overgrown plankton. Fuck shrimp."

Using the expletive brought a smile, and she wondered if Ansel would laugh at her outburst. The man helmed so many restaurants, he must have the skills needed to revitalize day-old shrimp and make her dinner bearable. Shaking off the thought, she climbed the stairs and focused on her work.

Until Ansel opened his restaurant in Cypress Creek, she had no idea of his capabilities outside the bedroom, but she appreciated his mastery of the bedroom arts.

****

The shrimp and the conversation were as bland as Riley expected, but reserved civility, white wine, and patient smiles let her weather the meal and the seared shrimp. When she heard Mikey suggest a round of cards before bed, she feigned a yawn and excused herself for the night. Dad and Papi could entertain their houseguest.

After a restless night's sleep, she trudged down the stairs, wearing running shoes and a loose pair of shorts.

If her body refused to rest, she would tip the scales with exercise.

In her dreams, Cypress Creek's newest restaurant burned to the ground. Shocked by another inferno, the building's limestone walls crumbled, and its poured concrete tables remained like lonely monoliths. Blackened, prickly pear cacti slumped in glazed pots while Ansel picked through the rubble. Standing on the sidewalk, she watched the dream unfold and wondered how she could have prevented the shuddering, sooty end.

"Oh good, you're up." Dad set down the newspaper.

She covered a yawn and dropped into an upholstered chair. "Barely."

"Mikey's in the kitchen. He mentioned running over to Houston tomorrow for a concert date. Maybe you should attend. You could listen to his new music and see if any of his latest songs resonate."

Bending at the waist, she tightened the laces on her running shoes. "Or not."

"Give the man a chance, Riley."

She raised her head and made eye contact. "Mikey's in my past. You asked me to come home to fix the restaurant build-out. I can't afford to take off a few days and stroke Mikey's ego."

He worked his jaw.

"Actually, I can skip town for a few days, but I don't want to. Let Mikey sweet-talk a groupie into warming his bed. I have zero interest in reprising my role." She tilted her head and chose her words. "Am I making myself clear? Zero interest. If you want Mikey next door, find him a different wife. I'm not the woman for the job."

"You're too committed to your firm." Dad fluffed the newspaper and raised it to reading height. "That kind of commitment can't last."

"No? Then how come you're using it to save your ass?"

Dad's face reddened.

She considered going on a spree. "With my commitment, the Percheron project would fall behind, and your reputation would suffer. Ansel wants excellence. He hired you for a reason."

Dad smiled. "Oh, it's Ansel, is it?"

She stood and stretched her arms over her head. The weather forecast said the break in the rain would last for an hour, and she refused to spend her time butting heads with Dad. "Meddle in someone else's life!"

"Whose life?" Dad asked. "Grant's?"

Her father could be such a jerk. Hiding behind his seniority and his professional reputation, he wielded Grant's death like a well-formed argument. Given a choice between arguing with Dad's motivations or banging her head against a wall, she chose the wall.

Past her parents' two-story home, a steep, bald hill parted the rain clouds. Once a watchtower for the county fire department, the top of the formation offered a paved limestone viewpoint and a panoramic overview of the surrounding hill country. The steep limestone staircase leading to the bald summit would test her muscles, but it would also wear down her frustrations.

She jogged in place to warm up, checked the skies for lightning, and ran up the first ten steps. Of course, Dad couldn't interfere in Grant's life, so he deserved the right to interfere in hers. His reputation helped launch her career, and he felt entitled to derail hers without concern for the consequences. Her thighs burned, but she kept climbing.

At the first turn, she glimpsed a brass plaque and repeated the message she knew by heart. Papi installed the plaques to commemorate his grief. Some referenced scripture, but others recalled Grant's favorite books and most-played songs.

Her stupid, beautiful brother had graced her life, but his death threatened to ruin it.

She had nobody to blame but herself and Mother Fucking Nature.

Thunder cracked.

She winced and decided to watch her language. Scanning the horizon for lightning, she climbed the steps. Ever since losing Grant, she felt adrift, and she hated the feeling as much as she hated the taste of margaritas. She used to *love* margaritas!

By now, she or Grant should be married Texans toting toddlers. Fate had other plans. If her dads wanted grandkids, they should adopt because the chances of her marrying Mikey were as likely as the chances of Bald Mountain growing a proper-sized tree.

At the top of the formation, she bent double and caught her breath. Exercise burned off her self-indulgent mood and confirmed her continued existence. Despite the inclement weather forming, her parents' house sat directly below her. The home's warm, yellow lights reminded her how much she had instead of how much she lost. She could yell as loud as she wanted without reproof, but an outraged scream died in her throat. Brass plaques, stylized urns, and unlimited tears would never bring back Grant. Instead of replaying the past, she had to look toward the future.

Taking a deep breath, she looked away from the house and admired the area's green, rolling hills. Dark stands of trees marked the creek tributaries flowing into Cypress Creek, and gray clouds blanketed the higher elevations. By July, the hillsides would turn brown, but she could savor the remnants of spring.

A dung beetle pushed its way across the hilltop.

"Just keep chugging, little buddy." She took a step, slipped on scree, and turned her ankle on the slick limestone. Coming to a shuddering halt twenty feet down the formation, she debated who to call. Her dads would worry, and few other people would understand her location. Gritting her teeth, she gripped a handrail and pulled herself to standing. Ansel was new to town, and calling Aubrey would take her away from her shop. Damn, her ankle was tender and swelling.

By the time she got to the bottom of the mountain, she needed more than stubbornness to extract herself from this situation. She pulled out her phone and dialed Mikey. "I busted my ass on Mt. Baldy. Will you give me a ride to town and let me hear your new album?"

"Give me a few minutes to make a graceful exit."

Twenty minutes later, he pulled his truck to a stop at the base of the trailhead, left the vehicle idling, and offered a hand. "You can skip the album. The ride's on me."

She leaned on his strength and wondered how many friends reached out after Grant's death. Guilt-ridden, she pushed away their condolences and holed up in her bedroom with old photo albums and unending boxes of tissue. She lost weight and listened to Papi roam the halls in high-heeled slippers.

Mikey kept calling. He showed up. Their romance was over, but his irritating presence held a certain nostalgic appeal. As long as he understood their relationship would remain platonic, she could return the favor and be a good friend, too. "I appreciate the ride, but I also want to hear the album. You've always had a knack for self-promotion. How many songs have you written? A hundred?"

"A thousand"—he laughed and led her toward the truck's passenger door—"but most of them don't see the light of day."

Glancing at the dark, stormy sky, she hoped the rain ended soon. Sometimes, the light of day was the only thing that kept her going. She focused on Mikey and cupped his shoulder. "I'm glad you kept writing. Song one thousand and one is bound to be a hit."

Chapter Twelve

After savoring the treats from Moeko's bakery, Ansel collapsed on the rental bungalow's leather couch and let the baked goods have their way with his digestive system. Carb comas existed, and although he preferred fresh, seasonal ingredients, he indulged in life's yeasty, buttery pleasures as often as he could.

A resounding crack of thunder roused him from a two-hour nap. Rubbing the sleep from his eyes, he sat up and checked his phone.

Collins left a voice mail with a status update on his wife, the restaurant group's lawyer forwarded an annotated summary of new food safety guidelines, and a PR representative sent a copy of his most recent interview.

If half his restaurant management team spent their Sunday afternoons working, he could, too. He swung his legs over the couch's side and shook off his stupor. On a lark, he checked his text messages and re-read Riley's text confirming her safe arrival in Cypress Creek. A follow-up message addressed to Ansel had never materialized, but he wished it had.

He padded into the kitchen, disposed of the bakery's white paper bag, and lamented not saving himself a snack. Maybe if he had offered Riley a piece of his prize, she would have indulged in an afternoon delight.

Chasing the shadows from beneath her eyes gave him an unexpected satisfaction, but he feared his pronounced reaction to her sighs. Most days, he used stress and nervous energy to power through his responsibilities, but he was proud of his output.

She missed her twin, but she pushed herself to create. That determination said plenty about her character.

Did they see each other's stresses and find comfort in providing release?

Bracing his hands on the counter, he accepted his limited, nine-to-five claim on her time. Even though claiming her lips would make a damn fine happy hour, he had to honor her request. Kissing her in the alleyway was a presumptuous way to end their discussion. After she watched him fall, she pressed her lips to his injured palm. A man could savor the feel of Riley's soft lips for the rest of his life, but he wanted more. Rubbing his hands over his face, he reminded himself to stop being greedy and enjoy his success.

If he wanted to maintain his momentum, he needed to keep innovating. He told Riley he wanted to move the kitchens toward the front of the house so restaurant patrons could walk into the space and see artistry and fresh ingredients. Her suggestion to open up the back room and provide patio dining required further thought. Who dined outside under the threats of a bug infestation and inclement weather?

Grabbing an umbrella, he risked the town's slippery, rain-drenched sidewalks and made his way to the old hotel. Under a dripping roof, he could admire the building's limestone arches and imagine a dining experience grand enough to cap his career. Walking through town, he imagined Riley's reaction to the falling rain. People often used corrective emotional experiences to get over their fears, but her grief and her fear of storms required more than a kiss in the rain.

His professional skills kept him in the kitchen and off a psychiatrist's couch, so he let himself into the old hotel and focused on the tasks he owned. Walking past pooled water where the roof caved after the fire, he made his way toward the building's back and considered his options for the new restaurant.

Rehabbing the building into a restaurant was a Herculean task, but he had resources. Restaurant reviewers noted his hard-working, motivated, and driven approach toward culinary innovation. He won awards for restaurant management, and despite his romantic failings, he was the definition of success. Why was he standing alone in the shell of a restaurant?

Aubrey's repeated betrayals haunted him. Her cheating pushed him to succeed, but her casual dismissal on the sidewalk dimmed his fires. For years, he envisioned giving her a piece of his mind, but he would only do it on his terms.

She looked as fazed as a chicken.

With hundreds of thousands of dollars sunk in the Cypress Creek project, he acknowledged coming to town might have been a mistake. He possessed the smarts, talents, and skills to reach the top of the culinary world. As long as he could innovate, he could stay there. Maybe he should have moved on long ago.

Thunder rumbled.

A rat scurried across the floor.

"Wannabe ground squirrel!" He tossed the umbrella to the floor and slammed two fists against the wall. His achievements felt as empty as this shell of a building. Collins' kids and his marriage were *real*. Ansel wanted what his right-hand man had, but finding someone to love felt like another man's dream. Before he could claim a shot at happiness, he had to wrestle with the doubts, the insecurities, and the unworthy feelings that kept him up at night. Who would lie next to him while he wrestled with self-doubts and insecurities?

His troubled childhood inspired his tears, his self-doubt paved the way for his ambition, and his ex-girlfriend just told him she faked her fucking orgasms. Did she fake how much she liked his cooking, too?

Staring at the haphazard pile of wooden siding he tossed in a corner earlier in the day, he shook his head and vowed to finish the work he started. The gauzy cobwebs and dark paneling had to go. "I'm not here to remake the 1980s Petroleum Club." He ripped another piece of siding from the wall and sent it clattering into the pile.

A second rat ran across the floor.

When more siding resisted his efforts, he put his back into it. "I'm not here to ruin Aubrey's life. I'm here to prove I didn't ruin mine!" Sweat mixed with humidity and ran down his back. As he exposed the wall beneath the siding, he registered a pattern and dropped his hands. Instead of pitted plaster, he found a smooth continuum of color and the beginnings of a mural painted on canvas.

He raised his phone and turned on the flashlight feature. Whatever artwork sat hidden behind the paneling had to go. The sooner he laid it bare, the sooner he could figure out what to do. An hour later, his shoulders ached, but the pile of discarded siding in the room's corner rivaled the fuel pile for a bonfire.

The sections of painting remaining on the wall depicted cowboys at work and play in the Hill Country. Horses grazed while young men strummed guitars, roped cattle, and branded livestock. Buildings that might belong to an older version of Cypress Creek conveyed a lively Gristmill Road brimming with chuck wagons, laughing children, and bonneted women. A particularly fetching woman looked suspiciously like Mrs. Golding, but he doubted the architect's wife had ever stirred a kettle of beans.

Standing close to the work, he wondered if the unknown artist had used oil-based house paint to create his work. Despite having spent its days behind wood paneling, the dusty mural looked in remarkable condition.

Floodwaters, smoke, and an unheated, uncooled building did little to dim its appeal, and the colors shone. The work would make a remarkable restaurant backdrop, but someone had hacked off sections of canvas, slapped siding over the gaps, and trusted that time would tatter and fray the evidence of their meddling. The remaining artwork would have to go.

He wiped his hair out of his face and considered his next move. The weather delayed his bungalow grocery delivery, but his stomach ached. A shower sounded better than any meal, but he doubted he had the patience to cook rice, let alone satisfying food.

Picking up the phone he left propped on flashlight mode, he grabbed his umbrella and put on his hat. Dodging puddles, he made his way to Kyle's place. Eating the food at the town's other restaurants would tell him a lot about his competition, and the pizza joint's proximity to his appetites made it a winner.

Given the downpour, nobody lingered under the freshly welded shade structure or enjoyed the swaying patio lights. Crossing Gristmill Road, he dodged a slow-moving car and its bright headlights. At the pizza joint's front door, he pushed his way into the dining room and found a thin crowd. With a stubborn squall line driving away tourists, he assumed the diners constituted the local crowd.

The greeter diligently erased a white board. "Twenty minute wait."

He counted three empty tables. A modern, steampunk vibe dominated the room, but vintage aviation posters softened the welded counters and leather banquets. He hung his hat on a coat rack. "Fine, my name's Ansel."

She looked up and noted his clothing.

Free to roam, he dropped his wet umbrella by the door and made his way to the bar.

A tall man with short, frizzy brown hair and honey-colored skin polished a glass. His medium-length goatee softened his angular face, but the piercings and gauges in his ears suggested he could hold his own in a bar fight.

Ansel chose a padded stool. "What's on tap?"

The man set down a glass and looked up. "The usual. What're you in the mood for?"

"A buzz."

Laughing, the man pulled a pint and slid it across the bar. "This should get you started."

Ansel took a long sip. The beer had a crisp, bright aftertaste. He offered a hand. "Ansel Percheron."

The man worked his jaw. "Kyle."

"*The* Kyle?" Ansel asked.

"In the flesh."

"Pleasure to meet you." Finishing half the beer, Ansel wondered if Kyle would be a friend or an enemy. Their restaurants would compete for different clientele, but a hungry patron could drop cash on a pepperoni pie or a chef's tasting menu. "You heard of a contractor named Nathan Thomas?"

Kyle jerked his chin toward the room's corner.

Turning and leaning an elbow on the bar, Ansel saw Aubrey sitting at a table with two girls and a commanding man with dark-brown skin. While Aubrey and the man toyed with their smartphones, the kids scribbled on their coloring sheets and made faces at each other.

The quaint family scene might have inspired the same reaction he had at the sight of Collins and his girls, but Aubrey's character dimmed her family's appeal. Riley proclaimed Nathan's merits, but her loyalties were as toned as her ass. Ansel had to find someone else to complete the build-out. "Never mind."

"He's good," Kyle said. "Knows his shit and how to work the system. I wouldn't trust anyone else with a construction project in Cypress Creek."

Ansel finished the rest of the beer. "Maybe it's time for fresh blood."

"Give him a chance to bid."

"Rather not." Turning his back on the family scene, Ansel picked up a menu and perused the dinner offerings. One pizza would be fine, but he wanted to try every dish the pizza restaurant offered. After a few bites, he would understand his competition, and the remaining food could feed the back-of-the-house staff. He slid the menu toward Kyle. "Give me one of everything except the pies."

Kyle raised his eyebrows. "Everything?"

Ansel laughed. "Trust me, I'm good for it."

"Fucking waste of food," Kyle muttered and pulled out his phone. As he tapped the screen and entered the order into the restaurant's point-of-sale system, he grumbled about out-of-town interlopers and arrogant city slickers.

Ansel absorbed the good-natured ribbing. A POS with online ordering took orders, routed them to the kitchen, and alerted the front-of-house staff when a customer or delivery person was ready to pick up the order. His restaurant would have a similar system, but his professional waiters would use it, and the patrons would never see it.

The front door opened.

The singer from Jacob's Hole shook off a cloud of raindrops and made his way straight to the bar. "Whiskey. Neat."

Kyle set down his phone and pulled out a glass and an open bottle of whiskey.

Ansel offered a hand. "Rough night?"

"My ex is a pain in the ass." Mikey Roberts took a hand and pumped it once. "Stubborn and as hard-headed as they come. One minute, I think she's softening up, and the next minute, she puts me in my place. God, I love that woman. Who wouldn't?"

Ansel kept his mouth closed. Riley's mix of vulnerability and tenacity kindled a tender flame that lingered longer than their echoing passion. His desire to protect, understand, and please her echoed in his heart.

The mixture felt suspiciously like love, but who could devote their life to another person after a fleeting encounter? He remembered Eagle Hawk and the man's unwavering strength. People made decisions in a heartbeat that altered the course of their lives. "I hear you," Ansel said. "Women are brutal."

"Since the moment I met her, I've had a crush, but I took her for granted. She refuses to give me another chance. I'm so firmly in the friend zone, I might as well roll over and let her scratch my stomach like I'm a good mutt."

Kyle choked back a laugh and set the whiskey on a napkin. He pulled Ansel another beer. "That bad?"

"Wants nothing to do with me." Mikey took a long sip and ran a hand through his wet hair. "She slipped and fell down a damn mountain today, and she barely let me bring her into town for an X-ray. Castrating myself might have been more effective, but at least, I know where I stand."

Ansel heard Aubrey laugh and glanced over his left shoulder. "Women are fickle."

"When do they draw the line?" Mikey asked. "I thought I had one more chance."

Nathan stood and walked toward the bar. "Let it go. You're better off with a woman you understand. At least, you know who you're getting out of the deal." He slapped Mikey's back. "I just thought you were too scared to show."

"Nope, just got hung up," Mikey said. "Fucking, beautiful, complicated women."

Nathan laughed. "We gonna play? We need a fourth."

Kyle wiped clean the bar. "Ansel, you any good at

darts?"

"Good enough," he said.

"Nathan Thomas." The man held out a hand. "I've heard about you."

Taking a deep breath, Ansel recognized the slippery slope and grasped Nathan's hand. Disliking a man on principle was easy, but sharing drinks and a dartboard tended to erode his reservations. "Nice to meet you. Ansel Percheron."

If a flicker of recognition narrowed Nathan's gaze, he let it pass.

Kyle walked out from behind the bar, holding the darts. "Let's go."

Ansel followed and avoided making eye contact with Aubrey. They could share the same space, but he had no desire to continue their acquaintance. Perhaps the media would capture her reaction to the restaurant, and he could savor her indignation from afar.

He eyed the dartboard. If Kyle played a standard game, each player would start with a score of 501 points and take turns throwing three darts. Bull's-eyes deducted fifty points, the outer rings deducted twenty-five points, and a dart in the double or treble ring doubled or trebled the segment score. Standing back, he watched Kyle take aim with a practice throw and knew he was in trouble.

As the food arrived, the server set it out on a nearby table.

Ansel took bites and made mental notes. The flavors melded, but nothing would threaten his establishment. However, as an hour passed, his principled rejection of Nathan collapsed into a pile of sawdust. The man was affable, had a mind like a steel trap, and checked on his kids between rounds. If only he had better taste in women.

Mikey Roberts, on the other hand, was close to being drunk.

The front door opened, and wind pushed rain into the restaurant.

Riley entered on crutches and scanned the crowd.

He wanted to go to her side and ask what happened, but she put him in his place, and pride kept him there. Whatever occurred hurt her body more than her spirit, and the story of her injury would come out. In solidarity, he rubbed his bruised tailbone and waited for her to make a move.

She made her way through the sparse crowd and headed toward his corner of the room.

He perked up and wondered if she sought him out, but he received nothing but a brief nod before she turned her attention to the other men.

Picking up a loaded potato skin, he sank his teeth into the salty treat, chewed, and considered his competition for her attention. If Riley had a thing going with Kyle or Nathan, her commitment to business ethics would have revealed her secret. He glanced at Mikey as the most likely suspect.

The man looked downright desperate for her attention, but too much beer glazed over his pining calf eyes. Ansel replayed Mikey's comments, and Riley's crutches suddenly made sense. If she told the singer to stuff his lyrics, then there might be hope for Ansel. He grinned, and his heart skipped a beat. Riley could tell off a man and look beautiful doing it. He should know.

She leaned against the table near the crooner. "Mikey, I'm done. Can we head home?"

Nathan threw a dart. "He's drunk."

Riley wrinkled her nose and turned to Kyle.

The owner nodded.

Riley settled onto a barstool and leaned her crutches against the bar. "So much for Mikey's coping mechanisms."

"We'll give you a ride home," Nathan said. "Aubrey's almost done with the kids."

Riley shifted and spotted Aubrey and the kids at the corner table. She waved at her friend, but she shook her head. "No, you stay and finish your meal. I don't want to intrude on family time."

Ansel snorted. Aubrey appeared to love her kids, but she had zero respect for her husband. Nathan seemed content to let her do her thing. Ansel liked him well enough, but he wasn't about to wade into the couple's family dynamics. He picked up a dart.

"I'll just call Papi to come get me," Riley said.

From Warrior's comments, he and his husband lived quite a ways out of town. Ansel paused his throw and looked over his right shoulder. The shadows under Riley's eyes looked deeper by the minute, but she could make her decisions. He and Mikey would rock out in the friend zone.

Mikey wandered behind the bar and made himself a drink.

A customer approached the singer.

Ansel questioned whether the customer wanted an autograph or a drink, but he let the pair make small talk and focused on Riley's measured progress. If she could get by on crutches, she had a mild sprain, but the injury must hurt. Clearing his throat, he weighed his options. As long as he kept his hands to himself, he could be a good friend. "I can run you home."

"I can't impose—"

He ignored her protest, let the dart fly, and hit the outer ring. His cooking credentials outweighed his dart skills, but Kyle and Nathan seemed happy enough with his performance.

Riley, on the other hand, looked ready to bolt. Every time the wind buffeted the restaurant, she glanced toward the door.

Wiping clean his hands, he slid a marinated, Italian salad toward her. The dish needed more kick, but it tasted better at room temperature. "It's fine. Grab a bite while we finish this game, and I'll take you back."

Picking up a fork, she hesitated. "You're sure you don't mind?"

He would have to dash back to the bungalow to pick up his car. He had nothing better to do until the sun came up, but availability was the least of his drivers. He liked the damn woman, and he wanted to soak up her attention until life dragged him away from Cypress Creek. "It's no problem."

She loaded up her fork and took a healthy bite.

Letting his shoulders relax, he turned his attention to the game, but her proximity distracted him, and his performance deteriorated. When the game ended near a draw, Kyle attended to restaurant concerns, Nathan pulled his kid onto his lap, and Mikey reveled in his position behind the bar.

Ansel checked Riley's plate, found it nearly empty, and pulled his keys from his pocket. "I'll grab the car." Before she could object, he smiled. "I really don't mind."

"Okay." She returned his smile. "I need to tell

Mikey I'm headed home and make sure he doesn't sober up and send out the fire department to locate me."

He wondered if the town's fire department would go looking for every wayward adult or just Riley. Clearly, she had deep roots. "No rush."

She considered the crowded restaurant and put weight on her ankle. She winced. "It might take me a few minutes to reach the door."

He thought about offering to carry her, but he flexed his fingers and kept the impulse to himself. She might bolt, and he would lose his chance to play hero. Accepting her pace, he grabbed his umbrella and his hat, slipped out the restaurant's front door, and sprinted through the rain. If the chance to be alone with a beautiful, accomplished woman made him this euphoric, he should spend more time dating. Dodging a large puddle, he admitted his reaction had more to do with Riley than a taste of romance, but he still grinned.

Sliding into the driver's seat, he started the car and covered the blocks to Kyle's place. Just behind the restaurant door, he spied Riley's silhouette on crutches. He put on the car's hazard lights, parked, climbed out of the vehicle, and stepped into a puddle deep enough to flood a pair of sneakers. Luckily, he wore boots.

Making his way toward the restaurant door, held the umbrella and opened the door. She warned him storms did her in, but he couldn't erase her reaction or the pain of losing her brother. He *could* make sure she got home in one piece. "Lean on me. The street's a mess, and I don't want you to fall."

She handed him the crutches. "I know it. Everything's saturated. Walking over from the urgent care clinic, I thought I might float away."

"I won't let you float away."

She took his arm. "Thank you."

From beneath the umbrella, the falling rain made a steady patter. Unable to gauge her reaction to the storm, he guided her toward the car's passenger door, leaned the crutches against the car, and risked a glance. "You're doing okay?"

"I'm making it." She offered a weak smile. "I can't control gravity, my clumsiness, or the weather."

He wrinkled his nose. "Pity. I had a few requests."

She laughed.

He reached for the door handle, brushed against her skin, and felt his skin tingle. Must be a charge to the air. He cleared his throat. "The weather's persistent, but it's not so bad when it leads to productivity. The storms kept me inside all afternoon, so I tore off the wooden siding in the restaurant's back room. There's an old mural back there. It has minimal environmental damage, but it's hanging in pieces. Might have to go."

She tightened her grip on his arm and peered across the street. "What kind of mural?"

"A bunch of cowboys doing Texas things." He pinned the umbrella to his chest with his chin and used his free hand to open the passenger door. "Kind of art deco."

"Let's go see it." She leaned forward. "If you have time?"

He opened his mouth to protest, but he wanted to spend time with her. Between the rain, the crutches, and the late hour, he should drive her to the Golding ranch and drop her off like a dutiful prom date. If he were lucky, he might get a kiss for his troubles, but he doubted landing on her parents' doorstep would give her reason to back off her pronouncement. Handing her the umbrella, he closed the passenger door, bent his knees, and scooped her into his arms. He would take what he could get.

"Ansel, put me down." She struggled to keep the umbrella over their heads. "I can walk."

"You have a plastic boot on your foot, and the street's full of water." He stepped into the inch-deep torrent and waded toward the restaurant site. She felt good in his arms, and he dropped his head to smell her hair. No doubt, she smelled a hell of a lot better than he did.

If he were lucky, he might catch the scent on his pillow, but he doubted he could convince her to stay the night. He plopped his hat onto her head and straightened it. "If I have to make up excuses to be close to you, I might as well enjoy the process."

She wiggled in his arms.

"Keep fighting, Riley, but if I put you down, you'll float away." An abandoned cup drifted on the small current. He jerked his chin toward the debris. "See."

"I'm not a plastic cup."

Tightening his hold, he wondered if his metaphor was more on target than she cared to acknowledge. How long could she balance her work, her grief, and her commitment to social networks? A bucket or a boat would have made a better metaphor. "You're definitely not a cup. More like a spork. A little bony at the edges, but supremely clever and useful."

"A spork?" Shifting the umbrella, she peered up from beneath his hat's brim. "When you fell off the spider swing, you might have hit your head. The rain will let up, and the road will dry, but you won't live down that quip."

Water dripped down his back, but he laughed and stepped onto the sidewalk in front of the old hotel. It wasn't his best line, but it got her laughing, and the sound did more for him than he imagined. Adjusting her in his arms, he climbed the few steps leading up from the sidewalk, set the key in the lock, turned it, and kicked open the door. "So, you plan to remember me?"

"Like a celebrity gnat. A corrupt inspector. A bad case of flu."

He could let her go on, but the sooner he brought her home, the sooner she could take care of her foot, and he could take care of his raging hard-on. Proximity felt like a good idea, but his memories were too sharp and pleasant for continued restraint.

Standing beneath a streetlight, he smiled. "I like the way you play nurse, but it's my turn."

Chapter Thirteen

Riley enjoyed being carried by a man who could handle her weight, but the sight would trigger savage gossip and probing questions. Plus, her umbrella and her bag made her look more like an unhoused mess than a hot siren. She didn't even want to think about the stale sweat and antiseptic cleaner permeating her clothes. "Put me down."

Ansel complied and lowered her down his chest. Belly to belly, he paused and raised his eyebrows. "Are you sure you want me to put you down?"

"Are you sure you're a spoiled celebrity chef who's used to getting what he wants?"

"Touché, but lately, I can't always get what I want."

"Tell me about it." She felt his controlled strength. She wanted to hang on to their connection, but she felt so off course she probably needed her crutches to remain upright. Too bad she left them by the pizza joint's front door. Instead of savoring the heated feel of his chest and wrapping her arms around his neck, she wiggled free, turned away, and focused on the lure he cast. She enjoyed his body far too much for common sense, but she respected art.

Streetlights cut through the rain and lent the old limestone building a weathered dignity. It persevered, and whatever secrets Ansel uncovered would see the light of day. Cypress Creek's most famous resident, Buckey Windstop, was known for his cowboy murals. Local historians thought they had inventoried his work, but they might be wrong. If Ansel discovered a new piece, then she could incorporate the art into her design. The inclusion would dim her plans for patio dining, but Windstop's work deserved center stage. Carrying her umbrella in her left hand, she hobbled through the exposed room and headed toward the building's rear. Given the pain in her ankle, she hoped Ansel uncovered a masterpiece.

Pulling her phone from her bag, she turned on the flashlight feature and shone the light around the room. From Ansel's description, she expected a single wall of color, but the painted mural ran continuously around the room's perimeter. The work had to be twelve feet tall and nearly three hundred feet long, but it was fantastic.

Windstop's familiar cowboys worked and played, but his depiction of Gristmill Road bustled with chuck wagons, families, and wandering animals. A familiar-looking vendor hawked a kettle of beans, and a woman wearing an apron passed out flyers while a toddler held onto her skirt. She sighed and took in the rich detail. "He finally painted women."

Ansel walked to her side. "Old guy was a bit of a misogynist?"

"Not on record." She shined the light at the pile of discarded siding in the corner and wondered how Ansel carried her. After putting his back into the muscle-wrenching work, he must be exhausted.

"This stuff is typical of his work?" Ansel asked.

She shook her head and lowered her phone to the

floor to cast a dull glow. "His work features proud, Art Deco cowboys and nuanced landscapes, but they're usually so lonely. Most of the time, he painted men with mythical fortitude. I wondered if he really saw the men as frontiersmen, or if he mirrored social expectations in his paintings. His father was a farmer."

"I'm sure his son's art career went down well," Ansel said.

She smiled. "Windstop studied at Washington University in St. Louis and the *Académie Julian* in Paris, France. Maybe he wanted distance."

"You know this because?" he asked.

Pivoting, she laughed. "Every school kid who grows up in Cypress Creek learns about Buckey Windstop. His work's in the high school and the welcome center. When the sun rises, you should see his murals in a proper setting.

He crossed his arms. "This one suits me fine."

She smiled, raised a hand to touch the mural, and drew back. "I'm glad you like it. These people he painted are more approachable. I can see them coming together outside the old hotel. This building would have been their gathering spot."

He picked up a shredded scrap of mural and held it up to the work. "Not the church?"

She scanned the mural and found a preacher welcoming parishioners into a white, clapboard church with a prominent steeple. "The church is there, too."

"Too bad the rest of the pieces aren't."

The beauty of Windstop's communal work receded, and she focused on the holes in the canvas. Whoever hacked off sections of the work and left the mural's remaining canvas to tatter and fray should be drawn and quartered. Preservationists could repair the work, but the repairs would be expensive. She rubbed her jaw and wondered if her foundation contacts would sponsor the renovation work.

Ansel set his phone on the floor, and the combined light cast the room in a dim glow. Rain pattered on the roof, but the sturdy structure held against the storm. "We can cut the mural canvas into pieces, pull them off the walls, and send them to the local museum. Maybe they can find a use for the work."

She gasped and widened her gaze. He looked like one of Windstop's painted cowboys considering a desert vista. The phone lights on the floor amplified his wolfish air, and rainwater plastered his shoulder-length hair to his head. She had no doubt he would dispose of the mural to maintain his restaurant's momentum, but she had to convince him otherwise. She pulled his hat off her head. "Are you out of your mind?"

He made eye contact and smiled. "Probably. What do you recommend?"

The heavy leather in her hands reminded her of material strength. Preservationists could salvage the mural. The restaurant could proceed. She could go back to Austin and forget how much she liked Ansel Paul Percheron. Of the three outcomes, her prospects looked the bleakest. Inviting him back to her Austin house for a quickie seemed less likely than the day she met him. "I need time to think."

A rat scurried across the floor.

She jumped and screamed.

Ansel moved closer. "Don't worry about them. They're escaping the rising water."

Shaking her head, she scanned the room's corners.

Rodent eyes reflected her flashlight. She would add extermination fees to her project proposal. "They probably made nests in the building. Aren't kitchen rats part and parcel of your profession?"

He slapped a hand to his chest. "You wound me. Unless rats become a delicacy, they don't belong in my kitchen."

"About that kitchen…" She approached the mural section where the woman stirred beans and wondered if the 1950s pioneer rendering borrowed traits from a maternal ancestor. Despite the dust on the woman's skirt and the long-handled wooden spoon she used to stir a cast-iron kettle, she looked like a prairie-inspired riff off of Mom. "You need to keep this work."

"Absolutely not," he said.

Before she could organize her thoughts, lightning struck a nearby tree, and the boom forced her to cover her ears. She closed her eyes and swallowed. Minor problems annoyed her, but she learned to address the gnats by systematically checking items off her to-do list. The geometric, romantic mural required preservation. Grant's memory necessitated safeguarding. Her fear of storms, injured foot, and attraction to Ansel Percheron could wait for sunnier days. She drew deep breaths.

He cupped her elbow. "Let me get you home."

His voice carried the concern and uneasy affection of a burgeoning friendship. She spent the morning defining their relationship within the confines of their business partnership, but every time she secured her boundaries, she crumbled. Why couldn't she shake his concern and her response?

Weakness had its place, but when a friend rushed

to render aid, the friendship grew. She had known him for forty-eight hours. If the painkillers prescribed by urgent care impaired her judgment, she should chuck them into the creek.

Peering past him, she looked toward Cypress Creek's flowing water. The town occupied a limestone island amid the creek's tributaries, but if rats started to take note of the storm, then she should follow their lead. The town sat above the surrounding countryside, but it remained vulnerable to nature's whims. Weighing her choices, she chose deep sleep and the start of a new day. "We should go. The mural's been here for decades. It can weather another storm."

He tipped up her chin. "You're tougher than I thought. That night at Jacob's Hole, you took one look at the rain clouds and jumped into my arms."

"Maybe I just wanted to jump you." She struggled for levity and rubbed her arms. "I'm making the right call. We can't discuss preserving this mural in the dark while you're half-drunk and I'm unsteady on my feet. It can wait until morning light."

"For the record, I'm not half-drunk. I told you I would drive you home."

"Then you carried me across the street." She rubbed her arms. "I can walk."

"And I can carry you!" He rubbed a hand over his face. "The mural's a pretty picture, but it's not worth derailing the restaurant's progress. It has to go."

She worked her jaw and weighed her words. How did a man helm a culinary empire and find time to amble around Cypress Creek like a good-natured rancher playing hooky? Come Monday, the rain would stop, and business would push him toward progress. If he out-ran his past, he would destroy his chance for peace.

Stooping, he scooped up both phones and offered one.

The glow lit up his features, and she saw the deeply etched worry lines radiating from his eyes. She took the phone and held it against her hip. "Hire Nathan."

He crossed his arms. "No. Find someone else."

"You like him! I just caught you playing darts with the man."

"Sure. I like you, too, but I'm not putting you in charge of helming a kitchen."

"I'm not asking you to put Nathan in charge of a kitchen. Let him build one!" She shifted her weight to take the strain off her pulsating ankle. "He's been in the construction industry since 1993. He paid his way through Texas State University building homes, and he hasn't slowed since he secured his license. He'll meet your performance, service, budget, and scheduling needs." She held out a finger for each successful project attribute. "What more could you want?"

Ansel raised an eyebrow.

Realizing she needed everything she had to illustrate the depth of Nathan's character, she spread wide her fingers and held up her palm. "He's nice, and you like him!"

Ansel's posture remained resolute, but he softened his dubious expression. "He's married to Aubrey. Find someone with better taste in spouses. If he can't see her true colors, he's a terrible judge of people. His subcontractors probably rob him blind, and I refuse to pay the overhead for his mistakes."

Slipping her phone into her back pocket, she turned

and exhaled. Hurt drove Ansel's career to such great heights that he couldn't see what he had overcome. She considered a section of mural showing two teenagers whispering behind a post. If real people inspired the painter, the couple was long dead. She could do nothing to help them, but she could help Ansel overcome his past. Taking a deep breath, she faced him. "You're hung up on Aubrey."

He rubbed his jaw. "Hung up isn't the wording I would use."

Eyes wide, she weighed spitting out the truth. Her family's architecture firms could survive losing Ansel as a customer, but she couldn't let the mural end up in a dusty storeroom or let an out-of-town firm blow through the property with the finesse of a limestone boulder. "I'm sorry Aubrey cheated. That sucks. She gave away your secret sauce, and she left you for another man"—holding up her hand, she rushed through her counterattack before he could interrupt— "but life happens. Stop letting your pride make your business decisions."

Opening his mouth, he stared.

"Get over her."

"Get over her?" He worked his jaw like he had a sour taste in his mouth.

"What she did was terrible, but she's more than a bad decision." She threw up her arms, held them wide, and encompassed the cavernous building. "Look at what you've become. You're rich and successful. I gave my father a jar of your brisket rub for a stocking stuffer."

"Oh, yeah?" Ansel cocked his head. "Did he like it?"

"It's salt and pepper, Ansel." Dropping her arms, she planted her hands on her hips and gave thanks that the relative darkness hid her frustration. "You found a way to charge ten dollars for salt and pepper! You're selling your reputation."

He cracked a smile. "Don't knock the ingredients. The salt's quality counts."

Lowering her chin, she met his gaze. "So does your contractor's quality. Let Nathan do the build-out. I can line up his services and get an expert on site to advise us on the mural's status. This weathered canvas might have a few holes, but it's beautiful, and it's worth preserving. I don't know who was selfish enough to cut out panels, but the deed's done. You have to move on. We have to finish this project!"

Stepping closer, he cocked his head. "Pick one."

"Ex-cuse me?" She let her jaw hang for a moment. "Pick a preservationist?"

"No, pick a favor. You want me to forgive the woman who cheated, gave away my recipes, and mocked them to my face. She took everything I am and stomped on it. Why should I give her husband business?"

Infidelity, thievery, and mockery were a triad of indiscretions, but Aubrey had always given Riley her loyalty. She struggled to reconcile Ansel's portrait with her experiences. Then she considered Aubrey's relationship with Kyle. People changed, and their motivations changed with them. She couldn't arbitrate the past, but she could plan for the future. "Nathan's a good contractor. You're desperate for his services."

"I. Am. Not. Desperate." Ansel drew a deep breath and ran a hand through his hair. "I'm a chef and a businessman. I make decisions that benefit *me*."

In another situation, she envisioned calling him out on his worldview or taking on his happiness, but she had to stick to her vision board. "If success granted people total control of their lives, Grant would be alive. Some things are out of our hands, and accepting that fact can be hard. Aubrey's my friend, but she betrayed you. Acknowledge it and move on. She can be a bitch, but her betrayal shouldn't ruin your life or your business."

"They're the same," he said.

She sighed. "They're not."

"When you lose everything, you hold onto what you have."

"But you've come so far," she said. "Whatever you had with Aubrey is in the past."

"You had no idea how far I've come. After my parents died in a traffic accident, Eagle Hawk put me to work on the reservation. I banged out my grief in the mechanic shop, slammed down skillets in the kitchen, and glared at anyone kind enough to meet my gaze. Hormones amplified my fury and desperation. I'm surprised Eagle Hawk didn't dump me at the welfare office."

Eagle Hawk sounded like someone who recognized life's rhythms. Tragedy excused Ansel's poor behavior, but by the time he met Aubrey, he was a grown man. Holding onto shitty cards was a poker player's most foolish move. She huffed out her breath. "When you lost your parents, you were a vulnerable teenager. How old were you when Aubrey dumped you?"

He slapped his chest. "Both times, I wanted to control my life. Now, I choose who benefits from my success. It won't be Aubrey."

The lines on his face deepened, as if the pain of losing family members threatened to spill out in a torrent of tears, but he looked like a man who had years of practice holding back his feelings. As much as he wanted to believe he moved on from his pain, the defiance behind his pronouncement proved his unwillingness to surrender his control. She missed Grant and longed for his laughter, but her memories were sharp enough to haunt her dreams. She carried part of him, but tears had failed to bring him back.

Ansel had found a way to carry his grief, but the decades of constriction kept him from growing into a man who could forgive the world for altering his plans. Would losing Grant haunt her, too? She softened her approach. "Raining spite down on Aubrey won't bring back your parents. Opening a restaurant in every city center won't cement your worth." She scratched the back of her neck and wondered if the humidity could go any higher. "You're a rich celebrity chef. Your ego's about as wide as a city block. This vendetta is beneath you."

He laughed. "Cypress Creek is hardly an urban stronghold. I'm here to prove good taste transcends"— he coughed and slapped his chest again—"location."

"Swallow a moth?" she asked. "Maybe you should return to San Antonio."

He cleared his throat. "I can deal with a few locational hazards, but I didn't expect you. When I said you were prettier than a javelina wearing lipstick and just as fierce, I had no idea how right I was."

She smiled and remembered the night they shared. Her muscles reveled in the glory, but a one-night stand should fade from memory. Ansel, née Paul, lingered. His unexpected depth and intensity intrigued her. Even if he hadn't turned out to be her pain-in-the-ass client, she would have wondered how often she would meet a man and get lost in his arms.

The morning after their hookup, when he promised future rainstorms wouldn't bother her, he meant the flashes of lightning and unexpected memories wouldn't sear her soul. Grant would always be with her, but she recognized time's healing power. When Ansel lost his parents and his trust in Aubrey, the grief hardened his heart, and she wondered if he could recover. He might be another sad-eyed adult if his adoptive father hadn't stepped in. "Is your Eagle Hawk onboard with your empire?"

"He wants me to come home. Doesn't every father want his children to come home?"

She smiled and imagined Dad lording over his library and his hilltop fortress. Papi had a softer touch. "Some fathers are tyrants. I have two of them, so imagine how agile I've become."

"So did I. My biological father and Eagle Hawk both shaped me. He helped me pick up the pieces of my life, but when I said he put me to work, I didn't tell you the whole truth." He exhaled and dropped his head in his hand. "My grief was so loud and so drenched in guilt that it kept me from hearing the breaths of life around me. Eagle Hawk helped me hear the wind. The rustling leaves and the croaking frogs proved I was alive. He told me the wind gave our grandfather his first breath and received his last sigh. If I was quiet enough, I could feel a connection to my parents. Each exhalation mingled our breaths. I found solace in the wind."

For a moment, she saw him standing on a lonesome ridge, wailing to his heart's content. Without anyone to judge him, he could turn his grief into a mournful keen his family might hear. Most likely, after he made his connection, he would kick a rock off the cliff and let loose a string of colorful expletives to tell fate what she could do with her whims. Riley doubted the old witch would enjoy being compared to a javelina, but she'd probably heard worse. Holding a palm to her chest, she focused on Ansel's confession. "That's beautiful."

"That's all Eagle Hawk."

"Is he a poet?"

"A man and a mechanic." He smiled. "You would have liked his practicality, too. He encouraged his peers on the Oglala Lakota leadership team to honor their past but to also concentrate on their future economic development. Over the last decade, revenues from a casino and alcohol sales enabled the tribe to build a hospital, a school, and housing. When activists proposed prohibition, he pointed out how much bootlegging occurred on other reservations. He doesn't pull his punches, and I miss his guidance. I wouldn't be here without him."

She heard his muffled angst and resisted the urge to cup his face. Smoothing away his pain held an appeal, but his restaurant was her biggest problem. She liked the man behind the project, and she savored her memories of him naked, but she had to work around his hang-ups. "He set a high bar. I see where you get your work ethic."

He clicked off the phone's flashlight feature. "You do?"

As the screen's light dimmed, she watched his features fade into the subtle shadows left by the streetlights, but she shored up her determination and trusted her ability to influence the remnants of their conversation. If Ansel remained so focused on his goals that he couldn't enjoy his success, then she would use his drive against him. The fine line between manipulation and capitulation hovered between them, but she held her ground.

Standing in the old limestone building, she planned to make Ansel's restaurant project a success without abandoning her hometown. If she could convince drought-wary tech bros to dig watering holes for wildlife, she could convince Ansel to preserve the mural. "I recognize where you get your work ethic, but I promise you, Nathan works just as hard."

He crossed his arms. "No Nathan."

"Fine!" She threw up her hands. "Then I need time to brainstorm alternative contractors. Nathan won't charge me ridiculous change fees to work around the mural. He's my friend, but if I have to improvise, I will."

Looking away, Ansel stared at the mural. "You're choosing to preserve this mural over everything else? It's in tatters."

"It's a work of art." She cleared her throat. "Also, I'm not paying for the mural's preservation. Kicking the can down the road sets up the opportunity for someone else to make an investment in the work of art." She pitched her voice toward a whisper. "I'm hoping someone rich enough to own a yacht and appreciate the finer things in life will pony up the fees to preserve the work. Think of the press coverage."

He turned and met her gaze. "Absolutely not."

Pushed to choose between Nathan and the mural, she leaned toward saving the mural, but she had to bide her time until she exhausted all her options. If Ansel's ego could resist the self-inflating appeal of writing a fat check, there might be hope for him yet. "Just think on it."

"Riley, the only time I'm thinking about this mural is when you're naked in my bed and I'm using chocolate sauce to draw it on you."

Her cheeks flamed, and she met his gaze. Manipulation could go both ways. Wetting her lips, she considered his implicit offer, but letting desire cloud her decision-making skills was a bad way to go down. Look what happened to Aubrey. "I'm tired, and my foot hurts. Can we talk about our options tomorrow?"

"What options?" He tipped up her chin. "The sex, the contractor, or what to do with the art?"

She tabled two out of three options and hoped the town's ancestors appreciated her support. Shifting her weight, she winced. "You might come around on Nathan and the art. In the meantime, what kind of nurse argues with a patient? I thought you were in caregiver mode."

"I am." He glanced down and frowned. "How badly are you hurt?"

Angling her boot, she hoped the streetlights picked out the medical device's industrial rivets. "Just a sprain, but the meds are wearing off, and I'm feeling the pain. Thanks for showing me the mural, but we can go. I'll figure out the next steps before we meet in the morning. My phone's vibrating, and my parents are probably worried. Urgent care wouldn't have taken this long."

He handed her the umbrella and scooped her into his arms. "I shouldn't have brought you to the construction site. This mess can wait."

She looked up. "How long?"

He narrowed his gaze. "Until morning. Unless you're reconsidering the chocolate sauce?"

She laughed and laid her head against his chest. Even when he was being a pain in the ass, he appealed to her, and his polished persona hid a tender heart. Too bad he was a client with an ego and a celebrity bent on cashing royalty checks. If she wanted to fall for a guy with an ego, she could have stayed in Austin.

Closing her eyes, she held the umbrella over their heads and enjoyed the ride through the downpour. For once, she was too tired to care when the clouds would depart. "Tomorrow will give me enough time to sort out this mess. I'll work all night, but I'll figure out how to do everything I want to accomplish."

Snorting, he adjusted his hold. "Tell me your secrets."

She smiled. "Stubborn perseverance?"

"I have it in spades."

Opening her eyes, she risked a glance and caught the soft smile tugging at his lips. "Then you should be golden."

Chapter Fourteen

Ansel drove the state highway toward the Golding house while Riley slept against the roadster's door frame. Pain and exhaustion had finally taken their toll, and he listened to the radio while delivering her home in one piece.

Stopping for a stop sign, he wiped condensation from the car's windshield and wished the early summer humidity would let up. Slick roads and flashing skies promised rising rivers, but as soon as the storm stopped, the waters would recede. Passing an old concrete bridge, he checked the water levels and found plenty of room beneath the bridge's arches.

His cell phone chimed.

He followed the directions Riley uploaded before she conked out. Pulling up to a locked cattle gate, he roused her by tapping her thigh until she blinked open her eyes. "Is this the right place? What's the code?"

She yawned and rubbed the sleep from her eyes. "0-0-0-0."

"You have to be kidding. That's your father's security code?"

"People never try the obvious answers. Life doesn't have to be complex."

Shaking his head at the absurd statement, he dashed for the locked gate. Of course life was complex, but he could make it simpler. If he brought her back to the bungalow, he could help her forget her injury, cook her breakfast in the morning, and start his week on a high note. He could be the definition of easy.

The oiled lock popped open.

Shirt soaked by the rain, he returned to the car and left open the gate. Who was he kidding? Someone named Paul who worked a nine-to-five and scratched out donuts in abandoned parking lots was easy to be around. Ansel Percheron had baggage, and he knew it. Rubbing his cheek against his right shoulder, he dried his face and put the car in Drive.

She straightened in the passenger seat and flipped down the visor. Running her hands through her hair, she shook off her catnap. "Thanks for the ride. I know it's out of your way. If Mikey hadn't gotten drunk, then I would have just ridden home with him."

He glanced over. Illuminated by the car gauges, she looked as alluring as ever, but he understood the shadows. "Mikey still loves you."

"Wrong." She cleared her throat. "He said he wanted to be friends."

"He lied." He scanned the vegetation surrounding the dipping road. "Men lie."

"So do women." She closed the visor. "We're all people."

"More specifically, I lied when I told you my name was Paul, and I omitted my plans in Cypress Creek. I could have been more upfront and given you my full name, but I wanted to let the moment at the gas station stand on its own. I wanted to help you without throwing around my wallet."

"Wait, you carry cash?"

He elbowed her. "Then I saw you again at Jacob's

Hole, and I wanted to savor you." He cleared his throat. "I just didn't know you were Riley Fucking Golding."

She laughed and rested a hand on his thigh. "It's Riley June Golding, but I appreciate the apology. I don't think using your middle name was being malicious."

Her touch's comfortable heat threatened to undo his good intentions. "What did you think I was doing?"

"Protecting yourself?" She sighed and leaned back against the passenger seat, but she left a hand in place. "I've seen fans go after Mikey. I wouldn't walk a mile in his shoes. How many drunk restaurant patrons have hit on you?"

He laughed. "They're not always drunk."

"I bet." Scratching her nails over the worn denim on his jeans, she flexed her fingers and settled her palm against his thigh.

If she wanted to scratch an itch, she could aim a few inches higher and find him ready and willing to indulge his automotive teenage fantasies. Instead of fantasizing about road head, he swallowed, kept the roadster's speed low, and navigated the unfamiliar road.

Native trees towered over thick shrubs, and the car's headlights picked out nocturnal animals hiding along the road. Puddles pitted the gravel and dirt drive. He did his best to avoid the traps, but the car's tire slipped into a deep spot and jerked hard to the left. He gripped the wheel with both hands and maintained a steady course. "Is the road always this bumpy?"

She peered through the windshield. "Yes and no. The rain's doing a number on the upper drive. We'll have to dump a ton of gravel to fill the holes."

He nodded.

"We're in the middle of nowhere, but I love this place more than anywhere else on earth. You can't replicate the smell of the cypress trees by the river. Tourists see shrubs, but I see thick stands of possumhaw holly, red yucca, and cenizo.

"When I was a kid, I walked up and down the drive, tossing out handfuls of seeds. I wanted to make the world a more beautiful place. I didn't realize how much beauty I already had."

He smiled. "Now, you create beauty from building materials and reclaimed objects."

She placed a palm against the window. "It's fleeting. Materials, weather, and nothing compares to nature's renewing bounty. Grant and I could wander these hills for hours until we ran into the deer fencing. We knew the wide world waited outside, but as long as we stayed at the ranch, we had family."

He swallowed the searing pain in his chest. "That's lovely."

She turned away from the window. Wide eyed, she dropped her hand. "I'm sorry. What a crass thing to say. Of course, you miss your parents."

"I have Eagle Hawk, but you're right, I do miss them. We always miss the people we love." He squeezed her hand. "Thanks for telling me about the ranch. I appreciate how special it is to you."

She returned his squeeze. "You're welcome."

He focused on the road. Past the ridgeline, the driveway dipped and transitioned to smooth, black asphalt. He loosened his grip on the steering wheel and exhaled. Raindrops assaulted the windshield, but the car was steady on the smooth road. A minute later, the drive dipped, and house lights shone through the acreage.

The two-story Golding home looked nothing like the grand mansions Warrior built for his clients, but the white ranch house offered floor-to-ceiling windows, large, shaded decks, rocking chairs, and a screened porch.

Ansel took in the restrained affluence and frowned. Warrior built this house before he got rich, or he was canny enough to play off his clients' egos. His sprawling, San Antonio estate reflected the size of his portfolio, but he asked for the monstrosity, didn't he? Reviewing his past few days in Cypress Creek, he realized he felt as at home at the bungalow as he did in his gilded bathrooms, and he doubted the bungalow's water bill was close to a thousand bucks.

"Just drop me by the garage," she said. "I'll go in the kitchen door."

A silhouette rose from a porch rocking chair.

Judging by the silhouette holding a stock, Warrior carried a broom handle or a loaded gun. Ansel doubted the architect spent his evening clearing out cobwebs. He slowed the car and parked in the circular driveway before the front door. "I don't think I have that choice. Are we late?"

"Um, I might have left with Mikey without telling my parents about the fall. My phone's been off. I didn't…uhh…want them to worry."

Ansel gripped the door handle. "I'm surprised we didn't see more police cars on the highway."

She laughed.

Warrior descended the steps and raised the rifle to his left shoulder. "Riley, is that you?"

Some men learned to shoot a rifle from the time

they were knee-high to a grasshopper, but Ansel's biological parents were academics. Instead of spending his summers oiling his .22, plinking tin cans in the woods, and clearing squirrels from the vegetable gardens, he read about other cultures.

Eagle Hawk took him deer hunting using a bow and an arrow. At least, the deer had a chance! If Warrior wanted to read Ansel the riot act for bringing Riley home late, he would have to weather the architect's barrage with his hands at his sides and the rain pouring over his head. He took a deep breath and opened the car door. He should have stayed on the yacht.

Riley threw open the passenger door. "Dad! Put down your silly gun. You're liable to shoot yourself in the foot, and then you'll never walk straight. I came home with Ansel Percheron, not a deadbeat I picked up at the bar."

Lowering the gun, Warrior raised a hand to shield his eyes. "Ansel, that you?"

Ansel raised a hand. "Yes, sir."

Warrior laughed. "Well, if I'd known she was getting a jump-start on the project, I wouldn't have worried so much. Mikey said he sent her home with a stranger. Fool couldn't remember his name. I thought a damn idiot stranger had my kid."

He extended a hand. "That'd be me. I'm the idiot."

"Welcome to the club." Warrior pumped his hand. "Come in for a drink?"

He looked past the older man.

Riley stood on the porch.

At least one of them had the sense to get out of the rain. Making eye contact, he smiled. Given how quickly

Riley fell asleep on the ride to the ranch, he doubted she wanted to stay up and make small talk or review her plans for the Cypress Creek restaurant. He looked back to Warrior and shook his head. "Another time?"

Warrior slapped his back. "Any time. I always liked you."

"Same." Ansel dropped his voice. "Riley took a tumble hiking. She swears it's just a sprained ankle. Don't worry if she gets a late start in the morning. I have plenty to keep me occupied."

Warrior looked over his right shoulder. He leaned his body toward the porch, took a step, and hesitated.

Ansel could feel the older man's need to check on his child. Returning the affectionate slap, he pivoted and made his way back to the roadster. "I'll catch up with you tomorrow. Thanks for the consult, Riley. Great ideas."

She flipped him the bird.

He laughed and buckled his seat belt as Warrior mounted the steps, set the shotgun on the porch, and inspected her medical accessory. She might be a grown woman, but Ansel doubted he would see her at the construction site before lunch. People might lie, but they loved fiercely, and displays of love gave him hope for the world. With or without his influence, Riley would find her way.

****

Laying in bed the next morning, Ansel wished he could start his day with Riley in his bed, but that option remained off the table.

So did the prospect of dry weather.

Setting aside the weather app's gloomy forecast on his phone, he sat up and made his way into the kitchen for hot coffee. The grocery delivery came through, and he swore he would never start a morning without caffeine.

Whistling, he rummaged through the bungalow's kitchen cabinets for a measuring cup. The bungalow's modern, American single-serve coffeemaker and the basket of single-use plastic cups could go to hell. He would improvise drip coffee and start his day with a solid caffeine kick.

He filled the electric kettle, set it to boil, and dumped coffee grounds into the glass measuring cup. The coffee's fresh, oily aroma teased his senses. He could almost taste the brew's caramel undertones. Picking up the paper bag, he read the beans' origin story and tasting notes. When the kettle boiled, he carried it toward the measuring cup and drenched the coffee grounds.

Steam rose.

Drool pooled in his mouth.

The glass measuring cup shattered.

"For the love of..." He grabbed a dishtowel, shoveled the watery mess into the kitchen sink, and braced his hands on the countertop. If glass pieces went down the drain, Moeko might kill him or leave a complaint with the rental agency. Either way, he would be screwed out of his bungalow or skewered in the media. *Famous restaurateur trashes short-term rental.* Collins would laugh until his balls fell off.

Sparing himself the thought, Ansel found the trash can and diligently picked up the glass shards. "I have people on my payroll who can make coffee blindfolded. Collins isn't picking glass out of his sink. What the hell am I doing?"

He looked past his left shoulder and considered the empty bungalow. Its spotless charm worked well for its owner, but he needed more than a three-ring binder and a six-pack of beer to feel at home. Letting his shoulders sag, he considered his motivations. Spite motivated him, but his petty schemes left a bitter taste in his mouth.

Only Riley's presence seemed to relieve it.

Looking out the kitchen window, he watched the rain pool on the grass and knew women should play little role in his decision making. San Antonio wasn't home. He planned to retire and travel the world visiting friends. If he returned to the reservation, nostalgia would swamp him, and he might never leave Eagle Hawk. Would that be so bad?

After seven o'clock, he gripped the coffee shop's door and pulled. The door flew open as if it weighed less than a feather. Losing his balance, he gripped the porch railing to steady himself. "What the…"

"Rowdy night?" Nathan sat at a corner table, eating a croissant. "Happens to the best of us. Too bad you're shit at darts."

Ansel stomped into the shop and left rainwater on the coffee shop's doormat. "I'm an excellent dart player."

Nathan sipped his coffee. "Sure you are."

The shop owner with the lined skin and girlish braids waved from behind the counter. "What can I getcha?"

"A large, hot coffee." He laid a twenty on the counter. "No room for cream."

She smiled. "You did have a rough night."

He rubbed his clean-shaven cheek and wondered

what constituted a rough night in Cypress Creek. Showing Riley the mural turned into a shadow-stained confessional. Leaving her at her parents' house left him unsatisfied. He came to Cypress Creek for a reason. As soon as he accomplished his task, he could figure out how to spend the rest of his life.

Picking up the coffee, he took a hesitant sip. Rich, bold flavors flooded his mouth. Closing his eyes, he sighed.

The whole rock-star-chef axiom fell apart when he remembered closing his first kitchen at two o'clock in the morning and waking up three hours later to run his business. Twenty years later, success gave him latitude, but low margins, high turnover, rising real estate, and fickle labor markets toyed with his psyche.

Coffee never let him down.

Despite the media's persistent glorification of bad-boy chef behavior, he and the top names in the industry knew how much work went into running successful restaurants. Without Collins, the burden fell on him, but he knew his business.

He also knew when he was being an ass.

Swinging a chair away from Nathan's table, he straddled the seat and set his coffee cup on the table. "Mind if I join you?"

"Go right ahead." Nathan smiled. "You're already sitting."

He laughed and considered how to approach business discussions. On paper, the commanding man had competency, two kids, and a pretty wife. He wondered if the builder was self-aware enough to know what kind of life he truly led.

Aubrey wanted to feel like Nathan's first passion,

but instead of articulating her needs, she chased thrills at the pizza joint. Riley must know, and yet, Nathan looked at him with cool composure. Ansel adjusted his seat. He could tear apart a line cook's presentation, but he had no business doling out life advice to Nathan or Cypress Creek's residents.

On the other hand, the person who took over the restaurant build-out needed an astute understanding of legal contracts, workforce management, and industry expectations. He weighed his options and limited the conversation to his business pursuits. Going all in on his emotions never worked out. "Riley tells me your crews do excellent work, and you know the county regulatory environment. Why aren't you on another jobsite this morning?"

Nathan glanced outside. "It's raining."

He frowned. "I have a restaurant to build, but I need progress more than I need excuses about the weather."

Setting down the croissant, Nathan interlaced his fingers and set his hands on the table. He leaned forward. "My company has a solid reputation. I can give you my elevator pitch, but you've already made up your mind."

He worked his jaw and prepared his rebuttal.

"You don't want to hire me." Nathan leaned back in his chair. "That's fine. Aubrey told me what happened between you two."

"She told you?" He narrowed his gaze. "What did she say?"

"When y'all were fresh out of culinary school, she felt lonely and made a bad decision. You never forgave her, and now you're making her feel like shit by building a restaurant in her hometown that proves just how wrong she was about you. It's petty, man, but it's your call. I would have just found another broad to warm my bed."

Suddenly, coffee might not be enough to salvage his morning. He jabbed his finger against the table. "She did more than make a bad decision. She gave away my recipes and set my career back years."

"You seem like you recovered just fine." Nathan took a bit of his croissant, chewed, and swallowed. "I don't care what you build or why you do it, but if you want the project done right, then I'm your man."

"You don't care you married a woman with a wandering eye?" He cupped the coffee cup and told himself Nathan could interpret his statement with respect to the past. One palm registered the heat, and the other palm registered the slightest pressure. Pulling back his scarred hand, he flexed his fingers. He was lucky he didn't drop more knives. "If you know what she did to me, don't you wonder if she's loyal?"

Nathan shrugged. "I know she's messing around with Kyle, but it's a phase, and she'll grow out of it. Society asks a lot from women." He looked out the window.

Ansel exhaled. If he could buy the man a beer, he would. Stress and loneliness failed to justify cheating. He turned his drink and wondered how to empathize with Nathan's predicament without sounding like a condescending ass. He opened his mouth.

"What kind of midlife crisis should a woman have?" Nathan shook his head, squared his shoulders, and faced the table. "Half the men I know feel threatened by their wives' success, and the other half of the men think opting into family life means opting into selfless servitude. No wonder so many marriages fail. You ever been married?"

"Nope." He swallowed past the pain of his admission. "It never happened."

"You probably work too hard."

Ansel drew back his chin and wondered how Nathan had turned the table. He replayed his long hours in the kitchen and the effect on his relationships. Putting more time into his romantic efforts might have made a difference, but professional success felt as fleeting as a summer storm.

Nathan tipped back his chair. "Construction's a hard gig. I'm gone a lot, but when I'm home, I try to be present. Sometimes, Aubrey and I make it work, and sometimes, we stray. The kids don't know the difference, and that's what counts." He let the chair legs clack against the wooden floor and tapped the table. "I know where to get my kicks, but I don't know how to replace Aubrey. She's a great mother."

He couldn't imagine tying up his emotions in a loveless marriage. Instead of arguing, he closed his eyes and recast Aubrey as a person who felt vulnerable and unloved. Memories of the months after his parents' deaths washed over him. He felt too powerless to influence his fate. If he expected Aubrey to wait patiently for his triumphant success, he expected more of her than he expected of himself.

She was never a small and polite woman. Steak *Frites* and giving away his recipes were mistakes, but his vision of success diminished her accomplishments. No wonder she thought she had nothing else to offer the world.

Hating her felt like a justifiable emotion, but he feared failure more than he feared her influence. He understood thinking of her as the woman behind the chef had been an error. For two decades, he cast her as the villain so he could play the hero, but the time had come to grow up.

"Now, Riley on the other hand." Nathan whistled. "You've got your hands full with that one. Mikey never could hold her. Ever since high school, she's had one foot out the door, and losing Grant kicked her into high gear. Her passion fuels her professional work and her commitment to the town, but man, it's a lot to handle. I couldn't do it."

"I can." His testament came without thinking. If Riley could commit, he could, too. Clearing his throat, he changed his approach toward Nathan and Aubrey. Their personal decisions had zero impact on his professional success. If he tied up his grievances and his career choices, he would still be the defeated culinary student bemoaning his first flop and blaming Aubrey for his failure. Granted, her hijinks didn't help, but he had moved on from his first concept. His new restaurant in Cypress Creek would be his capstone project. In some ways, Nathan's involvement felt fitting, and Aubrey could come or go from the premises as she pleased. He laid his palms on the table and spread his fingers. "I don't respect the way you and Aubrey handle your relationship, but it's not my business. Running restaurants *is* my business. If you can build what Riley designs, you have the job."

Nathan rubbed his chin. "You want a bid?"

He smiled. "Riley will make sure you don't screw me on the price. She might be a lot to handle, but I hear she's damn good at her job."

Slapping the table, Nathan laughed. "That she is."

He picked up his coffee cup, used a beverage napkin to wipe up the spills caused by Nathan's exuberance, and tipped his finger to the woman running the coffee shop. He hoped her hearing matched her weathered expression, but he had a feeling gossip was more than fair game in this town.

Instead of moving the car, he dashed toward the limestone building and walked into his future restaurant.

Riley stood in the middle of the covered area.

A folding table held drawings of the restaurant, and two floodlights illuminated the mural. He strode forward and planted his feet, "What the hell are you doing here?"

"Good morning to you, too." She erased a line on the topmost drawing.

"It's just after seven." He checked his phone to make sure the morning hadn't gotten away. Caffeine hummed through his veins. He sometimes lost himself in creative endeavors, but he wasn't in the kitchen. He was in rural Hays Country with Riley Golding and her medical-grade boot. "I told Warrior you could get a late start."

"My father isn't in charge of my schedule." She glanced up. "Did you bring me a coffee?"

He pushed the beverage toward her.

She picked it up and took a sip. "It needs cream."

Drawing a breath, he considered his options. Hating Aubrey brought him to Cypress Creek, but the time had come to grow up. Whether Riley liked cream in her coffee had zero bearing on their business relationship.

He swallowed and approached her project involvement with the same criticality he would apply toward Warrior. Lipstick marked his cup. Exhaling, he wished he had brought his hat so he could hide his warming cheeks. Riley was nothing like Warrior, and he wanted her to be just like herself. "I, uh, hired Nathan Thomas to be the contractor. I hope that's okay."

"You did?" She set down the cup and threw her arms around his neck. "Brilliant. I'm so glad you came around. He's really the best." She pulled back and patted his cheek. "You won't regret it."

Poor Mikey. Ansel understood the friend zone, but his body had other responses. He adjusted himself and stepped back. "I appreciate the case you made for Nathan's services. His professional competency means more than his taste in women."

She laughed. "You didn't bond over your good times with Aubrey?"

"Hell, no." He cleared his throat. "I mean, I shouldn't be having this conversation with you. We're colleagues. She's your friend. Save the gossip for a pint."

"Well, you made a good call." She gave him a side hug. "You're really not so bad."

Feeling her warm curves, he closed his eyes and wondered how he would survive the restaurant build-out without turning as blue as his balls. Opening his eyes, he shifted.

She shifted, too.

The side hug turned into full frontal contact, but he held himself in check. He'd removed a project barrier, and her reaction was nothing more than professional exuberance touched with a dusting of familiarity. Women's rights were people's rights.

His cock sprang to attention. He was an asshole. He had a lot to learn, and the lessons would be painful. Clearing his throat, he prepared to walk the building's perimeter until he could think of Riley, the professional architect, instead of Riley, the woman he wanted in his bed.

A heartbeat later, he felt her lips on his. A hint of coffee never tasted so sweet. Wrapping his arms around her, he held on tight and savored her kiss. Rain might be pooling inside the building, and the creek might be rising, but the woman kissing him was the same woman who warmed his bed and his scarred heart.

The relationship was new, fragile, and unprofessional, but as long as she granted him privileged tastes, he would savor the flavor of her kiss.

Chapter Fifteen

"Anyone in there?" Mimi Lewis banged on the old hotel's rear door and tried the handle. Her raspy question ended with a cough. "Riley? Your momma said you headed into town before the sun came up. When did you get the lights turned on in this old cave?"

Wincing at the intrusion, Riley pulled away from Ansel's kiss and apologized for the interruption with a brief, soft exhalation. She wanted to explore the exuberance that smashed her inhibitions and sent him into his arms, but she had a job to do. "The thing about small towns…"

He raised his eyebrows.

She smiled. Nothing she could say about Cypress Creek would surprise him. A dozen painted cowboys could watch their kiss, but their static opinions and asinine reactions would remain frozen in time. Mimi, on the other hand, could get tongues wagging faster than a whispered divorce.

Mimi rattled the handle again. "Did you call a locksmith?"

Ansel offered Riley a lopsided smile and ambled toward the door.

Hoping their kiss put the spring in his step, Riley smoothed her shirtfront, stacked the large-format printouts, aligned the edges, and brushed dirt from a pristine corner. The gesture left a sandy stain, and she frowned. Keeping her workspace neat kept her thoughts organized, but kissing Ansel made her clumsy. She brushed at the stain a second time, but the mark remained. Her lips tingled with the memory of his kiss, and she chewed her lip. Did she need pristine order to complete the job, or could she muddy the waters and crave the man paying the invoices?

Ansel opened the door and stepped back. "Good morning to you, too, Mrs. Lewis."

Mimi brushed past him holding an umbrella and a bag of baked goods. She gasped and dropped the pastries on the table and the umbrella on the floor.

Riley looked up. Mimi wore blue jeans and leather boots, but hairspray held her dyed-blonde hair in place, and she must have risen before the sun to apply her lipstick and penciled-in eyebrows. Given the things she had seen, catching sight of the mural for the first time must have given her a thrill. "Amazing, isn't it?"

"He shaved off his whiskers." Mimi cleared her throat and made eye contact. "So clean-cut and respectable. I love a man who shaves daily. Don't you?"

Frowning, she wondered when Mimi began tracking the town's grooming habits with such intensity. Buckey Windstop's artistic style was unmistakable to locals. If Mimi thought Ansel's smooth cheeks were more exciting than Windstop's mural, she had peculiar opinions of art. If Mimi wanted to reinforce the town's stodgy pecking order, she should share her opinions with the other gossips. "I stopped commenting on other people's bodies a long time ago."

Mimi blinked.

She smiled.

The silence stretched.

Ansel cleared his throat and rubbed the smooth skin along his cheek. "I did shave. I hate to scratch up a pretty lady's face, but if Riley likes the scruff, I'm happy to grow a beard. Wouldn't you do everything this pretty lady asked?"

Warmth flooded Riley's cheeks.

Mimi pursed her lips. "I see how it is."

"It isn't." She stepped between Mimi and Ansel before the conversation veered into personal territory. "What can I do for you? We're about to get started for the day."

Bringing his coffee and standing beside her, he took a long sip. "Getting a jump-start on reservations, Mrs. Lewis?"

"Ha!" Mimi crossed her arms. "I heard Riley came to town, and I brought her breakfast." She peered around the room. "What's going on here? When did you rip off the paneling? And what's with the retro wallpaper?"

Looking over her left shoulder, Riley wondered how anyone could view the hand-painted canvas in the same league as mass-market wallpaper.

"A gift from the prior owner," Ansel said. "Riley's calling someone to take a look at the work. As far as I'm concerned, it can go into storage until she figures out where to send it."

Riley resisted kicking his ankle.

Mimi tilted her head. "Looks like it's a mess. I have room in my storage shed with the rest of the boots. Feel free to toss the art in there until you come up with a plan. What a hassle."

"Thanks." Ansel offered a hand. "We might take

you up on that offer."

Blocking his gesture, Riley stepped between the pair. "Absolutely not. This work fits with Buckey Windstop's style. Local historians think they have a complete inventory of his work, but I've never seen references to a town scene. It's a discovery."

Mimi leaned toward the nearest wall and shook her head. "Nope, too many women. It's probably an imitator." She wet her lips. "The paint looks too fresh and modern."

Riley crossed her arms. "The paneling protected it."

Mimi turned and smiled. "Sweetie, I've lived here a long time, and I've never heard rumors of a work this size. I'd know, wouldn't I? Don't get your hopes up, and don't waste a professional's time."

"He was a prolific artist," she said.

"This is nothing but an old, nostalgic print. It's two shades shy of tacky. Let Mr. Percheron cut it off the walls and toss it in my shed. You'll thank me for keeping your project on track." Mimi patted her cheek. "Trust me."

She bit the inside of her lip and tasted blood. "I appreciate your feedback." Lacey and her public relations consultants would applaud her control. "If we need your shed"—she choked out the word—"we'll walk over and let you know."

Mimi waved a hand in the air. "It's no skin off my back. I can send over those high school boys who erect my tents and save you the time and effort of pulling this mess off the walls."

"Excellent," Ansel said.

Riley gripped his arm. "No!"

He worked his jaw and smiled as if he could play this game all day.

She wondered if his enthusiasm for Mimi's suggestion was a ruse if his aversion to art was a warning sign. He hired Nathan, so he had to be open to change, but his approach to the mural's preservation baffled her. The man created art from olive oil. Surely, he could recognize another man's achievements!

Before she could launch a counter argument, a sharp pain shot through her right shoulder blade, shot up her spine, and radiated toward her temples. Pressing a hand over her eyes, she inhaled deeply and waited for her vision to go hazy. These headaches happened at the worst possible times, and she had to get control of them.

The construction lights flashed. The colorful mural blurred out of focus. Gripping Ansel's arm as tightly as she could, she breathed through the pain. Innovation was her strong suit, but she had no control over her body's physical rebellions. "Help me sit before I fall."

He lifted her in his arms, carried her toward the table, and set her on top of the drawings. "I'll call a doctor."

She held up a hand. "Wait. I just need a minute."

"You swayed on your feet."

She breathed deeply and managed a weak smile. "I'm an art fan, and you're ready to make collages from Windstop's art. Give me your coffee?"

He picked the cup up off the floor and offered it.

Keeping her eyes closed against the light, she sipped the cooling coffee and hoped the caffeine helped ease the pressure in her head. Ansel could keep Mimi at bay until the pain subsided, but his intentions skewed in the wrong direction. If she heard anything approaching ripping canvas or shearing scissors, she would launch herself off the table and give the pair a reason to talk.

The threat amused her, but her inability to move without doubling her pain rendered her as useless as one of Mimi's pet kittens. When Ansel walked into the building, the morning went from productive to provocative, but now she felt downright pitiful. "Fuck."

"Riley Golding!" Mimi said.

She ignored the scolding and tried not to feel like an outsider. Cypress Creek was her hometown, and her firm provided full architectural services and finish selection. Kissing Ansel might have been an impulsive reaction, but she would regain her footing and her momentum. Mimi's reproof could wait.

Ansel passed behind her and trailed his fingers along her lower back. He applied the slightest pressure before picking up leaves skittering across the floor.

His touch was so brief, anyone might have questioned his intent, but the gesture reassured her. She squared her shoulders. "Ansel hired Nathan Thomas for the job. Within the hour, we'll have plenty of workers on-site." She breathed through the echo in her head. "I appreciate the help, but I've got it. We've got it."

"Fine." Mimi cleared her throat. "A bunch of fuss over some trash. I've never paid much attention to art, but I doubt it's in style."

Riley swallowed and opened her eyes. Mimi matched her lipstick to her nail polish. What did she know about style?

Ansel turned down the construction lights, and the room's colors dimmed.

"Thank you," she said.

Mimi clucked her tongue and made her way back toward the door. "Maybe tastes in the city have changed. I wouldn't know. I've spent most of my life in Cypress Creek."

"I'm so glad you came over to help." Impatience crept into her voice, and she blew out her breath. "Do you want to keep the pastries? I've already eaten."

Mimi picked up the umbrella, but she left the bag sitting on the table. "Ansel can try the muffins. I baked them myself."

He opened the bag and made a show of inhaling the scent of the contents. His nostrils flared, and he reached into the bag. "What a sweet gesture. How can I resist such hospitality?"

Mimi nodded. "I hope you like bran."

Riley wanted to roll her eyes, but the pain lingered. She took a slow sip of coffee and listened to the rain falling on the old roof. In a moment, Mimi's boots would crunch on the gravel, and she would be alone with Ansel. Kissing him would be more pleasurable than scolding him, but she might fall over, and she refused to abandon her plans for the mural.

"Love it." Ansel winked and escorted Mimi toward the back door. "Thanks for stopping by." He shut the door with a firm push and sealed off the alley between the restaurant site and Mimi's boot store. Turning, he leaned against the entry. "Can we talk about this?"

She touched her lips. "It was a kiss. I shouldn't have done it, but we're even for the alley kiss. Call off both sets of lawyers."

His lips quirked up in a smile, but he shook his head. "I'm not talking about the kiss, but I'll happily accept more of your moral failings."

"Failings?"

He walked across the dust-strewn floor. A maze of footprints from the last few days created a swirling, confusing pattern no sleuth could follow. "I'm talking about the pain that's laying you low. What is it? Migraines?"

"Just sudden headaches. Blame them on stress." She rolled her head and hoped the gentle motion failed to trigger vertigo. "Mimi can be the definition of stress."

He walked across the room and tucked her hair behind her right ear. "You eat people like Mimi for breakfast."

She smiled, but she shifted away from his touch. Aubrey or Lacey could see her weaknesses, but her clients should maintain absolute faith in her abilities. When Ansel called her "loyal" and "accomplished," he parroted the traits she projected. Calling her "sexy as hell" was icing on the cake, but she couldn't afford the calories. "I'm fine."

"Have you seen a doctor?" he asked.

She had three doctors on speed dial, but each offered her a different prescription. Her therapist said grief could increase the release of stress hormones like cortisol, and high cortisol levels could trigger headaches, shortness of breath, and stomach upset. It could also trigger migraine episodes, but for the most part, she escaped with brief flashes of pain. "The headaches come and go, but I'll be fine."

He crossed his arms. "How often do they happen?"

Raising her chin, she made eye contact. "Are you asking as my lover or as my client?"

"I'm asking as your friend, but let's revisit being

lovers."

She smiled. "I appreciate you shooing Mimi out of the building. I don't want her to start gossip. If she asks, tell her I was hungover."

"Alcoholism is more acceptable than pain?" he asked.

She rubbed her forehead. "In some towns."

"Not the best ones. I've lost more people to alcoholic cirrhosis than I've lost to car accidents. I still drink, and I still drive, but I don't make jokes about the danger. I don't want to joke about your health, either. Will you tell me when you need a break?"

Entitled assholes rarely made allowances for their peers' humanity. She told him she would abstain from kissing, sex, and side-alley shenanigans, but she could do her job in her sleep. She couldn't duplicate her attraction. Stuck in Austin's hippie-chic rodeo, she searched for renewed inspiration, but Cypress Creek and Ansel's hard-edged resilience swelled her creativity.

The restaurant build-out had more to do with overcoming his deepest doubts than sticking his success to his ex-girlfriend. She saw plenty to admire about the man Aubrey discarded. He compartmentalized his life and let his culinary creativity blossom while his heart slumbered. She could do the same. By separating her work and her grief, she could keep moving forward.

"I'm not a task master. You can take breaks." He glanced at her booted foot. "In fact, you should."

If she crawled under the sheets and let him hold her, would his skill set wear off? Would forty nights of pleasure unwind her nerves? She let her feet swing and exhaled. "The headaches are infrequent, but I'll tell you when I need a break, okay? We'll iron out the rest of our relationship as we go." Stilling her feet, she tilted her head. "We can do dinner tonight. Let me cook at your bungalow."

He laughed, caged her between his arms, and leaned his weight against the table edge. "Riley, your cooking is the last thing I want from you."

Proximity was a heady aphrodisiac. He smelled like sage, sweat, and fresh, crisp aftershave. She rubbed her right cheek along his smooth skin and knew she would spend the night in his arms. "Fine, you can cook."

"You're so generous."

She lifted her chin for a kiss.

An earth-shaking boom rattled the glass remaining in the building.

Eyes wide and gripping Ansel's arms, she waited for a second assault. "What was that? A direct lightning strike? Should we check for fire?"

He raised his head and looked past her. "No need. A driver delivered a roll-off waste bin, but he was as subtle as an earthquake. Nathan doesn't mess around."

She relaxed her shoulders. "Nathan. I told you he was good."

The building's front door swung open.

Nathan blocked out the sunlight, shook the water off his head, and scanned the remnants of the old hotel. "Whoo, this is a mess, but what a fun project. I can't wait. Time and materials?"

She smiled. "Fixed bid. Do I look like I was born yesterday?"

He skirted the rain coming through the building's destroyed front roof and edged along the walls.

"Honestly, you look a little pale."

"It's the boot." The lie tasted bitter, but she needed competency more than she needed compassion. "Have a look around, and I'll show you what we're planning to erect."

Ansel cleared his throat.

"Fair enough." Striding across the ground floor, Nathan kicked the pile of paneling and released a shrill whistle. "Jack, get your ass in here and start with this mess."

A twenty-year-old with a swooping fraternity haircut pulled on a fresh set of work gloves. "Yes, sir!"

Ansel straightened. "Your timing could use some improvement."

"Don't let me stop you," Nathan said.

Her cheeks warmed, and she slid off the worktable. When she felt confident her feet would hold her, she gathered up the papers she dislodged from the table.

Instead of Ansel's warm lips, she had to focus on a structure worthy of poured concrete that looked like leathered granite, diners' expectations, and Ansel's food. If she played her cards right, she would sample his cooking tonight.

"This has been here the whole time?" Nathan peered at the mural. "It looks familiar."

"I think it's Buckey Windstop's work. Don't let your crew touch it." She placed her body between him and the work. "As soon as I figure out what to do with it, I'll let you know."

Ansel snorted.

She avoided his gaze. If he thought her attraction had taken a similar course, he was wise enough to keep his mouth shut.

"Can you look at these beams and tell me what you think?" Ansel asked.

Nathan nodded.

The two men approached a wooden stairway leading to the second floor.

The stairs would have to go, but if Ansel wanted to check out the upper floors, the stairs might hold him. While they bonded *mano-a-mano*, she would call a Houston preservationist and find out how to restore the mural. Preserving artwork was an intricate marriage of art and science. Conservation involved assessing state-of-the-art techniques, implementing preventative treatments, and repairing unfortunate damage.

Her unspoken curiosity about the mural's condition also required delicate privacy. Someone in town knew about the work, removed portions, and left the remnants in tatters. If the panels made it to art auction sites, the preservationist might know who felt entitled enough to destroy a piece of art for personal gain.

Additional crew members arrived on-site. They made for the paneling pile, but the colorful art drew them up short. A few scratched their heads and went back to work, hauling debris to the trash receptacle, but the rest pulled out their cell phones and snapped photographs.

"I don't pay you to stand around museums." Nathan's voice boomed from the second floor. "After you remove the wood, get a roll of plastic and seal off the back room. I can't have people traipsing through and delaying progress. I have a reputation to uphold."

"Mimi suggested cutting the mural off the wall and storing it until Riley could find it a home," Ansel said.

"Yeah?" Nathan stomped on a loose board. Dust

and unidentifiable debris rained from the second floor. "Good call."

"Absolutely not!" Riley shouted toward the men above her. "Get me tape and plastic. I'll do it myself."

The men laughed.

She shook her head and glared at Nathan's underlings scurrying around the job site. Some looked as scared as the recent college kid, and others looked as hardened as criminals straight from a halfway house, but every person moved with discipline. Nathan was the right person for the job.

Until she had the answers to her questions about the mural, every person in Cypress Creek remained a suspect. The stout limestone building housing the artwork required twenty-four-seven surveillance. As much as she wanted to explore her attraction to Ansel Percheron, celebrity chef, creative lover, and occasional asshole, she had a feeling she would eat delivery food for dinner.

Chapter Sixteen

Ansel had half a mind to call Collins. After exchanging pleasantries, he would chew out his second-in-command for omitting details about the restaurant project that should have raised red flags. What had the prior contractor done to earn project draws and a large down payment? The place was a wreck.

When the project delays began, Collins mentioned unreachable references and vague contract language, but he assured Ansel he had the project under control. Nothing about this site was under control. Rainwater puddled near the front of the building, the second floor was as flimsy as a jury-rigged stage, and he swore a rat tracked his progress.

The prior contractor's slight gnawed at his pride. He demanded quality from his food suppliers, and he got it. Maybe he should call the former contractor and demand a refund. He mentioned the idea to Nathan.

Nathan laughed and slapped him on the back. "It's a new day. Let's move forward."

The man offered good advice, but he wondered how long Collins knew about his wife's distress. Four days ago, he met Riley, and he already tracked her movements around the dusty construction site. With her injured ankle and recent headache, he wanted to offer her a break, but he doubted she would take it.

Instead of dumping his frustration on Collins, he

focused on his role. Given how stubbornly he outbid the other auction bidders, he doubted anything Collins could have said would have dissuaded him from buying the old hotel and turning it into a restaurant. Cash and time would tell whether he gave up. In the meantime, his appreciation for Nathan grew. His interest in Riley threatened to distract him from his mission, but he could handle the distraction.

"At least the last guy hauled off most of the debris," Nathan said. "I hate that part of the work. You never know what you'll find buried at the bottom of a pile. We'll have to get an electrician in here as soon as possible. I think the knob and tube wiring is gone, but it might have pockets of rag wiring left in the walls."

He was thankful no injuries occurred at the construction site. Given the site's condition, he doubted the prior contractor had insurance coverage, a contractor's license, or the basic qualifications to do the job. No wonder his rates had been too good to be true. "Get someone here as soon as possible."

"In a rush?" Nathan asked. "The building's already burned down once."

Ansel tried not to laugh, but a chuckle slipped past his chapped lips. He pulled balm from his back pocket and covered his reaction with a cough. Once a person had accumulated enough regrets, he should prioritize empathy over amusement, but discretion was never his strong suit.

Several of Nathan's workers stopped and glanced his way. One man offered a tissue.

He waved off their interest. Being on-site during construction felt different from being the boss who barked out a punch list. With Riley and Nathan on his team, he could enjoy the process and find ways to make the restaurant better. "Too bad the fire left the mural intact. I guess we're saving it." The prospect made him feel lighter, and he jammed the balm back in his pocket before squaring his shoulders.

Nathan held a finger to his lips. "You know you won't win that argument. Let it go. She'll find someone to take it off your hands. Collectors go wild for that vintage, cowboy stuff."

"I don't see you cutting off a panel."

"Where would I put it?" Nathan asked. "I see one person of color on the walls, and he's holding a mule's halter. If I'm hanging art over my mantel, it's modern art."

Wondering how Nathan viewed Aubrey's curio shop, he watched Riley unroll a sheet of thin plastic and explain to a lackey how to tape off the mural. She moved with quiet precision, but she favored her injured foot. He looked forward to helping her unwind, and he could think of several pleasurable ways to exhaust her. If she woke up tomorrow with dark circles under her eyes, they wouldn't be due to a lack of sleep. He walked toward her.

She pulled out her phone. "Riley Golding."

Working his jaw, he wondered how long the call would take.

"That's very flattering, but I'm on a jobsite in Cypress Creek, and I can't attend the community service award ceremony. Perhaps you have another honoree whose work deserves the award and whose presence on stage would encourage donors to give generously?"

He scratched his head and wondered why she

turned down a professional award. The dinners could drag on, but the press would bolster her career. If Warrior knew about her demurral, he would probably drive to the award ceremony and accept the plaque himself.

Riley ended the call and slid the phone back into her jeans pocket.

"Feeling popular?" he asked.

She turned and smiled.

He knew a fake smile when he saw one and raised an eyebrow.

"Being nominated for a community service award always feels good. I do so many high-end, fee-based projects. To feel balanced, I need to give back to the community, but I don't want to rack up honors. I don't want to take the focus off of community needs. Why should they spend all that money on a big dinner? A kind email is thanks enough."

His cheeks warmed. He donated gift cards to local charities, but he rarely put in the time to volunteer one-on-one. If someone wanted to give her an award, they wanted to leverage her work and her personality to double the contributions from slightly inebriated, deep-pocketed guests. Imagining her dressed to the nines made him itch to pull out his wallet and contribute to the undefined cause. "What kind of work are they honoring?"

"Why?" she asked.

"I want to know how badly you feel about accepting my fees."

She laughed. "Fee-based work keeps me in business, but when I work with pro-bono services, I support organizations at the heart of social, economic, and environmental change. I've already won my award."

He handed her a roll of tape. "Good for you."

"I'm not the only Austin architect eligible for the Member Service Award. Plenty of my peers have made outstanding contributions to the community through service, design, or design thinking. The association won't have a problem finding another recipient."

"I doubt the backup recipient will look as lovely in an evening gown."

Her cheeks blushed.

He awarded himself a win.

"It's not about the dinner."

"It's always about the dinner," he said.

She laughed.

Scratching his jaw, he replayed her description and wondered how design thinking paralleled his profession. Lying in bed and dreaming up new dishes to stimulate his customers' palates fueled his creativity, but it also stimulated his wallet. Given his outlay on the Cypress Creek boondoggle, profitability was a poor reason to keep him from volunteering.

Perhaps his retirement could include a more active role in the community. Eagle Hawk put him to work in the garage and in the kitchen, but neither venue required deep conversation. By embracing him and giving him a safe place to grieve, the reservation community filled that void, but work could help people process their emotions. So could a sharp knife, bunches of onions, and a willing ear. "I still think you should accept the award. You earned it."

She looked over her right shoulder. "Now, you sound like Warrior."

Raising both palms, he shied away from the comparison. "I never want to hear you use that phrase again. He's your dad. I'm your"—dropping his chin, he wiggled his eyebrows—"celebrity crush? Once-in-a-lifetime bang? Secret lover."

She laughed, bent her knees, and finished taping up access to the mural. "Something like that."

He worked his jaw. If she would give him a clue about how she felt, he would know how to approach her. Hearing silence, he considered the mural. The flimsy barrier would keep people from wandering into the space, but it offered little protection. "You were right. Nathan's pretty unfazed by the artwork. He says the rest of the building offers plenty of labor opportunities."

Brushing together her hands, she nodded. "I'm sure the job will take months."

He rocked back on his heels. Could he spend months horsing around in Cypress Creek? She and Nathan had jobs, but his presence felt a little superfluous. Eying her boot, he hoped her ankle felt better and cleared his throat. "So, what do you want to do for lunch?"

"I'll skip it. I don't want to miss the conservator."

He slapped his chest. Skipping lunch meant skipping the chance to explore what made them click...or kiss. He doubted comments about her injured foot, growling stomach, or shadowed eyes would get him anywhere. He cleared his throat. "How about I order in?"

"From where?" she asked. "You don't have to feed me. It might be your impulse, but I can take care of myself."

Watching her wobble back to the design table, he believed her, but he doubted their care definitions aligned. Showing up with sandwiches failed to win Aubrey's heart, and the stakes with Riley felt higher. He walked to her side and looked over the drawings. "These are really intriguing. I don't understand everything I'm seeing, but I want to know more. If I pick up sandwiches from the coffee shop, will you walk me through the design?"

She tilted her head and made eye contact. "You're my client. I'll answer any questions you have."

"But will you tell me *why* you picked the things you picked?"

Tucking her hair behind her ears, she smiled. "Sure, but the choices might offend your sensibilities. I added a touch of Cypress Creek to the urban designs."

He pulled back his chin. "Does the men's room have a watering trough urinal?"

She laughed and shook her head.

"Then I think I'm good."

"Okay," she said. "Turkey and avocado on wheat."

He straightened and pushed his luck. "With mayo and bacon?"

"Absolutely not." She traced a finger along a foundation line. "I want to live to a ripe old age."

He did, too, and for the first time, he imagined retirement with someone at his side.

****

Balancing two paper bags and two drinks in his hands, Ansel walked into the jobsite and found it nearly deserted at the lunch hour, but two silhouettes stood near the worktable. Seeing Riley, he felt his heartbeat stabilize, but he wondered if the other person might be

Warrior Golding. He cleared his throat. "A consult?"

Riley and the man turned.

When the construction lights hit the visitor's face, he realized the man might be the same generation as Riley's father, but his soft, pale skin and meticulous pocket square suggested a life lived indoors, instead of a life spent roasting beneath the Texas sun.

"Ansel, I'm glad you're back," Riley said. "This is Saunders Reesuzn, the conservator from Houston."

Ansel set the lunch bags on the table and offered a hand.

Saunders pumped it. "A rare find! Absolutely brilliant. You're a lucky man."

Meeting Riley's gaze, Ansel smiled, but he felt luckier to have met her than to have discovered a moldering mural on his construction site. He ran a hand through his hair. "Life is full of surprises."

Riley turned to the section featuring the woman who looked like her ancestor. "Saunders cleared his schedule to see the work, but his news isn't all good."

"Oh?" Ansel propped a hip on the table, checked to make sure he wasn't destroying Riley's work, and crossed his arms over his chest. "What's the verdict?"

"The mural's in remarkable shape," Saunders said. "Restoring it can be done, but it might take a few months and a significant investment."

Ansel's nose twitched.

"We don't store works of this caliber in unheated, uncooled building shells." Saunders ticked the site's characteristics off on his fingers. "Imagine how much damage the fire, rainwater, and the broiling Texas sun inflicted on this work of art. Disgraceful."

"How much?" Ansel asked.

"For three thousand square feet of canvas." Saunders twirled his mustache. "I assume we're talking museum-quality restoration. Repairing and stabilizing one ten-foot-tall section would cost nearly ten thousand dollars."

Ansel plated two hundred and seventy-five dollar tomahawk ribeyes, but seasonings inspired by Eagle Hawk's Oglala Lakota heritage balanced the steak's ridiculous size. The juxtaposition earned him a tongue-in-cheek mention in the *New York Times*, but he knew how to manage his money. He stretched out his legs. "Come again? What will you use? Cotton swabs?"

"A quarter of a million dollars is a conservative estimate," Saunders said.

A bucket of lip balm couldn't ease Ansel's cough. He slapped his chest. "C-come again?"

Riley rolled her eyes.

Saunders peered at the damaged sections. "I'm not sure how we would address the torn canvas and missing sections. It's a shame someone found the mural before the two of you, but I'm glad you called me."

Unwrapping his sandwich, Ansel took a bite to keep his mouth full. The bakery's turkey sandwich barely calmed his reaction to the conservator's news. Before Saunders's arrival, he toyed with sponsoring the conservation work, but the restaurant's costs were already out of hand. He leaned toward removing the mural and sending it to Mimi's storage barn. Let a foundation or a university carry ole Buckey Windstop's flag. Then he looked at Riley.

She chewed her thumbnail and stared at the mural's section that first caught her eye.

If he would build a restaurant to spite a woman he

no longer loved, what would he do to please someone who cared for him? The slippery slope and the brevity of his connection with Riley brought him up short. The mural's colors shone, but floodwaters, smoke, and an unheated, uncooled building left their mark.

So did his experiences with women. The minute he laid out the cash to conserve Buckey's work, he might be flat on his ass looking for a new woman to hack off sections of his heart, slap sex appeal over the wounds, and trust that time would cauterize the wounds.

"I have contacts in the preservation world," Riley said. "I'll circulate images of the work and see if anyone bites. The last piece of Windstop's art that went to auction brought in plenty of cash. Worst-case scenario, you can sell off half the work and donate the rest to the local museum."

"Many owners have adopted the same approach." Saunders walked toward a cutout near the rear door. "I'm surprised the thief left the portraits of women. Their rarity increases their value."

Riley rubbed her arms.

Picking up her lunch, Ansel carried it toward her. "Why don't you sit a while?"

She perched on the table and riffled through the bag. "Thanks."

He wondered if he could find a camp chair at one of the neighboring stores.

Saunders pulled out his phone. "In fact, I wonder if this section"—he looked back and forth between the phone screen and the mural—"yes, I know what happened to this piece. It went to auction at the last Lone Star event."

"What?" Riley looked up.

"It's Texas' largest live art auction, and one never knows what will turn up. The buyer said the work was a family piece. Obviously, they lied." Saunders shook his head and sheathed his phone. "Some people."

She jumped to her feet, winced at her injury, and adjusted her stance. "Who was it? Do you have a copy of the catalog? I have to call Lone Star."

Ansel rested a hand on her right shoulder. "Come on, eat. You can track down the seller after lunch. Laying blame won't bring back the work. At a minimum, you'll have to involve the police, and you might as well do it on a full stomach."

Narrowing her gaze, she looked back and forth between the two men. She worked her jaw.

Indecision almost looked cute on her. Her professional success depended on deep pockets and limitless choices, but making concessions probably left a sour taste in her mouth.

Her stomach growled.

He shook his head. Running a kitchen was an act of service. If he couldn't take care of Riley, he might as well go back to chopping vegetables. Ignoring her audible concession, he walked toward Saunders. "Can I see the auction item?"

Saunders called up the image and handed over his phone.

A painted man polished his glasses on a porch swing. His friend spat chewing tobacco into a pocket spittoon bottle. Well, at least the cowboys had manners. Ansel sighed and handed back the phone. Superimposing the panel required little imagination. Who had access to the work?

"Anyone in there?" The raspy question ended with

a cough. "Anyone home?"

Ansel frowned.

Saunders leaned forward.

"Come on in, Mimi," Riley said. "We're just having lunch. Walk toward the plastic, and I'll pull back the tape."

"I'll do it," Ansel said.

"Thanks." Riley brushed her hair off her forehead.

He unstuck the taped parted the thin plastic protecting the mural.

Holding a cat and an umbrella, Mimi entered through the back door and wiped sweat from her forehead. Rain water flattened her dyed-blonde hair and smeared her eye makeup. "This blasted rain." She dropped the cat to the floor, closed the umbrella, and shook off the rainwater. "Will it ever end?"

"No," Saunders said. "Mind the artwork."

"The artwork?" Mimi scanned the mural. "Right, the artwork."

Saunders cocked his head. "Come again?"

The cat darted toward the room's shadowed corner.

A rat squealed.

"Nasty little creatures." Mimi coughed, slapped her chest, and lumbered toward the worktable. "I never could see the appeal, but I see you're coming along with your designs." She patted Riley's cheek. "Good on you. I shouldn't have lost my temper this morning. I'm getting too old for niceties."

"The designs are a work in progress," Riley said. "Is there something you need?"

Mimi cleared her throat. "As a matter of fact, yes. Too much banging this morning, and the waste container is taking up parking spots. I have a business to run. Take your trash out the back door like the rest of us." She lifted her chin. "We have to maintain appearances, or we'll descend into lawlessness."

"You!" Saunders rushed toward the table and circled Mimi. He reached to grab her arm and pulled a hand up short. Pointing his finger, he breathed deeply. "You brought the stolen Windstop work to auction. Thief!"

"Get away from me." She shuddered and turned her back. "I have no idea what you're saying, fly boy."

The conservator paled before his cheeks reddened. "Fly boy?" Waddling in place like a penguin, he pulled out his phone. "I'm calling the police. A disgrace!"

Ansel wondered if the conservator considered becoming a wine steward. He summoned indignation like the best of the best.

Holding the phone against his ear, Saunders pointed at Mimi. "I saw the interview introducing the missing piece at last year's auction, too. You said the work was a family heirloom from Aunt Becky's New York attic."

"Do I look like I'm from New York?" Mimi wiped her hair off her forehead. "You're mistaken."

Saunders planted his free hand on his hip. "I am not!"

Ansel looked toward Riley and raised his eyebrows.

Riley held her sandwich and scanned the exposed rafters. Her chest rose and fell with deep breaths, and the room's occupants waited for her reaction. When she lowered her gaze, cool disdain replaced the outrage he expected, and she held his gaze. "What if she didn't need room to expand? She might have bid on the hotel because of the mural. What if she needed access to the artwork? What if she started the fire?"

"Don't be ridiculous!" Mimi stomped her foot. "Do I look like a murderer?"

Turning, Riley faced the town eccentric. "Looks mean nothing. The boot business isn't very lucrative, is it?"

"For the love of God!" Pivoting on her heel, Mimi snatched the cat twirling around her ankles and stormed out of the building, holding her closed umbrella beneath her armpit.

The rain curtained around her, and the cat screeched.

In her wake, Saunders relayed his information to the call's recipient.

Thunder rumbled in the distance, and the rain pattered the roof.

Riley dropped her head in her hands. "The accusation is so far-fetched, it's possible. If Mimi were a doting, eccentric aunt with deep pockets, pride and the fear of scandal would keep her from indulging in larceny. But she sells boots, and the Boot Byre no longer looks like an eccentric hobby. She didn't deny it, did she?"

He shook his head and ached to hold her, but she insisted on keeping their relationship under wraps. Clearing his throat, he turned to Saunders. "Are you sure?"

Saunders covered the phone's mouthpiece. "Absolutely! After I'm done alerting the police, I'll call the major auction houses and inquire about additional sales. Your thief might have distributed Windstop's panels to avoid creating a pattern. Aunt Becky, my arse." He straightened his pocket square. "I should have known."

Riley rubbed a palm over her face. "What a mess."

Ansel scanned the room and wondered if yellow crime scene tape would add or distract from the restaurant's vibe. Closing his eyes, he counted to ten. One, Mimi Lewis and the mural's fate were none of his concern. Two, the theft upset Riley, but she held her composure. Three, he peeked through his lashes and saw Riley drop her forehead to her hand. Composure was overrated. Her forgotten sandwich sat at her side. Abandoning his consternation, he walked toward her and cupped her elbow. "Are you okay? What can I do to help?"

"I'm fine." She swallowed. "I should have known…"

"What?" he asked.

"I should have known the thief would be a local, but I let my love for this town blind me. Whoever took scissors to the work skimmed off sections like a kid unable to resist stealing icing from a cake. A little bit here, and a little bit there." She shook her head. "She felt entitled. What a two-faced…liar."

He had a feeling her first word choice had been stronger, and he took her measured epithet as a sign she would find her footing amid the betrayal. "Liar? How about 'brazen monkey baller' or 'sideways charcuterie hog'?"

Riley rolled her eyes, but she smiled.

He stroked her arm. "Saunders could be wrong."

She shook her head. "Professional thieves would have taken down the whole work. Maybe that outcome would have been better." She rubbed her temples. "At least, the mural would be intact."

"Saunders will track down the sales. If we can reunite the missing panels with the main body of work, we'll do it."

She chewed on her bottom lip and eked out a smile. "You were ready to throw the whole work into storage."

"Is that off the table?" He scratched the side of his lip. "It's still an option."

Her mouth gaped.

Handing her the sandwich, he turned his back and accepted the inevitable. The mural would come down, go into conservation, and return to the Cypress Creek restaurant.

Mimi's mug shot would grace the bathroom walls. The mural would decorate the bar along with vintage cowboy boots and glittering liquor bottles. Local color gave a building its character, and he could no sooner evict Buckey Windstop's masterpiece than he could ignore Riley's dedication. Their continuity pulled at his heartstrings, and twenty years had passed since he felt the same way about his Sioux Falls eatery.

"I'll front the conservation work, but I'd like to find partners from the art world," he said. "Preservationists. Endowments."

"You can't endow a piece of art," Riley said.

He imagined brass plaques marking barstools. If all press was good press, the restaurant would get a dose of media attention. "Watch me."

Riley laid her head against his back and wrapped her arms around his waist. "You don't have to sponsor the conservation. I'll find someone else."

"I want to do it." He lifted a hand and pressed a

kiss to her soft skin. "Let me give back to the community before the lynch mob runs me out of town."

She laughed and rubbed her cheek against his shoulder blade.

The rumble sent his heartbeat into overdrive, and he realized he would do whatever was in his power to make sure she smiled.

Chapter Seventeen

"Riley, you in there?" Dad asked.

Jumping back from Ansel's heated frame, she adopted a smile and wiped dry her lips.

Ansel dropped her off in the pouring rain.

Dad lowered his shotgun.

He looked surprisingly pleased with Ansel's actions. She could base his exuberance on her safe return, but his unexpected site visit tipped the scales toward interference.

He wasn't at the jobsite to review her work or offer his suggestions. He rallied his energy to meddle. Working her jaw, she settled on the easiest approach to handling him. "Yep, Dad. Come on back!"

"I brought Mikey and Papi," Dad said.

As if she needed the warning. Arranging the drawings, she picked up her sandwich and took a huge bite. Fuel would get her through the encounter and the long vigil night guarding the mural against Mimi's selfish tendencies. Wondering how the turkey tasted better after a kiss, she turned toward Ansel to express her thanks.

Holding his phone, he looked up from the screen and winked.

Whatever was going on between them would stay private until she figured out how to present it to the town, much less to her fathers. If novelty underpinned her attraction to Ansel, the lust would fade. No harm, no foul. She relaxed.

"My Gawd," Papi said. "Warrior, I thought you said you made progress!"

Her father's exasperated assessment teased out a real smile, and Riley swallowed her bite. Papi wore a blue linen shirt over designer jeans, and his rain boots were so immaculate they looked fresh from the box. How he managed to navigate the rain puddles without acquiring mud stains baffled Riley.

Skirting an indoor puddle, Papi pressed a kiss to her cheek and sniffed. "You smell like a man." He pulled back and waggled his eyebrows. "Lucky girl. Who is he?"

Setting down the sandwich, Riley felt her cheeks warm at the insinuation. She wondered how much of Ansel's cologne could have possibly worn off. Amid the burst of creativity that would make her dads proud, the room smelled like dust. If Papi could pick out Ansel's fresh, crisp aftershave, he should train his nose for perfume manufacturing. More likely, Papi was fishing for information, and she refused to indulge his lucky guess before she had a handle on her feelings for Ansel. She scratched an eyebrow. "Huh."

Papi narrowed his gaze but left his indulgent smile in place.

"This is progress!" Warrior walked the room's perimeter until he came to the plastic sheeting guarding the mural. "What's behind this curtain?"

Riley flipped her long brown hair over her right shoulder. "A job site. I thought your hip kept you from the construction site. What happened, you ran off another physical therapist?"

Papi waved toward his husband. "Don't get me started."

"No, really," Dad said. "What's behind the plastic?"

Steady rain falling on the roof kept the room's silence from feeling like a physical presence. Since her college exams, she couldn't remember a day she felt so tense and pigeonholed by expectations. Her clients knew the caliber of her work before they engaged her, but Ansel hired Dad.

The restaurant and its secrets belonged to Ansel, but family loyalty demanded honesty. She looked toward Mikey to break the ice, but queasiness lingered at the edges of his taut smile, and he held the open umbrella near his feet.

Ansel cleared his throat. "Riley and I discovered an old mural behind the wood paneling. It's in good shape, but the boot-barn lady has helped herself to sections of the work and sold them at auction."

Dad and Papi exchanged looks.

"The boot lady?" Papi mouthed.

"Mimi Roberts," Dad said.

Papi opened wide his mouth. "Ohh."

"We're right here." She waved a hand to break the couple's sidebar.

Both dads flushed and turned toward her.

They looked as crestfallen as a longhorn chewing fresh hay. Her heart rate skyrocketed. "Aren't you shocked? Outraged?"

Warrior rubbed a hand over his cheek. "Disappointed? Mimi's had her problems over the years, but this would be a new low. How badly damaged is the mural?"

"It's pitiful." She clenched her fists. Mimi's history with the town started before Riley's birth. Witnessing her dads' acceptance reinforced how quickly life could upend her idyllic notions of Cypress Creek. "How could Mimi be so petty?" She choked out the words. "She nearly ruined the work."

Ansel shifted closer.

His respect and proximity pulled the tension from her shoulder blades, and she forced herself to breathe deeply. First glimpses were powerful emotions, but trust could anchor a relationship. His respect for her boundaries made her want to break them, but she had bigger issues at hand. Mimi's theft left a sour taste in her mouth. She understood economic necessity, and she thanked her dads for sheltering her, but without honorable citizens, Cypress Creek was just another Hill Country town. "The theft's just pitiful."

Papi hugged her and patted her back. "I know." He brushed her hair from her eyes. "Life can be tough. Did I tell you about the time the governor left me a thousand dollar tip and the club owner…"

Dad cleared his throat.

"Right." Papi stepped back. "The artwork."

"It's not a complete loss. We're waiting on a conservationist to determine next steps," Ansel said. "What was his name?"

She exhaled. "Saunders Reesuzn."

"A good man!" Dad peeled back the tape.

"I'd rather you leave the plastic in place," she said. "I took pictures, but I don't want to keep re-taping the sheeting."

Dad stilled his hand, huffed, and dropped his arm. "Who painted it?"

"Windstop."

"Oh, I love his work!" Papi held out his hand. "Show me the pics."

Riley surrendered her phone. "Doesn't anyone want to see my design work?"

"I do," Mikey said.

Looking up, she made eye contact and smiled. "Thanks, but you look like you need a chair more than a bird's eye view of my work."

"You're not wrong," Mikey said.

His bright-blue eyes looked dim in the shadows, but hangovers had that effect. Riley turned to Ansel. "I brought two in my SUV, but I haven't lugged them in yet. Do you mind grabbing them?" She fished the keys from her pocket and offered them. "I'm parked out back."

Reaching for the keys, he let a hand linger.

The heat of his touch made an impression and offered release. Pleasure could obscure her doubts and uncertainties. She leaned into the touch and imagined indulging, but just as quickly, she blinked away the fantasy and focused on her responsibilities and her family's lingering presence. "Good deal."

"See you in a second," he said.

Forcing a smile, she watched him depart from the front door and looked forward to reclaiming a moment of intimacy.

Dad cleared his throat.

She turned and widened her eyes. "Soo?"

Papi moved aside the designs and perched his backside on the table. "Callie's been calling all morning about the rain. For a housekeeper, she has remarkably few limitations about issuing orders. She wants me to

261

round up the dogs' gear and bring it when we evacuate."

"Evacuate?" Riley frowned and looked away from the door. "I thought the weather forecast looked better. The chance of rain tapers off today. We're headed for clear skies."

Dad and Papi exchanged glances.

"Aren't we?" Riley asked.

Mikey leaned against a wall. "The rivers are high, and people are getting jumpy. You probably didn't see the water levels last night. You came home late."

She detected a note of reproach in his voice, and she ignored it. Mikey could sleep off his overindulgences wherever he wanted, and she could, too. "How high?"

Dad walked toward her and crossed his arms. The work lights cast his shadows on the wall. Even in a stripped-down space, he maintained a presence.

"Just below the bridges, but you're right, the forecast calls for clearing," Dad said. "I can't help it if Papi and Callie are Nervous Nellies."

"Don't I have a reason?" Papi twisted his favorite, gold cocktail ring. "You always say the rain will stop, but what if it won't stop? How much more can we lose?"

Riley looked away from Papi's worry lines and anxious habits. After three days of rain, the town wouldn't fall apart. Officials had mitigations in place. They installed gauges and replanted the flood plains. Ravines could hold a lot of water, but how much had already fallen? She rubbed Papi's back. "If you feel better leaving, go ahead. Nobody will judge you."

"But what about you?" Papi asked. "I can't leave

my girl."

She stilled her hand. "Let me secure the site, and I'll be right behind you."

Papi stopped twisting his ring. "Where will you go?"

The possibilities intrigued her. Austin made sense, but her dads had a condominium in Houston Heights. Proximity to Saunders would help her plan her next course of action on the conservation work.

Ansel walked in, carrying two camp chairs.

Her cheeks warmed. Did she want to go to San Antonio?

Unfolding the chairs, Ansel gestured for Mikey to sit.

Mikey's pasty skin blanched, and his signature pompadour, wet from the rain, flopped over one eye. "Actually, man, I'm good. I'll check in on Mimi and see if she needs help moving her stock to higher shelves. The old broad's a piece of work, but she's part of this town."

"Welcome to Cypress Creek, home of muralists and kleptomaniacs," Riley muttered.

Mikey saluted her. "Don't forget country music stars."

She saluted him. "Of course."

Dragging the open umbrella behind him, Mikey made his way outside.

Dad peered at the design work laid out on the table. "You were up late, and you left near dawn. I didn't get a chance to see your sketches."

"They're a mix of Texas romance and industrial design." Riley ran a finger along the soft paper. "I want to take advantage of the building's heritage, but I also want to mix in charcoal-black seating, finished concrete tables, and romantic lighting to highlight Ansel's creations."

Looking up from the drawings, Dad considered Ansel.

Ansel looked toward the hotel's burnt-out second floor. "I always said the restaurant would be an ode to Texas glitz and glamour. Spaces evolve. If Riley wants to mix urban sophistication with country intimacy, I trust her." He met her gaze. "You do, too."

She grinned. His support obliterated her exhaustion, but she might also have a creative high. Focusing on his sincerity, she melted into his gaze's warmth. "Thank you."

Ansel cleared his throat. "The mural's remnants can anchor the bar, but the martinis will still be lethal."

"Of course," Dad said. "You're spot-on."

"Well, that's a first." Ansel winked. "I've been known to rework menus and issue enough change requests to give a man gray hair."

Dad snorted. "Trust me, son, Riley and Grant inspired mine."

She laughed and wondered how easily Ansel accepted Dad's past suggestions.

"Let's move the kitchen toward the front of the house, too. The social set can stay near the bar and the high-energy activity. The lovers and entrepreneurs can gravitate toward the shadows. There's a place for everyone."

Dad huffed. "I told you to move the kitchen six months ago!"

Papi placed a hand on his crossed arms.

Ansel rocked back on his heels. "You did. Seeing

the building again pushed me toward the right decision."

"Are you sure it wasn't Riley?" Papi pushed down his cuticles.

Dad glared. "Don't meddle."

"Oh, that's rich." Papi stood. "Look who's talking."

Riley cleared her throat before her charming, out-of-touch fathers made the room feel infinitely smaller. "So, you're headed to Houston? Callie will meet you there?"

"Yes." Papi tilted his head. "Has the rain stopped?"

One by one, Riley, Ansel, Dad, and Papi turned their ears and listened.

Raindrops no longer pelted the roof, and without a breath of wind, the blue covering lay quiet. Riley exhaled. "I think it has stopped."

"We could stay," Dad said.

Papi shook his head. "This is the perfect time to go. Riley will follow, and Ansel will head home to San Antonio." He leaned toward the chef. "Give the creeks a day or two to subside, and we'll open the house by Wednesday. Come by for a drink."

"A good plan." Ansel adjusted the pants slung low on his hips. "Everyone needs a break from the weather."

Riley gave him points for the deflection. Noncommittal statements got her through tough client situations, and hearing his strategic feint threatened to trigger a smile. She rolled up the design plans and sheathed them. "Thanks for coming by!"

Nathan and a crew of three workers walked into the building holding power tools.

Taking his cue, Dad kissed her cheek, took Papi's hand, and skirted puddles on his way toward the front door. He shook Nathan's hand and looked over his right shoulder. "Riley, we'll expect you late tonight or early tomorrow?"

"I'll call as soon as I'm finished here. Houston sounds good." She ran her tongue over her teeth and considered her alternatives. "Unless I go to Austin."

Dad's step faltered. "Come to Houston for a few days. It will put Papi at ease."

Reminding him of her age and professional achievements seemed petty. He and Papi were down to one offspring, and she understood their tendency to hold her tight. They grieved as a family, but remembering her fathers' loss helped her calibrate her feelings. She would do anything to minimize their loss. "Houston sounds good. I'll meet you there."

Nathan revved a cordless reciprocating saw and approached Ansel. "You know how to use this?"

"To cut up a mural?" Ansel asked.

Riley gasped.

Nathan laughed. "I had the stairs in mind. We'll knock out a better set so no one falls and busts their ass or their insurance policy."

"Yeah, I can take down a few stairs," Ansel said, "but I'm only good with demo."

Slapping him on the back, Nathan nodded. "Leave the rest to us."

Riley pulled her laptop out of her messenger bag. With Ansel and the work crew occupied, she could transfer her plans to the computer, refine them, and get a jump-start on the next stage of her design. She pulled out headphones and settled them over her ears. The clearing forecast and her parents' departure were icing on the cake, but she hoped Ansel had a thing for Hill Country takeout. Until she secured the mural, she would remain in Cypress Creek.

Chapter Eighteen

Looking up from her computer, Riley surveyed the deep shadows cast by the setting sun. She wondered where the afternoon went, but it came back to her in flashes of inspiration and loaded looks from Ansel.

The constant drum of raindrops stopped mid-afternoon. Her parents texted to confirm their arrival in Houston, and the weather forecast held out. Cypress Creek and the surrounding Hill Country could expect clear skies, and she could call an end to her day. Standing, she rubbed the back of her neck.

"Ready for dinner?" Ansel asked.

Hearing his voice, she turned toward the front of the building and found him holding a bottle of wine from the local liquor store. "Um…"

He furrowed his brow. "Why don't I like the sound of that sentiment?"

She could think of several reasons for his suspicions. Her on-again, off-again approach to their flirtation, her family's hovering presence, and her marathon work session made her a candidate for a hot bath and an early bedtime. He looked like a man with passion on his mind, and she had enough energy left to meet him halfway, but she refused to leave the building.

"I found quail and wild rice. Do you like sage? Some people can't stand the smell. I'm surprised the co-op had dried chokeberries. Once people think a food has cancer-fighting properties, I guess it's all the rage."

She rubbed her throat. "Did you say chokeberries?"

"Aronia berries. They look a bit like small cranberries, and they grow on North American shrubs. Native American tribes ate them and made medicinal teas." He skirted the remaining puddles and put the wine on the table. "I think you're like them."

"The thing is"—she looked behind her at the plastic sheeting—"I think I should stay here and protect the mural. All the construction workers passing through glimpsed it, and Mimi might get desperate."

He crossed his arms over his chest. "You said Nathan was the best choice."

"I can't vouch for all his subcontractors!"

Exhaling, he kicked at the old, dusty flooring. "You're turning down a private dinner with Chef Ansel Percheron to guard an aging mural from an unspecific threat." Looking up, he made eye contact. "That's where you're placing your priorities? Work trumps life any day?"

She extended a hand and gripped his forearm. Feeling him flex, she hoped the involuntary muscle movement was more surprise and less recoil. "I'm not turning you down, but I need to stay on-site until Saunders develops a plan. I'm sorry I didn't tell you earlier. Maybe the quails and the chokeberries can go in the freezer?"

He opened his mouth.

"And…" She tightened her grip. "You're more than the food you cook. I don't need a fancy meal to enjoy spending time with you. A grilled cheese would do."

"A grilled cheese?" He scowled.

269

She lowered the hand. "I'm more interested in what you have to say than what you can whip up in the kitchen. I like listening to your stories. They're unique, and so are you. Let's just do takeout."

He threw up his hands. "Well, hell."

"Okay, what if you cook the quail and bring them here—"

He held up a palm. "Forget the quail."

"I'd rather forget the chokeberries."

He laughed. Scanning the room, he focused on toolboxes Nathan left. "If my contractor thinks the building's safe enough to leave supplies, it's probably safe enough to house the mural."

"Nathan probably has a dozen toolboxes," she said. "I only have one mural."

Rifling through the supplies, he returned to the table with a long screw and a hammer. Screwing the metal fastener into the cork, he left an inch showing, locked the hammer's backside under the screw, and pulled out the cork.

The *pop* echoed in the limestone building.

"Impressive party trick," she said.

He took a sip of the wine and offered the bottle. "Desperate times call for desperate measures. Thirsty?"

She took the bottle and followed his lead. Sharing a bed was one thing, but wrapping her lips around the warm wine bottle felt incredibly intimate. The room's humidity made her sweat, and Ansel's proximity amplified the effect. Stripping off a layer of clothing and swapping stories sounded like the perfect beginning to a stripped-down meal with a man who intrigued her. She set down the bottle and unbuttoned the top of her shirt.

"I like where this is going. Maybe I should have bought a case."

She laughed and rolled up her sleeves, too. "Just getting comfortable."

"By all means." He lifted the bottle and took a second sip. "Get comfortable."

"What about the quail?" she asked.

"They're in the refrigerator," he said. "They'll keep."

Sinking into the chair that supported her weight for most of the afternoon, she stretched out her legs, wondered if she could slip off the medical boot, and reached for the bottle. The rich, red wine carried a slight chill, and its balanced acidity and berry undertones would have gone well with chokeberries. She savored the wine's mouth feel. What did she know about chokeberries?

He mimicked her pose and kicked out his legs. "Why aren't you heading to Austin to accept your community service award?"

Swallowing the mouthful, she bought time to formulate an answer. "I'm too young to win that award. I worry the honor has less to do with my professional achievements and more to do with my peers' empathy. I understand why people feel sorry for me and for my family, but I don't need a hotel banquet or a glass obelisk to shore up my emotions."

Raising the bottle, he took a sip and nodded.

"Grant's death hurts." She took the bottle and swallowed a hefty mouthful of wine. Her cheeks warmed, and she fought off a cough. "Despite what experts say, grief has no stages. It doesn't proceed in a predictable, linear progression. It hurts, and that hurt is the linear, universal truth." Returning the bottle to the table, she leaned back her head and closed her eyes. "Anyone who has grieved has grieved in their own way. A community service award won't help."

"You might be underplaying your contributions," he said. "I don't know anyone who would trade my quail for a watchman's vigil."

She laughed at the mockery behind his indignant rebuttal. Instead of shaping her reaction, he accepted it, and she wanted to believe the honesty came from more than a shared bottle of wine. She might have a taste for booze, but alcohol needed time to set in. This easy camaraderie between them just…was.

"I'm not much fun right now." She hefted the boot and wondered if she could turn its weight into an exercise regime. She would need to alternate sides, but anything would be better than sitting on her backside as time passed. "You're probably saving yourself from a shitty date. Finish the wine, go back to the bungalow, and enjoy the quail."

"I don't cook for myself," he said.

She straightened in the chair. "What?"

"After a twelve-hour shift, my body is exhausted. I might make a turkey burger and a salad, but I rarely make gourmet food for myself. When I go home, Eagle Hawk and I cook, but he razzes me for my success. The old man would eat bison pot roast with corn, beans, and squash for every meal. If I offer to cook something more complicated, I find myself relegated to the garage. He says it's hard to get lost amid pistons and steel."

She tilted her head. "So, you're not a fan of turkey burgers."

He laughed. "Is that all you heard?"

"You have to do better." She leaned forward and braced her elbows on her knees. "Turkey burgers are terrible."

He winked. "Not when I make them."

She smiled at the display of self-assured confidence. Despite his feelings toward Aubrey, the trait must account for most of his success. If he decided on Wall Street or real estate, he would have also succeeded, but she wondered what he would be like on vacation. "I'm not buying it. You don't work twelve-hour days in the kitchen. You have people."

"I'm always working." He cleared his throat. "Relaxation isn't an option."

Rest could be a curse. She scratched the side of her neck. "Where is the next restaurant?"

Tipping back his head, he looked toward the ancient roof. "I'm planning to retire. This is it. The grand finale."

She gripped the chair's flat armrests. "This is it? A spite restaurant is your capstone? Aubrey doesn't deserve that power. Go out on your terms."

He lowered his gaze. "Isn't she your friend?"

"Yes, and she's…imperfect!" Struggling to her feet, she paced the bare room. Standing by the gas station air pump on a hot summer day, he looked relaxed, but after three days in Cypress Creek, she knew him better. All afternoon, he worked on-site, and she tracked his movements with awareness that bothered and thrilled her.

All his little touches, light brushes, and glancing hands against her back kept her aware. His piercing, intense gazes told her he felt something, too, but he deserved more than inattention and spite. "Rework the site to leave behind a monument to your creativity."

"It wouldn't be in Cypress Creek," he said.

She threw up her hands. "Perfect. Someone else will come along and take over this venue."

He rubbed the side of his mouth. "I'm replaceable, huh?"

"Intense people are never replaceable." She pursed her lips. "You're also stubborn and a micromanager. If you weren't so hot, I would have kicked you off-site six hours ago. With you around, my productivity plummets."

"I let you rearrange the entire restaurant," he said.

She pushed back from the table. Hearing the chair scrape, she winced, but she held her ground. "My plans are better, and you know it!"

Laughing, he strode across the room and stopped on the opposite side of the table. "They are better, and just so you know, my productivity plummets around you, too. Instead of playing with power tools, I should be designing the restaurant's menu, reviewing food and beverage vendors, and scouting staff." He cocked his head. "Come to my place, and we'll reclaim our identities in the morning."

She exhaled. "I can't leave the site. I have to protect the mural."

He braced his hands on his hips. "Now, who's stubborn? You're so stuck in the past, you're forfeiting your future."

She gasped, but so few people knew what happened the day Grant died, and so few could understand her remorse. Ansel could. She failed to protect the most important person in her life, and she refused to trade her pleasure for the possibility of another selfish mistake. If he understood her remorse, he might understand her desire to protect whatever she could. "You're wrong."

"How am I wrong?"

Pushing away the wine, she dropped her head into her right hand and looked up. "The day Cypress Creek flooded, experts responded within hours, and rescue crews pulled hundreds of people from the floodwaters. Media coverage shows swift water rescue teams from Texas Search and Rescue making heroic choices, but their presence wasn't enough."

His stance softened. "I'm sorry about your brother."

Clearing her throat, she nodded. "You would have liked Grant. Everyone liked him. When the County Office of Emergency Management announced they had contacted the last person on their missing persons list, they didn't know Grant was missing. But I did."

He frowned.

"I was in Mexico at a boozy brunch, and Grant called. Imagine fielding a phone call while your best friend pours you tequila shots."

Turning his bracelet, he nodded.

Most people would have smiled, but she gave him credit for knowing how the story ended. She summoned the memory of her last conversation with Grant. The mix of laughter and the unreliable cell connection rekindled the pain in her temples. She should have stepped away from the celebrations. "I told Grant I would call him back later, and I let his next call go to voice mail. It was the last one I would ever receive."

Ansel's face paled.

Watching him connect the dots, she looked past

him and saw twilight's last glow pouring through the building's compromised roof. "Grant wasn't a member of TEXSAR. He was a volunteer first responder with a heart of gold. When county officials realized the severity of the flood, they ordered first responders to start evacuations and prepare for rescue efforts.

"With the community reverse alert system activated, emergency alerts sounded, and sheriff's deputies and constables went door-to-door. People like Grant stepped up and helped any way they could. He relocated our neighbors' stock like herding cattle was more fun than field day."

Ansel dropped into the second camp chair and stretched out his legs.

As she unburdened her conscience, she watched for signs of boredom. Their brief connection and the building's stark interior caged his focus on her pitiful tale. Hoping his attention stemmed from a deeper interest, she settled a leg against his and gauged his reaction.

One side of his mouth tipped up in a lazy grin.

If she were a more compassionate person, she would restrict her grief and ignore attraction, but she needed his empathy like she needed air. The alternative, rigid self-control and a polished demeanor, would smother her.

"I'm listening."

She wet her lips. "When the water rose, Grant joined boat and vehicle responders to rescue people from attics and roofs. The people running out of breathing space were a higher priority than the ones hanging onto trees, but rescuers couldn't reach the creek's south side. Grant split from the group and considered his souped-up truck. His voice mail said his stomach was churned up, and he had a bad feeling about the flood, but he thought he could reach the other side."

Ansel released an audible sigh.

"Minutes before the floodwaters went over the Ranch Road Bridge, Grant crossed with his truck and a boat. I should have been with him. I should have been on the phone, telling him to stay with the rescue group." She dropped her chin into a hand and closed her eyes. "Instead, he went rogue, and the only person who could convince him he was an over-confident idiot was taking tequila shots with her friends. I've listened to his voice mail a thousand times. My parents don't know about it, but I can hear the fear and uncertainty in his voice. He didn't want to be a hero, but he didn't want people to die."

"You didn't know what he faced," Ansel said. "Maybe the water levels dropped."

She opened her eyes. "I've pieced together what he saw. Logs, lawn equipment, and household debris hurtled downstream. Entering the water wasn't safe. If I'd been there, I could have stopped him. He took risks, and I moderated him."

Ansel worked his jaw.

"Except, I wasn't there." She closed her eyes. Carving out her identify shouldn't have come with such dire consequences. Swallowing, she faced Ansel and waited for his censure. "By sunrise, the water rushed downriver, and the flow of 911 calls slowed enough for rescue crews to return calls from the creek's south side. Rescuers arrived on-site and said the flood's aftermath overwhelmed them. Debris littered trees, and broken houses looked as if a tornado cut a path through the city."

Ansel offered a hand.

She gripped it. "They found Grant's body wedged in a tree. He still wore a helmet with a flashlight. The light still shone through the hazy morning and guided them to his location. A local woman who placed a 911 call said she watched the light throughout the night. The beacon barely penetrated the rain and the fog, but it held steady and gave her hope. Every time lightning cracked, she looked for movement in the tree, but the light's beacon never wavered."

"He was dead before the tree caught him?" Ansel asked.

She nodded. Any number of hazards could have taken him out. Propane tanks rammed submerged vehicles and exploded with flashes of light. Huge cypress trees tumbled into the creek with ear-splitting cracks. She understood Grant's impulse to help, but his ego baffled her. "As best I can figure, Grant approached the woman's house and realized the boat wouldn't make it. He jumped into the water and swam toward the house, going from tree to tree like his training taught him, but he lacked team members to support him. He should have stopped and turned back. He should have waited for help. Maybe he was stupid, or arrogant, but I doubt he would have put me in that position. I don't know how long he was in the water. When they retrieved his body, they said he looked like he braved a war zone."

She exhaled. "The past is more valuable than the future. The wrong twin died, Ansel. If I could do anything, I would trade places with him. He was the better, nobler person. I can sit here, cynical and rich, and call him an idiot, but he cared enough to risk his life. What have I done?"

"Well, shit." Ansel looked toward the rafters. "I didn't know this place was haunted."

She frowned.

He lowered his head. "You think I wouldn't have stopped my parents' accident? Jumped in front of their car to steer them toward a safer landing? We all regret our inability to shape the past, but I wasn't anywhere near my parents. If I had been, I'd be dead, too. You loved your brother, but you weren't in Cypress Creek." He stood and paced. "You have to let go of that possibility. You just weren't there."

The work lights cast his shadow and compelled her attention. Her therapist delivered the same pep talk, but advice without experience sounded like it came from a lecture hall.

Grief was so personalized and nonlinear that she refused to accept a standard progression, but Ansel's self-reflecting intelligence encouraged her to mourn her brother without rehashing her culpability. He was a celebrity chef and an excellent lover, but personal loss sharpened his credibility. She might need to hear his advice a hundred times before it altered her outlook, but she would listen.

Then again, what were his motives? If he wanted to spend the evening tumbling the sheets, what wouldn't he say to lure her to his bed?

"And as for being the better twin, you're wrong. There is no such thing as a better person. We all make mistakes, and living for tomorrow is the best thing we can do." He stopped pacing and pivoted. "You'll find a way to move on."

Her mouth felt dry. She waited for his argument to pivot. Maybe he would tell her sex and a bottle of wine could erase her regrets and make her feel alive for a brief moment.

"But moving on takes time. Hell, it's taken me twenty years to realize I'm no better than Aubrey. Pinning my happiness on her misfortune makes me a prick, and I've worked with enough hot-tempered chefs to know better. I shouldn't benchmark my success against her regrets. You can have all the time in the world to grieve your loss."

"So…" She stared.

"I shouldn't have asked you to leave. I understand why guarding this mural means something. We can sit here all night."

She swallowed. "All night?"

"I'll stay until the sun comes up."

"And then?" she asked.

"You trust Nathan?"

She nodded.

"Let him handle the daylight shift."

Letting her shoulders sag, she reached for her wine. "So, takeout for dinner?"

He tipped back his head and stared at the second floor. "Do you know how hard I worked to find those quail?"

An apology danced along her lips, but she believed he would stay in the humid, empty building to keep her company. Given another glass of wine, she might test the table's ability to hold their combined weight. She ran her tongue along her front teeth.

Lowering his head, he smiled. "Don't worry about

the quail. They'll keep." Nudging forward her laptop, he cocked his head and reclaimed his chair. "Show me what you've dreamed up."

She could put her heart into her plans, but she feared he already held it.

Chapter Nineteen

Ansel's preferred method of romance eschewed dinner by construction lights, but Jed deserved an accolade. Despite the honky-tonk BBQ's terrible marketing plan, the ribs were tender, sweet, and satisfying.

So was Riley. He bided his time until he could get his hands on her.

In the meantime, she walked him through her digital designs.

Each view exhibited her creativity and focus. As the building came alive under her descriptions, he understood the passion that made her a successful architect. She had an innate understanding of how people moved through a space, what they wanted to see, and what staff needed to thrive.

He envisioned the restaurant in a new light. The mural above the bar would create a welcoming vibe and a place to gather and mingle. The full-service bar and lounge would feature craft cocktails, local beer, and an extensive wine list.

A wood-burning grill and brick pizza oven in the open kitchen would tempt appetites. The menu would include small plates, contemporary comfort food, and fine dining specials featuring local, fresh produce. Organic proteins were de rigueur, of course.

Diners who wanted privacy and a seated meal

would gravitate toward the back of the restaurant, and the flow of food and laughter would create a profitable gradient that culminated on the alfresco patio.

If he played his cards right, Cypress Creek by Ansel Percheron would leverage traditional Mexican, Creole, and Southern Comfort foods with a Native twist. The waiting list would be booked for weeks, and the restaurant would be as successful as every other restaurant he opened. "Fuck."

"What did you say?" she asked. "An actual expletive?"

A rat perched on the new staircase and held a food scrap.

If he swiped the table's contents to the floor and had his way with Riley, he could ignore the opportunistic rodent. If the mammal stole a piece of rib meat, it came far too close. He jerked his head toward the furry pest and raised his eyebrows.

Riley looked over her right shoulder and shrugged. "You told me not to worry about them. They're escaping the rising water."

"But the water should be going down," he said.

She straightened in her chair and nodded. "If we can't control the bugs, we'll screen in the limestone archways. A few construction rats are the least of our concerns."

He liked the inclusive term, but after the build-out, the restaurant's success rested on his shoulders. Tipping back his head, he rubbed his forehead and considered what bothered him.

The rat was a joke. While scouting restaurants, he had dealt with cockroaches, ants, and termite infestations. Warm, humid states like Texas, Louisiana, and Florida had a well-deserved reputation for creepy, crawly critters, but the states' patrons loved to dine out. The Northeast harbored too many small rodents, but he would kiss a rat before he swapped the furry mammals for desert scorpions and snakes. Why hadn't Aubrey hailed from a snow-encrusted state like South Dakota?

Why hadn't he waited to fall in love with a woman like Riley?

"Lighting is key." Riley annotated her drawings. "It sets the tone for the meal."

"You're right."

She looked up. "I am?"

"The minute you walk into a restaurant, the lighting tells you if you'll receive fast-casual efficiency or shadowed luxury. I don't have to explain to you what concept we're chasing. This isn't a roll-your-own-burrito farm."

She laughed.

The sound warmed his heart. She deserved something new and fresh and so did Cypress Creek. If his restaurant mirrored every other venue he opened in the last twenty years, it would cement his legacy. It would also feel as hollow and impersonal as the rest of his culinary empire. When he held Aubrey, he drifted to sleep, refining his ambitions. When he held Riley, he drifted to sleep, scheming ways to make her happy.

Raising the bottle, she moved to fill their glasses, but scant drops landed in the takeaway cups. "I guess we're out of wine."

"I can get more." He braced his hands on his knees and prepared to stand.

"I don't need more."

Cocking his head, he waited and held his breath.

"I don't need to be intoxicated to feel attracted."

"Is that so?" He wet his lips and ignored the rib-induced stupor dulling his senses.

Unbuckling the medical boot protecting her ankle, she dropped it to the floor. "I'm sure the boot's helpful, but it's kind of a buzzkill."

His mouth went dry.

No matter how long she had been batting her eyelashes, he refused to miss a silver-plated opportunity to show her how much she captivated him. Beyond the laptop's glow and the set circles beneath her blue-gray eyes, she carried a warmth and vulnerability that called his name. He scooted forward. "What do you need?"

"Clean bedding would help." She patted the table. "But this will have to do."

"*Mi* bungalow *es tu* bungalow."

She laughed. Standing, she put her weight on her ankle and pulled her shirt over her head.

He might not be the brightest bulb in the chandelier, but he could take a hint. Mirroring her stance, he pulled off his shirt and met her gaze. "I like this game."

She grinned. "I do, too."

"What happens when your mural thieves arrive and find us buck-ass naked on this worktable?" he asked.

"Well, they'll enjoy the show, or they'll fleece us while we're in the throes of passion."

His cock jumped to attention. "Lucky thieves."

Tossing her hair over her right shoulder, she unhooked her bra.

"God, you're so beautiful." He rounded the table and took one of her breasts in his hand. The heavy warmth and her soft sigh centered his attention on her pleasure. Lightly squeezing the handful, he lowered his mouth to the other breast and sucked in her nipple between his lips.

"Oh!"

He looked up. "Too hard?"

She shook her head and smashed his face against her breasts.

Taking the hint, he continued his caresses and cupped her hip with a free hand.

Her moans grew a little louder, and she pressed into him.

She begged for more, and he intended to provide it. He moved his mouth to her other breast until she withered against him and thrust her pelvis into his groin. His dick was pleading for attention, too. Raising his head from her chest, he grinned. "How long have you been thinking about sex?"

"Since I met you at the gas station."

"All righty, then." Grinning, he lifted her to the table, dropped her laptop in his abandoned chair, and unbuttoned her jeans. "Last chance for a bed."

"Ever?"

He made eye contact and caught the teasing smile curling her lips. "Not ever. My door's always open."

"You'll forget me and move on."

She couldn't be farther from the truth. Her vulnerability and intensity were like a brand on his heart. He worked his mouth down her stomach to the waistband of her thong. The lacy, white silk begged for admiration. Right now, it also blocked his way to her soft folds and the one taste he couldn't erase from his mind. He dragged his tongue along the edge of the silk, around her belly button, and breathed air across her skin.

Goose bumps rose on her flesh, and she gasped.

Indulging in a smile, he pulled her thong down an inch and kissed the top of her pubic bone. He could feel her heat, and it beckoned him.

Her legs spread wide, and her breathless pleas intensified.

He was on the right track. Despite her evident need, he wanted to tease her the same way she teased him. He moved his mouth to her inner thigh and pressed kisses along her skin until he reached the slip of fabric. With one slide, he could feel her heat.

Her muscles tensed. "Ansel."

He raised his head. "Riley."

"You're killing me."

Grinning, he dropped his chin. Wanting her languid and breathless, he traced a similar pattern on the other side of her thong and moved his mouth up her stomach.

"Ansel." She drew a heavy breath. "I'll pull the same trick on you."

"So, you're saying there will be a third time?"

She gripped his face. "Only if you hurry."

He chuckled against her heated skin and lowered his mouth between her legs. Instead of teasing his rough skin along her thin, sensitive legs, he dragged down her thong and tossed it to the side. It probably landed in a pile of wood chips, but he would buy her a thousand replacements. Pressing his palms against her inner thighs, he spread her wide, lowered his head, and planted a kiss just above her arousal.

She squirmed in his arms. "Why are you torturing me?"

Her breath heavy and desire-soaked folds tempered

his control. "I want you to remember this night. No matter how many times you doubt yourself or my feelings, remember how this feels." He stroked her clit.

She gasped and nodded.

He dragged his tongue from her belly button to her slit, licked her where she wanted him, and pulled away to lavish attention on her inner thigh.

"I hate you," she whispered.

"In my bed, I wouldn't have nearly this much control. You'd be flat on your stomach, clutching the sheets and chanting my name."

Gripping his hair, she pulled him away from his attentions. "Braggart."

He held back his smile while he made his way to her other leg. She could believe what she wanted to, but he would take his time. He spent a few more minutes, making sure she realized his control.

When he pulled up and found her panting, her arm draped over her eyes in complete surrender, he found his goal in life. Dragging his tongue over her clit, he circled the bud and steadied his breath. If he thought about her wetness, her taste, or her breathlessness, he would blow his load and leave her hanging.

Losing himself between her legs, he licked, sucked, and kissed her until she writhed and clenched around his fingers. As he felt her release building, he tasted her, and his breath hitched. She was heaven and smoke on a cloudy day.

Her hips rode his tongue, and her hands fisted in his hair.

Like he would ever move. He continued his pace and listened to her moans grow faster and more urgent. Flicking his tongue across her clit, he pushed her closer to the edge.

She pulled his hair and tightened her legs around him. "Ansel!"

He could die a happy man, but he let her move against his tongue and ride her pleasure until her limbs loosed, and she lay sated on the table. Stepping away from her curves and rising chest, he stripped off his pants and pulled a condom from his wallet.

She propped herself on one elbow and raised her head. "Let me return the favor."

"Absolutely not. Stay out of my way."

Laughing, she flopped back on the table.

It shook beneath the impact, but he kept his gaze glued to her sex. Rolling on the condom, he was eager to get inside her. There was no possible way he could slow and prolong his pleasure. The sound of her orgasm echoed in the old building, and he hoped the late hour and thick, stone walls muffled the sounds of their pleasure.

Then again, let the whole town know he claimed this woman.

He climbed onto the table, braced himself on his knees, and entwined his left hand with her right hand. Pressing their hand above her head, he raised his eyebrows.

She grinned and nodded.

He guided his cock to her entrance, thought about the accidents that brought her into his life, and dropped his head to the soft, sweet spot below her ear. "You make me feel alive. This passion"—he swallowed—"is just the tip of my feelings. If you'd let me, then I'd take you around the world."

"Take me here."

Raising his head, he made eye contact and wondered if her sweat-soaked eagerness had eclipsed his declaration. His cock begged him to proceed, but as much as he needed her heat, he held back.

"I heard you." She looped her free hand around his neck and brought his lips to her mouth.

Lightning cracked.

He waited.

Her hazy gaze and warm smile held, and she lifted her hips. "Now, I want to hear you come."

Slowly entering her, he kissed her and reveled in the silky, perfect feel of her wrapped around his cock. Grabbing her other hand, he pinned that one against the table and thrust in and out of her heat.

The moments of connection and uncertainty might have slowed his lust, but the results were intimate, generous, and everything he had ever wanted from a woman. His connection to her felt so strong he wondered what could break it.

Lightning cracked a second time.

She stilled.

He released a hand and cupped the back of her head. "I've got you."

Resuming the kiss, she rocked her hips.

The connection intensified. The slow, leisurely buildup turned feral. Before he could judge the table's sturdiness, he stuffed a discarded shirt behind her head, released her other hand, and lifted her legs to his shoulders. Deep in her heat, he moaned into the new position.

She gripped the edge of the table above her head and raised her hips.

Thrusting, he tempered his passion against her

response. He could bang out his pleasure in a moment, but he wanted her with him.

"Ansel." She groaned. "More."

Adjusting his knees on the table, he gripped her ass so when he thrust, he could fill her and press a thumb to her clit. At the edge of his control, he watched her eyes go wide and her mouth part.

"Ansel! This is so good. You're so good."

As she clenched around him, sweat dripped down his back, and his climax gathered at the base of his spine. "Riley, I'm so close. Stay with me."

"I'm with you." Her whispered moans grew heavier. "I'm here."

Her commitment centered his pleasure, and his connection to the vulnerable, beautiful, intelligent woman writhing beneath him felt stronger than anything he ever experienced.

As she contracted around him, her fingers gripped his back and dug into his skin. "Yes!"

The echoes of her pleasure reverberated in the great, stone room. He pumped his hips as white-hot satisfaction tightened his balls and ripped through his system.

For a moment, they breathed.

Still inside her, his cock throbbed as her muscles pulsed. He gripped the condom, withdrew, and lowered her legs from his waist. Bracing his weight on one hand and his knees, he let his head hang.

"Again."

He laughed and nodded. A moment later, he dragged a thumb over her heated cheeks and smiled. "Riley, you astound me."

She wet her lips. "You did all the work."

Raising his head, he scanned the shadows and exhaled. Without the intimacy of sex, he feared letting his emotions bubble over. He came into her life like an unexpected storm, and his interest in spending more time with her could overpower her warm, willing embrace. If she wanted to live in the moment and keep their attraction at the center of their relationship, then he would keep his emotions in check. "I might have done the work this time, but I expect all's fair in love and war."

She chuckled. "And in the kitchen. Does this mean I can cook?"

He met her gaze and rose on his knees. "Absolutely not."

Looking up, she smiled. "Tyrant."

"I've been called worse." He climbed off the table. "I can run back to my place and get you a towel. Clean clothes."

"That would be nice." She toed a wet wipe from Jed's Pit. "Do you hear anything outside?"

He cocked his head. The rattling thunder had interrupted his pleasurable quest, but gathering storm clouds held their rain. "It's quiet. It's late." He met her gaze. "Are you ready to go home?"

Pulling up her legs, she threaded a hand through her hair. "I want to park my SUV by the trash bin and leave on the overhead lights. If anyone outlasted us, they might think we're still here."

"I doubt anyone's awake in Cypress Creek." He offered a hand. "Do you know the coffee shop doesn't even open until seven?"

Taking his hand, she slid off the table and reached for her shirt. Slipping it over her head, she skipped the bra and panties littering the floor. "You've mentioned that defect."

He ran a thumb along his whiskered cheek. "If Moeko added an espresso machine to her pop-up bakery, she would put the coffee shop out of business in a heartbeat."

She tossed him his shirt. "She's happy with her setup."

He worked his jaw and tugged the smooth cotton over his head. "Would Moeko bake for the restaurant?"

"Probably not." She shimmied into her jeans. "Are you always this worked up after sex?"

Wrapping an arm around her waist, he gathered her close and stole a kiss. "No."

She placed a hand on his chest. "Your heart's still beating fast."

"So's yours." Shifting her hips, he lowered his head. "Skip the clean clothes. Let's do it again."

Shaking her head, she slipped from his grasp and checked her phone. "It's three in the morning. Take me to my parents' house? I'll get Mikey to bring me back in the morning."

"Mikey?" The sound of another man's name on her tongue soured the taste in his mouth. In an instant, he wondered if he leapt out of the gate and let his emotions get the better of him. "He's in love with you."

She furrowed her brow. "We're friends."

He crossed his arms. "So are we. What about the no-sex-with-customers policy?"

She shrugged. "You'll move on, and I'll go back to Austin."

Conquering the Lone Star State never held such appeal, but he took in her guarded posture and focused on what he could do to preserve the present. Tossing the used condom in the remnants of their takeout food, he gathered the empty wine bottle and added the glasses to the sack of trash. "Let's get you back to your parents' house."

Her laptop and papers slipped into her bag.

A whoosh of fresh air would sweep the evidence of their desire from the room, and he hoped the voyeuristic little rat enjoyed the show. Running his fingers through his hair, he held open the front door, waited for Riley to slip past, and locked the door. Tossing the trash into the construction waste, he offered Riley an arm.

She scanned the sidewalk and took it.

"Afraid to be seen with me?"

"Afraid to be seen at all."

A wordless walk to the old roadster left room for the sound of night bugs and distant thunder. At the passenger side, he opened the door and stood back.

She slipped into the seat and looked up. "It's still raining upriver."

He held her gaze. "It's not raining here."

She clutched her bag to her chest and nodded.

Closing the door, he walked around the trunk and slipped into the passenger seat. Starting the engine, he waited for her to change her mind, but her silence persisted. Driving out of town toward her parents' ranch, he watched Cypress Creek's streetlights recede in the rearview mirror. The engine rumbled, and the car's wheels ate up the highway.

"Stop!"

He slammed on the brakes.

The car shuddered to a halt before the old bridge leading out of town. At the other end of the concrete expanse, a highway patrol car turned on its lights and illuminated a series of orange-and-white barricades.

The patrol lifted a megaphone. "Bridge is closed. Water's too high. Turn around."

Ansel tilted his head and spied the creek water lapping at the bridge's underside. He looked at Riley. "Is there another way to your parents' place?"

She shook her head.

Despite her silence, he saw the bloodless way she gripped her bag. "The water came up fast."

"The limestone hills sluice off the water in sheets. Soil would act as a sponge, but that's not how this area formed. I'm surprised the storms don't uproot more plants and shrubs. Have you ever seen a field of flattened wildflowers? It's intense."

"But they keep growing."

She wet her lips. "They do. Short of terracing the hillsides, I don't know how you could slow the deluge. The vegetation finds a way to persevere."

This seemed like a poor time to compare her beauty to a rosebud. She might be a prickly, ice-blue, Texas wildflower he'd rather avoid picking, but watching her push through her trauma inspired him. It also inspired him to take care of her. He draped an arm across her seatback and shifted in his seat. "I can take you back to the restaurant site or to Aubrey's house. The water will come down, Riley. The rain's stopped."

"The rain never stops." She shuddered and closed her eyes. "Maybe we should leave town tonight."

He nodded. "I can book a hotel room or bring you wherever you want to go."

"I can't ask you to drive. It's too late to be out on the road." Closing her eyes, she audibly exhaled. "I'd rather spend the night at your rental. At least, I'll have something to take my mind off the weather."

"Okay." Putting the car in Reverse, he turned the vehicle and headed back to Cypress Creek. Laying a hand on her thigh, he waited and counted his heartbeats.

She cleared her throat and placed a hand in his. "Thanks."

He squeezed her fingers. "You'll be okay."

"I know."

Did she? He cleared his throat. "On the bright side, anyone who vandalizes the mural will be stuck."

She summoned a weak smile. "Good point."

Exhaling, he remembered his anxiety after his parents' deaths. Whenever Eagle Hawk slid behind the wheel, Ansel placed anxious landline calls and pinged Eagle Hawk's bulky, black beeper. If Eagle Hawk could patiently accept his needs, he could honor Riley's fears. Squeezing her hand, he offered reassurance.

She clasped a hand in return.

Keeping his gaze on the road, he alternated between watching distant lightning and scanning roadside shrubs for deer. Somewhere, rain roared through flash flood alley, but the water would recede.

He glanced in the rearview mirror and found the patrol car parked at the bridge. Alone on the dark highway, he and Riley drove toward the quiet bungalow. No matter how hard the storm raged or she shook, he would hold her while she needed him.

Chapter Twenty

Riley stepped out of the shower and headed toward the bungalow's living room.

"Do we have to get up at the crack of dawn?" Ansel asked.

She stilled. "Why not? Nathan texted his crew will arrive by six, and with the bridges blocked, they'll be on edge and looking for work to keep their minds occupied."

"Two and a half hours of sleep." He flopped back on the bed. "I should have spent the morning buried inside you, instead of snoring in your ear."

"True." Rubbing the towel over her wet hair, she shrugged. "There's always tonight."

He sat up and raised his eyebrows. "I'll take an advance on tonight."

She shook her head and marveled at his ability to rise to the occasion. Men might lead with their cock, but their anatomy left little need for interpretation. Her system was more temperamental, and as much as she enjoyed testing the worktable's weight and Ansel's creativity, she couldn't summon the interest to take him up on his offer. "Saddle up, cowboy. We're off to work."

Pressing his head into the bed, he spread wide his arms. "I could find easier women to love."

Surely, he didn't mean it. With a decade of

Mikey's insincere lyrics bouncing around her brain, she ignored Ansel's offhand affection, slipped on yesterday's clothes, and padded into the kitchen. Fresh fruit filled a bowl, and neatly washed glasses rested in the drying rack. She wondered if his commercial kitchens operated with the same finesse. Picking up a green apple, she washed the skin and bit into the tart fruit. One day, she would find out.

The more time she spent with him, the more she wanted to know him. His strong arms and muscled torso should have given her the best sleep of her life, but sex could only consume a fraction of the night. The rainfall and her reaction weren't his fault.

While he slumbered, she listened to the soft rain and reloaded websites. She watched radar patterns swirl on the weather app she downloaded and deleted twenty times in the last two years. Technology gave her a measure of comfort.

Warm, moist air swept in from the Gulf of Mexico, hit the area's limestone hills, and warmed as it rose. When the wet air mass collided with cooler, lower atmosphere layers, intense thunderstorms formed and drenched the Hill Country. Occasionally, the area's mix of topography and prevailing winds let storms reform over the same locations. The onslaught of water hit downstream locations like a full-speed locomotive, but tonight's storms looked like they were moving through the area.

She watched the red and yellow waves traverse an area map and traced their progress with her fingertip. Forecasters called for a let-up, but they could be wrong.

When the sun rose, she texted her parents and conveyed her status. If things got rough, she would use the new bridge and join them in Houston.

"It's still dark outside," Ansel said.

"How about a cup of coffee?" she asked.

"Don't touch that single-cup contraption! It's an insult to caffeine addicts, and the local coffee shop doesn't open at a reasonable time." He strode into the kitchen stark naked. "I'll make the coffee."

His muscled ass caught her attention, but his confidence amused her. She set the apple onto the counter. "You don't trust me to make coffee?"

"Do you want to make it?" He ran his hands through his hair, turned, and braced his hands on the counter's edge. "By all means, have at it."

She eyed his morning erection. If she wanted to have at something, it offered more appeal than ground beans, but summoning the energy for sex seemed an impossible feat. Clearing her throat, she picked up her phone and noticed the remaining battery life was close to zero. Three messages from Lacey and waiting emails reminded her she had an architecture firm to run. "You make the brew. I've heard you're good at it."

He raised an eyebrow.

One more scan of his lithe muscles would lighten her day, and then she would bury her instincts beneath a mountain of responsibility. "I'll settle in on the couch, but I want to be on-site as soon as possible."

"The mural." He turned on the water. "I get it."

"Among other things." She sat on the leather couch and tucked up her legs. Holding her phone in a hand, she opened her email app, but she couldn't shake the dread pushing bile into her throat. Looking out the window, she watched rain slant through the glow of streetlights and splatter the windows. Trees heavy with new growth swayed in the wind, and she wondered when rainstorms would stop bothering her. She could look at dark clouds without thinking of Grant, but days of rain left her on edge.

Last night, when they discovered the State Route Bridge's closure, she had wanted to jump from Ansel's car and race across the concrete expanse toward the safety of her parents' ranch. The rising hills would hold her in their arms. Responsibility would keep her on track. She reached for the door handle, but the sheriff's flashing lights and Ansel's calm acceptance had tempered her impulse.

The adrenaline remained.

They said the storm that took Grant was a hundred-year flood. It shouldn't happen again.

The hand holding her phone shook. It could happen again. Tipping back her head, she closed her eyes and breathed deeply. The bungalow's flagstone flooring and leather sectionals could be cold, but the smell of Ansel's coffee grounded her senses. Somewhere in the room, lilies gave off a sweet scent. She breathed deeply.

The couch cushion shifted, and Ansel sat. "The coffee's ready."

"Thanks." She kept her eyes closed.

"Do you want cream?"

She shook her head.

"Whiskey?"

Opening her eyes, she turned her head and found him wearing a fresh set of clothes. Nudity might have swayed her impulse toward stress relief, but his red shirt looked good. "Maybe."

He smiled and sipped from his mug. "You're nervous about the rain."

"A little. Closing the bridge isn't an idle step. I checked the Cypress Creek gauges. Last night, it was at thirty feet."

"And when Grant died?"

She swallowed and ran a hand through her hair. The tangles hardly bothered her. "The flood stage peaked near forty feet. After the last flood, the US Geological Survey installed more gauges, but real-time data doesn't predict the future."

"If the authorities foresaw a threat, they would have started an evacuation. When county officials realized the severity of the last flood, they ordered first responders to start evacuations and prepare for rescue efforts. I scrolled through the local news alerts. I haven't seen anything. If the authorities sent out a mobile alert, Moeko would look out for me and knock on my door."

"The alerts use GPS to monitor location. You wouldn't have to rely on Moeko."

He nudged the coffee closer. "I know, but you seem to take a lot of comfort from the community's presence."

She laughed and picked up the cup. "They gossip from sunup to sundown, but they take care of their own. My parents couldn't stand another loss. If I so much as sneeze, then the mayor offers me a tissue, and his wife reports on whether I use it."

He pulled her legs into his lap.

His suntanned skin looked so dark against her pale legs. She needed to spend more time exercising her body instead of her fears.

"A bunch of state and local agencies collaborated on something called the Flood Decision Support

Toolbox. It's an interactive online app, and it provides maps and data regarding possible flood events. All night, I alternated between the toolbox, the weather forecast, and the real-time water gauges. I trust the authorities, but if my phone had run out of batteries, I would have slept better."

He stroked her leg.

"The USGS stream gauges don't lie. My head knows the water's going down, but I can't convince my heart."

"What do you need?" he asked.

She looked up from the tangle of their limbs and the images burned into her mind. "A distraction."

He unbuttoned the top button on his shirt.

Leaning forward, she stilled a hand but noticed his smile remained. "Let me go to work. It's how I handle stress. It's how I've coped."

Grasping her fingers, he raised them to his lips. "You're the boss."

The soft, warm kiss soothed her. "Does that mean I can have the keys to the building?"

He wrinkled his nose and dropped her hand. "Don't push your luck."

****

Holding her breath, Riley breezed past Ansel, flipped on the work lights, and headed straight through the old building. Removing tape from the thin plastic protecting the mural, she inventoried the artwork's integrity and let her shoulders drop. "All good."

Ansel walked up and peered over her right shoulder. "I like the animals the best."

She hip-checked him. "On your menu?"

Clasping a hand to his heart, he shuddered. "You

302

wound me."

"The quail…"

"Will be delicious." He grinned.

Shaking her head, she backed away from the opening and turned to face the building. Without a large format plotter, Nathan would have to work off her laptop. She pulled it from her bag.

The front door banged open.

Looking up, she saw Nathan enter. Raindrops sparkled on his dark-brown skin, and he held his smartphone in a hand. "Riley, you're here."

"I told you I would be."

Nathan glanced behind him, took a deep breath, and approached. "They closed the bridge last night. Aubrey was up half the night packing bags. It gave us a chance to talk." He frowned and looked up toward the damaged roof. A deep exhalation helped lower his shoulders, and he met Riley's gaze, opened his mouth, and then shook his head. "Aubrey's worried about the kids and the rising water. I think we're headed out of town, but I want to secure the restaurant site."

His withheld comment intrigued her, but she had limited social reserves. Forecasting mistakes could have lethal consequences. Her lip quivered. "The wa-ater's going down."

Gripping her shoulders, Nathan squeezed before he loosened his grip. "The main gauges agree, but the swollen creeks beg to differ. The ground can't hold much more water. Your parents already left?"

She puffed out her cheeks and slowly exhaled. "Yes."

"Come with us."

Ansel moved to her side.

She turned her head and met his gaze. "Nathan's leaving town, too."

"I heard."

Dropping his hands, Nathan nodded and jerked his head over his right shoulder. "Aubrey won't risk the kids' safety. She's next door unplugging electronics. The kids are at my parents' house, but we'll be gone within the hour."

"But evacuations haven't started," Riley said.

Ansel placed a hand at the small of her back.

"The experts have a toolbox." She swallowed. "They're monitoring the situation."

"They're also filling sandbags at the fire station."

Rubbing small circles against her back, Ansel waited.

Nathan held her gaze.

Sudden, intense anxiety flooded her system. She felt disorientated, and nausea roiled her stomach. Pulling her phone from her back pocket, she gripped it, but a hand shook, her heart raced, and her mouth went dry. Trying to breathe through the panic attack, she feared she might faint.

Ansel pulled her to his side and supported her weight. "Thanks for the heads-up, Nathan. Don't worry about the site. We'll lock up and follow you out of town. Riley's SUV can handle a little street water, and we'll be long gone before anything threatens the town."

She managed a weak nod. He was right, and voluntary evacuation was a calm, sensible response. "Can I borrow a phone charger?"

Nathan nodded, then retrieved one from his truck.

She plugged in her phone.

"Nathan?" Aubrey walked into the building,

carrying a shopping bag brimming with electronics. "It's all backed up, but I won't risk it."

Riley stared. Aubrey's short, light-brown curls hung limp, and her wide, brown eyes looked bloodshot. Believing her friend had been up half the night, she wondered how bad she looked, too.

Reloading scientific websites calmed her unease, but Aubrey's exhaustion grounded her fears. They grew up together in Cypress Creek. Grant's death hurt, but Riley pieced together the sequence of events from news coverage and anecdotes. Aubrey had weathered the flood, and her fear of a repeat disaster was obvious.

If the conditions had shaken Aubrey's confident, easy smile and cracked her sleek, colorful image, then Riley knew better than to fight reality. She would follow Aubrey's lead and depart as soon as possible. She pulled Aubrey to the side. "You okay?"

"I don't know which way is up," Aubrey said. "Cypress Creek was supposed to be my refuge, but ever since I moved home, I've been on edge. Last night, I went to my parents' house, sat in my momma's kitchen over a plate of cold food, and told her everything I've done lately. It all came out."

Riley shifted her weight and listened.

"I've never cried like that in my entire life, but she patted my back and let me wail like a ten-year-old who broke a window." She wiped away a tear. "No wonder she let me go on. The things she's seen. Everything could be worse."

"She's your mom," Riley said. "She loves you."

"I thought messing around with JJ was a game. Nobody knew. Turns out, half the town knows, and so does my husband." She chewed a nail. "What does that say about me? People accept my bad decisions?"

"It says you're an adult, and you're allowed space to figure out your life." The words seemed to lodge in Riley's throat. Messing around might be a selfish mistake, but it wasn't the end of the world. "Everyone makes bad decisions."

"You make the affair sound like a pint of ice cream."

Riley wet her lips and refrained from passing judgment on Aubrey's choice of bedmates. "Well, if you and Nathan can iron out your differences, that's all it has to be, right?" Living in Austin broadened her perspectives. If you met enough people and listened, you developed empathy toward the human condition. If she could apply that empathy toward Aubrey's choices, could she give herself a break, too?

"I can't keep laying my problems at other people's feet." Aubrey wiped away a tear. "I chewed my nails to the quick last night, but nervous energy and fear brought out my confession. Nathan and I stopped seeing each other as individuals because we were too proud to admit our needs. That cowardice has to stop."

"I've never viewed you as a coward."

Aubrey squared her shoulders. "This town needs heroes. Maybe we should stay."

Riley reached toward her. "No! Don't be a hero. Take care of yourself."

Aubrey cupped her right shoulder. "I won't take risks. I have kids to protect, but how many times can we fight to live here? Maybe we should relocate."

"We'd miss you," Riley said.

"It won't come to that." Nathan folded Aubrey under his right arm. "We'll keep shaping the lives we want in Cypress Creek."

Riley chewed her lip and considered her determination. Could she make the same pledge? For most of her life, her fathers provided everything she needed. Their power stopped at saving Grant, but their work ethic and love set an example she strived to follow. Aubrey was always the impulsive counter to her well-thought-out schemes, but she assumed her friend found her happiness returning to Cypress Creek.

Her affair with Kyle and her history with Ansel said otherwise. Distance made the heart grow stronger, but separation highlighted flaws. The older she and Aubrey grew, the more her friend seemed like the type of person who would do anything, or anyone, to advance her objectives. If entitlement justified the harm she inflicted on people, then the rising creek had something to say about her living life on its terms. "I don't think we have any rights to this area. Judging risks and making choices are our options."

Aubrey looked at Nathan and squeezed his hand.

He returned the gesture and smiled.

His response looked so forlorn, Riley wondered if his bravado hid a broken heart. Who could say which person stepped away from the marriage first? Spurned lovers had a litany of complaints, and each justification summoned a prior fight. She pulled Aubrey close and squeezed out a hug. "You'll pick up the kids?"

Aubrey looked over her right shoulder. "They're waiting."

No matter what lapses of judgment the pair committed, they united to protect their children, and she recognized that bond. Its strength seared through her fears, and she nodded. "Go. We have this place covered."

Dropping her husband's hand, Aubrey stepped forward. "Just leave now with us. Family means nobody gets left behind, and you're part of my family, too. We can rebuild this whole damn town, but we can't replace the people."

Riley wrapped her arms around her friend. "I'm right behind you." She gave Aubrey a light squeeze and released her. "Just go, already. You look like shit. You'll probably scare the kids into quiet time."

Nathan laughed. "They'll be so busy with their tablets they won't notice where we're going until we arrive." He shook the remaining water droplets off his shoulders. "Oh, to be young and oblivious."

Ansel cleared his throat.

The two men exchanged glances.

She doubted either courted obliviousness. Despite differing physical descriptions and differing professions, they plowed through obstacles and pursued success with single-minded determination. If their quests left scars, time would give them room to heal.

"Let's go," Aubrey said.

Nathan nodded and escorted her toward the door.

Ansel shoved his hands in his jean pockets. "Ready to clear out, too?"

She took a deep breath. "Absolutely not. We can't let the mural get wet."

His jaw dropped

"I think we should cut it off the walls and bring it with us. If Mimi can do it, we can, too. It won't take more than an hour or two. We'll be gone before lunchtime."

Rocking back on his heels, he worked his jaw.

"This is rich."

She hobbled past. "Don't say a word to anyone. We'll load the canvas into my SUV. Whatever doesn't fit will go on the second-story floor."

"Riley…"

Turning, she made eye contact.

"You're injured. The building will hold. The artwork survived the last flood."

She turned and considered the space. It would come to life as a new restaurant, but it needed help meeting the future head-on. "The wood paneling protected the mural. You're right, this site never flooded, but we've left our mark, and we've exposed everything. What if the water crests higher than last time?"

"What if the water keeps going down?"

"The gauges aren't crystal balls. Look how much damage Mimi did to the remaining work. Losing entire sections will destroy the artist's legacy. We can't sacrifice the bottom portion to floodwaters and mold. It comes with us."

"But your ankle." He pointed and raised his eyebrows.

She flexed the tendons and felt stiffness, but in the grand scheme of things, the joint would hold. Minor inconveniences were little annoyances she could handle. They toughened her resolve during a Hill Country childhood, and she carried the resilience into adulthood.

Faced with a looming disaster, art and preservation mattered. Life and limb mattered…just not her limbs. She'd already failed once, and she wouldn't fail again. "My ankle's fine. Help me find a pair of shears in

Nathan's toolbox." Twenty minutes later, she held shears and searched for canvas seams near the mural's base. She called Saunders for advice and ignored his conniption fit. Faced with two options, he endorsed removing the mural.

Conservation involved techniques, treatments, and repairs, but to get anywhere, a conservator needed art. She would do the brute work of saving it and leave the intricate marriage of art and science to the professionals. Taking a deep breath, she made her first cut and felt tears gather. Blinking past the wetness, she held the canvas in place.

Ansel rolled it from the bottom and carried it toward the door.

He was a good sport. He had better things to do than babysit her whims, but he carried the canvas like a kettlebell at a high-end gym. She should have found the time to savor him, the coffee, and the apple. Instead, she came here to salvage what she could. Her stomach rumbled, and her phone vibrated. Pulling out the device, she read the notification for a Flood Watch.

Flooding or flash flooding was possible in her area. The alert warned her to pay attention to changing weather and flood conditions. She should prepare to move to higher ground. In an instant, her life could turn upside down. Resting her forehead against the exposed plaster, she closed her eyes. "No shit."

Before the installation of new flood gauges upstream of Cypress Creek, officials relied on a network of local ranchers and property owners to relay water level changes. Urgent voices marked the creek's progress up tree trunks, bridge supports, and local landmarks.

Technology negated the town's dependence on their expertise, but she had no doubt the neighborhood watch was still in full effect. The summer G died, the river rose higher than the old-timers had ever seen. They wouldn't let it happen again.

"Riley June," Mikey said. "What the hell are you still doing in town?"

Her cheeks flushed. Turning, she held the shears and swallowed.

Mikey stood in the entryway with his hands braced on his hips.

"Thinking of the future."

He stomped a foot. "Think of yourself."

Experience let the admonition roll off like water off a duck's back, but Mikey was really more like a swan. He threw around his celebrity status. When people challenged him, he hissed, but he ultimately retreated. She stuck out her chin. "Forget me. What are you doing here?"

Working his jaw, he remained quiet.

"You don't even live here." She waved her right hand. "Shoo! Get in your truck and beat it. If I needed your help, I would have called."

"Shoo?" He cocked his head. "Did you just shoo me?"

"Did you try to pull me off a mountain in a rainstorm? I have a reason for being here. What's yours?"

Letting his boot slide back and forth against the floor, he looked down and took a deep breath. "Mimi needs help. She called me last night, and she's worried about her cats and her inventory. I told her I would swing by this morning and see what I could do."

"The bridge's closed from my parents' house," she said. "How did you even get here?"

He looked up and blushed.

She narrowed her gaze.

"I'm not celibate." He cleared his throat. "I, uh, met someone staying at a short-term vacation rental. She invited me over for a drink. I never left town."

She rolled her eyes. He thrived on attention, and the crowd provided it in spades. When they were together, her life revolved around his needs, and she struggled to find the space to breathe. Whichever long-legged, honky-tonk groupie had lured him into bed could have him. They had history, and she wished him the best, but he could spare her the details. "Good for you. Where's she now?"

"Uh. On her way back to Oklahoma, I guess."

She turned to the mural and cast her voice above the rumbling town drama. "Follow her. If you don't leave, you're liable to get yourself killed."

"Do you care?"

"I do, but you need to stop playing hero and focus on what Mimi needs. The Boot Byre has flood insurance. Catch the cats and leave town."

Someone cleared his throat.

She turned and spied Ansel. If he heard half of what she said, he would urge her to follow her own advice, but flood insurance excluded priceless works of art. He could leave at any time, but he would stick by her. The implications floored her. A man who could carry a grudge for twenty years could also keep a candle lit. She didn't need fine dining and exotic ingredients to feel love. She needed someone to hold her through the night and stand by her side.

As soon as they left Cypress Creek, she would tell him she wanted to see him again. She might not be ready for love, but she was open to it.

"There's a line of cars headed out of town." Ansel climbed down from a window ledge. "They're moving slower than an expeditor with the shits."

Hearing the unease in his voice, she straightened. "People are evacuating?"

"The smart ones," Mikey said.

Staring, she wondered what that made her.

"All right, I'm leaving," Mikey said. "You'd be smart to leave, too."

She clapped his shoulder. "Thanks for the warning. You're a good friend."

Mikey nodded, turned, and bumped into Ansel's left shoulder.

Ansel absorbed the blow.

"Sorry," Mikey muttered.

Walking past, Ansel shook his head. "Safe travels."

She made eye contact and caught his smile. "What?"

"You're finally done with that clown?" Ansel winked. "I think you like me."

"I like you naked." She returned his wink. "When we get ourselves out of this mess, we can discuss the rest."

"Deal." He hefted another roll of canvas and followed Mikey toward the dreary skies that refused to stop dumping rain.

Feeling her phone vibrate again, she checked the battery power. Calls from her parents, her assistant, and her friends whittled away the last battery reserves, but she let the calls go to voice mail and snapped the shears. "Let's do this!"

The empty building echoed with her proclamation.

Car horns honked, and brakes screeched.

Swallowing, she continued her work.

Halfway through the extraction, sweat dripped down her back. She would take a blizzard over blanketing humidity and unending rain. Massachusetts held a lot of charm. Her phone powered down, and she ignored the warning to focus on the panel sporting the woman and her pot of beans. She refused to let today be the day Mother Nature obliterated the woman's historical presence.

Ansel tossed her a bottle of water, opened his, and downed the contents. He set the empty plastic on the worktable and pulled his phone out of his pocket. "Flood warning. Flooding is occurring upstream. Avoid low-lying areas and review evacuation plans. Seek higher ground."

"I can't work any faster." She set the bottle at her feet and considered how much work remained. Ignoring the seams and blindly cutting the canvas would result in a frayed disaster. If she had any doubts about her methodology, she could look at the mess Mimi left behind. "What does the radar say?"

"What's the difference between weather and climate?" He waited for a beat. "You can't weather a tree, but you can climate."

"Seriously?" She lowered the shears and stared. "You're making jokes?"

Closing the distance, he gripped a hand holding the shears. "I'm working my ass off to save a cowboy muralist's forgotten canvas because it means something to you."

"I know." His dedication registered, and she swallowed. He smelled like sweet sage, fresh sweat, and aged wood, but he came into her life like a whirlwind. Submitting to his needs went against everything that kept her sane in recent years. She tightened her grasp on the tool. "Thank you for everything you've done. We're making progress, but you can take your car and go."

"Let's get in the car and listen to the local news station for the latest information. If the warning expires, we can come inside and finish the work."

"The SUV might get stuck in high water."

He released his grip. "Then why the hell are we loading the mural into the back? We should move to higher ground and stay there. Did the public safety officials mandate an evacuation?"

Her legs shook. "I don't know. My phone's dead."

"Did you check on your neighbors? Has Rickie Hays evacuated? Mimi?"

The gray-haired proprietor lived above his silver jewelry store. He could dump his inventory into a duffle bag, but he had to be willing to go. Mimi could rot among her boots, but the store cats deserved a fighting chance. At least, Riley could catch them and bring them to the old hotel for higher ground. She cleared her throat. "You're right. Let's make sure the street's clear, and then we'll go. I don't want to risk lives."

He held out his palm. "All righty then."

She handed over the shears. "But if the forecast changes..."

Taking the clippers from her, he pocketed them. "We'll finish cutting down the mural. You think Nathan will adjust his bid to reflect our contributions?"

"I haven't seen the bid yet. It could be expensive."

He scanned the cavernous workspace. Wind flapped the roof covering. Critical expectations echoed between the rafters. "The bid's not what worries me."

She wiped her palms on her jeans and headed toward the front door. Pushing it wide, she found cloudy skies and a line of cars inching toward the new bridge. Red taillights flashed, and water flowed along Gristmill Road. Judging the water's depth against the car tires, six inches of floodwater filled the road. Stepping off the elevated walkway, she let water soak her shoes. Its brazen chill accentuated the perspiration drying on her skin. Retracting her foot, she rubbed her arms. "How long has the water been up?"

"About twenty minutes."

The moving cars sent ripples through the swiftly flowing, light-brown stream. Public service admonishments filled her mind. *Turn around, don't drown!* An onslaught of recalled information weakened her knees and paralyzed her.

He shifted the rolled canvas to his right shoulder and took her hand. Stepping off the walkway, he let the water circle his leather boots. "Riley, let's go. I don't want you to panic, but it's still raining north of here. More water's coming."

She stepped forward, but history called her back.

He tugged her hand. "Forget the mural. It's not worth your life." Between balancing his load and moving her forward, his balance teetered. He released his hold.

Caught between possibilities, she craned her neck and checked for lights in the small business lining the road. Every outlet remained dark. Her family left yesterday, and Aubrey left this morning. Riley and Ansel might be the last idiots in Cypress Creek. They should climb into the SUV and join the slow-moving evacuation. In twenty minutes, they would cross the new bridge and climb the limestone hills toward higher ground and guaranteed safety. "Okay."

Lifting their clasped hands to his lips, he pressed a light kiss against her fingers. "I doubted you would leave."

She met his gaze. "Another loss would destroy my dads."

Frowning, he lowered his hand. "You're not worried about yourself?"

"No." The cold admission stole her breath. "Compared to eight billion people living on this planet, I'm just a drop in the ocean."

"A drop in the ocean?" Shaking his head, he tightened his hold and pulled her toward the SUV. "Well, hell, I might as well trade you for a blow-up doll. I'm just a cook. Have you tried Steak *Frites*? It's a little better than a chicken sandwich." He tossed the canvas panel into the rear storage area and slammed down the liftgate. "Get in the car. I'm driving."

She frowned. "You're driving?"

"If you think you're insignificant, I'd rather have you in the passenger seat."

Standing beside the vehicle, she rubbed away the chills racing up her arms and considered the limestone edifice that survived decades of development, a raging fire, and human greed. Drawing inspiration from its persistence, she focused on being a survivor, too. Her laptop bag sat on the worktable. Without a strong Wi-Fi signal to facilitate uploads, the bag held the only records of the designs she and Ansel dreamed up. Saving them would avoid weeks of rework and free up her time to help the town rebuild. "Give me a minute."

"It's time to go." He started the SUV's engine.

Ignoring the rumbling prompt, she headed into the building to keep her priorities in line.

Chapter Twenty-One

Ansel watched Riley rush into the old hotel and exhaled. He'd have to lure her away from the mural. If she balked, then he doubted the SUV could accommodate another canvas roll. He would find a way. One day in a person's life couldn't define it, but one woman had upended his life. His body temperature skyrocketed, and his ribs ached. For a moment, he felt like laughing at the improbability, but he held his breath.

Aubrey's betrayal should have taught him a lesson. Wiping wet hair from his eyes, he scanned the storefronts. Aubrey's syrupy interior design business sat shuttered against the storm. She might be the queen of throw pillows, but she had her priorities in check. The kids came first, and the adults followed in their wake.

For decades, her unfaithfulness left behind a bitter, metallic aftertaste, but the lingering memory had an outsized influence. He came to Cypress Creek to spite an ex-girlfriend, but twenty years dimmed the allure of exacting vengeance. Instead of giving her the middle finger, he should thank her for bringing Riley into his life and hire her to redesign his San Antonio mansion. Hell, she might get a kick out of sprucing up the yacht.

Making peace with Aubrey would free up his emotions, but securing Riley's affections wouldn't be so easy. He no longer viewed her as an uptight, well-manicured woman with shadows beneath her eyes. Lost in the midst of her work, she was as passionate as any creator. In his arms, she chased her pleasure with headless abandon.

No wonder she found herself in Mexico, downing tequila shots. She craved sensory experiences, and without Grant's death to temper her appetites, she would have gotten her kicks from Paul and moved on with her life. The woman had zero interest in tranquility.

He couldn't let her move on without telling her how he felt; he had a feeling twenty years with her would never be enough. Given enough time, he could court and woo her, but Mother Nature had other plans.

He considered telling Riley about the changing weather conditions, but fear paralyzed her. When he relayed the flood warning, he left out the purple bands moving over the radar screen.

Fifteen inches of water had fallen upstream, and some riparian devil kept the rain bands locked in position. He could deal with the slow-moving thunderstorms drenching the area, but the upstream deluge forming and reforming over the same area spelled trouble. Replanted floodplains and cleared tributaries could slow walls of water headed downstream, but the water flood would eventually hit Cypress Creek.

Best case scenario, the overflow spilled into valleys and dissipated. Worst-case scenario, debris clogged waterways, roadways collapsed, and a hulking wall of water slammed into the quaint, Texas resort town. He aimed to be on the other side of the bridge before the water arrived.

Checking the side-view mirror and his watch, he waited for Riley to return, but nothing moved. He shook his head, left the engine running, and climbed out of the SUV. "Riley June Golding!"

Thunder rumbled in the distance.

Shielding his eyes, he stomped toward the building to find Riley and get her to safety. When things went to shit in his restaurants, he trusted his management team and his culinary abilities, but nobody had his back in the Hill Country. He climbed the steps leading to the old hotel. "Riley, I'll paint you a new mural. I'd endow a whole art wing dedicated to Buckey's legacy. Get in the car!"

The work lights flickered, and the city power failed.

Plunged into dreariness, he caught the glow of a flashlight in Mimi's Boot Byre. If he found Riley over there, he would throw her over his right shoulder and carry her kicking and screaming out of town. A mural was one thing, but if she had a thing for boots, she could have a new pair every day of the year. He considered the alleyway separating the two buildings and his plan of attack. She went inside the old hotel. He expected to find her there. Mimi could fend for herself.

The street water rose above his boots and flooded his socks. He peered through the rain and spotted a dark, looming tide surging through Kyle Road's Pizza Joint and Brewpub. Rising water toppled chairs and spilled into the roadway.

Drivers honked car horns and split from the flow of traffic, searching for shortcuts.

Vehicles stalled and occupants unbuckled their seat

belts. Seeing no escape, they fled their automobiles and stormed surrounding buildings carrying small children, pets, and precious mementos.

Water sloshing from his boots, he pounded the steps leading into the hotel. "Riley?" He slammed the door at his back, grabbed her bag, and slung it over his left shoulder. "Riley! Get upstairs. Now!"

"I am upstairs!" Backlit by midday sunlight, she waved from the second floor. "I'm already up here."

Closing his eyes, he took a deep breath. The old stone building stayed dry during the last flood. He might be in for a long day, but he and Riley could take shelter and wait for the water to recede. His muscles grew heavy, and he gripped the newly constructed railing and hauled himself to the second floor. Life, like fine recipes, could collapse in an instant.

The moment he saw the storms stall on the radar, he should have laced Riley's coffee with barbiturates and bundled her lovely ass into the car. He was too old for this stress. Summiting the stairs, he scanned the second story.

She stood at the window. Clouds rolled past the opening and cast her in silhouette.

He waited for her chest to move. Every muscle tensed, he let the enormity of his love for her tear through his consciousness until his clenched hands shook at his sides.

She sighed.

He gasped for breath, ran a hand over his face, and wiped away the wet evidence of his fears. Regrets could drown a man, but hope gave him a destination. He lowered her bag to the floor, wrapped his arms behind her, and buried his face in her hair.

She shuddered and pressed against his chest. "I'm sorry I stalled out."

"It's fine. We're fine." He stroked her hair.

"The water's rising, Ansel. We're not fine. It's too late, isn't it?"

After a minute of memorizing her scent, he lifted his head and followed her gaze. The water's momentum sent the heavy, empty vehicles bobbing along Gristmill Road like a child's playthings. Foot by foot, the creek rose, and buoyant vehicles crashed into each other and the surrounding buildings.

Riley covered her mouth. "The vehicle occupants will die!"

In their haste to swamp the town, the churning, brown floodwaters seemed to agree.

He made soothing sounds. "People are resilient."

A cypress tree crashed onto the roadway leading from town. Its towering branches rested on a building across the street, and a large, empty truck smashed sideways into the barrier.

Before the tree could break, a second vehicle magnified the jam. Within minutes, the blocked chute prevented vehicles from floating downstream. It also trapped Cypress Creek's fleeing residents amid a charming patchwork of wooden walkways and elevated porches.

Evacuees broke windows and fled to the surrounding shops.

"They'll be okay," he said. "They'll find higher ground."

She rubbed a hand over her mouth.

Her silence worried him. He gripped her shoulders and pulled her to his chest. "How high did the water peak last time?"

She pointed toward the last shop and a dark, black line painted along the building's perimeter. "Midway up Jed's."

He took the restaurant's racing stripe for a cosmetic accent, but its symbolism struck a chord. Every day, Cypress Creek's residents walked past the innocuous mark and shuddered at its implications. Tourists visiting the town would never know their heartache.

"I didn't think it would happen again," she said. "The storms frightened me, but I didn't think lightning could strike twice." Turning in his arms, she looked up. "Maybe this town is cursed."

"It's not." He rubbed her back and made soothing sounds. "Storm's stalled upstream."

She raised her head. "When?"

"This morning. I didn't want to alarm you. I know how much the mural means."

Closing her eyes, she shuddered and exhaled. "I don't blame you for the omission. You're not from here. You didn't know."

He stilled his hand. "I should have told you, shouldn't I?"

"Yeah." She cleared her throat. "We could have made the decision together."

"Why does that statement sound so final?"

Toying with a button on his shirt, she sighed. "Computer models are good at broad, general predictions, but they misfire with small watersheds like Cypress Creek. The new river-level gauges will let forecasters build a historical record, but their precise, real-time information about rainfall and rising waterways are no match for local intuition. If I'd seen those upstream storms stall on the radar screen, I'd have known to run. Everyone in Cypress Creek is an amateur meteorologist."

"But Grant stayed."

"Grant knew better, too." She pulled away and smoothed his shirt. "So does Mimi, and she's still next door herding cats. Literally. I saw her flashlight and waved her toward a window. She looked scared, but at least, she's in the hayloft."

"That's why you're upstairs?" he asked.

"We've seen springtime floods, but the one that killed Grant was the worst on record. I can't imagine the destruction this one will bring. The people trapped in their cars." She shuddered. "I know them. Even if they whisper behind my back, I know them."

"You sent Mikey to Ohio."

She smiled. "Oklahoma."

He laughed. "Either way, you told him to leave before you were willing to evacuate. You're a good friend."

"I know, but what am I supposed to do now?" She slid her back down the wall and sank to her heels. "Throw a rope out the window and rescue people from their cars? Call 911? I don't even have a working cell phone."

"Do you have a rope?" he asked.

She scanned the upper floor.

A helicopter buzzed overhead.

The logjam of vehicles might destroy historical edifices, but as long as it held and the cars floated, the vehicles' occupants had time.

Riley, on the other hand, looked ready to fall apart.

She could be literal and precise, but he respected her hidden vulnerability and her strong dedication to this town. Sinking to his heels, he waited for her to look up.

Wetting her lips, she sighed.

He took her hand. "Riley, you're an architect. I'm a chef. We're doing the best we can. We'll stick together and wait for rescue, or we'll wait for the water to subside. The power grid's knocked out, and cell phones aren't working. It'll be a scary ride, but we'll be fine. We'll keep each other warm. You can tell me all about Grant and your regrets in life."

She laughed.

"You don't have regrets?"

"I regret not meeting you on a dating app."

He cupped her cheek. "I'm a celebrity chef, Riley. I don't use dating apps."

Raising her eyebrows, she waited.

He dropped his hand. "Fine, I use them, but I call myself Paul."

She smiled. "Of course, you do."

About to remark on her stalwart coping skills, he saw her smile tremble. Before he could stop himself, he settled by her side, pulled her into his lap, and held her tightly against his chest. "Shhh, we'll do everything we can to help, okay? There isn't much we can do right now, but help's coming. We just have to ride out the flood."

"I just…"

He cupped the back of her head and leaned back so he could look her in the eyes. "Want everyone to be okay?"

She nodded.

"Not in your power."

She gasped and strained against his embrace.

He tightened his hold. He was tempted to push her stray hair behind her ears and cup her cheeks, but he refrained and met her fear head-on. "The only things you can control are your actions. Your intentions matter, but adults are accountable for their own shit. I'm here because I want to be here. Kids need love and security. Adults need love and honesty"—he cleared his throat—"also, money helps."

She laughed and laid her head against his chest. "I heard you."

"Glad we had this pep talk."

"I meant earlier," she said. "You said you could find easier women to love."

He exhaled. "But you're worth it."

With her arms wrapped around him and her head on his chest, she was close enough that he could press his lips against hers and show her how he felt. Instead, he held her tight, leaned his head against the wall, and listened to the eerie rumble of rushing water.

He knew her taste and the heady allure of a long, intoxicating kiss, but he reveled in the feeling of comforting her. Last night, while she tossed and turned, he held back and waited for her to signal her needs.

Instead of planning a menu, he found himself admiring her qualities. Convenience sat at the bottom of the list, but the list was so long, he hardly cared. "Should we write love poems on the walls? A hundred years from now, someone might find them and preserve them. We could be Romeo and Juliet. Isn't that romantic?"

She pulled away from his chest and shook her

head. "That won't help me feel better. It's a romantic tragedy. They die."

He scratched his beard. "Huh. Who knew?"

"Most of the global population."

He smoothed a hand up her leg to just above her knee. "Are you saying you don't like grand acts? I shouldn't name my restaurant or my yacht after you?"

She shifted her fingers through his hair. "You have a yacht?"

He laughed and pressed a kiss to her palm. Her touch captivated him. Envisioning her stretched over a teak deck chair might be enough to get him through the coming hours. It might also give him a raging hard-on. His romantic skills might require honing, but he knew better than to use sex as a distraction. On the other hand... he worked his jaw. He was good with his hands.

"Let's see. I'm sitting on the floor of an old hotel, my legs draped over your lap, while my town floods. Again. You're an excellent distraction. This is much better than sitting in a traffic j-jam."

Her voice wavered, and he cupped her cheek. "I'm here. Tell me a story. Grant must have gotten you in trouble a time or two. Mikey must have drunk too much and peed his pants. If I'm spending time in Cypress Creek, I want to know the town's dirty secrets."

"Because you're a gossip?"

He snorted. "I prefer earnest citizen."

She tilted her head. "I live in Austin."

He smiled. "And I live in San Antonio, but here we are in the middle ground. Did I win you over with my charm?"

She raised her eyebrows. "It certainly wasn't your culinary skills."

Slapping a hand to his chest, he stared. "You wound me."

She wet her lips. "I've eaten at your San Antonio restaurant, but it didn't turn me into a stalker. I had to meet you in Cypress Creek, when I needed you the most. Also, you look good naked. We just mixed up the order of our acquaintance."

He waggled his brows and opened his arms wide. "Consider me an all-you-can-eat buffet, Vegas-style"

"If I wanted sex, I'd straddle your lap and compliment you." She rolled her eyes. "Men are too easy."

"Don't hold yourself to a strict standard. Be easy."

She snorted and pressed a hand to his chest. "You're not *that* easy. I could tell you how ridiculously inappropriate this is, but I want you to hold me. Will you do that?"

"I can do that." He adjusted his seat and settled his hands at her waist. "Holding you is the best part of my day."

"Is it?" She sighed against his chest. "Ansel, if anything happens, I want you to know I kind of loved you the moment I met you. I was just a stranger at a gas station, but you had such a willingness to help me. The world needs more people like you, but I need you more."

Taking a hand in his, he kissed her knuckles. "Are you telling me you love me, Riley? Is that what you're doing? Declaring yourself while half of Cypress Creek is under water?"

"No." She looked up, met his gaze, and then stared at the raindrops. "I know my timing's terrible. We can do this tomorrow."

He turned her chin away from the unfolding disaster. Raindrops fell like pebbles after a mudslide, but he wouldn't let her tears follow. "I'm okay with today. Any day of the week, you can say you love me. Wake me in the middle of the night and shout it in my ear. Show up at my restaurant, climb on a table, and declare yourself at the top of your lungs. Have you considered a tattoo?"

She snorted and laid her head against his chest. "That would make an impact."

"*You* make an impact. You helped me realize I need to be truer to myself. Instead of giving customers exactly what they want, I'm returning to my favorite recipes and the communities that shaped me." He took a deep breath. "All of them."

Stroking his chest, she exhaled and nestled against his warmth. "This restaurant build-out has more to do with overcoming your doubts than sticking your success to an ex-girlfriend. You have so much to celebrate. I can't wait to see the finale."

"Will you be my first restaurant customer?" he asked. "Tell me if I get it right? I could use an honest review."

Sighing, she flicked his ear.

"Ouch!" He rubbed away the brief pain and admitted he became exactly who Aubrey told him to become. He might as well get a tattoo honoring Steak *Frites*. At least Riley saw through his veneer.

She sighed again.

Her exhalation sounded like defeat, but he didn't need her dissecting his insecurities. For twenty years, he turned toward critics and customers for affirmation, but trusting his intuition offered the greatest rewards.

The moment he produced a quality dish, he recognized it, and the flash of inspiration fired his soul.

Riley did, too, but he doubted he deserved her. When Aubrey's exposé highlighted his weak connection to the Pine Ridge Indian Reservation, she questioned his restaurant's authenticity, but she also gutted his identity. He could never be more than a tourist in other people's lives.

He wasn't a member of the Oglala Lakota tribe, but he loved and respected Eagle Hawk. If honoring the old man and his life lessons made him a weak man, he would gladly take the emotional hit, but he would embrace his experiences.

Until he figured out what he needed, he should go slowly with Riley. She would find her equilibrium after losing Grant, but he also had to reclaim his experiences.

Looking back on his life, he saw how experiencing loss and acceptance defined his reactions. His biological heritage, reservation adolescence, and professional success shaped him, but Riley deserved to see the finished product before he asked her to commit.

He stroked her hair. Would she embrace the final outcome? If the Cypress Creek restaurant failed, he would absorb the loss, but the venue could reflect his life. Hell, he might even name a cocktail after Aubrey. Losing Riley would sear his soul.

"I can hear you thinking. It'll be a fusion menu."

He laughed and shifted his position. In the culinary world, that term carried so many negative connotations it should be banned, but he understood her intent.

"Fusion makes things stronger."

He stroked her back. "Is that so?"

She nodded against him.

"I'll give diners the options to eat what they recognize or to experience the diversity nature provides. Dinner at Cypress Creek might not be as luxurious as meals at my other restaurants, but it will open eyes and honor the area's native offerings. I might be a bit of a magpie, but I've discovered plenty of treasures."

"Local sourcing is a tall order for this town. How much can you do with a prickly pear cactus?"

"Sioux Falls isn't a metropolis, either. Cypress Creek will be the same restaurant I opened twenty years ago, but it will be richer and more complex."

"Like you."

He captured her right hand and held it tight. The sincerity in her voice told him how much she understood. Coupled with her passion, he feared releasing her hand or her heart. "I hope I've aged well. Given all the people who've poured their love into me, I can't do anything less than honor them."

Chapter Twenty-Two

Secure in Ansel's arms, Riley blocked out the water damaging Cypress Creek's businesses and homes. As brown water reached higher marks, the toll grew more ominous. Cypress Creek's residents could only bear so much.

An hour ago, her SUV and the hotel's roll-off container joined the jam. She watched the air space inside the vehicle and worried about the mural segments. Would they survive their downriver float? The car's blaring alarm annoyed her. "Why won't it just give up?"

"It's resilient. I doubt the roadster put up such a fight."

"I'm sorry." She laid a hand on his arm, but she gazed at the pileup. She should have left the mural intact. Pride let her cut down the canvas sections, but her impact on the world hovered near zero. Ansel thought her stubborn perseverance was a good thing, but it could have killed him. "That car meant a lot."

He pressed a kiss to her hair. "It's a car. I can replace it."

When the rushing water slowed, she let herself breathe. Residents sat on rooftops and peered from second-story windows. She waved, signaled her safety, and watched for signs of distress. When the water retreated, first responders would arrive, and the residents would shelter at the local emergency response center.

"Is there anything you need?" Ansel asked. "Popcorn? Snacks."

The joke triggered her smile, but shifting her weight, she avoided thinking about her base needs.

Ansel turned her from the window and rubbed her arms. "Really, Riley. Are you okay? Do you want to talk about Grant? Is there anything I can do to help?"

"I need to pee." The admission heated her cheeks. "Get lost or turn your back."

He laughed, dropped her arms, and strode toward the opposite wall. "Nature calls."

His absence gave her room to breathe. He might enjoy peeing from a rear window, but she refused to bare her ass for her neighbors. Pacing the second floor, she doubted the hotel's prior occupants left behind a chamber pot, a mop bucket, or a forgotten houseplant.

"All done?" he called.

"Not even close!" She spied her bag near the stairs and grinned. Small miracles would get her through this disaster. Thanking Ansel for bringing her bag upstairs would be next on her priority list. "Keep your back turned."

"I've seen you naked!"

"Not on the toilet. I've known you for less than a week."

"You're ridiculous. Also, you don't have a toilet. What's your plan?"

At any moment, her bladder might burst. Pacing the floor accentuated the pressure. "Just stay over there for a moment?"

"No problem."

She eyed the stairway. Creeping downstairs, she gauged the waterline. It looked steady, and the building's walls blocked any chop. Choosing a step above the flood, she dropped her pants and relieved her bladder. Her contribution to the damage hardly mattered. The cleanup crew would need bleach and cleaning supplies to scour the building. Fans and steady electricity would help dry the walls.

The mural—she closed her eyes and wished the water would swallow her—was at least two feet under water. Spending the morning hacking it from the hotel's walls was not only pointless, but it endangered her and Ansel's lives. Her abandoned water bottle bobbed beside the floating worktable. What had she been thinking?

"Riley?" Ansel asked. "Is your ankle okay?"

She stood and secured her pants. "I'm done."

"Want some toilet paper?"

Frowning, she looked up.

He held her bag and dangled it from his fingers. "I'm sure you can part with a few printouts. Tissues stashed in the side pocket? You let me know what you're willing to sacrifice."

"How can you laugh at a time like this?" Climbing the stairs, she took the bag and dropped it against the second-floor wall. "You should be in San Antonio, sipping a beer while you watch this flood unfold on the news."

He steadied her shoulders. "I'd rather be with you."

"The day I met you, I thought you were a sunbaked road warrior. Then I worried you were someone who bought a surfboard and used it once, or you wore string bracelets to ward off the evil eye like some pseudo-

Jewish folk enthusiast."

"Really?" He eyed his jewelry. "That's what you thought?"

"I mean, reality was *far* worse."

Jerking up his chin, he stared.

"You're too good, Ansel. You see beauty in the world, and you share it with other people. I shouldn't have pulled you into this mess."

"I want to be here…with you."

His lagging statement, as sweet and unaffected as sun-warmed strawberries, rang true. She could brush off his raging declarations, but his simple sincerity cracked her resolve. The resulting outflow, a tangle of love and self-doubt, stole her breath. She swallowed and faced her reservations. "Even if I ruined the mural and put your life at risk?"

He ran a hand through his hair. "Riley, did you flood the town?"

"Maybe?"

He rolled his eyes. "My life insurance is pretty impressive, but Eagle Hawk's not ready to collect it. We'll get through this mess, okay?"

She nodded and silently looked away. As soon as the excitement wore off, he would lose his good humor and return to reality. His willingness to help broke through her reserves, but adrenaline mainlined their feelings for each other. When she said the world needed more people like him, she meant it, but as much as she needed him, too, she didn't deserve him. Lifting a hand, she rubbed her temple.

"Head bothering you?"

"Too much stress." She squatted and riffled through her bag. Finding a charger, she plugged in her phone. Her parents, associates, and friends would be desperate for news. She might have to send a bland group text or post to social media, but she would let the people she loved know she and Ansel were okay.

"Riley?" Ansel asked.

She stood and turned. If he offered another declaration, she might collapse. Keeping Grant out of her mind, staying calm, and breathing deeply taxed her emotional control. At some point in the future, she would crumble and book another self-indulgent, all-inclusive weekend, but for now, she would hold it together.

Ansel peered out the window and cocked his head. "Your Boot Byre neighbors request your attention."

Frowning, she joined him at the building side fronting the alley.

In the boot store's recessed shadows, Mimi clutched Mikey's hand and waved a bandana.

Their clothes looked dry enough, so the floodwaters hadn't reached the hayloft, but their refusal to evacuate strained the limits of their neighborly relationships. She waved and offered a reassuring smile. "I'm glad they're not alone."

Mikey lifted a hand and pantomimed making a phone call.

"I can't!" Riley cupped her hands. "Phone's dead, and the cell towers are probably out."

Ansel offered a thumb-down. "No signal."

Mimi slumped against Michael.

Mikey wrapped an arm around her waist. With his free hand, he slashed at his throat and tapped his chest above his heart.

In an instant, Riley understood Mimi's flagging

stamina was more than an alcoholic coping mechanism. She leaned out the window. Less than ten feet separated her from people she'd known her entire life. "What's going on?" She pitched her voice to carry. "How bad is it?"

Ansel gripped her waist and anchored her.

Lowering Mimi to a chair, Mikey matched Riley's pose. A string telephone would have lightened the mood. "Mimi's been sipping from a Texas-sized flask. The stories"—he rolled his eyes—"incredible. Did you know she had an affair with the governor?"

"Charming." She honestly didn't care which elected official had welcomed Mimi into his bed. "I'm glad you're keeping her company, but what's wrong? Besides being alone during this flood. That would scare me into a heart attack, too."

Ansel squeezed her hips. "You're not alone."

"Mimi feels terrible about stealing sections of the mural," Mikey shouted, "but she's broke. The stress is crippling her."

"Save it. I thought she was ill." She straightened and backed into Ansel's chest. Turning, she met his gaze. "Sorry for the false alarm."

He shrugged.

"Riley, she *is* ill," Mikey shouted. "Something's wrong with her heart."

Hearing a need for immediate crisis management, Riley looked out the window. "Mikey, tell her to calm down." She cleared her throat and projected her voice. "I've done as much damage to the mural as she did. When the water subsides and she sobers up, we can figure out how to move forward. No hard feelings. No need for alarm."

"That's just it." Mikey looked at Mimi slumped in the chair. "I don't know how long she'll make it. She had a rapid, chaotic heartbeat. I thought she was scared, so I put my smart watch on her and let her keep drinking."

The man had the coping mechanisms of a teenage boy. She bit her tongue.

"Twenty minutes later, she clutched at her chest and complained of shortness of breath. I think she's having a heart attack. I've never had anyone die on me, Riley. Help us!"

Riley considered her options. Mikey's skin looked paler than usual, and unless his road crew arrived to offer assistance, he might join Mimi's medical crisis. "Can she walk?"

He looked toward the chair. "No, shit." His voice rose an octave. "She's passed out."

"Are you sure?" Riley asked. "Try waking her!"

Mikey dropped to his knees and slapped Mimi's cheek. "Come on, you old hoot. Are you still alive? You're too quirky to die."

Mimi's head rolled.

"Atta girl! Stay with us."

The country singer looked ready to propose to keep Mimi's heart in motion, but Riley doubted Mimi owned any of his albums. In times of crisis, shared history mattered as much as capitalistic bonds. Riley turned toward Ansel. "What should we do?"

"I'm a chef and an amateur mechanic." He held up his palms. "Unless she has a food allergy or a supercharged engine, I have no clue. Medical school never entered my radar."

Pacing before the window, Riley considered her

options. Mikey might be a vain, manipulative prick, but he'd never actually lied. She worried Mimi could be moments away from a stroke or heart failure. The vibrant woman came from a different age, but she deserved to see the next one.

A helicopter buzzed nearby.

"Thank God!" She wanted to kiss Ansel, but she gripped his shirtfront. "We have to signal the first responders."

"How?" He cupped her elbows and tilted his head. "Tell me what you need."

She wondered if a red shirt would draw enough attention. Thinking through her plan, she focused on what she needed. "The boot store has a pitched roof, but if we get Mimi over here, we can bring her to the hotel roof. The first responders might medevac her."

"She can't swim." Ansel dropped his hands and rubbed his jaw. "How will you move her?"

She scanned the second floor. Her inventory of contractor castoffs revealed a freshly constructed staircase and a plastic table floating in the floodwater. She wouldn't risk entering the cold, murky depths to nab the table. "We'll build a bridge."

"Out of what?" Ansel asked. "Century-old wooden beams? We'll never get them down."

"The two-by-fours on the staircase."

Ansel worked his jaw and peered over his right shoulder.

She slapped his chest. "Come on, big boy, you can do this. Just rip them apart."

Shaking his head, he approached the staircase. "Easier women…"

Letting him work through the demolition logistics,

she braced her weight on the window's edge. "Mikey, do you have anything sturdy enough to support your weight? I want to get Mimi to a level roof so the emergency responders can reach her. Any metal bookcases or storage units? Shelves?"

"Cardboard boxes, endless boots, and whining cats," Mikey said. "It's another level of hell, and it's too far to jump."

"Mimi can't jump," she said, "but you're a good sport."

He made eye contact. "Am I?"

She nodded in reassurance. No matter their history, he had to believe she had his back. Mimi's life depended on their shared history and deep-rooted bond.

Mikey wiped the sweat from his forehead. "She's barely breathing. We need help, and we need it fast. Tell me what you want me to do."

"Ansel?" She looked up. "Where are you?"

He approached, carrying four planks of wood. "You know, the Fugu Puffer Fish is one of the hardest dishes in the world to cook. It's a Japanese delicacy, and its organs contain a neurotoxin one thousand times more powerful than cyanide. I cooked it."

"Moeko would be impressed."

He dropped the boards at her feet. They clattered. "I bet she would. You, on the other hand, are hard as hell to please."

She smiled and memorized his bemused expression. So far, he made her drip coffee. When the floodwaters receded, she would tell him the coffee was divine, but helping Mimi superseded supporting his ego. "Slide the boards across the alleyway and see if they're secure."

341

"What if I drop one?"

She toed the wood. "Don't."

He snorted.

"Mikey?" she shouted. "We'll build a plank bridge and get you and Mimi into the hotel. Can you help Ansel? Catch the wood so it doesn't fall."

"Okay!" Mikey leaned out the Boot Byre window. "I'm ready."

"Here goes." Ansel cupped one end of the lumber in his palm, tipped the other end toward the gray sky, and lowered the free end toward Mikey's outstretched hand. The wood wobbled, but he kept its trajectory steady.

She swore she would adopt whatever fitness regime kept Ansel in shape. Sweat beaded on his brow, and his muscles shook, but he remained focused on the task.

Minutes later, planks spanned the two windows.

She looked down. Brown water flowed through the deep alleyway like a roiling river spilling into a treacherous canyon. Miscellaneous household items bobbed in the water, and leaves and branches swirled in mysterious eddies. If anyone fell from the wooden walkway, they would be gone. She swallowed, looked up, and found Mikey staring at the water, too.

"Riley, I'm not s-sure…"

"You can do this!" She kept her voice light and upbeat, but her heart pounded in her chest. "It's a quick scoot and an easy push. You'll have her here in a moment. Imagine the news headlines. Country star saves ailing woman."

"Damn, Riley, I don't need more headlines," Mikey said. "I need to live!"

"We all do," she whispered. Swallowing, she pushed down the rising bile. "Don't worry, Mikey, I've got you!"

Looking between Mimi and the water, Mikey nodded.

Ansel rested a hand at her lower back. "I have more upper body strength. If your ankle gives out, and you lose traction, you might struggle to pull them into the hotel. Let me receive them, please?"

Cypress Creek was her hometown, and she helped her friends and her neighbors in times of crisis. Chewing on a thumbnail, she considered whether ceding control would help the evacuees. Mimi might panic and refuse Ansel's open arms. Mikey could lose his grip and pull Ansel into the water. She couldn't lose either her friend or her lover. Dropping a hand from her mouth, she cupped his face. "Please, let me do it. If something happens, I can take full responsibility for the outcome."

He pulled her close and nuzzled into her neck. "Riley, I'll get them across the board. I swear it. You can trust me."

The fear of losing control paralyzed her. She should have been beside Grant. Chiding him to stay with the rescue group might have saved his life. Would Ansel take her advice? Instead of Mikey's fear and uncertainty, Ansel projected confidence, but the threat of losing another person she loved stalled her decision-making skills.

For two years, she powered through work and dealt with her grief in a myriad of ways. Her control teetered on the edge, but she made progress. She found joy in Ansel's arms and inspiration in the restaurant he brought to Cypress Creek. His vulnerable, determined approach to life made him a brilliant celebrity chef. For his birthday, she would find a beautiful agarwood pendant for his jewelry collection. A red cord chain might give him a laugh. Would they have time to learn each other's smiles? He *had* to live.

He tipped up her chin. "Riley? Please?"

She swallowed. Charting rainfall amounts and floodplain maps bought Cypress Creek time, but the authorities had little control over the storm's outcome. She could grieve Grant for the rest of her life, but she couldn't let her loss destroy her ability to move forward. Ansel was right. His strength gave him an advantage, and she would be foolish to insist on being the hero. She pressed a kiss against his lips and pulled back. "If you drop them, I will haunt you."

Laughing, he stole a longer kiss. "I hope you're always with me, but I prefer your corporal form. It's much easier to love a woman I can embrace."

She caught his hand, and in gripping him, she felt her limbs tremble. His physical abilities meant less than his tender heart and his exquisite creativity, but she had no right to jeopardize his success. "I do love you, Ansel. Please, don't forget that fact—"

He squeezed a hand in return. "I love you, too, Riley. For a long time, I thought I needed to spend a heap of time in a place for it to sink into my soul. The minute I met you, I knew I was wrong. I instantly wanted you in my life, but I was too afraid to claim you. What right did I have to your happiness? Only the rights you give me. No matter what happens in the coming days, remember how much I love you."

"Are you sure? Your survival instinct's making

you loopy."

He laughed. "Well, it feels damn good."

Faltering, she acknowledged the sincerity in his gaze and wet her lips. "I hear you, but you should give things time to settle down. Risking your life for my friends is a huge ask." Exhaling, she stepped back from the pain triggered by her self-preservation. "Work on flagging down first responders. I'll figure out what to do with this pair."

He caught her right hand. "That's my call. I can help you, or I can wait in the corner, but I'm not leaving your side."

She blinked back tears. Her heart raced. The farther she shifted from Ansel, the more her limbs shook. When she thought about guiding Mikey and Mimi across the gap, she shivered. She rubbed her arms, steadied her muscles, and straightened her spine. Grant gave everything to help his neighbors. Collapsing on the floor would be the worst thing she could do. "You're right. It's your call."

Ansel nodded and released her hand.

"Guys?" Mikey asked. "We're running out of time."

Wiping a hand across her eyes, she hoped she wasn't out of her league. Letting fate unwind above the flood's swirling, muddy waters might be the hardest thing she'd done. To give Mikey and Mimi the best chances at life, she had to set aside her pride and trust Ansel. Leaning forward, she tried not to sway and pressed a kiss to his warm skin. "Thank you."

He nodded and squeezed her hand a second time before loosening his grip. Approaching the window, he widened his stance and put his hands on his hips. "Is

Mimi conscious?"

"She's moaning, but she's awake." Mikey looked down. "Mimi, can you stand? We're getting you out of here." Dropping to one knee, he hefted her and wrapped an arm around her waist. "We're going next door where the roof's better for rescue. Help's coming. That's right. Just follow my lead."

Riley peered around Ansel and saw the fear in Mimi's wide eyes. Uncertainty, peril, and pain muted her response.

But she laid a hand on the wooden bridge and nodded.

How could anyone recognize another person's pain and refuse to help? She released her breath and absolved her vivacious, golden brother. Until the moment she learned he succumbed to the floodwaters, she believed he was invincible, but now, she respected his choice.

"Mimi, between the two of us, you'll never be on your own," Ansel said. "I'll lie along the boards, stretch out my arms, and lead you. Mikey will do the same and guide you forward. There won't be a gap."

Guiding Mimi to her knees on the boards, Mikey caged her in his arms and followed her across the ten-foot gap until his knees rested in the Boot Byre.

Ansel stretched out in a similar position.

They were wrong. A gap remained. Mimi would have to inch across the unaided expanse. Riley clutched a hand to her chest. She wanted to flee and hide her gaze. Images of what could happen flashed through her mind. Time slowed, and she mistrusted her judgment in the same moment she held her breath.

A steady rain fell.

Mimi sagged against Mikey. An arm hung limp.

Refusing to let her teeter over the floodwater, Riley gripped Ansel's legs. "I'll hold you. Don't let her fall."

He edged out farther. "Come on, Mimi. Don't close your eyes, and don't look down."

"I'm an old woman," Mimi said. "I can go."

"You're a spring chicken." Ansel stretched out his fingertips. "Just a little farther."

Cracking wood echoed between the buildings, and the water in the alleyway surged toward the street.

If the cypress tree damming Gristmill Road finally broke, a torrent of cars and debris would flow downstream, and the current would intensify. Riley wordlessly squeezed Ansel's calves, urging him to hurry.

Mimi scooted along the wood.

Riley held her breath and closed her eyes. Feeling Ansel's weight shift, she opened her eyes, watched him snag Mimi, and pull her toward the hotel's limestone wall.

Relief stole her breath, and she focused on maintaining her grip while giving him room to retreat from the boards.

Having Mimi grip the window opening, Ansel dropped to the floor, wrapped his arms around her middle, and pulled her through the gap.

Sinking to her hands and knees, Mimi hung her head.

Riley dropped to her knees and felt Mimi's pulse. Her racing heartbeat surged and ebbed. As soon as Mikey made the transfer, they would escort Mimi to the roof and flag down help. She hoped they weren't too late.

"Almost there," Ansel said.

Leaving a hand on Mimi's back, she looked up.

Ansel braced his weight against the limestone and stretched out his hand.

Mikey edged along the wood and reached for Ansel's grip.

"My cats!" Mimi shuddered. "We can't let them drown."

Riley swallowed a response. How long could a cat survive without food? Surely, the town's rodent population would suffice until the water went down.

Mimi collapsed to the floor and clutched her chest.

Looking behind her, Riley made eye contact with Ansel and raised her eyebrows.

One hand gripping Mikey's arm, he mirrored her expression.

It was her call.

Except, the call wasn't hers. Scrambling across the boards to catch and retrieve cats was the last thing she wanted to do, and she wouldn't risk Ansel's or Mikey's lives in pursuit of the pampered pets. If they wanted to conduct a feline rodeo, it was their call, but she would never ask them to make that decision.

"Oh, hell," Mikey said. "I'll go get the cats." He pivoted on the two-by-fours and scooted toward the building.

Rain splattered his face.

"Mikey, please don't risk it." She rushed to the window and edged between Ansel and her ex-boyfriend. "You've already done enough."

A truck slammed into the wooden boot store, and the building shuddered.

Stuck on slick, smooth plywood, Mikey absorbed

the reverberations, lost his grip with one hand, and slipped over the planks. His legs dangled over the floodwaters.

Riley saw the fear in his eyes and lunged forward.

Ansel's right shoulder hit her as he grabbed Mikey's right forearm. "Either swing your leg back over the bridge, or let go and hang against the hotel. Either way, I have you."

Her breath stalled in her lungs, and she wanted to squeeze closed her eyes. Mikey wasn't part of her life, but watching him fall into the floodwater would be too much to bear. The visceral pain would remain for the rest of her life, and she might be foolish enough to follow him. She gripped Ansel's waist. If Mikey fell, he would take her and Ansel, too.

"You sure, man?" Mikey asked.

She heard Mikey's words, but she heard Grant's voice. Facing a raging flood, had he asked himself the same thing and decided to proceed? She squeezed shut her eyes.

"I have you. Come on, leg up?"

Ansel's voice sounded strained, but it resonated beneath her cheek. She gripped him as tightly as she could.

Mikey rocked and found the momentum to swing his leg back over the wood. The boards clattered with the impact.

Ansel surged and pulled Mikey into the hotel.

The transfer knocked her onto her backside, and two men sprawled over her. She struggled to breathe, but the pain never felt so good.

"I can't believe..." Mikey crawled out of the dog pile and hung his head. "What a rush! Did you see that shit? I was hanging over an abyss!"

Ansel rolled to his side and pulled her close. He slowed his heavy breathing. "You okay?"

She cupped his cheek. The rough rescues tore his shirt and left a rash of blood along his chest. Easing a hand beneath the damp fabric, she felt his heartbeat. "I'm okay. Thank you. You didn't have to risk your life to save my friends."

"I would have done it for anyone," Ansel said. "Don't tell the cats, but they're on their own."

Mimi moaned.

Riley smiled and brushed hair off his forehead. "They'll live."

He kept his eyes closed and breathed deeply.

"I hate to tell you this, but I need your shirt to signal the helicopter."

"Take it." He started on the remaining buttons. "It's seen better days."

She helped him wiggle out of his shirt. The fabric smelled like him, and she wanted to stash it under her pillow, crawl into bed, and hide until the flood felt like a newsreel. Instead, she planted a knee and stood.

"Riley?"

She looked at him, lying on the old, wooden floor.

"There are easier ways to get me naked."

Laughter slipped past her lips. As soon as she found privacy and a hot shower, stripping him would be the beginning of a long, indulgent rest period. "Good."

He grinned and hung an arm over his eyes.

She didn't blame him. The lines in his face looked deeper, his lips seemed chapped, and his weary gaze lent him a haunted look. After his heroics, he must feel as exhausted as he looked. When the waters receded, they would reconnect.

Chapter Twenty-Three

When Ansel heard the whirl of helicopter blades, he and Mikey escorted Mimi to the hotel roof and waited for instructions.

Within minutes, soldiers from a Texas Army National Guard medevac unit hung from a UH-60 Black Hawk helicopter and asked for their status.

Ansel explained the situation and prepared to transfer Mimi. He nodded toward the National Guard soldiers and squeezed Mimi's hand. "They'll take good care of you."

"But-t." She rubbed her upper arms. "What about y'all?"

"Mikey can care for himself, and I'll look after Riley." He flicked his gaze toward the soldiers shouting orders and admired their smooth efficiency. He depended on an army of professionals to prop up his success. As much as he valued them and his position, he valued Riley more. If push came to shove, he would give up his happiness to ensure hers. "She's as resilient as those soldiers. Hell, she'll probably look after everyone and reorganize the refugee center."

Smiling, Mimi glanced toward the hovering helicopter and kept a hand pressed to her heart, but she made the stumbling transition.

Ansel hoped the team would give her respite and the medical attentions needed to prevent permanent heart damage. A badge for the 36th Combat Aviation Brigade caught his attention, and he wondered how often the National Guard members trained for missions like this one. The woman operating the hoist looked blasé enough that she could rescue people in her sleep. If he had to guess, she shared personality traits with his badass yacht pilot.

He had heard of medevac training and exercises at places like the National Training Center at Fort Irwin, California, but he never thought he would see one in action. The sobering experience put his priorities in check, and he swallowed past a lump in his throat. Feeding people was one thing, but actually helping people in need felt rewarding. He might be too old for the National Guard, but he could refocus his retirement plans toward search and rescue.

Riley might kill him.

Taking oxygen in the aircraft's backseat, Mimi sat between two crewmembers. As soon as she stabilized, she would give the staff sergeant and his crew an earful about life in Cypress Creek and her poor, sodden cats.

The Black Hawk helicopter lifted upward.

The relentless wind waned.

Turning, Riley made eye contact. Tears streamed down her face.

He rushed forward and wrapped her in a hug.

"I'm just so grateful for you, and Mikey, and the Guard's assistance. As soon as I saw that helicopter, I started crying. I knew Mimi would get much-needed help." Riley shuddered and wiped away the tears. "But what if we hadn't been there?"

"We were there," he said. "You did it."

"I couldn't have hauled her across those boards."

"Sure you could." He wrinkled his nose and tried not to think about the muscle-clenching pain of moving Mimi and keeping track of Riley with every fiber of his being. "Everyday people can surprise you."

She laid her head against his chest. "That's true. We're all doing our best, aren't we?"

Mikey coughed. "Man, I want to fly in one of those birds. Do you think the United Service Organizations still provides live entertainment to members of the United States Armed Forces? I'm all over it!"

Of course, he wanted to fly in a military aircraft. He probably wanted to pilot it, too. Faced with life-or-death situations, emotions ran high, and rescues summoned the best intentions from people who witnessed them. "Me, too."

Mikey offered him a high five. "You can be my backup singer."

"Thanks, man, but I'll stick to the kitchen." Absorbing the slap, he savored the feel of Riley in his arms and the quiet interlude after the storm. Emotions would calm, but the devastation required weeks to reveal itself. Would she find room for him in her life, or would she let their adrenaline-fueled escapade fade from her mind?

****

Ansel lifted his head from Riley's shoulder. Hours after exhaustion stole her focus, she slept deeply. He looked out the window and spied a rescue boat arriving at the hotel. Men and women wearing life vests and reflective clothing charged through the receding water and offered respite from a harrowing day. "Up here!"

Riley stirred.

"What happened to the staircase?" a rescuer asked.

With his back against the wall, Ansel smiled. The staircase railings helped rescue Mimi, but the structure's remaining supports sported nails like cactus spines. If Nathan's crew had used screws, the charming, rhinestone-clad thief might be dead in her boot store, and his body wouldn't feel like it'd been raked over coals.

After Mimi's medical evacuation, Riley, flush with accomplishment, had danced around the rooftop. She kissed him and heaped on the praise. His need to protect her allowed him to accept her affection, but he had steadied her hips and kept his focus on the changing environmental conditions. A loose wire, sudden windstorm, or errant explosion could still upend his day and harm her.

Mikey, scribbling on a notepad, could fend for himself.

"Ansel used it to bridge the two buildings," Riley said. "He saved Mimi Roberts."

"He saved Mikey, too!"

Mikey scratched his head. "That's not exactly what I meant. I'm the person who got things moving. I could have gotten her help."

The responder climbed up the remaining stairs and offered him a life vest. She patted his arm. "Sure, you could, sweetheart. Let's get you warm."

Riley giggled. "I like her, Sweetheart."

Mikey glared.

Ansel closed his eyes and knew everything would be okay. Sitting in the vessel with Riley, Mikey, and other evacuees, he clutched a warming blanket to his shoulders and let the wind from their progress blow his hair from his face. Oil, gasoline, and raw sewage stained the floodwaters. He ached at seeing the damage, but he refused to comment on the destruction. For Riley and Mikey, it must be devastating.

Outside of downtown, a fire blazed where a propane tank smashed into a house. The flames licked up the sides of a honey mesquite tree, and the tree's dense, aromatic wood burned hot and smoky. The wood had a long history of flavoring grilled foods, and he feared the smell would mark the end of his time in Cypress Creek.

The boat captain navigated around downed utility lines to avoid electrocution. The farther the boat traveled from downtown, the lower the waterline looked.

Riley leaned against his right shoulder. "How're you holding up?"

"I've been better." He shifted her closer. "How're you?"

"I don't know." She cleared her throat. "It's just, so much, you know?"

He spent a week by her side, but once the adrenaline subsided and shock set in, she needed people who understood how she'd evolved into such an amazing woman. She needed her dads. Wrapping an arm around her, he made a noncommittal noise and wondered how to manage his blazing, painful desires to stay close, support, and avoid smothering her.

She demanded professional boundaries, but the lines blurred. His priorities shifted. She meant more than anything he'd achieved. How would she grapple with that role? She was incredibly resilient, but challenges drew on her reserves until they might grow so thin that they snapped. He didn't want his love to feel like a burden. His chef's whites defined his life, but he refused to burden Riley. She loved Grant, and losing him pained her.

What if Ansel couldn't hold up his end of the bargain? He respected her and wanted her, but he couldn't honor her until he made peace with his life. Responsibility and love went hand in hand, but loving a person required accepting oneself *and* the other person. Until he had his bearings, suppressing his emotions with cold practicality was the only answer. His heart would suffer, and she might move on, but he would take the risk. Instead of answering her, he pressed a kiss to her hair.

She turned her head. "I'm sure when you came to Cypress Creek, this is the last thing you thought would happen."

"Loving you?" he asked.

Mikey grumbled. "She's very lovable."

Ansel glared.

She angled her shoulders and blocked his view of the melodramatic musician. "The flood. With all your success, it's amazing how different our worlds were, but we're in the same motorboat, yeah? Like, no matter how hard you plan for the future, fate has a way of throwing people into impossible situations. Whether you sink or swim is your choice."

He tightened his grip. Thinking about her drowning sent white-hot terror through his heart. Mikey's presence kept him from declaring just how much she reset his perspectives, but the musician wouldn't be a third wheel for long. Ansel would wait for privacy to remind Riley how good they were together. He probably needed to return to San Antonio for a few days and put wheels in motion, but technology would ease the ache of separation. He willed himself to relax. He and Riley were alive, and at the moment, the comfort of feeling her steady breaths was the only thing that mattered.

At the shelter parking lot, volunteers greeted the boat and held it steady. Broken bottles and nails covered the asphalt, and mud slicks captured tire imprints. Yellow lights flashed from the tops of white emergency vehicles.

Ansel stood, offered Riley a hand, and assisted her from the boat. The blanket fell from his shoulders, and he considered what to say.

"Life is so strange. I'm in Austin, and you're in San Antonio. Who knew we would meet in Cypress Creek." She cupped his face. "What an adventure we had."

"You make it sound like it's over." He grasped for the right words, and not finding them, he leaned into her touch. "How do you feel about partnering with a cocky chef who happens to have a small restaurant empire?" He cleared his throat. "There's a yacht."

She laughed and dropped her hand. "I don't know. You have a thriving career, and I have…don't know. Looming therapy bills? Waning twin syndrome?" She cracked a smile. "Limited hang-ups in bed?"

"I love your inhibitions." He pressed a kiss to her cheek. "You're also an amazing architect. I can't wait to finish building the restaurant."

"It'll take time." She placed a palm over his chest. "I shouldn't have run back to Austin. I should have stayed with my dads and accepted our family of three would thrive without Grant. Who else but my parents could understand our new normal? Families give people strength. I have to remedy my mistake and thank them for everything they've done."

Placing his hand over hers, he swallowed. In his lowest moments, he felt like a blank, unbound page, but squeezing himself into the rhythms of someone else's life was an impossible solution. Riley didn't need a groupie. She needed someone who complemented her brilliant creativity. He was so wrapped up in the pleasure of finding her that he forgot the difficulties of merging their dynamic lives.

The past few days, they'd swanned around Cypress Creek like two creatives without outside obligations. Tucked into a cabin he didn't own, he played house with Riley and imagined their relationship was his only existence. They could pretend Cypress Creek was their real life, the same way they pretended Warrior hadn't contrived to throw them together, but everyone knew the truth.

When Ansel envisioned his relationship with Riley, he saw himself with classic cars for sports cars and speeding to Austin on weekends. He would ensure Riley wasn't a nameless person on his arm at restaurant opening and industry events. She deserved to be more than a supportive girlfriend. Outside of the culinary world, she could maintain her professional identity and architectural creativity. She forged ingenuity from Austin's base materials and produced unexpected variations from her customer's whims. Her track record proved her capabilities, and her ingenuity stole his breath. He could no more ask her to move to San Antonio than he could ask her to give up her career.

He squeezed her hand. "I'll tell Eagle Hawk how

much he means to me, too. Take all the time you need. Your family should be your top priority." He looked away before his affirmation felt too much like a good-bye. "I'll be in San Antonio for a while."

"You could stay here."

Her offer hovered somewhere between genuine and perfunctory, but he wanted to understand his place in her life instead of questioning it. Keeping his chin from wobbling, he gritted his teeth and hoped the rain dripping from his hair disguised his watery eyes. "I appreciate the offer, but don't worry about me."

She lowered her hand and stepped back. "You need to go?"

He nodded. If she had time to learn his subtle expressions, she would understand how much the distance hurt him, but they'd fallen in love in a week. When he left Cypress Creek, the things that might happen terrified him. Giving her space to ground herself felt like a responsible approach toward establishing their future happiness, but damn, it hurt worse than a cactus to the backside. He would do what he always did. He would soldier on, but he was adamant she understood how much he loved her. "When—"

"Riley June Golding!" Warrior strode through the debris field and wrenched Riley from Ansel's arms. He clutched her to his chest and smeared dirt and tears over his three-hundred-dollar dress shirt. "What the hell do you think you're doing? Do you know how worried Papi and I have been? We can't lose you, too!"

"I know, Daddy." She sobbed and clutched her father. "I'm here."

Tears streamed down Warrior's face.

Ansel recognized a family's need for reconnection. He swallowed his emotions, squared his shoulders, and stepped back to make some calls. At the right time, Riley would find him.

"Clear out!" Papi rushed past wearing a yellow raincoat and coordinating boots. He slammed into the pair, spun Riley from Warrior's arms, and clutched his daughter's face. "Honey, what would I do without you? I couldn't bear losing you. Don't give my old heart such a scare."

Riley's sobs intensified. "You're not old."

"Shhh!" Papi rocked her. "This is my moment."

She laughed and laid her head against his chest.

"Don't hog her!" Warrior bellowed.

Sandwiched between her two fathers, Riley wiped her nose and grinned.

Ansel looked toward the shelter and swallowed. Riley and her dads would never have Grant to hold, but they had each other. Love could alter behaviors in a matter of days, or it could disappoint in a moment. Where did he fit in their embrace?

Walking away from the trio, he let a near-death experience unearth his innermost thoughts. He barely knew who he was, but he cooked for the same reasons he loved life. He was an optimist. What was he supposed to do? Stop trying and eat Steak *Frites*? For too long, he'd become the man Aubrey had predicted. Success pulled him toward mainstream expectations, and he forgot the feelings of baking summer days and cool lake breezes. Riley and her family understood those pleasures.

Glimpses of other people's lives thrilled him, but whether he visited Collins' and Jia's family in Korea or indulged in Moeko's savory confections, he could only sample their experiences. Hopping from restaurant to restaurant padded his bank account, but it deflated his soul. He didn't want to feel that way about witnessing Riley's connection with her dads. He should spend more time with Eagle Hawk and tell the old man how much he meant. Eagle Hawk saved him, but he couldn't define him. Only Ansel could navigate his future.

A car crash uprooted his life, but Eagle Hawk gave him refuge. An exposé smashed his dreams, but The Chow Channel gave him an opportunity. What would he and Riley make from the flood?

Before they could look back on this moment and be proud of the outcomes, he had to find a way to riff on the foods and pleasures he held dearest. For too long, he kept his head down and created joy for other people. In a moment of folksy passion, he fell for a gray-eyed woman, but in order to claim her, he had to define what he brought to the table.

Approaching the shelter door, he exhaled. The community volunteers could give him a hot cup of coffee and space to pull himself together. Whiskey would be better. He had a feeling he would need it.

A woman wearing a white, belted raincoat met him at the shelter door. Her honeyed curls and worried expression looked as threatening as a glass of iced tea on a hot summer day.

"Come in, Mr. Percheron." She beckoned. "You must be exhausted."

He wiped wet hair out of his eyes and entered the shelter's air-conditioned, low-humidity chaos. "Do I know you?"

"I'm Lacey, Riley Golding's assistant."

"Ahh." He scanned the folding tables and eager volunteers for a place to rest. "She's outside with her fathers."

"I saw them," Lacey said. "I'm glad everything worked out. This week's been a whirlwind of sample requests and oddball emails. I'm glad she's coming back to Austin. She can do everything remote, right? I mean, it's the future, isn't it?"

He needed a break from Lacey's uptick and vocal fry. He didn't know whether she aspired to influencer status or not, but she sounded like a woman used to leveraging her good looks and expecting results. Riley must trust her skill sets, or she wouldn't employ the woman. Too exhausted to think, he dropped into a chair and rested his chin in his right hand.

"Should I call you a car to San Antonio?" Lacey asked. "Riley said you're off to your next adventure."

"Did she?" Raising his head, he scooted his butt to the chair's edge, let his aching limbs sprawl, and closed his eyes. Pulling Mimi to safety had terrified him. Rescuing Mikey had been touch and go. Walking away from Riley might kill him. He needed rest and a bathtub tall enough to submerge his body neck-deep. Opening his eyes, he realized Lacey hovered. "Just give me a few minutes."

"No problem. Riley told me to get you squared away." She laid a portable battery pack on the table. "Would you like to charge your phone? I can find you a hot meal before you get on your way."

He covered a yawn. Lacey was adept at giving him the boot. "You're efficient."

"Taking care of Riley is my job." She preened, but then she looked toward the parking lot, and her smile faltered. "Riley pays me well, but I don't know what I would do without her. I never want to leave Austin. Some parts of the country are"—she dropped her voice—"cold."

Stifling a laugh, he fished his phone from his pocket and plugged the device into the charger. The screen lit up. Messages from Eagle Hawk, Collins, and concerned friends overwhelmed his alert page. Collins could resume the restaurant build-out under Nathan's guidance. Somewhere in the wide, blue Caribbean, *Tranquility* waited. He cared, but exhaustion blurred his ability to process the words. Riley wasn't hovering, and Lacey wasn't his flavor of efficiency. A million social media followers might have inflated his ego, but he could take a hint.

His black, chauffeured SUV arrived an hour later.

Ansel tried one last time to look for Riley, but he only glimpsed her back and her fathers' bracketing embrace. What was he supposed to do? Pry them apart? Shaking his head, he walked into the parking lot and waited for Collins to climb from the car.

Dark clouds cast a shadow and threatened to release a torrential downpour. Oaks and mountain laurel claimed the ridgeline. A buzzard crowned an Ashe juniper. It circled the parking lot, landed on the SUV's luggage rack, and flexed its wings.

Collins finally climbed from the driver's seat and shooed away the bird.

Ansel tipped his head toward the animal's hostile retreat. "Point taken."

Dusting his hands, Collins swallowed a final bite of food and swiped a thumb across his lower lip. "Mr. Percheron. I'm so glad to see you."

Ansel offered a hand and neglected to mention the salsa staining Collins's white shirt. "Thanks for coming to get me. I didn't give you much notice. How's the family?"

"Good, thankfully. We were worried about you." Collins scanned the controlled chaos surrounding the flood victims. "Do you have any luggage?"

Holding out his arms, he shrugged. "Take me as I am."

Collins blinked.

The shadows beneath Collins's eyes rivaled his sleep-deprived bags. Instead of prodding, Ansel sank into the rear passenger seat, left the door ajar, and wondered if Riley would notice his departure. She might have kept track of his movements. Lacey might have seen the SUV arrive. He rubbed the large, white scar on his palm. She'd seemed to love him without the trappings of his success, but their liaison started as a fling. Maybe it should end that way, too.

The carrion bird circled as if looking for prey.

Collins climbed into the driver's seat and cleared his throat. "This flood wrecked the project, huh? What a mess. We'll have to start from scratch…"

No longer listening, Ansel looked out the window. Who was he kidding? Riley kept her emotions close to her chest. He spied Moeko's family huddled together in front of the shelter. She paced the sidewalk and spoke into her cell phone.

He suspected somewhere in Japan, a worried mother clutched her shirt and second-guessed her daughter's updates. In another life, he might have been the person calling loved ones. A charming bungalow and a loving family could be twice as potent as fame, but he had Eagle Hawk and his empire.

Moeko looked up.

When floodwaters inundated the town, she focused on her family. Her baking tins might have floated to the Gulf of Mexico, and she didn't need to worry about him. For so long, he wanted to control his life. Mother Nature might not have laughed in his face, but she had damn well spit into it. Acknowledging his camaraderie with the townspeople of Cypress Creek was the least he could do. He raised a hand to signal his safety to Moeko.

She dipped her head and continued her call.

Dropping his hand, he ceased waiting for Riley to validate his departure. A few days of connection paled against the lifetime of love she shared with her fathers. Remembering the times he brought her back to her family ranch, he realized he had houses around the world, but he had never stepped foot inside her home. "Come on, Collins. Let's get moving and save the restaurant renovations for the office. Tell me about the kids." He pulled closed the door, shut his eyes, and sank into the SUV's buttery, soft leather while he listened to Collins live his dream.

Chapter Twenty-Four

Autumn sunlight shone through Riley's tall office windows, and she gazed at her plans for a new technology campus. After seeing her residential designs, the technology chairman had asked her to focus on a project in Northwest Austin. He planned to revitalize the Parmer Corridor. She appreciated the challenge of applying her skills on a larger scale, but preserving the area's character would be as tricky as pretending Ansel had good reasons not to call.

"Just, like, no sleeping pods." Lacey sat perched on the desk's corner, holding a notebook and a pencil. She shuddered. "Eww."

Riley smiled. "I don't think sleeping pods have a future in America. We're too tall and too accustomed to space."

Lacey chewed on the pencil. "Like astronauts in space?"

She shook her head and ran a finger along a landscape elevation. The Parmer Corridor offered suburban home prices in attractive communities like Cedar Park and Round Rock, but the growing towns risked predictable restaurants and mundane entertainment. Thousands of white-collar workers would soon take up residence.

She appreciated a good strip mall, but miles of them created mundane blight. By building community space into the technology campus, she could blur the border between work and play. "More like we're too accustomed to moving on. Do you know anyone who enjoys being beholden to bad choices?"

"I enjoy carbs."

She laughed and marked the elevation for a new stand-alone café. Looking up, she smiled. "I know you love carbs, and I appreciate your effort to diversify my diet. Without your help, I'd probably live off bean-and-cheese burritos."

"You've had a rough summer." Lacey twirled her hair and looked away. "After all you've been through, it's the least I can do."

If Lacey wanted to downplay her role, then Riley would give her space…and a hefty holiday bonus.

Focusing on the Palmer Corridor street plan, she checked window placement at the technology office. Intersecting hallways created opportunities for greetings, but couches and lounge areas supported collaboration. Should she add a beverage station?

"Are we almost done?" Lacey asked. "The awards ceremony starts at eight o'clock. I want to see you in your dress. It's hanging in the bathroom."

For the first time this week, she wondered what Ansel would think. A week without dreaming of him was a new record. He doubted the awards committee could find a backup recipient that looked as lovely as she did in an evening gown. If he saw her tonight, would he still feel that way?

After the flood, she had finished the design work for his restaurant and helped Cypress Creek residents rebuild, but he never touched base. Throwing herself into work let her ignore his silence and the nagging sensation she left something undone.

Once or twice, she called him, but Collins answered and made vague excuses about Ansel's exhaustion.

She played off her surprise and brought the conversation back to the restaurant design. She made such a show of moving on that she started to believe the performance. How could two people go through something like a flood and walk away from each other? Had she done something wrong to Ansel?

Clearing her mind of her nail-biting anxiety, she annotated her thoughts on the campus design. She almost forgot about the preservation award, and it had nothing to do with the way Ansel ghosted her. "Thanks for ordering the dress."

"And your car will be here at seven. I don't want to be your designated driver."

She set down her pencil and looked up. Austin traffic could be extreme. "What, you didn't find me a plus one?"

"Did you want to bring someone?" Lacey clapped. "I can make it happen."

Jerking away from the possibility, she held up a hand and noticed her chipped nails. "Absolutely not."

Lacey pouted. "Spoilsport."

Rubbing the back of her neck, she wondered if she had time for a manicure, but nobody would notice her nails.

Tomorrow morning, she would leave Austin near dawn, and she would arrive at her family's ranch house before her fathers woke for brunch.

Papi would get a kick out of the new glass tower honoring her preservation work.

Dad would size it against his awards.

Both reactions would thrill her. The high-elevation ranch seemed like the only place she could relax. Her therapist called her weekly migrations a coping skill, but setting foot in the sprawling compound released the tension in her soul. As long as she remained under Dad's and Papi's watchful care, she could pretend all was well.

After the manicure and slipping on the gold dress that fit like a second skin, she rode to the awards ceremony.

The driver opened the car door.

Stepping onto the sidewalk, she smiled for the press photographer. Yellow leaves drifted from the Drake elms, and they contrasted nicely with the red carpet. She made a pretty sight, and she made a beeline to the hotel's front door.

Inside the lobby, reporters jostled for attention.

"Tell me about the flood." A brunette reporter thrust out a microphone. "Were you scared?"

"Will Cypress Creek rebuild?" a second reporter asked.

A woman shouldered her way between her colleagues. "Do you believe in climate change?"

Riley believed in spending time with her family. Agreeing to this ridiculous evening had been a mistake. Instead of cozying up by the fireplace with Dad and Papi, she would endure a night of hard drinks and industry gossip. To combat the reporters' questions, she intensified her smile.

"Your brother died—"

She held up a hand. "Losing Grant hurt, and this year's flood did nothing to minimize that loss. If I wanted a round of immersion therapy, I would go to the hotel pool."

The brunette reporter laughed.

Thinking she should have saved her joke for the awards presentation, she chewed her lip and hoped her lipstick resisted the abuse. "Until I found myself caught in that natural disaster, I didn't realize how powerless flood victims feel. People refuse to evacuate because they're poor, infirm, or guarding something too precious to lose. They think they're in control, but they're not."

An elderly couple wearing black tie stopped and listened.

Conscious of her role in her professional community, she returned their smiles and decided to wrap up her impromptu interview with the red-carpet reporter. "During the Cypress Creek floods, Grant had his reasons for staying, and I had mine."

"But you're twins…"

"With different passions," she said. "The restoration of Buckey Windstop's lost mural is almost complete. Cypress Creek is rebuilding its charms. In the coming months, you'll see more and more businesses opening their doors and welcoming day-trippers. It's a beautiful story of birth and renewal. You should visit my hometown."

The reporter scratched his jaw. "I should."

"But tonight's not about Cypress Creek. It's about community service in Austin."

Flicking the side of his nose, the reporter nodded. "Okay, then."

"Ms. Golding?" An assistant from the architectural association beckoned toward the ballroom doors. "Are you ready to take your seat?"

"Just a minute." She pointed to the reporter's recording device and waited until he activated it. "Being nominated for a community service award feels like an honor I don't deserve. When I perform pro-bono work with organizations, I see the benefit of social, economic, and environmental investment. I appreciate the honor, but I've already won my award."

He clicked off the recorder. "Absolutely perfect. You're stunning. I'm sorry I asked about your brother."

"Are you?"

His face reddened.

The gentleman wearing black tie clapped.

Drawing a deep breath, she acknowledged the feedback and made a beeline toward the ballroom. She couldn't wait to return home.

****

After making the rounds at the awards ceremony, Riley set an early alarm and then fell into bed. Dawn cast the drive to Cypress Creek in soft, pastel light. She slowed for her parents' gravel drive and let herself in through the garage. Muted yellow lights illuminated the first floor.

"Warrior, she's here!" Papi cried out.

"But is she sober?" Dad asked.

Her fathers' exasperated responses teased out a real smile, and Riley stepped into the kitchen with views of the sun climbing over the river.

"Hush now!" Papi swatted Dad with a kitchen towel. "You're the only person in this household who considers whiskey their best friend."

Dad wrapped an arm around Papi's waist. "Says the man with an unknown credit limit."

She smiled and set down her purse. "I thought you both would be sleeping."

Papi rounded the expansive marble island.

He wore a yellow housecoat, and his highlighted, dark-brown hair stood on end. Without hair gel and gold jewelry, he looked like a man who needed a shave and a hot cup of coffee. At least it was too early for food poisoning. "Is Callie here?" She listened for paws on wood. "What's for brunch?"

"Callie went into town to pick up our dry cleaning." Dad braced his palms on the island and raised his eyebrows. "The restaurant opens tonight.

Her hands went cold, and she gripped her arms. "Tonight? I must have lost track. I didn't bring the right clothes."

"Wear that gold dress!" Papi filled a coffee cup. "You looked stunning at the awards ceremony. I reposted your speech on *every* platform."

Hearing the pride in his voice, she pulled the glass obelisk from her purse and set it on the island. "You mean *this* award?"

"Oh! So phallic!" Papi picked up the award and carried it toward the office library. "I love it. Just wait until I stage it behind my morning selfie."

She could mock him, but his daily outfits received more likes than her company posts. So much to the Internet leading to an enlightened experience. Shaking her head, she wondered what Papi would wear and understood exactly why his followers liked him.

Dad cleared his throat and tapped his right fingers on the countertop. "You are attending the opening, aren't you? You designed most of the concept."

Reality felt like a lead weight. Dropping to a

barstool, she lowered her head into her hands and ran her fingers through her hair. "I designed it, but it bears your company's name. Go without me."

"We have plenty of tickets."

She looked up and met his gaze. "I can't do it. You don't know how much effort getting through this project took. Ansel reworked the restaurant to highlight Cypress Creek's uniqueness, and every tweak thrilled me, but he sent the change orders through Collins. What does that say?" Dropping her head to the counter, she laid her cheek against the cool marble. "The action says I'm an employee. It says I got exactly what I wanted. We crisis-bonded. I have to get over him."

"You're both chicken!" His voice boomed. "If age is a luxury, I'd rather be poor!"

She started and braced her hands on the counter.

He waved off her wide-eyed expression. "I remember being young and nervous. You are neither of those things! Claim your involvement in this project and add it to your portfolio. I didn't raise my kids to hide from their fears or their involvement with celebrity chefs."

"Dad…"

"Riley June Golding…"

"Before the flood, you were a meddling matchmaker!"

"I was not." He narrowed his gaze. "I said I've always liked the man. I love you."

"I love you, too, Dad. Life's just…harder than I expected." She blew out her breath. Tackling design challenges and finding solutions required grit and a holistic design approach. No matter her feelings for Ansel, she had to show her face at the high-end cocktail party. "Thank you for raising me and Grant to be tough."

"Tough enough to face Ansel?"

She swallowed. "Tough enough to put business first."

He slapped a hand on the counter. "That's my girl!"

Standing, she walked toward a window and surveyed the limestone slopes. Life in Hill Country could be rough, but the area rewarded those who persevered. The restaurant's grand opening party attendees would include investors, friends, and family. The guests had money to burn and imaginations that outstripped seasonal social media trends. She preached about reducing inequality and achieving sustainability, but to keep her name circulating among this crowd, she needed continuous exposure. Her firm bore her name, and her staff depended on a pipeline of new projects to keep on the lights. If her feelings for a man altered her professional behavior, she needed a new line of work. "I'll be there."

"You're going?" Papi walked into the room rattling ice in a tumbler.

"Yes!" She turned and hoped he had enough gossip to fill the next twelve hours. "I can't let a great dress and a beautiful restaurant go to waste. After all, I am a designer."

Papi saluted her. "One of the best!"

Squished between two loving, space-invading, overly-cologned men, she acknowledged how lucky she and Grant had been to bask in their love and count on their continued support. If life had turned out differently, Grant would be with her, but she had to make the best of what she had. Frankly, she had a lot, and she would rock it.

Sunday morning dawned brisk and bright. On her way to the dry cleaners, she passed Ansel's restaurant and risked a glance. Set to open at sunset, the restaurant was a hive of last-minute activity. Employees flitted around the entryway and turned shrinking lead time into last-minute adjustments. Florists delivered bouquets, and painters touched up trim. The sound of a drill made her wince, but Nathan could handle the last-minute adrenaline rush.

An opening wasn't Ansel's first rodeo, either.

She wondered if every restaurant opening was just as chaotic. After the flood, Ansel would be collected and focused, but neither he nor Nathan needed her to pop in and revisit the awkwardness that defined their week in Cypress Creek.

So much changed after the flood. News write-ups touted Buckey's mural, Saunders' conservation efforts, and Mimi's conviction. In light of Mimi's age, the judge shortened her sentence. Aubrey suggested they lengthen it, but she and Nathan had weekly appointments with a marriage counselor, and she needed ways to vent her ire. Rickie Hays directed traffic at the Boot Byre, and Riley wondered if the old romantic would be there when Mimi returned. Kyle, on the other hand, fired up his welding equipment more often than he opened his restaurant. His pizza joint wouldn't last the year, but she already had ideas to flip the restaurant space.

Being a local had benefits. Parking near the dry cleaners, she scooped her dress off a hook and bundled the plastic-wrapped treasure into her new electric SUV.

Her old vehicle sheltered the mural segments, but the flood damage totaled it. Had Ansel's classic, blue gas-guzzling roadster lived to rumble another day? Collins' dry reports felt no room for personal comments. Each time she read one, she steeled her heart, but she was about to experience the culmination of thousands of hours of work and millions of dollars of investment. Why did her apprehensions center around one man? Palms sweaty, she gripped the steering wheel and navigated toward the ranch house. He was just a customer. She would muster her strength to make it through the coming night, but she would do it.

By five o'clock, her hair set in smooth curls and her feet sporting high heels, she took a whiskey shot and accompanied Dad and Papi to the opening. Riding in the backseat, she wondered what Grant would have made of the ground-lit, stone edifice that once housed a hotel. Now, it was a culinary cathedral poised to redefine Cypress Creek. A crisp sign crowned the old hotel's façade, and a string of sports cars idled in front of a valet stand. The cars' owners threw their keys to the valets and probably walked into the cocktail party without considering the town that rebuilt itself for the second time in as many years. Maybe they saw everything they needed on the news. Chewing the inside of her cheek, she wondered if her design and Ansel's ambitions reached too far. Thank goodness he approved all her change orders.

"Good size crowd," Dad said. "I can't wait to see the space in action."

"Me, too." She scanned the attendees and looked for familiar locals.

A young assistant in chef's whites greeted guests

and offered hors d'oeuvres from a silver tray. Half the guests wearing ten-gallon hats accepted his offer, and the other half rolled through the restaurant's front doors as if the assistant never existed. Press members recorded quips and snapped photographs.

"I thought Ansel would be at the front door."

"He's probably in the room's middle." Dad checked his teeth in a visor mirror. "Best to avoid a bottleneck."

"Right. He's the main draw." The crowd of technology executives, professional athletes, and old-money patrons would shield her until she felt ready to face Ansel. Climbing out of the car, she followed her parents, declined the young chef's offerings, and stepped into the restaurant holding her chin high.

The mural above the bar created a show-stopping, vibrant vibe. She and Ansel couldn't save every inch of artwork, but they'd altered the mural's future. The strips of salvaged canvas they bundled into the SUV hung in museums and displayed Buckey's creativity to a new generation of admirers. The portion of the mural below the water line required more than museum lighting and rough-hewn frames could provide, but conservationists salvaged Buckey's intent and recreated what they couldn't save.

Then again, tonight wasn't about Buckey. The event was about Ansel and his team. Tuxedo-clad servers passed out glasses of wine, and bartenders poured craft cocktails and local beers. Electric pillar candles flickered in tall, hurricane vases. If she closed her eyes, she felt the hum of excitement. Cypress Creek's newest venue was a success, and her staff deserved the recognition heading their way.

She walked up to the polished wood bar and picked up a heavy, cardstock menu. The highlighted drinks were Mimi's Mescal, the Creek Rises, and Your First Love, a dirty martini. Curious, she flipped over the menu, but none of the offerings referenced her existence. Why should Ansel honor her with a drink? Their relationship was just a trauma-fueled fling. Forcing a smile, she chose a glass of dry, red wine and wondered if Aubrey had tried her namesake cocktail. Mimi would have to wait until she no longer received her meals behind bars.

Turning her back to the bar, she admired the gas lanterns illuminating limestone arches and the alfresco patio where servers offered delicacies. A wood-burning grill and a brick pizza oven sizzled with atmosphere. The restaurant's guests wore a mix of rhinestone boots, leather blazers, and haute couture, but most importantly, they smiled. In between bites, they also snapped images on their phone. Tomorrow, her name would be all over the news.

She took a minute to anticipate the torrent of inquiries. The restaurant was the product of a successful team, but Cypress Creek held a piece of her heart. Experiencing the venue warmed her soul, and she felt lighter than she anticipated. No matter what happened with Ansel, attending the opening was the right move.

"Do you like it?"

She froze with her wine glass halfway to her lips. Turning, she found Ansel standing at her side dressed in immaculate chef's whites. He looked more handsome and more untouchable than the sweat-tinged cowboy who caught her eye outside a service station. Then again, she also wore designer heels. Maybe she looked untouchable, too. Instead of answering his question, she waved a hand toward the crowd. "I thought you would be mingling."

"Just shaking hands and kissing babies." He turned his back to the bar and stood shoulder-to-shoulder. "Texans are set in their ways, but this is a good reception and an eager crowd. Their jealous friends will happily drop fifty dollars for eight-ounce filets and candlelit ambiance."

She turned her head and raised an eyebrow. "Filets?"

"That's what we sell." He smiled and scanned her dress. "Life's finer things aren't on the menu."

Was she a cut of meat? After so many months of silence, his innuendo made her see red. If he thought she was set in her ways, she had a few comments about South Dakotan chefs and their ability to drop off the face of the planet. Instead of acting out, she slowed her breathing, sipped her wine, and watched patio bartenders flirt. Ansel sought out her presence. If he wanted to make small talk, he could carry the conversation.

He cleared his throat. "Your designs are more beautiful in real life than they are on paper." He shifted until their shoulders brushed. "Just like you. I appreciate your hard work and willingness to show up tonight. I wasn't sure you'd come."

"Of course, I came. I spearheaded this project." Staying detached in such close proximity was like asking a cat not to purr. Even though she was mad, she was also thrilled to confirm he was okay. She risked a glance. He was so annoyingly tan and handsome that she wanted to look away, but she held her ground.

"Sadly, I didn't make enough of an impression to land the cocktail menu. The free publicity would have helped my firm."

He stroked his chin. "How would I describe you? Rye aged in a rum cask with a hint of sweetness. Grenadine and lemon juice for a little spice." He dropped the hand and shook his head. "Every night, I sipped that drink and missed you. You're too complex to bottle."

The restaurant industry peddled romance. Putting stock in his flattery was like asking for a hug from a cactus. She tilted her head. "Just a hint of sweetness?"

He leaned close. "Honestly, I couldn't bear to share you."

Something deep and warm thrummed in her soul. She bit the inside of her cheek and replayed the sleepless nights she worked herself into exhaustion. Of course, he could capture her in a drink and savor her from a distance. He didn't rise to the top of the industry by stumbling over mundane challenges. "You ignored my calls and sent everything through Collins. Would you call that outsourcing?"

He worked his jaw, opened his mouth, and straightened his shoulders. "I funnel everything through Collins. He's my best project manager."

She snorted. "And your best defense. As long as you have people around you, you don't have to get too close. You don't have to risk people asking too much of you, Ansel. Not your restaurants, but *you*."

"You never wanted to be friends." He frowned.

She swallowed. "I never wanted anything from you."

Shaking his head, he stared into the crowd. "Funny,

it feels like you have it all."

What did that mean? She watched the crowd and replayed the conversation until she felt sure she misheard him. Finishing her wine, she set the glass on the bar and waited for him to wander off. People who saw them chatting would mark their friendship, not her bad behavior.

Ansel rubbed his temple. "How's your family? I wanted to give you time. Everything you went through in the past few years"—he loosened his stiff, white collar—"you've managed it beautifully. You didn't need drama from a capricious chef with limited design skills."

If they defined themselves by their professions, what they had was nothing more than a fling. She pushed from the bar and hoped the press had something more interesting to capture than her tantrum. "What I need in life is *my* call, and I *did* call you. Twice. Don't slide up to me, half-drunk on success, and expect me to welcome your cheap compliments. I'm not a filet, and I didn't wear this dress for you. I wore it for myself and the people who depend on me." She pounded a fist on the bar. "Damn, Ansel, you should have left me alone!"

Snagging her hand, he held it fast. "Riley, did you really call me?"

His gaze held her captive. "Yes"—she ground out the admission—"and the second call hurt."

Dropping her hand, he took her face in his hands and kissed her.

Eyes wide, she told herself she would limit him to a taste, a sizzling confirmation of what they had or a dim reminder that it was nothing special. She held herself rigid and waited for his impulse to fizzle.

His lips were slow and tender upon her lips.

The tenderness shattered her resolve. Tugging his bottom lip between her teeth, she let her eyes flutter closed. *Forget the wine. His taste was headier than an aphrodisiac.* The cocktail party could come to a screeching halt, and she would still forgive his transgressions. The hum running through her system was more than a celebrity crush. Compared to being in his arms, running a design firm and cashing million-dollar checks were cheap thrills. She understood how women could give up everything for the men they loved. She also understood why they hid their feelings. Love made people too vulnerable. How much more could she possibly bear to lose?

The possibility of Ansel walking away now sobered her response. Hearing laughter and cheers, she knew she had an audience, but she also knew she had to take control. She pushed against his solid chest and tore away her lips. "I'm not here to put on a show."

His arms snapped around her waist, and he dragged her closer before pressing a kiss below her ear. "Why are you here? You could have sent someone."

She fingered the stiff chef's uniform and ached to remove it. For a few magical nights, she and Ansel were alone in the world. His tender caresses were the only things that mattered. Then, life came crashing in on her fantasy. "I missed you. I wanted to know if I made up everything I remembered."

"And?"

She swallowed and remembered her strength. Heart pounding, she angled her head and claimed another kiss. The moneyed crowd witnessing their spectacle could go to hell. His embrace felt right, and the pressure and texture of his lips were far headier than any cocktail. She pulled out of the kiss. "You're as potent as I remembered," she whispered against his lips. "The question is, why did you find me?"

"I meant to say hello"—his forehead crinkled—"but when I saw you, my heart thudded in my chest."

"And now?"

He stroked her cheek. "I don't want to share you."

The prospect of being a shared commodity sobered her high. She stared at the ceiling. "Selfishness isn't enough. If you only want to be friends, walk away."

He snaked a second arm around her and pulled her close. "What do you want? Kissing you is the best impulse I've ever indulged, but I don't want it to be my last memory of you."

Impulses could also saddle a person with regrets. Tired of fighting storms, she pulled out of his arms; she gestured toward the crowd, most of who had returned to their conversations. "We should have this conversation somewhere more private. You're here to open a restaurant. I'm here to work the room."

He rubbed a hand over his mouth. "That's it?"

"Why else would I be here?"

"Because you're ready—"

Saunders Reesuzn walked up and slapped Ansel on the right shoulder. The Houston conservator's soft pale skin glowed from a recent facial, and his meticulous pocket square stood starched and crisp. "Absolutely brilliant." He offered a hand. "You're a lucky man."

Ansel returned his handshake, but he held her gaze.

Was she ready? Had he given her space, or had she hidden behind her professional identity? Calling was one thing, but leaving a voice mail was a completely different animal. If she admitted how much she missed him, would she have received a return call? She swallowed and flipped the last few months. Maybe Ansel had put her needs above his. Should she believe him or hold his restraint against him?

"I want you to meet some Texas-based art collectors," Saunders said. "They're all young museum trustees with socialites and scions on their arms. If I know them, then you probably should, too." He tugged Ansel away from the bar. "It's now or never."

Brows furrowed, Ansel stepped away from the bar.

"Love doesn't have deadlines," she said.

Saunders laughed. "Ahh, but art does!"

Ansel followed him but looked over his shoulder. *I love you*, he mouthed.

Or was it *elephant juice? I'll have two?* Two what? Martinis? As she watched him disappear into the crowd, she fought months of doubt muddling her decisiveness. She wiped Ansel's kiss from her lips and replayed when he compared her to a javelina. One kiss did not make a relationship. Neither did spending one week in the arms of a man she loved.

Papi parted the crowd, joined her at the bar, and sipped a Negroni.

His sashaying walk outlived his time on Miami stages, but he still drew admiring looks.

"The place is booked out for two months. You did good, honey."

"Thanks, Papi." Chewing her bottom lip, she lost sight of Ansel, watched the cocktail party unfold, and stole a sip from his sweet drink. The restaurant's curated, high-dollar beauty would delight Cypress Creek sales tax collectors, but the town needed attractions to draw in high-dollar spenders for more than one night. "The crowd's here for one thing."

"The man ruining your lipstick?"

She touched her lips. "The one."

Papi sipped his cocktail. "But you gave his concept life."

She spotted Ansel on the patio and remembered falling for a cocky, rural highwayman before she fell for a polished, celebrity chef. Knowing both sides of him, she appreciated the man behind the whites as much as what he accomplished.

Saunders handed him a cigar, and the DJ shifted the house music toward a Sinatra-inspired ballad.

Any minute, a server would walk past and offer her a Steak *Frites* slider. Only she and a few other people in Ansel's life could appreciate the irony behind the menu choice. She straightened. "I shouldn't be here. I'm not ready. It's too much."

Papi cupped her elbow and leaned close. "Honey, life is too much. If you run away from challenges, you'll end up rambling around Hill Country mansions like a deranged lunatic with too many shoes."

She laughed. "Would that be so bad?"

"Terrible." He downed his drink. "Without Warrior, I would be lost. He anchors me, and he flatters me. You can't ask for a better conversation starter. Following him to Cypress Creek was the smartest thing I've ever done. Having you and Grant"—he shook his head—"well, the pair of you proved how far Cypress Creek's Calf Scramble Champion went to make me happy. To love someone, you give them everything and expect everything in return."

His pronouncement restarted her stalled heart, but

she focused on the anecdote underpinning his announcement. "Dad was a Calf Scrambler? Really?"

He adjusted a large, gold belt buckle. "You think I won this thing? Warrior knows I have an eye for bling. I know it, too. This buckle was a perfect gift. Knowing what you want is the first step toward getting it. The night's still young, honey, and so are you."

She pressed a kiss to his smooth cheek. "Thanks."

"I'm always here."

"I know." She held his gaze. He was always there, standing with Warrior and smoothing over Dad's rough edges with laughter and joy. Who else would have sent them to their rooms and then assembled s'mores to dry their tears?

"Get on with it." He urged her into the crowd.

Smiling, she made her way toward the restrooms and admired a sensuous, glowing neon sign Ansel had issued a change order to place in the recessed hallway. *Don't you want me?* The sign was both a plea and a tease. If she could anticipate the answers to her own questions, she wouldn't have to ask them. *Of course, I want you. Do you want me, or am I reading too much into the art?*

Stepping into the hallway, Ansel yanked open a storeroom door and tumbled her against a bare wall. Metal shelving rocked. He flipped on a bare light, kicked shut the door, and braced his hands on either side of her head. "I should have waited to kiss you, but I can't wait forever."

In the tiny room, his scent suspended reality. She pressed her hands flat against the freshly painted wall and focused on the lingering paint fumes. She could dismiss the bar kisses, but if anyone found them in the storeroom, tongues would wag. She wanted them to hang low. She chewed her bottom lip and knew it was bare. "I didn't ask you to wait."

"I know, Riley. I thought I was doing the honorable thing." He dropped his lips to her neck. "To avoid thinking about you, I'd have to be dead. I missed you so much."

At his touch, her senses went into overdrive, and she couldn't think of a reason to stop. Wasn't that how she ran away from a lightning storm and found release in his arms? Every time they came together, logic slipped out the window. For a glorious week, she had a taste of everything she wanted. Then the flood rocked her foundations and her expectations.

After months of silence, Ansel's declarations were so unexpected that she wondered if he kick-started the party before she arrived. Fearing he might be drunk, she steeled herself for heartbreaking sober regrets. Meeting him changed her outlook on life for a week. She was a better, freer version of herself. Spontaneous, sexy Riley had a lot to offer the world, but she couldn't maintain her impulsiveness without Ansel's steady anchor. His perseverance and his outlook on life channeled her passions, but she couldn't bottle his influence or chain him to her side. Turning her head, she remembered the day his kisses stopped and life returned to normal. The minute she saw his car pull away from the shelter, she felt his absence. "The night's gone to your head."

"*You've* gone to my head." He lifted her dress, ran a hand up her leg, and pushed her panties to the side. "I'm only ahead of you when we're naked."

Inhaling sharply, she felt herself grow wet and let him explore her exposed skin.

He slid his fingers along her sex. "Say what you want about my relationship skills, but indulge me. What I can't put into words, I can put into sex."

Arguing during sex had never been her strong suit.

Spinning her around, he anchored her hands to a shelving unit and ripped away her underwear. Boxes tumbled to the ground. Cans rolled. He replaced his fingers with his ready cock, but he stopped at her entrance. "I missed you so much. I missed this. I missed *you.*"

She forgot the crowd of well-dressed patrons and arched her back. She and Ansel might as well have been strangers sneaking away from a midsummer concert for a well-deserved tryst, but she knew exactly how good he would feel. "I missed you, too."

"Keep talking." He nudged her entrance. "My fragile, celebrity ego needs praise."

She laughed. "No, it doesn't."

"Maybe it does."

His hesitation emboldened her. She tested the steel rack, found it anchored to the wall, and wondered how much indulging her impulses would cost her. Maybe trauma overemphasized their connection. Maybe the thrill of a fling and the rush of survival short-circuited her impulse control. Then again, maybe he was just right.

Before she could set boundaries, she felt him slide in deep, and she let her eyes roll back in her head. He was more than an impulse. His heady humor and lean muscles fit her needs and her body like no one else. If she stripped away the things that separated them, their bodies flew. She moaned and met his thrusts.

A can rolled along the floor.

After pulling out, he slipped inside her and set a punishing pace.

His rhythm pushed her higher.

"I missed you every day we were apart." He moaned. "Fuck me."

She should stop him. She should pick up the can. Lock the door.

"I dialed your number a thousand times."

"Liar," she gasped and clenched her muscles around him.

He stilled, his chest heaving against her back and his hands tight on her hips.

In an instant, her tears fell. Caught between what she needed and what she had, she pulled away, turned, and braced a hand against his chest. Her dress fell against her hips, a whisper of silk and a slow good-bye. "We can't do this. You walked away last time. It's my turn to set limits."

Cupping her shoulders, he backed her against a free wall. "You can't admit you love me. Fine, but the moment I touch you, you come alive. You want to talk about taking turns? I love you, Riley. I have no problem saying it. Now, it's your turn."

Chest heaving, she closed her eyes. She loved him, but fate sculpted his ambitions for a bigger stage. Austin was the farthest she could be from Cypress Creek. She treasured her quirky, resort town, her eccentric, loving family, and her successful, design firm. Who was she to ask for more? "I can't risk losing you."

"Fuck, you can't say it, can you?" Grabbing her ass, he lifted her and pressed into her heat. "Tell me I shouldn't have left you. Tell me you'll use me for sex. I don't care what you say."

She wrapped her arms around his neck and held on. "I care about failing you."

"You never lost me, Riley. Do you love me as much as I love you?"

She wet her lips and considered his question. Admittedly, she held his cock inside her, her arms wrapped around his neck, and her legs clutching his ass, but she struggled to articulate her vulnerable feelings. If everything fell apart, she would be happy with him. "I love you so much it hurts, Ansel. Choosing between you and the rest of my life feels like an impossible choice. I can't have it all."

"You can, Baby. You've always seen through my disguises. You didn't care who I was, but you wanted to be together. That counts. I've spent months missing you and making sure I can be who you need. You lost Grant, but you won't lose me or anything else you've created." He pressed a kiss to her shoulder. "I'm not going anywhere."

She clung, rocked her hips, and let the cathartic pleasure burn through her. Her tears would dry, but hearing his declaration wasn't enough. She needed the hard, searing heat of his presence. When he was inside her, she felt alive.

"I'm here." He stilled and cupped her cheek. "I promise."

Burying her face against his neck, she closed her eyes and inhaled deeply. "I thought I lost you."

He set an easy pace, rocking her against his hips and pressing kisses to her temple. "You didn't, Riley. I'll give you everything I have. I need you to claim it."

A million rebuttals sprang to mind, but she

tightened her grip on his shoulders and urged him deeper. Within seconds, his deep, slapping thrusts pushed her past her limit, and she no longer cared if Texas' elite knew she was banging the head chef in the restaurant's storage room. Ansel felt so good that his labored breathing goaded her, and his glazed eyes fueled her release. She unmade him.

He gripped her calf muscles and changed the angle.

She needed him as much as he needed her. Her orgasm hit her like a freight train. Shuddering hard, she gripped his shoulders and held on.

Arms shaking, he came in a rush and dropped his head to her shoulder.

She waited and felt their heartbeats slow and owned this moment in time. Despite the party raging outside the storeroom, she had never been with a man who was so completely hers. How could she get anything done with him in her life?

Pulling back, his gaze searched her face. "Been on many dates?"

She snorted and unwound her legs from his hips.

He reached out a hand and steadied her. "Downloaded all the dating apps?"

"Hardly." If the storage closet held paper towels, she could clean up without darting toward the bathroom. Stripped of wealth and status, she loved him, but she refused to say it in a storage room that now smelled of sex, cologne, and volatiles.

He buttoned his chef's whites. "Indulged in one-night stands and torrid affairs?"

She fixed her dress and looked for her underwear. "Ready to smoke another cigar?"

"I never smoke cigars." He looked up. "Ruins

palates."

His life revolved around his work. She needed to escape before she collapsed in his arms and begged him to move to Austin. Physical intimacy was one thing, but admitting how much she loved him would lead to questions she couldn't answer. She looked toward the door.

"Then again, there's a first time for everything. I've never banged my architect in the storage room, either."

She reshaped her curls and debated what she wanted. Worst-case scenario, she would come to the party and be too mad to make small talk. Best-case scenario, he would apologize for ghosting her. Stealing kisses and disordering the storage room were so far off her roadmap that she needed to regroup. They met at a roadside air pump. Trauma brought them close. He loved her. She loved him, but what did that mean? The moment she stepped into the hallway, she would circulate like a boss. The restaurant's patrons were probably too drunk to realize she smelled like sage, sweat, and fresh, crisp aftershave. She smelled like Ansel Percheron.

Reaching for the door handle, she paused and tilted her head. "I'm not your architect. I don't know what I am."

"Whoever you want." He cleared his throat. "I bought a ranch."

One hand on the doorknob, she fixed her heels. "Where?"

"What do you mean, where? Here! I wanted retirement, but I have more restaurant ideas. Cooking is like taking care of people. I want to take care of you.

We fit together, Riley. You love this town. I can't imagine living here without you. I hope I won't have to."

She stared and struggled to organize her arguments. Ansel was a global celebrity. The prospect of him putting down roots in Cypress Creek felt as surreal and intoxicating as his kiss. "Here? In Cypress Creek?"

He stepped closer. "Have you seen the menu?"

She shook her head.

"It's more than fifty dollars steaks." He grazed a hand along her cheek. "You taught me how valuable life's relationships are when they're done right. I brought back all the dishes I debuted in Sioux Falls—"

She raised her eyebrows.

He dropped the hand and stroked her lower back. "—but, the dishes are better. I added experience and expertise. I added everything you've taught me."

She picked out tile for millionaires. Reshaping a person's life carried infinitely more weight. Pulling back, she met the calm resistance from his hand on her lower back.

"Riley, don't run away from this."

She swallowed. Honing his menu and buying a ranch were something, but the way he looked at her melted her resolve. Her throat tightened, and she feared losing her determination to stay strong. With enough warning, she could have bluffed her way through this evening. Instead, the arrogant asshole cornered her in a storage room and reminded her how good they were when they were together. She feared she loved him for the prompt.

He lowered his head. "The only thing worse than

losing people you love is losing yourself. I know who I am, and I'm ready to be that person...hopefully with you by my side."

She let out her breath.

He twined a string of her hair around a finger.

Without his leather bracelets and celebrity gear, his strong forearm looked bare and capable, but his tanned skin tempted her kisses. Hadn't that always been her weakness? She'd seen the banked heart beneath his handsome exterior and wanted everything. What would happen if she claimed it?

"I love you, Riley. From the moment I met you, you've been honest, brutal, and authentic. We're stronger when we're together. I shouldn't have stayed away all summer. I should have known you could handle the flood, me, and anything else life throws your way."

His speech was worthy of a podium, but his load dripped down her thighs. She swallowed and worried hormones might overpower her reason. "Ansel—"

"You don't have to let me down easy. I can handle rejection. Tell me what you want."

Looking at the bare bulb, she blew her hair from her eyes and met his gaze. "We had sex in a storage room."

He rubbed his thumb along the side of his mouth. "I have poor impulse control."

She snorted. He could give lectures on impulse control. A man who held a grudge against an ex-girlfriend for twenty years knew how to keep his eyes on the prize. He needed redirection, but he excelled at many things. Loving her could rise to the top of his list, but she refused to be a nightly special. "Don't lie to get what you want. We can fuck without falling in love."

"I think about you non-stop. I want everything."

His declaration sounded much sweeter in person than over voice mail. She laid a hand against his chest and felt his heartbeat. For a man who lost everyone in life who cared for him, he had a remarkable capacity to love. Being the beneficiary of his attention was like finding herself frozen on the red carpet, but she could shake off her nerves and embrace the attention. "I love you, too, but I refuse to start a relationship after a one-night stand or a storeroom hookup. You let me leave first. If anyone asks, we had a last-minute consult in this storage room. When the dust settles, we'll sort out what's happening between us."

"Go back to saying you love me."

She laughed.

He dropped his hand from her lower back and scratched his head. "What was this? A consult?"

She tried the door handle and looked over her left shoulder. "After all, you're a client. We can be discreet."

"Are you sure you love me?"

The uncertainty behind his question broke her heart, but she couldn't craft their futures in a storeroom. "Of course, I love you." Cracking open the door, she scanned the empty hallway and eyed the restroom. A mad dash would be entirely appropriate. Pausing, she replayed his admission and looked over her shoulder. "Where's the ranch?"

He grinned. "Next door to your dads' place."

The hall light cast his cheekbones and wicked smile in sharp relief. She considered staying in the storeroom for round two of spine-tingling sex. Crafting a life beneath a bare bulb might be rash, but they had the ingredients to make something brilliant. "How convenient."

"Stay in town awhile." He walked toward the door, swatted her ass, and strode past into the hallway. "I'll give you a tour."

"Wait, where are you going?"

"I have a restaurant to run, Riley. You'll keep."

Her mouth hung open. Relief coursed through her in happy waves. She yearned to end the night in his arms, but she wasn't about to let him leave her standing in the storeroom. However, she had a role at the cocktail party and a reputation to maintain. Also, if he thought she would *keep*, he had another think coming.

He braced a hand on the doorframe and swung back to face her. "Before I go, I want you to know the only thing worse than losing someone is losing yourself. You know who you are, and I admire your resilience, but I need you to look forward. I'm ready to be authentic. Are you?"

"Authentic?" She swiped her hair out of her eyes. Despite his achievements, he was still a little boy swinging his dick around to see what would happen. She shook her head and approached him. "You named the restaurant Cypress Creek. When did you put yourself out there? When did you pick up the phone and tell me how you felt? When did you get authentic?"

He released the doorframe and grinned. "Didn't you read the press release?"

She shook her head.

He spread his arms wide. "Welcome to Percheron. Sink or swim, the place has my name . If you'd let me, I'd put your name on it, too. We're stronger when we're together, but we can't lean on propriety. Call me until I pick up. Let me interrupt your meetings. *'Til death do us part* is for sissies."

Sissies? Picking up the wayward can, she set it on the shelf and planted her hands on her hips. "Okay."

"Okay?" He raised his eyebrows. "You can make the leap?"

She stepped past him and trailed a hand along his chest. "Of course, I can. Can you?"

"With you, I can do anything." Saluting her, he exited toward the main dining room.

She dashed into the bathroom and pulled herself together. His public kisses and private tactics would anchor her memories for the rest of her life. She was too afraid to make an aggressive move, but he made moves on a grander scale.

Thinking of her campus plans, she wondered if some of his ambition had rubbed off. Branching out and making waves had always been her plan, but she considered his empire and planned her own. She and Ansel had a future to embrace, a culinary empire to run, and a love story to top the charts. Her egotistical, brilliant celebrity chef had claimed a home, and she would fall asleep in his loving arms.

Slipping from the bathroom, she took a deep breath and entered the main dining room.

"Who's the lucky woman?" a reporter asked Ansel.

"Riley Golding. She's an amazing architect, and she saw the best in me." He made eye contact with Riley and raised his eyebrows. "Some days, I think she even loves me."

The crowd erupted into cheers and wolf-whistles.

Heat flamed her cheeks. Heels beating out a

staccato beat, she strode across the room, pressed herself to his side, and turned her body so only he heard her remarks. "Subtle."

He rubbed his jaw along her cheek. "About as subtle as a bedazzled armadillo."

She chewed her bottom lip. "Is that the best you can do?"

"Maybe." He pulled back. "You think you can do better?"

"I can't make up a four-letter word, but I can claim you." Gripping his lush hair, she pulled him close and pressed her lips against his in a branding kiss. Satisfied she made her point, she pulled back. "And you're the best."

The crowd cheered.

He wrapped his arms around her. "Damn straight."

Cypress Creek and Texas' elite could gossip until the sun came up. She had her man. "I think you'll do, all right."

"I'll do?" He tipped up her chin. "You want me to name the restaurant after you or somethin'?"

Observers laughed.

She swatted his chest.

He softened his gaze. "If you want everything, you have to claim it. Marry me or brand me, the choice is yours."

Someone hooted. "Brand 'im!"

Shaking her head at becoming a spectacle, she remembered the night she slipped into town to help Dad, soak up time with Papi, and mourn Grant. Meeting Ansel rocked her world, but she couldn't stop thinking about him here, in Austin, or anywhere else she might roam. Gripping his waist, she held him tight and marveled at his steady concentration and even breathing.

No matter life's setbacks, people found ways forward. Scanning the mural depicting the best parts of Cypress Creek—the people working hard and making the best of what they had—she acknowledged the decades of hard work and perseverance flowing through her veins. Life offered setbacks, but she found her way, too. Ansel's confident swagger and tender heart were the perfect complement to her controlled diligence and creative impulses. Together, they could stand against anything life offered. "We'll work our brand." She smoothed his chef's whites. "In the meantime, get me a drink. Something potent, but a little sweet."

He tightened his grip and pressed a kiss against her temple. "My favorite."

Surrounded by glitz and candlelight, she buried her face against his chest and breathed deeply. He was steady, strong, and capable, but he was also creative and impulsive. Most importantly, he was hers.

A word about the author...

Amy Craig lives in Baton Rouge, Louisiana with her family and a small menagerie of pets. She writes contemporary romances and women's fiction with intelligent and empathetic heroines. She can't always vouch for the men. She has worked as an engineer, project manager, and incompetent waitress. In her spare time, she plays tennis and expands her husband's honey-do list.

https://linktr.ee/authoramycraig

Other Titles by this Author

A Winter Rose
The Crevasse
The Peninsula
The Starlight Motel